TENDER EMBRACE

"I think, Wade Cameron," Clem heard herself whisper, "that you want to kiss me."

"Yes," he answered, his voice ragged, "I do."

Her heart began to race. "Then do it, because I want you to."

First his warm breath tickled her lips, then his mouth touched hers in a delicate kiss. So fragile was the touch, yet she felt it all through her body. When she shivered, he drew her closer, and she seemed to melt into his strength and warmth.

"Oh, Wade—" she stammered as his lips brushed back and forth over hers, as his hard body firmly acquainted itself with hers to create delicious sensations, "this is wonderful."

Her words were stopped when his arms tightened around her, his hands pressing her even closer, and his lips claimed hers in a full kiss. She clung to him, snuggling against the hard muscles of his chest.

She never dreamed that something as glorious as this existed in the whole wide world, and that it was hers for the taking . . .

HISTORICAL ROMANCES BY EMMA MERRITT

RESTLESS FLAMES (2203, $3.95)

Having lost her husband six months before, determined Brenna Allen couldn't afford to lose her freight company, too. Outfitted as wagon captain with revolver, knife and whip, the single-minded beauty relentlessly drove her caravan, desperate to reach Santa Fe. Then she crossed paths with insolent Logan Mac-Dougald. The taciturn Texas Ranger was as primitive as the surrounding Comanche Territory, and he didn't hesitate to let the tantalizing trail boss know what he wanted from her. Yet despite her outrage with his brazen ways, jet-haired Brenna couldn't suppress the scorching passions surging through her . . . and suddenly she never wanted this trip to end!

COMANCHE BRIDE (2549, $3.95)

When stunning Dr. Zoe Randolph headed to Mexico to halt a cholera epidemic, she didn't think twice about traversing Comanche territory . . . until a band of bloodthirsty savages attacked her caravan. The gorgeous physician was furious that her mission had been interrupted, but nothing compared to the rage she felt on meeting the barbaric warrior who made her his slave. Determined to return to civilization, the ivory-skinned blonde decided to make a woman's ultimate sacrifice to gain her freedom—and never admit that deep down inside she burned to be loved by the handsome brute!

SWEET, WILD LOVE (2834, $4.50)

It was hard enough for Eleanor Hunt to get men to take her seriously in sophisticated Chicago—it was going to be impossible in Blissful, Kansas! These cowboys couldn't believe she was a real attorney, here to try a cattle rustling case. They just looked her up and down and grinned. Especially that Bradley Smith. The man worked for her father and he still had the audacity to stare at her with those lust-filled green eyes. Every time she turned around, he was trying to trap her in his strong embrace.

Available wherever paperbacks are sold, or order direct from the Publisher. Send cover price plus 50¢ per copy for mailing and handling to Zebra Books, Dept. 3334, 475 Park Avenue South, New York, N.Y. 10016. Residents of New York, New Jersey and Pennsylvania must include sales tax. DO NOT SEND CASH.

BENEATH A TEXAS STAR

EMMA MERRITT

ZEBRA BOOKS
KENSINGTON PUBLISHING CORP.

ZEBRA BOOKS

are published by

Kensington Publishing Corp.
475 Park Avenue South
New York, NY 10016

First printing: March, 1991

Printed in the United States of America

Chapter One

Sure enough it's winter, the lone rider thought. Her gaze slowly moved back and forth across the dismal horizon, where dry, barren earth melded into a single mass of black storm clouds.

Everything's dead or wished to God it was.

As if she had spoken blasphemy, lightning, accompanied by an ominous boom of thunder, flashed across the heavens. A cruel north wind assailed, tossing grit and sand into her face. It whipped her jacket and trousers against her body, and repeatedly slapped the brim of her Stetson down over her face. She lifted a gloved hand, pressed the collar of her jacket about her neck, and settled lower into the saddle, but still she was cold. Dear God, but she was cold.

Cold to the bone, the Sheriff would say.

A checkered bandanna secured her hat to her head, and she wore several layers of clothes, a fleece-lined jacket and gloves, thick wool stockings and trousers, and knee-high boots. Yet they were no barrier to the icy blue norther that howled across the desolate plains of West Texas and announced the late winter storm.

"Yeah, Clemmy girl," the Sheriff would say, "this is a blue norther, the worst storm of 'em all. Freeze you dead in a minute, it will."

Against another brutal attack by the wind, Clem

forced her head up and stared once more through grit-swollen eyes at the menacing sky and the spindly but deadly streaks of lightning. She only hoped she could make it to town before the bottom fell out. Although she — as well as all the other inhabitants of Lawful — had prayed for rain for the past six months, now was not the time for it to come. Dear Lord, she would freeze to death for sure. She had no rain slicker! She twisted in the saddle, the leather creaking as she moved to look over her shoulder at the black stallion following behind. This morning a glorious mount; now a mere packhorse. The wrapped burden had been laid carefully across the silver-laced Spanish saddle, the gun belt slung over the pommel. The saddle and revolvers were the Sheriff's pride and joy, she thought with a smile that went as quickly as it came.

The Sheriff was dead, her best friend gone.

Unable to look at the stiff, lifeless form wrapped in her rain slicker, Clem turned around, twin revolvers biting into the tender flesh of her thighs. She shut her eyes tightly, but not before a tear slid from beneath the lid to run down her cheek, the cold wind quickly transforming it into a sliver of ice. She lifted a hand and angrily swatted her cheeks, regretting her action as soon as the rough glove touched her chafed skin. She considered tears a weakness. It would not do for the inhabitants of Lawful to know she cried. She was their Deputy Sheriff. Besides, she had already done her crying.

For the past five years she had ridden with the Sheriff. At first the townsfolk had given her a rough time, and the city council had questioned the Sheriff's judgment, but he had remained steadfast in his desire to have her at his side; his confidence in her never wavered. Finally the citizens of Lawful came to accept her as one of their peace officers. Now she was their only peace officer.

She unbuttoned her jacket and slipped her hand between the fleece lining and the flannel shirt she wore, but she was not seeking warmth. Her searching fingers soon closed around the badge the Sheriff had pinned to her shirt seconds before he died.

"Pretty bad, isn't it?" he had asked.

Tears burning her eyes, her lips trembling, she could only stare at the gaping wound, at the blood seeping through the serrated flesh. More than bad, it was fatal.

As if reading her mind, he said, "I thought so."

"No!" She shook her head vigorously. "You're going to be all right . . . I promise. I'll get you to town."

His rough hand had caught hers in a tight grasp. "Let's face it, Clem. I'm gonna die. Now it's up to you to take care of the star." Blood dribbling out of the corner of his mouth, he lay on a blanket spread for him on the ground of the shallow mountain cave. Tears running hotly down her cheeks, Clem knelt beside her dearest friend, her mentor.

"You can't."

"Even sheriffs die, Clemmy girl."

"Sheriffs can," she cried, "but not *you!* Dear God, Papa! Not you!"

"All of us have to go sometimes, Daughter," he said gruffly and drew her into his arms.

"Don't leave me, Papa! Please, don't leave me." Disregarding the blood-soaked jacket, she laid her face against his chest and wrapped her arms around him. Like a fearful child, she clung to him. She had lost her mother; she could not stand to lose her father also. "You can't leave me."

He drew a hacking breath, death rattling in his chest. She felt his large, callused hand gently rub her back. "The big fellow up there has called my name, and I can't ignore Him. I'm sorry, Clemmy."

"No!" She lifted her head and stared into his gray,

7

pain-filled eyes. "What am I going to do, Papa?"

"You're not Clement Jones's daughter for nothing." A slow, sad smile played across his weathered face. Amidst the pain, love shone in the depth of those eyes, the corners of which were deeply creased from years of staring at the relentless West Texas sun.

"I don't know what to do, Papa."

"Yes, you do. You're the only one who does know. Most important, you're the only one who can do it. Besides, Hokie and Turbin will be there to help you."

In spite of her grief, Clem smiled as she thought about the two surveyors who served as part-time deputies for the Sheriff.

"You got to make sure a scared, hungry boy gets a fair trial," her father insisted.

"Scared and hungry maybe," Clem muttered harshly, remembering the arrogant seventeen-year-old who had shot her father, "but not innocent, Papa, and not a boy. Alarico Olviera is not a boy."

"Innocent until proven guilty," her father gently reminded her. "Besides, Rico didn't mean to do it, Clem. He was desperate, and desperate people do desperate things."

Like kill my father.

"The man responsible for this shooting, Clem, is Antonio Borajo."

"Slim chance of our getting the *Reverend Father* Borajo! He's hiding behind his priestly robes. If only the Mexicans understood that he's not satisfied with controlling the salt supply at Guadalupe Lakes. He's using them to get a monopoly on all the salt in the region."

She lifted her head to gaze into the desert valley below at Chupedera Lakes, three small lakes commonly called the Chupedera Salt Flats. These "lakes" covered about one hundred and fifty acres, and were about eighteen inches deep with a glittering surface of white

8

salt almost four inches thick.

"It's up to you to convince the people." Clement coughed, then took in deep gulps of air before he said, "You have to find the evidence to expose him. You got to do it the right way. You hear me?"

Clem heard but could not answer. All her life she had believed in her father's way, and had thought it was the right way. Now he was dying. If that was the right way, she did not know if she could accept it. From now on, she would do things her way—right or wrong.

"Wearing the star means shouldering responsibility," the sheriff continued. "You got to protect all the citizens. All of 'em, Clem."

"Yes, Papa," she murmured.

"Remember, as soon as winter is over, Doña Pera Antonia Montelongo will be making her yearly trip to San Antonio. You'll be responsible for her safety while she's in Lawful, daughter, and you know how the rumors fly when she travels. You never know when some lowlife—thinking she's traveling with lots of money—is gonna try to rob her."

Doña Pera Antonia Montelongo was the elderly matriarch of the vast Montelongo holdings that stretched for thousands of miles across West Texas and included several farms, a large ranch, and salt lakes. Every spring she and her entourage traveled to San Antonio to spend several weeks with relatives. Always she stopped in Lawful for a few days' rest before proceeding on her journey.

The townsfolk looked forward to these visits and marked them with a celebration, equaled only by the Fourth of July festivities. People from all around gathered into town. Early in the morning the men built cooking pits. During the day, as they slowly barbecued the beef, pork, and chicken, they celebrated. The men played games, competing against one another in horseshoes, wrestling, shooting, and horse racing. The women usually swapped recipes and quilting and dress patterns; they passed around their latest fashion journals. In the afternoon a prize was given for the best tasting preserves. That evening all ate, then danced the night away.

However, there was a more somber side to Doña Pera's annual pilgrimages. They gave rise to many rumors. As the *haciendada's* empire and wealth had grown and prospered, many speculated that Doña Pera—feeling that her money was safer in a San Antonio bank than in one on the isolated frontier of West Texas—made large annual deposits.

"I don't have to worry about it too much, Papa," Clem consoled her father. "Dona Pera always travels with her vaqueros."

"Don't be so casual about it. It doesn't matter how many cowboys she travels with, or how well trained they are, there's always the potential for trouble. Especially when someone is as wealthy and prominent as she is. You—the peace officer—have got to keep your eyes and ears open." The Sheriff barked the admonition, then succumbed to another bout of coughing. "Always the potential for trouble. Be aware of it, so you can avoid it."

"Yes, Papa."

Drawing in a deep gulp of air, his face creased in pain. He grasped the badge and struggled to unfasten it from his shirt. Finally his lips tipped into a pleased smile, and he held the star up to the light to look at it. A sigh slipped out, and regret darkened his eyes as he caressed it between his thick fingers. With a shaking hand he pinned it to her shirt.

His voice growing weaker, he asked, "Can you handle the responsibility?"

She could. Perhaps not like her father would, but then she was not Clement Jones. She was his

10

daughter.

"Clem?" the sheriff prompted, and she nodded. "Clem—Clementina Jones—" He paused and smiled. "Your mother would be happy to hear me call you by your given name."

"Yes," she murmured, doing her best to return his smile.

"Clem, about your mother—"

"Not now, Papa."

"Please, Clem—"

"No, Papa, I can't. I can't talk about her now." He had held her in his arms a long time as she sobbed into his chest.

When she finally lifted her head, he smiled weakly and said, "By the authority invested in me by the citizens of Lawful, Texas, I hereby appoint you deputy sheriff. Do you swear—"

Yes, she thought as she rubbed the smooth metal star between her fingers, she had sworn as Papa had known she would, and by damn she was glad. At the same moment she had taken an oath to be the deputy sheriff, she had taken another silent oath. She had solemnly sworn to track down Alarico Olviera—the man who had shot her father. By damn, she would kill him. He had shown no mercy to her father, and she would show none to him.

"Damn you, Alarico Olviera!" Tears, a mixture of anger, hurt, desperation, and fear, rolled down her cheeks. At the same moment that a jagged streak of lightning serrated the sky and thunder rumbled in its wake, she jabbed her fist into the air and screamed, "Damn you, Chupedera Salt Flats! Damn you to hell!"

Elm Jackson, doctor and caretaker of Lawful, stood beside the black stallion and stared at the dead body. The wind flapped his huge white surgical coat around his legs, and his gray hair stood on end.

"Damn those salt lakes to hell!" he muttered.

"I already have." Clem lifted her father's gun belt from the pommel of his saddle. "It didn't do any good. They're still there."

Elm's long, sure fingers untied the Sheriff's body from the back of the stallion, and he grunted softly as he heaved the body onto his shoulder and carried it into the two-story shotgun building. The bottom story consisted of two rooms, the funeral parlor and the doctor's office. The upper story was the doctor's residence.

Clem followed Elm into the building and dropped her father's holsters on the table, her stride never slackening until she reached the black potbellied stove on the other side of the room. Peeling off her gloves and shoving them into a back hip pocket, she spread her hands over the stove to savor its warmth. His burden on his shoulders, Elm passed her and opened the door into the adjoining room where he did the undertaking. Cold air swirled around her, causing her to draw closer to the heater. Clem heard the thud as he laid her father on a table, but did not turn.

She could not remember a time in her life when she had felt so alone, or her heart had been so heavy — perhaps she had experienced this depth of grief before, but at the moment, she could not remember. She had not even felt this way when her mother abandoned her and Papa, to run away with Clement's adopted younger brother. The Sheriff had changed after that; always there was the shadow of Deborah and Rand's infidelity hanging over their heads, but Clem was glad she and Papa had had the past five years together. She did not regret one minute they had spent together, riding the range and keeping law and order in Lawful.

Brushing the painful thoughts aside as she had

taught herself to do through the years, she moved to a nearby shelf where she picked up a cup and poured herself some coffee.

"Nothing like good strong, hot coffee in a norther." She raised her voice so that the doctor could hear her in the other room.

"Nope!"

Struggling for self-control, Clem stared into the steaming black brew, then out the window as a quicksilver flash of lightning illuminated the room. Above the aroma of the coffee, she smelled the faint acrid stench of sulphur. Although she did not look into the room, she knew Elm had struck a match to light a lamp—a light to see by so he could prepare her father's body for burial. How ironic! Elm had lit a lamp to shed light in the room where her father would be prepared to be buried six feet deep in the dark, wet earth. He would never see daylight again; he would never see the sun he loved so much.

Clem clenched her hand into a tight fist and bit back the tears. She could hardly stand the thought of putting her father in a wooden box that would be buried beneath the soil he had loved. She would no longer see his crooked smile or hear his laughter or feel his arms around her. When Papa was buried, he would be gone . . . forever.

"Where's his badge?" Elm called.

Still she kept her back to the door.

"I have it." She slipped her hand beneath the coat to grasp the star—the star that Papa had loved and worn for so many years of his life—the star that was Papa's life.

"I've emptied his pockets into a small bag," Elm called again.

Clem thought about the pocketknife and the gold good luck piece her father always carried. He had won both of them in a poker game in New Orleans when he was a young man, and had carried them ever since.

"Do you want his possessions now or later?"

"Later," she answered.

Not quite ready to admit that her father was in the funeral parlor, that he really was dead, she refused his belongings. To accept would mean that she was alone, and at the moment she was not ready to do that. Acceptance would mean he *was* truly gone, never to return. On the ride back from Chupedera Lakes she knew he was dead, but he was not gone; she felt as if he were still with her. Not now. Not in there with the wooden boxes.

Elm entered the room where Clem was, heavy footsteps jarring the floor as he walked beyond her to a wall cupboard. He opened and closed the cupboard door and moved nearer to her. She heard a pop and turned to see an opened whiskey bottle tilted over her cup, the amber liquid spilling into the coffee.

"Reckon you can stand some of this." Elm's voice was slightly gruff, almost teary. "It'll help you a little."

"I'm not going soft." Clem leveled a suspicious gaze on the older man. "Don't treat me like I am."

She was speaking unkindly, but knew if she let down her guard, she would go to pieces. That she would not do. Papa might forgive her for losing control, but she would never forgive herself. One of her hands curled over the butt of her revolver, her fingers caressing the carved and inset handle. She had to be tough in order to survive in her world, and tears were a sign of weakness. She had to be tough in order to be the deputy sheriff of Lawful. No matter how deeply she hurt, she determined not to show it; no one would ever see her cry. She would be brave.

Courage, Papa said, was a healthy amount of fear, wrapped in larger amounts of determination and wisdom. Enough fear to be cautious and to temper the

14

overconfidence; enough determination to act; enough wisdom to know when and how to act. Clem figured Papa's definition of grief must be similar to courage. A great amount of hurt and loneliness, wrapped in larger amounts of determination and nonchalance.

Elm ran his fingers through his hair, giving it some semblance of order. After clearing his throat, he said, "Didn't think you were going soft, Clem. You're a tough one. There isn't a person here in Lawful that would argue that point." Again he brushed his hair flat with his hands. "I just figured you needed thawing out, what with this norther and all." As if to give credence to his words, the wind howled around the building, clapping the shutters against the wall and whining through the cracks. "Your Pa always liked whiskey in his coffee in weather like this. Just figured you would, too. I'm gonna have a cup of it myself."

Clem lifted a hand from the revolver and slowly nodded, her gaze only now moving to the door that led to the second room, to the room that held the body of her father, to the room that held the wooden casket—Elm always kept one on hand. From where she was standing, she could not see her father's body, and she was glad. Appreciative of the liberal amount of whiskey Elm had poured, she cradled the cup with both hands, lifted it to her lips, and drank greedily, welcoming the fire that spread throughout her body. She and Elm lapsed into silence as they drank their coffee, Clem standing in front of the heater, Elm sitting at his paper-cluttered desk.

The front door opened, and a tent came billowing into the room on a gust of wind. "Elm, Clem—" a low, raspy feminine voice came from beneath the layers of fabric as a hood was tossed back, and a small, round face framed with strands of fading brown hair appeared to stare curiously at the doctor who slowly rose, "I got here as quick as I could."

15

"Howdy, Maybelle," Elm said. "Right glad you're here. Figure we're gonna need your help before this day is done."

"I thought it was you I saw riding in, Clem," the older woman said, stripping off her gloves and shoving them into her cape pocket. "Brought someone in, didn't you?"

Clem nodded.

"How about shutting the door, Maybelle," Elm said and walked toward the stove. "No sense in wasting all the heat."

"Who?" Maybelle's gaze never left Clem's face.

"The Sheriff." Clem referred to her father in third person and by his title, as she was accustomed to doing in public.

Color drained from the woman's face, and it was a second before she exclaimed, "Oh, my God! I . . . knew it was possible for Clement to die, but I never figured on it's happening. Certainly not so soon." She held out her arms, moving toward Clem. Her eyes misted with tears. "Oh, you dear child."

Glad for comfort, needing it desperately, Clem willingly embraced the small woman whom she had known all her life, and who was now the closest person to a family she had.

"Oh, Clemmy baby, I'm so sorry."

Tears burned Clem's eyes and grief knotted in her throat. With all her heart she wanted to remain in Maybelle's arms and to receive the love and reassurance the older woman promised, but this was a luxury she would not allow herself. She was too close to losing control of her tightly coiled emotions. Gently she moved from the embrace.

"I'm all right," she said tremulously, then paused. After she swallowed several times, she spoke in a stronger voice. "I'm a little tired because I've been riding all day, but, otherwise, I'm fine."

Maybelle fumbled through her pockets, finally extracting a wrinkled handkerchief which she dabbed to her eyes. "What happened?"

"Shot," Clem answered in a staccato voice. "Salt thieves."

Because she had promised to get Alarico Olviera herself, she deliberately withheld his name. In time she would tell, but not right now. Vigilante committees were too prominent out West where the law was scarce; in fact, they were an institution, and she was not about to take the chance of a group of them hanging Olviera. Her thoughts, however, were not charitable. She did not intend to save him from death. She simply wanted to make sure that she — and she alone — was the one who punished him for killing her father.

"Were Hokie and Turbin with you?" Maybelle asked.

"No, they were surveying for Quirt Fisher," Clem answered. "I don't look for them to be back in town until late tonight."

The door flew open again, and this time the owner and editor of the *Lawful Tribune*, accompanied by two strange men and an icy blast of the north wind, stomped into the room. The slamming of the door blended into an ever-nearing clap of thunder. An unbuttoned jacket and disheveled hair gave evidence of Hadley Moore's haste.

"Howdy, Elm. Saw Clem ride into town. Figured she and Clement had a story for me."

"Reckon that's the way you would figure it, Hadley, or you wouldn't be a newspaper man." Elm walked to the oak washstand on the other side of the room. Lifting the pitcher, he filled the basin with water and washed his hands. "Won't be long before all of Lawful is in my office, and all my heat outside."

As Elm grumbled, Clem's gaze swept over the two

strangers who stood near the entrance door. One of the men looked to be in his early twenties, the other in his thirties, and neither had taken the time to put on overcoats. Dudes, Clem thought. Both of them were dudes, more interested in finding out what had happened than they were in their own health or welfare.

"Well, Clem," Hadley said, "what happened? Who's dead?"

"The Sheriff," she answered for the second time in a matter of minutes.

"The Sheriff!" Hadley wheeled around. Staring disbelievingly and taking several faltering steps toward Clem, he said faintly, "He can't be! My God, what are we going to do without him?"

"Reckon we're gonna soon find out." Elm's flat words echoed through the building as he walked into the undertaking room.

Chapter Two

The room was uncomfortably quiet after Elm left. Maybelle moved closer to where Clem stood. Hadley gazed fixedly at the two women; and the strangers remained by the door. Clem sensed that her friends wanted to say something to comfort her, but lacked words. Everyone, including her, had thought the Sheriff was invincible.

"Clem . . ." Hadley finally spoke. "I'm so sorry. Your father was one of the finest men I've ever known."

"Yes, he is . . . was." Clem's words were subdued.

"I couldn't grieve more if it were my own father," he murmured. "This is a sad day for you, Clem."

"A sad day for Lawful," Maybelle murmured. Then silence, heavy and suffocating, once again hung like a blanket over them. In time Maybelle asked, "Who're your friends, Hadley?"

"Sorry," Hadley apologized. "In all the excitement, I forgot to introduce them. Wade Cameron and his cousin Prentice Fairfax."

Wade Cameron, Clem thought. The name seemed familiar, but she could not place it, and at the moment she really did not want to exert the energy necessary to think. Again her gaze swept over the two men, this time more thoroughly. The younger one, despite his

19

moustache, dapper haircut, and expensive suit, had an innocence, an almost endearing naivety about him. The older one, cosmopolitan in bearing, leaned back against the door with his arms folded over his chest and his legs crossed at the ankles. Because he was looking in the other room, in the room where Papa lay, Clem could see only the profile of a strong, almost arrogant face. A shock of black hair, burnished to a high sheen by the muted light from the overhead lamp, fell across his forehead to touch brows the same color as his hair.

"Right smart suit you have on, Mr. Cameron," Maybelle said. "I can tell by looking that it didn't come from around these parts."

"I had it made in New York City."

While his attention was on Maybelle, Clem continued to study him. He must be all of six feet two inches, she thought, as her gaze slowly slid down his frame. He wore a black suit with a gray polka-dotted shirt, a gray, black, and white-checkered waistcoat, and trousers that fit his long legs rather snugly. His black shoes, square-toed and slightly heeled, were made of smooth black leather and polished to a high sheen. Yes, he was an Easterner all right, and a wealthy one at that. His clothing was tailor-made and expensive. One could tell by looking. She lifted her head, her gaze meeting his. The encounter was shocking.

Blue eyes! Blue eyes ringed in midnight! Just like her father's! No, she corrected herself, they were not like Papa's. They were not filled with friendly warmth. They were cool and aloof and analytical. Unmindful that he might consider her gauche, Clem continued to stare curiously into those startling blue eyes. Papa had always said the eyes were the window to a man's soul.

"Look straight into 'em, Clem," Papa said, "and you'll know exactly what a man's thinking and when he's a'thinking it. You'll always be one step ahead of 'im."

Clem had believed the proverb, and evidently this man did, too, because his gaze never wavered from hers. Wade Cameron seemed to have invisible shutters over his eyes that kept her from learning anything about him, but she suspected his eyes could penetrate to the depth of a person's soul, that they could read a person's most intimate thoughts and secrets. While she had no concern about his reading other peoples' thoughts, she did not want him to be privy to hers.

She shivered and had a momentary impulse, which she restrained, to fold her arms across her breasts, to hide her vulnerability from him. She certainly did not want anyone to see her inner thoughts and grief at the moment, and in particular she did not want a reporter and a stranger, at that, to do so. The mere suspicion that he had this power over her disturbed Clem, and made her distrustful of him. Although she wished he would stop staring at her, she would not be the first to break the gaze.

"How'd you happen to come to Lawful, Mr. Cameron?" Maybelle asked.

"The stagecoach threw a wheel."

"So you'll be in town for a while."

"Seems so." He continued to gaze at Clem.

Hadley, walking into the adjoining room to join Elm, said over his shoulder, "They're guests at my house until repairs can be made or another westward bound stage arrives."

Clem realized that if the gaze were going to be broken, she would have to do it herself. Wade Cameron was not. She turned her head, her gaze sweeping over Prentice, who sat at Elm's desk doodling on a piece of paper. Then she looked out the window. Again the only noises heard were the crackling of the fire, the wind howling around the building, and Elm working in the other room.

"Wade Cameron," Maybelle finally murmured. "The name is familiar."

"Possibly," the man answered. "I've been a correspondent for the *New York Times,* and I publish a new magazine called *Cameron's Journal.* Perhaps you've seen my name in reference to either or both of them."

Now Clem knew why she recognized his name. She had read a copy of the journal.

"No," Maybelle drawled, her brow furrowed in thought. "No, I don't reckon so. I've read the *New York Times,* but not any of your articles."

"I have," Clem announced.

"Articles or the *Journal?*" He looked at her curiously.

"*Journal,*" she answered.

"If anybody out here read it," Maybelle said, "it would be Clem. She's right smart, just like her ma who was educated back in a convent school in New Orleans. She taught Clem to read and write and cipher. Yes, sir, she did."

Wade smiled. "What did you think of the *Journal?*"

Clem found pleasure in saying, "I found the articles to be biased and controversial."

"Items of interest sometimes are controversial." The tone was smooth; yet there was a hint of amusement in it, as if he were patronizing her. "My readers seem to be happy with the kinds of articles I'm publishing."

"Readers probably would," Clem conceded. "But I wonder about the people you write about. I have a feeling they feel victimized, and their families must be humiliated."

"I write only the facts." There was an edge to Wade's voice.

"It's the careless way you put them together and the conclusions you draw that bother me," Clem said. "You journalists are interested in nothing but sensationalism, and it doesn't matter how many lives and reputations you must ruin to get it."

"How many issues of the *Journal* have you read?" Wade asked.

"One." She wished her answer could be different. To have read several more issues would substantiate her conclusion, but she refused to give in to the inclination to squirm beneath his glare.

He smiled smugly. "I would say, madam, that this is an instance of the pot calling the kettle black. You have read only one issue, yet you're condemning my publication out of hand."

"Just stating a fact," Clem said.

"No," he said. "Facts are true. This is supposition."

"Well, now," Maybelle said, "I reckon both of you are a little testy over that journal. But if I'm gonna believe either of you about it, it'll have to be Clem, no matter that she's only read one of 'em."

Metal grating against metal sounded through the room, and Clem turned. Maybelle had opened the door of the stove and was shoving in more wood. A piece of it slipped from her hands, fell, and rolled across the floor. Wade bent to retrieve and toss it into the stove.

Slamming the door to and dusting the wood shavings from her hands, Maybelle asked, "How do you like it out West, Mr. Cameron?"

He straightened, his gaze again pinned to Clem. "It gets more interesting by the minute."

Maybelle laughed softly. "I do have to admit, life certainly isn't boring around here."

Out of the corner of her eye, Clem saw Prentice glance up from his doodling, as if doubting Maybelle's statement.

"Nor predictable," the woman added. "And speaking of predictable — why, I remember, one time when . . ."

Having heard Maybelle's "predictable" story hun-

23

dreds of times, Clem had no interest in the retelling. Not wanting to stare at Wade Cameron longer, or at the artist, she gazed at the door of the undertaking room. Elm moved around the table where Papa lay. On the other side of the room, Hadley stood beneath one of the wall lamps, the soft light spilling over his tousled hair.

Clem liked Hadley, but in general did not like, trust, or even tolerate reporters or journalists—especially those who exaggerated the truth in order to create sensationalism. The press had not been kind to the Sheriff during his early life, and Clem would never forgive them for that. Her father had been wild during his early years. Some even considered him to have been an outlaw, but hardly a man on the frontier had not been wild and unruly and a tad outside the law at one time or another. The West spawned a breed of hard men who were an enigma to the Easterner, and Clement Jones had been one of these.

"No, ma'am, my friend isn't a correspondent," Clem heard Wade Cameron say, and her attention returned to him. He was just such a reporter, and she wanted nothing more to do with him.

"Actually, ma'am," Prentice said, "I'm an artist. I'm here to—"

Maybelle waved a silencing hand through the air. "I know what you're here to do, boy. You'll draw the pictures that go along with any story Cameron writes. We've had your likes through here before."

She snapped her fingers. "Why, I declare, I remember your name. Didn't you do some illustrations for *Harper's Weekly* about the West?"

Fairfax nodded his head and rose from the desk.

"I thought so. You and an Eastern Senator made a trip out here a couple of years ago."

The man's eyes glittered and his smile broadened. Bobbing his head all the more, he ran the tip of his

24

finger over the thick moustache. "Yes, ma'am, we did. My experience is one of the reasons why Wade asked me to accompany him. It's mighty kind of you to remember."

"Why, thank you, son," Maybelle said, dismissing him. She turned to Clem. "I know Clement had a Sunday suit, Clem, but it was kinda old. Not really good for burying, especially at the church. I have a new suit at the store that will fit the Sheriff. Well, now it might be a tad small, but I can alter it, if you'd like."

Clem swallowed the tears that were never far away. Many were the times that Papa had sent her over to the general store to buy burial clothes, but this was her first time to give the order to buy them. Again she slipped her hand between the jacket and her shirt to brush against the star, a gentle reminder of the promise she made to her father and to herself.

"Dear . . ." Maybelle touched Clem's arm, "I said—"

Clem smiled into the kind face. "I think the Sheriff would be mighty obliged to you for that, Maybelle."

Elm moved to stand in the doorway between the two rooms, a palm pressed against the frame. "Clement will be laid out by morning. Reckon we need to get the word around. People are going to want to come to pay their last respects."

"Yes," Clem said, a catch in her voice.

"Clement was well liked and respected, and those who didn't like or respect him feared him." Elm shook his head. "I shudder to think what will happen to Lawful now that he's gone."

I shudder to think what will happen to me, Clem thought. Although she stood in the center of the room surrounded by people, she was alone, all alone. She quickly pushed her self-pity and loneliness aside. She was a tough woman, able to take care of herself.

She had gone out of her way to prove to herself and to the residents of Lawful that she was as rugged and strong as any man. The thought reassured her. Besides, she was certain that Hokum Smith and Turbin Davis would serve as her deputies. Her only concern was how many hours a day they could give her. She would speak to them as soon as she could.

"Why don't you go on home, honey," Maybelle said. "You've done all you can tonight. Elm and I will take care of Clement. We'll call you when he's all laid out."

Clem nodded, then said, "If you see Hokie or Turbin—"

"We'll be sure to let them know," Maybelle assured her.

"Tell them I'd like to see them."

"All right, dear." Maybelle pulled her gloves from her pocket and pulled them on. "Do—don't you think we ought to send word to Deborah? I think she ought to know. And Rand?"

Clem hesitated before she answered. "You can send word of the Sheriff's death to anyone you wish."

Although Clem gave her permission, her entire being screamed no. She had seen neither Deborah nor Rand in the five years they had been gone. Rand's coming back did not bother her. Since he was not a blood relative and had not abandoned her, he had no power to hurt her. It was her father whom Rand had hurt the most, and now that the Sheriff was gone, Rand's presence in Lawful did not matter. Naturally she preferred that he did not come, but he was inconsequential to her.

Not so Deborah! *She* had hurt both of them.

Clem's hand closed around the points of the star, and she clenched it so tightly the points pricked her palm. Trust Maybelle to resurrect more disturbing memories, memories Clem had learned to push to the back of her mind.

26

"I'll send a telegram then," Maybelle said, the words lost in the heavy silence that engulfed the room.

Go ahead, Clem thought, *Deborah and Rand didn't come to see Papa and me when he was alive. They didn't care what happened to us after they left. They certainly won't have the nerve to show up now. Deborah is a weak woman. She didn't deserve the Sheriff, and he deserved better than she. Rand's a coward. When the going got tough, he turned tail and ran. Neither of them will have the gall to show up for Papa's funeral. Neither can face me after what they have done to Papa and me. They wouldn't dare!*

"I still can't believe Clement's dead," Hadley said, breaking into Clem's thoughts. "Tell me what happened."

Clem, relieved to take her mind off the possibility of Deborah's and Rand's returning to Lawful and to her life, spoke to the editor. "He was shot by salt thieves at Chupedera Lakes."

"Damn it!" Hadley muttered, the expletive followed by more muttered curses. "I wish to God Sam Harper, Kent Thompson, and Leon Howard hadn't bought all that acreage around those lakes. I know they had a right to, but I just wish they hadn't. At least, not until the local Mexicans can understand the difference in Mexican and American law regarding underground minerals."

"Well, none of the three is going to give an inch," Maybelle said. "And I can't say that I blame them. They own the salt, and feel it's their right to demand payment for it. You can't blame them because the locals are getting angry, stealing the salt and shooting the law enforcers."

She pulled the hood over her head, hitched her skirt in both hands and moved toward the door. "So we're going to have to live with this thieving until someone comes up with a solution to the problem."

"I could live with the thieving." Hadley spat the

words. "Clement couldn't."

His words were lost in the gust of wind that followed Maybelle's departure. Wade Cameron closed the door and settled back against it, his gaze moving around the room in a slow, calculated motion.

"May I go see the body?" Fairfax asked.

The question in itself was innocent, the request natural, but rage boiled within Clem. She could not answer, not even when both Hadley and Elm looked at her. As if Prentice sensed an undercurrent, he stopped and turned around to look first at Hadley, then at Elm, and finally at Clem.

"Is it all right?" he asked again.

Clem drew in a deep breath, then exhaled slowly. "Yes, it's all right," she answered, knowing that cooperation was her best defense.

An outright refusal would only cause Fairfax and Cameron—she cast a cautious gaze at him—to be more curious and determined to pry into her father's life. Reporters had taken little interest in him after he became the sheriff of this small west Texas town, when he was alive and protecting the citizens of Lawful with his own life. She did not appreciate this journalistic interest in him now that he was dead. Clem especially did not want a stranger digging into her father's past. It was over, done with, and best laid to rest along with him.

"Do you think we have a story here, Mr. Moore?" Prentice called. Clem's heart skipped a beat.

"Don't reckon the passing of a local sheriff will cause much of a stir back East." Hadley followed Prentice into the second room, his voice growing fainter as he moved away from Clem. "But it's a sad story for us. Clement Jones was the best thing that ever happened to Lawful."

"He looks old to be a sheriff." The artist's voice carried.

Hadley laughed. "Compared to you, I guess he was old."

"He was only fifty-five," Clem snapped, her voice loud enough to be heard in the adjacent room.

"Maybe that's why the salt thieves killed him," Prentice suggested. "Because he was so old, he was slow on the draw."

"That's an assumption that cost several gunmen their lives," Clem declared, not caring that she sounded defensive. "He was the fastest draw in the West. You have no right to talk about him like this. Not now. Not when he can no longer defend himself."

"Whatever you say," Prentice said. "It's of no consequence."

But it was of consequence to Clem, and she resented — strongly resented — the Easterner throwing aspersions on a local sheriff, and especially on her father. Then Clem felt an eerie feeling scurry up her spine, and knew she was being watched. Without looking she knew Wade Cameron was staring at her. Slowly, as if she had no will of her own, she turned and met the compelling gaze. Wade Cameron said nothing; in fact, his expression never changed. Yet she saw the curiosity — pure, undiluted curiosity — that swam in his eyes.

"I'm sorry about the death of your father, ma'am. I can only imagine how painful it must have been for you to bring his body back to town." The softness of Wade's voice did nothing to disguise the deep resonant timbre. His words easily carried across the room. "How did you happen to be the one who brought him in?"

His concern startled Clem, but not nearly as much as the mellifluous voice and the steady gaze. Fearing that he read too much in her eyes, in her stance, in her defensive outburst about the Sheriff, she changed positions and turned her head, but not before she observed him pull a small notebook and pencil out of his jacket pocket and begin to write.

Anger quickly quelled her curiosity. *Damn correspondent!* He was not really concerned about her at all. His only interest was a story. Although she and Papa meant nothing to him, he was taking notes . . . just in case he could use them. Clem imagined the kind of sensationalism he would fabricate (or perhaps would not have to fabricate) around her father, in order to make this an interesting story to Easterners.

Angrily, she rubbed the palm of her hand down her trousers. She stopped when she realized that he was watching her, that he was looking at her thighs. She looked down at her travel-soiled clothes, and for the first time since she had entered the room Clem was aware of how she must appear to him. She realized how bizarre this entire scene must seem to him.

"Clem—" Cameron's gaze lowered to focus on the twin revolvers. "That is your name, isn't it?"

"Yes."

She walked to the small wall mirror to look at her eyes, and was relieved to see that the swelling had abated since she had come out of the weather. Her cheeks and the tip of her nose, however, were still red and chapped from the pounding by the north wind. She tugged her hat a little lower over her forehead.

"How did I happen to be the one to bring him in?" she repeated his question. "Well, Mr. Cameron, I brought the Sheriff in because I happened to be the one riding with him when he was killed."

"Just the two of you?"

His gaze caught her reflection in the mirror, and she nodded. Making no attempt to hide his curiosity, he said, "Why do you call your father the Sheriff? It sounds rather odd coming from his daughter."

"That's the way he wanted it. Kept things on a business footing, and kept family and sentiment out of the way."

How many times she had answered banal questions about other men whom she and the Sheriff had brought into town, and it had not affected her. Just went to prove that even in calling her father by his name and title, she had not been able to keep family and sentiment out of the way.

Well, she had given out all the information she intended to give out tonight, especially to this man. She walked to the door, her determined steps snapping cadence on the hardwood floor.

"If you'll excuse me," she said. "I'd like to leave."

Her gaze locked with his, as it had done so frequently since she had met him. She was convinced that his eyes were magnets drawing hers to them, and refused to look away. She stood in front of the stranger now, close enough that the fragrance of his cologne teased her nostrils, close enough that she saw the dark blue ring around irises the color of the sky, close enough that she saw the lamplight playing over his thick black hair. He lifted a hand to brush the errant wave from his forehead, and she noticed the planes and texture of his face, the lower portion shadowed with evening beard stubble.

"I suppose you'll know me the next time you see me," he said.

Slowly she tilted her face to stare into the intense blue eyes. In their depths lurked a gentle—although quizzical—smile. "Yes," she drawled softly, "reckon I will. I make it my business to know everybody who comes into my territory. Never know when you've got a polecat among you."

A grin easily slid across his lips, softening the hard planes and angles. "I'm the polecat?"

Refusing to smile although she had an inclination to do so, Clem slipped her gloves on. "Reckon that's for me to find out. Now, if you'll just move, I'll be on my way."

He made no effort to obey. "Where are you going?"

"Had I wanted you to know, I would have told you."

"I suppose you're going to report this to someone?"

"To whom?" Clem lifted an eyebrow. "The Sheriff's in there . . . dead. Our two part-time deputies are out of town. Right now I'm the only semblance of law and order Lawful has, and I already know. Now, will you please get out of my way."

She laid her hand on his shoulder to push him aside. Her mistake. The man caught her hand in his, in a warm, binding clasp. His mistake. With lightning speed, Clem whipped out her revolver and raised it, the tip of the barrel touching the tip of his nose. The click of the hammer echoed through the room. He never flinched, and the hard blue eyes never left her face. Their eyes locked together once more—hers defiant, his steely. Clem knew the firm grip could have been as steely as his gaze.

He laughed softly, then said in an equally soft voice, laced with mockery, "That was a bad move."

It was humor Clem could not bear; it was laughter that set all her frayed nerve endings aflame. Another time she could have ignored it, but not now. Nor could she ignore the tingling sensation that coursed through her body.

Feeling like an idiot and wondering why she had done such a foolish thing, she demanded, "Turn my hand loose."

Why had she allowed herself to react to a stranger like this? She had no right to push him aside, and absolutely no cause to whip out her revolver. Somewhere out of the cluttered thoughts that spun around in her head, she heard a little voice that chided, *Use that brain of yours, Clem.*

"Remove that revolver from my face unless you mean to shoot me." Wade Cameron's voice was now as hard as his eyes, as firm as the hand clasping hers.

"Don't ever touch me again *unless I give you permission.*" Good sense chastised her, but pride refused to give an inch.

Still he did not turn her loose. In that deceptively quiet voice he said, "If you ever pull a gun on me again, you'd better be prepared to shoot."

The first rule Papa had stressed to her when he taught her to use the gun, and now some city slicker was taunting her with it! Embarrassed but refusing to let him know, she slowly released the hammer, lowered the revolver, and dropped it into the holster. Still, it was a full second before his clasp loosened on her hand.

"If you ever touch me again without my permission," she said, "it will be your last move. Now, get out of my way. I want out of here right now."

Clem was a mass of contradicting emotions. She had to make her escape before she burst into tears, before she made more of a fool of herself in front of this Eastern dude than she already had.

He did not move.

"Please move," she repeated. "I'd like to leave."

Slowly he stepped aside. She lowered her face, blinked back the tears, and grabbed the door handle. She gave one vigorous pull on the heavy oak, welcoming the cold blast of air as she stepped out of the building, casting him a last defiant glance before heading down the street.

"Clem," Hadley Moore ran onto the boardwalk and shouted, "wait a minute. I want to talk to you. I want to know the details about what happened today. Who killed your pa?"

"Not now, Hadley." The wind whipped her words into oblivion.

"Leave her be, Hadley," Elm said. "Can't you see she's in no mood to be talking tonight. It can wait until morning."

"No, it can't—"

Clem heard no more of the argument. Tears streaming down her cheeks, she unhitched the roan and stallion, and leading them, made her way to the darkened cottage on the edge of town. First she went inside to light the lamps and to build a fire in the parlor fireplace and the wood stove in the kitchen. She filled two large kettles with water, and while they heated for her bath, she returned to the barn where she groomed and fed the horses. The task finished, she moved to the barn door and stood for a minute looking up at the cloud-covered night sky, void of stars.

No longer fearing the imminent downpour, she pushed out of the building and slowly walked toward the house, toward the silent, empty house. Lightning flashed and booming peals of thunder followed in its wake. The wind slapped her scarf across her face and molded her clothes to her body. Nearer came the lightning; louder cracked the thunder; but she never lengthened her stride. By the time she reached the bottom steps of the back porch, large drops of rain splattered against her hat.

Blackness covered the small western town, as surely as it covered her heart. Soon the rain would clean away the impurities of the earth and give new life, but Clem knew the tears she shed would never wash away her hurt and grief; they would not give Clement Jones new life. Once more the sun would shine upon Lawful, but would it ever again touch her soul with its warmth and cheer?

Chapter Three

Listening to the gentle patter of the rain and to the sporadic roll of thunder, Wade stood in the shadows at the edge of the porch, while Hadley knocked on Clem's door. It was quite late, but the light in the parlor indicated that she was home and still up. Wade would not have blamed her if she did not answer. For most, grief was personal and certainly natural at a time like this. But this was an unusual woman—this Clementina Jones—daughter of the late sheriff.

The door cracked opened, a wedge of muted light filtering onto the porch. She said in a slightly husky voice, "Yes?"

"Clem, it's me." Hadley held his hat in his hands, water dripping from his raincoat onto the porch. His breath was a cloud of silver vapor.

"I know." She sounded tired. "I saw you through the window. I wouldn't have answered otherwise."

"It's late, and I hate to bother you, but I'd like to have the story about your father's death in tomorrow's news."

Curious by nature as well as by vocation, Wade quietly moved closer to the door, in hopes of seeing Clementina Jones again. Having learned more about her from Elm and Hadley, he wanted to study and to know her better, but as if she divined his purpose, she

35

remained hidden behind the door. Only a small shadowed portion of her face was visible. Through the crack and above her head, he could see into the small parlor where a welcome blaze burned in the fireplace, and several lamps were lit, their gentle glow adding to the homey scene that was cozy and inviting.

"Clem, I know you're tired, and I won't keep you up much later," Hadley pleaded. "But I do want to do this story. You know how I and the citizens of Lawful feel about Clement."

"You never give up, do you?"

"No." Hadley chuckled softly. "Tenacity is a newspaperman's best trait."

Wade could tell from the tone of Clem's voice that she was going to give in to Hadley's request. As a seasoned correspondent, he knew the scenario quite well. Clem was exhausted, having traveled all those miles from the Chupedera Salt Flats with her father's body, and it was easier to submit than to fight.

Under any other circumstances, and with any other woman, Wade would have thought she was under too much stress and grief, but not this woman, not this Clem Jones—who according to both Hadley and Elm rode and shot and cussed like a man. Although the dead man was her father, she acted as if he were of no relationship, merely the sheriff and an acquaintance. She actually spoke of him in the third person—to separate family and sentiment from business, she said. He supposed he could understand that, but at the doctor's office earlier this evening she had displayed absolutely no trace of grief over the sheriff's death. He had never seen a more composed person in his life.

"I might as well talk to you tonight," Clem said, "and get it over with. I have work to do tomorrow, and I don't want to spend the day spinning tales about the Sheriff's death."

Clem Jones had attracted Wade's attention from the

minute he walked into the doctor's office earlier in the evening. He had not thought about the sheriff's death as much as he had thought about the sheriff's daughter. At first, it was merely journalistic curiosity, but as time passed, he became interested in her as a person, as a woman. He had begun to compare her with other women he had known, and realized there was no comparison. His interest was thoroughly piqued. He wanted to discover what she was really like beneath that tough, tomboy veneer—and he had to believe the tough, cold exterior was a veneer.

He was glad Hadley had invited him to come to Clem's house tonight. He wanted to see her again. She was an enigma, and he liked that. One who loved to piece puzzles together and to unravel a mystery layer by layer, he was ready to uncover Clementina Jones to find out what she was really like—intellectually, spiritually . . . yes, and to be quite honest, physically.

The rounded buttocks and length of leg revealed by those trousers she wore had been quite alluring, and had given him a desire to see more, in particular the color and texture of her hair that had been hidden beneath the hat. He was most curious to see how well it complemented those frosty green eyes. Excitement kindled as he thought of getting to know Clementina Jones better, of melting the frost in her eyes.

She flung open the door, and Wade followed Hadley Moore into the house and was standing in the center of the room when she spoke, the sound coming from behind them.

"You didn't tell me you had the *tenderfoot* with you," she said, "but I should have guessed."

Venom would have been sweeter than her tone—far, sweeter, Wade thought as he turned around, a retort quickly leaping to his tongue. Then he saw her, and all thoughts of speaking vanished. She walked to the fireplace, auburn hair cascading down her back and a long cotton robe flowing with the movement of her body. He had been prepared for Clem Jones, for the tough gun-toting woman who had brought the sheriff into town for burial, but he was not prepared for Clementina Jones, the daughter of the sheriff. No, nothing he had seen or heard tonight had prepared him for this woman. She far exceeded his expectations.

"The artist didn't come with you," she said.

"No, he said he was going to visit a little longer with Elm, then go on over to the house," Hadley answered.

"How about Hokie and Turbin," she asked. "Have they returned yet?"

"Haven't seen them if they have," Hadley answered. "I'm sure they'll stop by Elm's place, and he'll give them your message. If he doesn't, Maybelle will. Probably the whole town knows Clement's dead by now. The preacher and his wife stopped by Elm's. They said as soon as Maybelle told them about Clement's death, they came over to see you."

Clem nodded.

"They also said you wanted Clement's body moved to the church as soon as he could. You having the funeral there?"

"Yes. Tomorrow afternoon . . . if tomorrow ever comes."

She crossed her arms over her breasts and hugged herself. She remembered the way Papa would begin his day, standing on the edge of the porch, breathing deeply and gazing at the rising sun. *Just embracing the dawn,* he would say. *A hug with her makes for a good day.* Clem wondered if she would ever see a good day again. At the moment her future looked bleak and lonely.

"Morning will come," Hadley promised her. "It

38

might take it a long time, but it'll come, Clem. Always does."

Wade watched the exchange with interest. Unlike the women with whom he associated in New York, this one was not beautiful in a sophisticated or artificial sense. And he was glad; he was tired of women who were artificially beautiful. Many times their beauty was a mask, hiding an ugly, deceitful inner person. Those with whom he had been acquainted were shallow and conniving, for the most part, with one purpose in life: to ensnare any man they could get into marriage. So far he had managed to avoid the trap.

The doctor had said Clem was twenty-one years old, well past the marrying age. Yet she was single. Wade wondered why. Since there was a scarcity of women on the frontier, he doubted she would have difficulty finding a husband.

Although she wore a white cotton dressing gown, buttoned from the top of her neck to the bottom of her feet, she was slender and—surprisingly—sensual. A little too slender, he decided as he studied the lines of her face, but it made her all the more attractive. Her hair, brushed back from her face, hung in deep waves down her back.

Her breasts were high and firm, gently molding the bodice of the gown; her waist was small—too small and fragile for those revolting revolvers she had worn strapped to herself earlier. Wade's gaze dropped to her hands—utterly feminine with long, slender fingers, her nails clipped short. He could not imagine that hand holding one of those pistols, much less shooting it.

"Clem's a dead shot, she is," Elm had declared with the same parental pride that an eastern mother displayed when she said of her daughter, "She's as accomplished with her domestic duties as she is beautiful. She'll make some man a wonderful wife."

"Mr. Cameron, would you like a cup of coffee?"

Slowly Wade's gaze rose from her hands to her face, in particular to her eyes. The chill he had noticed earlier in the doctor's office was gone, and they were the color of the forest in the springtime. Like her body, they were now soft and alluring.

"In case you didn't hear me," Clem began. "Would you like—"

"I did hear you," Wade answered, quickly regaining his aplomb, never off balance for long. "And yes, Miss Jones," strange she was not a Miss Jones; she was either Clementina or Clem and he fought to keep from calling her by her first name, "I would like a cup."

"Black?" she asked.

The material of her dressing gown pulled across her hips as she walked toward the door, making Wade even more aware of her femininity. He was amazed at her gracefulness when earlier she had appeared to be a tomboy.

"No, sweet."

Clem stopped walking and stared at him for a few seconds before she laughed. The sound was deep and husky and not the least bit masculine. For a moment her guard dropped, and her entire countenance relaxed and genuine laughter touched her eyes and mouth. Wade was unsure which was more beautiful, her utter femininity or her laughter. Both thrilled him, and sheer pleasure spread through his body.

"One teaspoon of sugar," said he.

"All right," she answered, then with amused tolerance in her voice said to the newspaper editor as she began to walk again. "A dude for sure, Hadley."

Sitting down on the sofa, Hadley laughed with her. "Indulge the boy, Clem. He'll grow up before he gets out of Lawful."

Clem stopped at the door, one hand on the frame. Once more she stared at Wade. This time a slow, quiet smile touched her lips, coaxing them up at the corners. Then it traveled to her eyes. She gazed at him for a long time before she dropped her lids, letting thick, curling lashes form a dark crescent on her cheeks. He already thought her handsome, but this smile completely transformed her into a vision of loveliness. He caught his breath in surprise and admiration. Unlike the sophisticated beauties to which he was accustomed, Clem was wild and untamed and spirited. She excited him.

"Yes, Hadley," she murmured, "I have no doubt he'll grow up before he leaves Lawful. The West will make a man out of him."

"I think, ma'am," Wade said, "I'm already very much a man."

"As you told me earlier," Clem said smiling, "that could be supposition on your part."

"Given the opportunity," he said, enjoying the verbal sparring, "I'll prove it's fact."

"If you're around here long enough, we'll find out. The West has a way of separating the boys from the men." They disappeared into the kitchen.

Wade was accustomed to flirtatious and pretended indifference, but not to genuine indifference. And this woman who had disconcerted him from the first moment he had seen her and had filled his thoughts ever since, sorely dented his confidence and ego. She gave him a feeling of vulnerability that made him most uncomfortable. Hell, he felt uncomfortable with the entire situation.

His attraction to her was causing him to behave like a callow youth. Clementina Jones was years younger than he, yet she spoke as if she were his mother's age. He walked around the room, finally coming to a halt in front of the reading table. On it were a large family

Bible, an equally large album, and several loose photographs. Having no qualms about invading Clem's privacy, he opened the Bible and began to read the entries. When he read the last one — small but poignant — he knew Clementina Jones grieved for her father.

"Here we are," Clem said.

She returned to the room to set a silver tray on the coffee table in front of the divan. She straightened, her gaze going directly to the opened Bible, then up to his face. Her glare accused him of invading her privacy, of reading what he had no business reading; it filled him with remorse — a first for Wade. He closed the book. Clem clasped her hands together, not nervously, Wade observed, but as if she yearned to remove the objects from the table where he sat. This further aroused his curiosity in her and her background.

"You may add sugar to suit yourself, Mr. Cameron."

Hadley took a swallow and said, "Good coffee, Clem. Now, sit down and let's talk."

"Exactly what do you want to know?"

"Everything that happened after you and Clement rode out to the salt lakes."

Clem sat in the chair opposite Hadley and curled her feet beneath her. Wade walked over to the low table between Hadley and Clem and stirred a teaspoon of sugar into his coffee. Picking up the cup, he moved to the chair next to the reading table.

"I'm curious, Miss Jones —" he began.

"Please call me Clem," said she.

Wade nodded and smiled, a deliberate gesture he had cultivated to devastate and to manipulate. Fleetingly he wondered what impact it would have on Clem Jones. None apparently. Her expression never changed; her steadfast gaze never wavered. "Why were you the only one with your father?"

"I was his deputy," Clem answered. "His full-time deputy. Since Hokum Smith and Turbin Davis are surveyors for the county, they worked for the Sheriff when he asked them. He didn't feel like this was an assignment that called for more deputies. Also, since I was the second best gun in town, I was the one the Sheriff always wanted by his side. No matter what the situation, he knew he could count on me."

"That's right," Hadley agreed. "While her ma was teaching her how to read and write and cipher, Clement was teaching her how to ride, rope, and shoot. He taught her everything she knows about handling guns. He was the best, but Clem ran him a close second."

"Now I'm the best shot in Lawful." She evinced no conceit, only a matter of factness that comes with knowledge.

"There must be at least one man who can shoot as well as you!"

Clem's back straightened, and her green eyes narrowed. "I'm sure there are many men who can shoot as well as I can, Mr. Cameron, but none of them are in Lawful at the moment."

"She's right, Wade," Hadley said. "You ought to see her in action. As Elm said earlier, this little woman here is one of the deadliest shots in the region."

"What's going to happen when news of her father's death gets out, and she's touted as the fastest gun in Lawful?" Wade asked softly, leaning back in the chair and already speculating the answer himself. "Gunmen will flock here to take her on."

"Yes," Clem answered without hesitation or any evidence of apprehension. "I expect so. Certainly it's a frequent and real part of life out here. I'm sure with you being from the East, you don't understand our way of life, Mr. Cameron."

Oh, but he did. He was much too familiar with the

43

code of the West. Having been a gunman himself, and knowing only too well the dangers inherent in such a vocation, he was irritated by Clem's casual attitude. He also knew that a gunman was respected—perhaps feared was a better choice of words—until someone a little faster than he came along. Has-been gunmen had tough lives. People never let them forget their past, especially young guns who wanted to use them as target practice; thus, they usually spent their latter years running and hiding.

"Some men pride themselves on being the quickest and deadliest shot in the west," Clem continued, "and while they can grudgingly accept another man as being quicker and better than they, they can't accept a woman as being quicker and better. So I have no reason to believe that they won't be coming after me. My only protection at this point is the badge."

"Looks to me like that's going to offer you little, with the sheriff being dead," Wade said. "Seems to me that you're on your own with a reputation to uphold."

"That's a chance I'm willing and going to take."

A quick stab of fear shot through Wade. He found the idea of Clem having to face a gunman in a shoot-out repugnant. "You're too young to have your life taken from you for such a useless reason." He was surprised to hear himself voicing his apprehension aloud, even more surprised that he actually cared what happened to her.

Clem arched a brow. "Thank you for the concern, Mr. Cameron, but I have more confidence in my ability than you. I figure that it will be the gunman's life taken, not mine."

Still in a daze, Wade did not answer. He could not remember the last time he had genuinely cared about a woman. Yet he did care about this one, who was virtually a stranger to him. The revelation that he was concerned—really concerned—stunned him.

44

Clem rose and walked out of the room, the whisper of fabric about her feet catching Wade's attention. His gaze fastened to the soft material, then steadily moved up from the tip of her slippers, past the gentle mounds of her breasts, to the lace circling her throat. When he imagined the bodice of her gown covered in blood, he grimaced and closed his eyes—as if that would erase the picture he saw.

Puzzled by his reaction to Clem, he wondered why she was getting to him when none other had managed to do so. *She's getting to you because you're allowing her to,* a small voice said. Initially the idea that he cared about Clem stunned him. Now it startled—certainly it un-settled—him. He was going to have to be most cautious where this woman was concerned. His caring made him vulnerable.

Clem returned with her father's badge resting in the palm of her hand. The silver star glinted in the lamp light. "I figure it's going to offer me a lot of protection. Clement swore me in as deputy sheriff before he died," she said. "So until we can elect someone, I'll be keeping law and order in Lawful. This star is mine to wear."

"Well, good, that's settled!" Hadley slapped his hands against his thighs.

"How can it be settled?" Wade asked. "Surely you have a city council who will have some say in the matter!"

"I've been riding with my father for the past five years," Clem replied softly. "At first they objected, but they haven't said one word about it during the past three years. As sheriff, Clement had the right to appoint his deputies."

"I'm not talking about anyone's right to appoint deputies." Moving closer to her, Wade gazed candidly into her face. "I'm talking about his right to appoint you his replacement. I'm even questioning his judg-

45

ment. I can't imagine any father doing this to his daughter."

"Since you're not a citizen of Lawful," Clem said in the same soft and deadly voice, "this is really none of your business."

"That's right," Hadley said. "You don't understand us westerners, Wade. Clem's more able to defend this town than any man I know, including myself. And she's right. During the past three years none of us council members has objected to her being one of Clement's deputies. Why should we mind her being the deputy sheriff now that her pa is dead? Besides, I have no doubt Hokie and Turbin will work with her as they did her pa. Now," Hadley turned his attention to her, "tell me about the man who shot Clement."

Thinking Hadley a coward to hide behind a woman's skirts, and thinking her insane for taking on the thankless job of protecting cowards, Wade gaped but said no more. War raged within him, but Clem Jones was right. This was not his battle or his cause. He had given up fighting for causes a long, long time ago. He was not about to start again. No, he had no need for the pain and hurt that accompanied caring. Biting back his arguments, he returned to his chair and sat down, his gaze flickering toward the window where rivulets of rain ran down the glass pane.

Clem began to talk. "As you know, Thompson's survey was completed, and he now owns the last section of land around the lakes. He, Harper, and Howard posted notices that these lakes belonged to them, and warned people not to take salt without paying a fee. They asked Clement to oversee the collecting of the fees. We thought we were doing a pretty good job of it . . . or we did until today." Her voice trailed into silence.

"Those damned salt lakes," Hadley murmured. "They'll be the destruction of this county yet. How

46

many Mexicans were there?"

"Two wagons," she answered.

"Only two wagons!" Hadley's brow rose in disbelief.

"Only two," Clem repeated dryly and walked to the window to pull the curtain aside. Her back to the men, she lifted a hand and drew designs in the condensation on the pane.

Not really interested in local politics or the death of the old sheriff, but quite interested in the new woman deputy sheriff, Wade idly thumbed through Clem's album. True, she had been displeased to see him reading her Bible, but photographs were not as personal. And they would surely tell him something about her. While he was searching for Bryan Dillon, he would be gathering information for interesting and new stories for the *Journal,* and one about a woman peace officer would certainly be an interesting one.

She said, "The fact that the Mexicans had brought armed guards should have tipped the Sheriff and me off, but it didn't. We weren't expecting trouble. The Mexicans know that—knew that—the Sheriff was a fair man, and they trusted him. At least, they've listened to him."

Wade looked up as she spoke, a brilliant flash of lightning silhouetting her in the window. He lowered the page at which he was looking and gazed instead at her.

"Do you know who killed him?" Hadley asked.

Clem waited a long time before she said, "Maybe."

"You do." Hadley accused sharply.

Without turning, Clem dropped the curtain.

Hadley settled back in the chair and stared into space for a few minutes; then he snapped his fingers and grinned. "Rico Olviera. He's the kid who refused to pay the salt tax several weeks ago and promised to lead the Mexicans in an uprising. It is Rico, isn't it?"

Ignoring the question, Clem turned to say, "This

47

salt war is a bad thing, Hadley, and the Sheriff knew that. It's turned family against family and friends against friends. The Sheriff understood what taking the salt from the Mexicans meant, and he didn't take what Rico said as a threat to him personally. In fact, he really liked Rico and believed that he was right. The Sheriff knew the citizens were ready to fight for what they considered their domain, but he didn't count on Rico's becoming so militant and belligerent. That's why—that's why we weren't prepared for the shooting. The Sheriff—Papa—"

Her shift from referring to her father in third person to first caught Wade's attention completely; the photographs forgotten, he closed the album. For the first time since he had met her, Clem Jones was showing her feelings about her father. She had not looked directly at him since she turned from the window, but even with her head slightly averted, he could still see her features clearly. Her eyes were misty, her chin trembling slightly; she was close to tears. She looked alone and forlorn. Strangely, Wade wanted to take her into his arms to comfort and to reassure her.

Clem drew in a deep breath, swallowed, and said clearly, "Papa thought these people were his friends."

Returning the photograph album to the table, Wade sat back in the chair, bridged his hands in front of him, and continued to stare pensively at Clem Jones. *Yes,* he thought, not for the first time, *she is an enigma, one that I shall enjoy discovering.*

Clem clenched her hands and said, "After the shooting started, the Mexican guards ran away, and we gave chase. I didn't even know that he—that the Sheriff had been shot until—until we reached the base of Black Mountain, and he fell off his horse. I stopped the chase and stayed with him, until—" She paused, then said, "I brought him home, and you know the rest."

"When are you going after Olviera?" Hadley asked.

"I didn't say it was him," Clem replied, "and I would rather you didn't mention his name in the paper."

"Couldn't be you're suppressing news, Deputy?"

"No, Hadley. I don't want to see a man lynched without the benefit of a trial. Like the Sheriff, I don't hold with citizens taking the law into their own hands." Clem's glance strayed to Wade, then returned to the editor.

"If you're worried about me talking," Wade said, "you're worrying over nothing. While I'm developing an interest in the story, the early release belongs to Hadley."

At the moment, my primary interest is you—first to discover who and what you are, and second to write a story about you.

Admirers as well as critics had often praised Wade on his ability to find a story where there appeared to be none. One of his greatest virtues was tenacity. No matter how difficult or elusive his quarry, he never gave up until he had the story. Then he squeezed it for every ounce of use he could. Most of all, Wade knew when to stop; he inherently recognized that delicate, paradoxical moment when the story was over, and one more word would be cheap sensationalism or exploitation. Wade knew he had a story in Clementina Jones; he felt it.

Hadley leaned to the edge of the sofa. "What you're saying is well and good, Clem, and knowing you as well as I do, I believe you. But *what you're saying* isn't your only reason for withholding Olviera's name, is it?"

Her voice was low and controlled when she spoke, "No. I just don't want anyone to get him before I do. He's mine . . . all mine."

The harsh declaration jarred Wade. The delicate woman he was intent on saving was gone; in her place stood a gunman as bloodthirsty as the worst of them.

"My God!" he exclaimed. "You can't mean what you're saying!"

"Yes," she was poised and determined, "I do. I fully intend to kill the man who murdered my father."

Chapter Four

"You can't go out there and kill that man in cold blood!" Wade exclaimed.

"Why not? He killed my father in cold blood."

Dumbfounded, Wade could only stare at her. He had been forced to kill men during his lifetime, first in the War Between the States, then in his former line of work, but he balked at the idea of Clem stalking this man to kill him. She could not be this cold and callous.

Clem's cool gaze continued to focus on him. "Don't you believe in justice?"

"Justice! This isn't justice. It's revenge."

"Perhaps we're using different words, Mr. Cameron, but the outcome is the same."

Wade pushed his hand through his hair. "For God's sake, the man could kill you! You're not invincible. Isn't your father's death testimony of that?"

He saw the hurt in her eyes, and while he was not sorry he had made the point, he regretted that he had used her father as an example.

"Yes."

"Of course, she knows it," Hadley said. "She's been flirting with death ever since her pa taught her to use those revolvers." A faint smile on his lips, the editor nodded his head, lifted his hand, and rubbed his neck. Finally he said, "I'll make a deal with you, Clem. I'll not run Olviera's name, if you'll take me with you so I can have an exclusive story."

"It's too dangerous for you out there, Hadley," Clem said softly. "Besides, you'd get in the way."

"I won't. I promise. Take me with you, Clem."

"No." She was emphatic. "I'm not going to make a deal like this with you. I've told you why I don't want you to use Olviera's name, but the decision is yours, Hadley. Whether you print it or not, I have my work cut out for me."

"Well . . ." Disappointment flickered in the editor's eyes as he rose and stared at her. When she did not relent, he turned, walking to the clothes rack to get his hat and raincoat. "I guess it's time for me to go. I have a lot of work to do tonight. Coming, Cameron?"

Dropping his hand to his side, Wade stood. When he took a step and swung his arm, the crocheted doily on the table came with him. As he caught the lamp to keep it from falling, he realized the ring on his little finger had become entangled in the delicate stitching. He was unable to save the empty cup and album. Both fell, the cup shattering, photographs sliding across the floor. By the time he untangled his ring from the doily, Clem was kneeling beside him.

"I'm sorry," he apologized, and leaned down to pick up the broken pieces of glass.

"Don't worry." She scooped up the album. "It's nothing."

A photograph, faded with age, slipped from her hand. Moving quicker than she, Wade reached for it, but Clem slid it from beneath his fingers. A fleeting glance had identified one of the men as Clement Jones.

As he straightened, he asked, "Was one of them your father?"

He was curious to see how her father looked as a

young man. He really would have liked to have a photograph in his possession, to compare it to the drawings he had asked Prentice to make of the Sheriff. The seed for a story—a story about the Sheriff and his daughter—was already germinating in his mind.

"Yes." She rose also and tucked the photograph into the album.

"May I see it?"

She paused, her gaze flitting from Wade to Hadley back to Wade. She looked like a small animal that had been trapped and was not sure what to do next.

"They're just family pictures," she answered.

As if fate intervened, the photo slipped from the album and fluttered to the floor. Wade bent again, picked it up, and looked at her. When she made no attempt to reach for it, he moved to the table and held the photograph so that the lamplight reflected across the faded features of three men, one of whom was Clement Jones, and a beautiful woman who stood next to him. Despite the fading, the woman and two of the men were discernible. While the face of the third man—the one who stood on the extreme right of the photograph—was a sienna blur, the rest of his image was intact. All of them were dressed to the nines.

"Your father was much younger here," he said. When Clem did not respond, he asked, "Who are the others?"

"Old acquaintances of the Sheriff's. People you wouldn't know even if I identified them." She gently tugged the photograph from his hands, this time securely tucking it into the album. "If you don't mind, Mr. Cameron, I'm quite exhausted and would like to be alone now."

"Of course," Wade answered smoothly, but his journalistic and investigative curiosity was fully piqued. He wondered about the beautiful woman who posed with the men, and he sensed that Clem was disinclined to discuss this particular photograph with him. Of course, she *was* exhausted, but she was also being deliberately secretive. Hadley had been wrong earlier when he said the death of a local sheriff would be of no interest to the Eastern reader. During the time Wade was in Lawful awaiting the repair of the stagecoach or other transportation to El Paso, he would do some investigating. "May I come back and look through your photographs at a later time?" he asked.

"As I said earlier, they aren't of interest to anyone but the family."

"Perhaps I'm interested in your family."

"No, you're just interested in another story, and right now Clement Jones seems to be as good a topic as any, if not better."

"That's probably the truth of the matter, Clem. You've got this young rascal pegged right." Hadley laughed and playfully slapped Wade on the shoulder. "Well, we'll be going, Clem. Thanks for seeing me tonight, and if you change your mind about my going with you to find Olviera, let me know."

Walking them to the door, she smiled. "I won't change my mind, Hadley. You can count on that."

"About the photographs," Wade began, but Clem cut him short.

"Good night, Hadley, Mr. Cameron."

She closed the door on them, the key grating in the lock.

"I'm going to drop by Elm's for a spell, then mosey on over to my office," Hadley said to Wade as they walked down the porch steps. The wet cold chilling him to the bones, he turned up the collar of his coat and clamped his hat on his head. "I want to get this story written and typeset for tomorrow. You want to come with me or go on to the house?"

"I'll go to the house and change into some dry clothes," Wade answered. "I'll see you later."

"Don't wait up for me. I won't be home for a long time." The wind whipped Hadley's hair about his face as he pulled his coat tightly about his body and led the way down Main Street. He was tired but had no time to rest. His story came first. "Philana Oxford, my housekeeper, will be in about six in the morning to cook breakfast. If I'm not there, you and Prentice go ahead and eat. I'll eat when I can."

Wade nodded, and at the doctor's office, they parted company. Glad to be out of the weather, Hadley walked to the center of the room and spread his hands over the stove. The wind, with renewed fury, howled and slammed the shutters against the wall.

"I believe it's getting colder," he said to Elm, who sat at his desk.

"Feels like it," Elm muttered.

"I thought maybe you wanted some company."

"Thanks," Elm said, "but the preacher has seen to it that I'm not going to be lonesome."

"I take it Pastor James is already visiting and talking with his flock," Hadley said.

Elm nodded. "The first sheep he visited was the mayor."

"Oh, God!" Hadley exclaimed. "Arnold had to know, but I wish we could have waited a little longer."

"Yep," Elm said, "he's already bleating."

"I'm in no mood for one of his council meetings," Hadley grumbled. "A funeral's bad enough; a council meeting is too much."

"Nothing else we can do," Elm said. "We got to get another sheriff appointed quicklike. Lawful's too far from civilization, and close enough to Mexico to attract riffraff. Word of Clement's death has spread pretty far by now. And from what I hear, Doña Montelongo is planning another trip to San Antonio this year. God, Hadley, rumors fly when she makes the trip in the spring. No telling what's in the air now that she's making this one in the winter."

"I don't think we have to worry about a thing, Elm. Clement swore Clem in as deputy sheriff before he died. She's got the star."

Elm shoved long, slender fingers through his graying hair. "I figured that when I didn't find the badge on him." He shook his head. "This is gonna make it hard, Hadley."

Hadley lifted a brow in surprise. "Why? Are you thinking she shouldn't wear the badge?"

"Aren't you?"

"Look," Hadley said, never flinching from the direct gaze of his old friend, "as far as I'm concerned, there's no one more capable of being the deputy sheriff than Clem. If she wants it, let her have it. It's her choice."

"It's not her choice alone," Elm barked. "It's ours, too."

"I'm not so sure about that, Elm," Hadley said. "At first I didn't approve of Clem's riding with her father, but he didn't ask the council's permission. He simply allowed her to become a part of his law enforcement team. And none of us, Elm—*not one of the members of the council*—has objected for the past three years. You've got to admit that's encouragement of a sort. The people of Lawful accept the role Clem plays, or they have until now . . . until Clement died. Do we have the right to take this away from her? To say that she's not capable of doing the job?"

"Good Gawd almighty, Hadley!" Elm's palm landed heavily on the table, an empty cup rolling on its base. "We didn't say anything because she had her pa riding with her to protect her. She's alone now. We can't let her assume that responsibility by herself. She's nothing but a kid, and a woman at that. Clement wouldn't have let her take on the sole responsibility for being sheriff of Lawful."

"Reckon he did, Elm. He deputized her just before he died. You're forgetting, she's one of the best guns in the West. Clement didn't forget. Why, Elm, I'd put her up against the best."

"Yep," Elm grumbled, "I guess you would, but, damn it, this isn't a Fourth of July turkey shoot."

"You're forgetting Hokie and Turbin. They'll help her, I'm sure."

"They'll help her for a little while, but they aren't going to give up their surveying job," Elm pointed out. "They can't afford to, and the county can't afford to lose them."

"Speaking of Hokie and Turbin," Hadley said, "have you seen them?"

Elm shook his head. "I won't stand for Clem to keep the star. It won't be good for her or Lawful. If we allow her to be the deputy, every fast gun in the West will be coming here to challenge her. She'll be up against the best, and it won't be long before another a little better will come along, and down she'll go. And it'll all be our fault. Besides, Hadley, we'll have to answer to Rand."

The door opened, and Maybelle swept into the room to announce, "Well, the telegrams have been sent. Both of them."

"I suppose it's too soon to hope for an answer."

Maybelle laughed. "You suppose right. But I do have some good news to tell you. Barney Joiner, just in from El Paso, brought word that Doña Pera is traveling behind him on her way to San Antonio. He said we could expect her in three or four days. Since the weather is so bad, she's going to stop over in Botello before coming here." After Maybelle threw the hood of her cape from her face, she stripped out of the gloves and turned a red, chapped face to them. "Reckon Deborah will be here in time for the funeral?"

"Depends on when she receives the telegram, and how travel conditions are between here and El Paso," Elm answered. "Weather's pretty bad, so chances are she won't. Clem's going to be a mite upset, Maybelle. You know she's still bitter about what happened."

"And she has a right to be," Maybelle pronounced. "Deborah shouldn't have done what she did, but no matter, it's not right to keep her from the funeral. After all, Clement was her husband."

"You're right," Hadley agreed. "She should be allowed to be at the funeral. That is, if she wants to."

"Where's the two newspapermen?" Maybelle sidled closer to the stove.

"At the house," he replied.

"I'm not sure I trust those two."

"Oh, Maybelle," Hadley groaned. He really liked the woman, but she always expected the worse of everyone and every situation. If she were unable to find it, she fabricated it. Tonight he had enough on his mind without Maybelle adding to it with her worries. "Don't get worked up about these two. They'll be leaving as soon as the stage is repaired, or another westbound one comes through. We got enough to worry about without you getting in a tizzy over two strangers."

As if she never heard Hadley, she shook her head and frowned. "Something mighty familiar about the tall one. I know the name, but I can't figure out from where."

Elm scoffed. "Of course, you know the name. He told you himself, and he also told you what he did."

"No," she drawled thoughtfully, "that's not it, Elm. I haven't read any of his articles, and I haven't seen one of his magazines. There's something else about him that bothers me. It's like I know him, like he's associated with something besides writing and publishing.

58

Oh, well," her forehead cleared, and her face brightened, "it'll come to me one of these days. I never forget anything."

"It might be a blessing if you did," Hadley muttered under his breath, and moved closer to the stove as the wind hammered a shutter against the wall.

"What did you say?" Maybelle turned to peer at him.

"Nothing that would interest you," Hadley said. "By the way, I have a copy of *Cameron's Journal* at my office. After hearing Clem's opinion, I'd like to read it to find out just what kind of articles that boy publishes, but right now I'm too busy."

"Well," Maybelle drawled, "I guess I could read it and give you my opinion for what it's worth, Hadley. What are friends for, if not to help out in time of trouble. I don't really relish the idea of reading Cameron's book, since I figure it's—"

"I know," Hadley interrupted. Despite her constant talking and her infernal memory, Hadley liked Maybelle, and he trusted her judgment. She had an insatiable desire to read, and at the moment that desire was focused on *Cameron's Journal* in particular. Now that she had planted the seeds of curiosity in his mind about the journalist, Hadley wanted her to remember. If she did know something about Cameron, perhaps reading the journal would jar her memory. "Thanks, Maybelle, I would appreciate your doing this for me."

"Well," Elm drawled dryly, with no apparent interest in the conversation between the two friends, "tomorrow should prove to be interesting."

"Yep," Hadley murmured.

"Wonder who all will be showing up for the funeral?" Elm's words, like an ominous threat, hung suspended over the three of them.

"God only knows." Hadley moved to the window to stare down the night-blackened street. From a few windows where shades were raised, slivers of light escaped to dance across the muddy thoroughfare. "Riders coming," he announced.

"How many?" Elm asked.

"Two," Hadley replied. "They stopped by Clement's office first; now they're headed here."

"Reckon it's Hokie and Turbin?"

"Don't know," Hadley said. "I can't make them out."

Shortly footfalls could be heard on the porch, then a knock. Elm answered the door, and two men, wool scarves wrapped around their faces and heads, long great coats covering their bodies, walked into the room.

"Evening." The first man, pulling the scarf from his face, moved farther into the room; the other remained near the door.

"Evening," Elm and Hadley answered simultaneously, both of them eying the strangers suspiciously. Maybelle backed farther into the room, hovering near the stove.

One of the visitors doffed his hat to Maybelle. "Ma'am."

"Howdy." She drew her cape closer about herself.

The stranger's gaze flickered between Elm and Hadley. "I'm Jeb Ramson. That's Dulles." He nodded his head toward his companion by the door. "We're personal detectives the Sheriff hired to find Lionel Porter."

"Oh, yes," Hadley murmured, quickly translating the words personal detectives into bounty hunters and gunmen for hire. In order to stay close to town and to protect the people better, Clement often hired men whom he trusted to capture and bring in outlaws. These were two bounty hunters he had used off and on. "I remember."

"He hired us," Ramson said, "because he figured if we didn't catch Porter, he'd end up on the other end of a vigilante's rope. Clement said the council would pay one third more than the stated reward on Porter, if we brought him in alive. Just the stated amount, if he was dead."

Remembering the meeting when the council had voted on the procedure, Hadley nodded. "That was the agreement."

Jeb rubbed his hand against his whisker-stubbled cheeks. "If it had been left up to us, we would have brought Porter back alive, but he was dead when we caught up with him. Strung up in a tree on the road north of the Mexican village of Botello. What remains of him is wrapped in a tarp on that pack mule out front. Wish we could have left or buried him, but we didn't know but what you'd want proof of his death."

Jeb fished in his pocket to pull out a crumpled sheet of paper. "Vigilantes got to him before we could. They left this note attached to his body. Porter's unlucky day. At least, if we had caught him first, Clement would have seen to it that he had a trial. Most likely Porter would have gone to prison, but he'd be alive. Brought his belongings. Figured Clement would want to give them to the family. But his office was closed. We saw light in your windows and came on over."

Hadley looked at Elm, then he glanced back at the bounty hunters who had arrived at a most inopportune moment. Clement was dead, and Rand was not here yet. And if one excluded Clem, which Hadley knew Elm did, Lawful was virtually without a law enforcement officer. Hadley's gaze ran the height of Jeb Ramson. No matter how affable the man might appear, he was a bounty hunter, a gunslinger, who earned his living tracking down other human beings and bringing them back dead or alive, more often dead than alive. Clement had been wise in suggesting that the council always pay a third more than the stated reward; that way he usually got his man alive.

Clement was also a tough man, accustomed to handling riffraff like this, but Hadley knew no one else in town could.

"Don't reckon Clement is here with you, is he?" Jeb asked impatiently, his words whipping through the silence.

"In a manner of speaking," Elm sighed. "Clement was killed today at Chupedera Lakes by salt thieves. His body's in there."

Both of the men glanced toward the undertaking room, but neither moved. "What's going to happen now? Who's gonna be the law and order around here?" Jeb asked. "That daughter of his?"

"Maybe. Maybe not," Hadley hedged, not because he was unsure about Clem, but because he was apprehensive of these men and their motives. He did not want them to know any more than was necessary. "She always worked with her father and can handle a gun better than most men. I'm sure she'll be considered for the post."

Jeb lifted his hand and pulled at his bottom lip. "Yep. I mind the time that she outdrew us all, one by one, at the Fourth of July fast-draw contest."

"She can handle herself good with guns," Hadley repeated, as much to reassure himself as the bounty hunters.

"Yep." Jeb continued to rub his lip. "That gal's better than most with them guns. How-some-ever, there's a lot of difference in quick-draw contests and turkey shoots than in killing people. I don't figure she's ever had to stand up to a real gunfighter or had to shoot a person before. I figure some man's gonna come along and take her down."

"We also have two other deputies on the payroll," Hadley said. "You may know them, Hokum Smith and Turbin Davis."

Jeb shook his head.

"And we've already sent a telegram to Rand McGaffney," Elm said quickly. "It's just a matter of time before he arrives."

"Rand McGaffney. Clement's brother," the man repeated thoughtfully. He stopped rubbing his lips to scratch his chin and neck. "Well," he drawled, "it's mighty bad for Lawful to be without a sheriff, and it's bad for us, too. Always knew we could count on Clement to give us a fair deal, and we liked his idea of paying us more if we brought a man in alive. Just hope to God people around here don't turn to vigilante justice!"

The bounty hunter dug into the large pocket of his coat to extract a handkerchief, the corners of which were tied together. Setting the bundle in the middle of the table, he said, "Guess I'll just leave Porter's personal belongings here, and ya'll can decide what to do with them. Me and Dully's gonna head for the saloon. Figure we need a drink . . . mebbe several. This is purty bad news. When we was in El Paso, we saw some real mean guns. Sure hope they don't head this way when news of Clement's death gets out."

"Who?" Hadley asked.

He was filled with conflicting emotions. He was excited about the possibility of a story. At the same time, he was repulsed at the thought of men like Jeb Ramson and Dulles Hammond swarming into town, and he was frightened by the mere thought of big guns meeting in a town as close as El Paso. That Ramson and Hammond would throw in with them was more a probability than a possibility.

"For starters, Ike Perry and Soloman Wise."

Hadley whistled. "These *are* mean guns!"

Jeb laughed. "Yes, sir, that's my thoughts exactly. Rumor's out that they've been hired by Borajo. He's tired of the Anglos buying the salt deposit. Cuts into the padre's profits." He paused a moment, then added softly, "Also, there's a rumor that old lady Montelongo is making a trip to San Antonio."

"That's nothing new," Hadley replied casually, not wanting the bounty hunters to know that her trip was an actuality rather than a rumor. He wanted to give them no reason to prolong their stay in Lawful. "She makes a trip to San Antonio every year."

"In the spring," Ramson pointed out. "Not in the winter. Some say she has a niece who's getting married. Others think she's delivering some old family treasures to the San Fernando Cathedral."

"Such as?" Hadley asked. This sparked his interest. When Elm had told him about Doña Pera's trip earlier, he had been surprised to learn that she was traveling five hundred miles this time of the year. A winter trip was hard on a young person; it would be tremendously difficult for an elderly one.

"Solid gold altar pieces inlaid with emeralds from the mines in South America," Ramson said. "A huge cross, candle holders, cups. Things such as that. They were crafted when the Spaniards first came over. Some say this stuff is worth several million."

"Could be." Hadley sloughed it off. "But I doubt it. You know how these rumors fly about, and with each telling they get bigger."

"Just repeating what I heard. Well, gentlemen, ma'am, me and Dully need to be on our way. We've got a job down San Antone way, so's we'd appreciate the council paying us as soon as they can. They'll find us at the saloon 'til it closes tonight, and at the hotel in the morning."

"Of course," Hadley answered. "I'll get word to the mayor and see that you get your payment as soon as possible."

After the bounty hunters left, a pensive silence filled the room. Elm sat down behind his desk, Hadley walked over to the window, and Maybelle edged closer to the stove.

"Well, *gentlemen*," she eventually said, "I smell trouble. Bad trouble. Hadley, why don't you give those men the money tonight, so they won't have any reason to delay their leaving in the morning? Arnold will be thankful and will gladly repay you."

"Yeah," Hadley drawled, looking out the window at the bounty hunters, "I guess I could."

Jeb and Dulles rode down the street, dismounted, and swaggered into the saloon. The two of them tonight, Hadley thought, but how many more would be riding into Lawful in the next few days? Maybelle was right: trouble was brewing.

Again the room was silent. Outside the wind howled, but above it could be heard the raucous noise of the nearby saloon — yelling, then shooting. The three of them looked at one another in silence.

"It's already started," Elm said.

"Reckon we should go get Clem?" Maybelle asked.

"Hell no!" Elm exclaimed. "Let her rest."

"I sure wish Hokie and Turbin would get in," Hadley said. "We sure need them. We're sitting on a powder keg with a short fuse. One wrong move, the fuse is lit, and we blow to bits."

"Good thing Rand's coming," Maybelle said. "He'll know what to do."

Elm snorted, then muttered, "If he does, he's a lot smarter than he was five years ago."

"I'm counting on that," Maybelle said. "I sure am."

Chapter Five

Although the rain had slacked to a drizzle, lightning continued to flash and the thunder to roll. The temperature dropped for a record cold, and the wind blew continually. Winter had come early to West Texas, and promised to be hard and long.

The house was dark, and Clem, wearing a heavy wrapper and house shoes, sat in the chair in front of the fire in the parlor. The box of photographs and the family album sat on the floor beside her. Hours had passed since Hadley and Wade Cameron had left, but she could not sleep. Neither did she wish to be bothered with company, no matter how well-meaning their visit might be. The mayor had come by a short while ago, but she had ignored him. She needed some quiet time to herself, time to compose her emotions and to decide how she was going to set about finding Alarico Olviera, and at the same time how she was going to protect the townsfolk.

She heard steps on the porch and several repeated raps on the door. She fully intended to ignore the visitor. More knocks came, louder this time.

"Clem, it's me," Hokie Smith called. "I know it's late, but me and Turbin just got into town, and Elm said you wanted to see us as soon as we got in." Again the knocks sounded through the room.

Grateful the deputies were in town, Clem quickly moved across the room. She slid the bolt and opened the door.

"Sorry to hear about the death of your pa," Hokie said, taking off his hat, rain dripping from it and the slicker to puddle on the porch. "And I'm sorry to disturb you, but I figured it'd be better for me to see you tonight than to wait for morning."

"Thank you for coming." Clem motioned him inside. "Where's Turbin?"

"He's in town, keeping a lid on things. Hadley and Elm was afraid emotions might get a little high tonight, so we decided to go on duty right now."

"Why didn't they call me?" Clem demanded. "Both of them know that Clement swore me in as deputy sheriff. I'm the one who should be keeping law and order here. I'm the one who should be on duty, not the two of you."

"Now, don't go getting your feathers all ruffled," Hokie soothed. "The trouble ain't nothing we can't handle. Me and Turbin figured you had enough on your mind tonight, without having to take care of town drunks. With what's in town tonight, we don't need no fast guns. Just somebody big enough to knock 'em out and haul 'em to jail. Me and Turbin are good at that."

Clem nodded as she walked to the reading table and lit the lamp, the soft light illuminating the room.

Holding his hat in one hand, Hokie brushed his other hand through thin, gray hair. He was a small man, but no one mistook his slight build for weakness. Hokum Smith was all muscle. Although he would never win a fast-draw contest with his revolver, no one stood a chance against him in a fistfight.

Knowing that Hokum and Turbin would be working with her, gave Clem even more confidence that she could be an effective peace officer.

"Me and Turbin, well, we decided that it would be best if one of us slept tonight, so we could relieve the other." He grinned. "We drew straws, and you can guess who won."

Clem smiled at him.

"And we wanted to let you know that you can count on us to help you out, Clem. We'll work for you just like we did for your pa. Only we'll be full-time deputies for you."

"Won't this affect your surveying job?"

A smile creased the weathered face. "We figure we can still do that. Don't you worry about it none."

"Thanks, Hokie. I appreciate the offer, and I'm going to take both of you up on it."

"Just wanted you to know you didn't have to be up and out early, lessen you want to. Weather's bad, and it don't look like the rain's gonna let up any too soon. You just take it easy. I'm headed home for some shut-eye, so's I can relieve Turbin about eight o'clock."

During the long sleepless night, Clem alternately sat in the chair in the living room in front of the fire, or stood at the window. Finally the rain stopped, and morning broke. Like the day before, it was gray, dreary and cold, and storm clouds, promising more rain, remained to hover menacingly in the sky. Thinking of her father's death—having thought of little else since he had been shot—Clem decided to wear a dress to the funeral. Still clad in her nightgown and dressing robe, she turned, walked to the armoire, and flung open the door. In the pale shadows of the bleak morning light, she studied her choices, which were few indeed.

For once she was angry because her wardrobe was so sparse. However, she had no one to blame but herself. When Deborah had lived with them, she had insisted that Clem wear dresses. After she left, Clem had chosen to be a tomboy, deliberately shunning any signs of femininity. The Sheriff and Maybelle had encouraged her to have dresses fitted for herself, as well as trousers, but she had never taken the time or expended the money to do so. As if femininity were a fatal disease—certainly it was a constant reminder of Deborah—Clem deliberately avoided softness of any kind.

Clem reached out to touch the only decent dress she had: a green taffeta gown her father had given to her on her sixteenth birthday. Because it had been a special gift, Clem was not willing to part with it, or to have it redesigned so she could wear it now. She brought it out of the wardrobe and walked to the oak dresser. Holding the dress against herself, she looked at her reflection in the mirror. Five years had changed her figure drastically. She had not gained all that much weight, but her breasts and hips were more fully developed and rounded. Even if the dress did fit now, she thought, it certainly would not be decent— not with the scooped neckline. Sighing, she turned and replaced the dress in the armoire, and began to dig through another drawer, throwing garments on the bed.

Soon she was dressed warmly in long, thick underwear and socks, and a new wool shirt and trousers Anona Cuellar had sewn. Once again moving to the mirror, she tied a pretty bandanna around her neck, the little flecks of gold and green complementing her eyes. What she wore definitely was not a dress, but it was garb more in keeping with who and what Clem Jones was. Papa would understand, she thought, tears pricking her eyes.

Putting on her fleece-lined jacket, gloves, and her Stetson, she headed for the barn, where she saddled Rusty-Be-Dusty, the roan Papa had given to her.

Later she rode into town, past the parsonage that sat next to the church on the outer periphery of town, down the narrow main street of the only home she could remember — Lawful, Texas. Although it appeared that none of the citizens had ventured out yet and, considering the inclement weather, probably would not for several hours, Clem was alert for trouble. Her gaze habitually swung from one side of the muddy thoroughfare to the other. Years of working with her father had taught her to observe anything that might appear to be amiss. Nothing was, but ironically the only sign of life was the team of horses hitched to Elm's funeral hearse. Fighting back the tears and loneliness, Clem averted her head and guided the roan into Lester McLean's Livery Barn. Normally she would have ridden the length of the street, but not today. The town was quiet enough. No trouble seemed to be stirring.

Later, when Rusty-Be-Dusty was stabled, Clem walked toward the sheriff's office. Tucking her head against the wind, she pushed her hands into the pockets of her jacket. Her footfalls were a lonely cadence against the boardwalk. When she reached the building, she looked in the window.

Turbin was asleep in her father's chair, his feet propped on the desk and his hat over his face. When she opened the door, he jerked awake and looked at her in surprise.

"Morning, Turbin. Looks like you had an uneventful night."

Dropping his feet to the floor and pushing his hat back, he straightened up and grinned at her. "Willie Blankenship got a little rowdy and started to shoot up the saloon, but me and Hokie took him home and put him to bed. After that we had no trouble. I'm surprised to see you. Hokie said he was going to tell you not to come in."

70

"He did," Clem said, "but I couldn't sleep. I figured I'd rather be here than at home by myself."

"Yeah, I can understand. I'm sure sorry about the Sheriff, Clem. I couldn't believe my ears when Hadley told us what had happened."

"It's hard for me to believe," Clem said. "I guess Hadley told you the funeral is going to be this afternoon."

Nodding his head, Turbin rose and walked to the window to look up and down Main Street. "Fresh pot of coffee on the stove. I had it ready for Hokie."

"Thanks, I'll get a cup later. Why don't you go ahead and turn in," Clem said. "I'll take over here."

"Believe I will." Turbin stretched. "I'm dead on my feet. I haven't had much sleep for the past two nights."

"Stop by Hokie's place and tell him he doesn't have to come in early this morning. I'll be all right."

"Clem, me and Hokie, we agreed we'll work with you. We're not going to let you handle this alone."

"Thanks. I'd like to meet with both of you tomorrow, so we can work out a schedule. That way you can continue to do your surveying."

Turbin lifted his coat from the wall rack and slipped into it. "I'll see you this afternoon, Clem."

After Turbin left, Clem shed her jacket and gloves and moved around the room, knowing she had to remove her father's belongings, but not quite ready to do so yet. She sat down behind the desk at the same time that the door opened and Hadley entered. He looked as if he had not slept in a week. His overcoat was unbuttoned to reveal the same suit he had worn last night. His hair was mussed, and his face shadowed with beard stubble.

"From the looks of it, you spent the night working," Clem said.

"Sure did," he muttered, running his hand through his hair, leaving it even more disheveled than before.

71

"I'm surprised to see you. I thought I'd find Turbin."

"I sent him home to get some rest," Clem said.

Hadley nodded. "That coffee smells good. How about a cup?"

He moved to the window where he raised the shade halfway up, curled a gloved hand into a fist, and wiped a large circle of condensation from the pane. Clem poured his coffee.

Peering down the boardwalk, he said, "If you have any whiskey, Clem, put that in it. I'm going to need something mighty strong before this day is over."

"That bad?" she asked.

"That bad." He turned so that he was looking at her, and yanking off his gloves, he stuffed them haphazardly into his overcoat pocket.

The door opened again, and Wade Cameron walked into the office. His hair was wind-tossed, the collar of his coat pushed up about his face. "Good morning," he said.

"You're up early," Hadley said, taking his cup of coffee from Clem.

When she offered Wade a cup, he shook his head.

"What about you," he retaliated. "I was curious when you didn't come in last night, and thought I'd check over here to see what's going on."

Hadley shrugged.

Clem said, "Not much." She was not pleased with his visit. She distrusted the man. He seemed to hear and see too much for her comfort.

"By the way, Ramson and Hammond returned last night," Hadley drawled after a few minutes of silence. "They found Lionel Porter strung up outside the village of Botello. They figured a vigilante committee got him. His stuff is over at Elm's."

"Are they still in town?" she asked, her gaze on Wade.

He walked around the office, reading all the wanted

posters.

"They're having breakfast over at the saloon," Hadley answered.

"I'll get their money," she said.

"No need. I—well, Elm and I didn't want to bother you last night, so I've already paid them. As soon as they finish eating, they're gonna head for San Antonio."

"Thanks for the consideration," Clem said, "but in the future, I'll appreciate you letting me handle my job."

Wade sat down at her father's—at her—desk, and leaned back in the chair as if it were his own. He irritated her to no end.

"Don't worry, Clemmy," Hadley said. "You'll have plenty to handle. Ramson reported that a lot of guns were meeting in El Paso. He thinks Borajo hired them. Looks like we're going to have a full-scale salt war on our hands." He shook his head. "It's bad when folks hire professional gunmen to be their law enforcers. Even worse when men of the cloth do."

"Seems like that's the way with the frontier," Clem said. "People use whatever proves effective, including gunfighters and vigilante committees."

Wade had taken out his notebook and pencil and was writing. *Dear, Lord, why hadn't he slept in this morning? Why was he over here bothering her? She needed her wits about her, and Wade Cameron disconcerted her, totally, absolutely!*

"Also heard some more disconcerting news," Hadley said, breaking into her troubled thoughts. "For a fact, Doña Pera Montelongo is making a winter trip to San Antonio for the wedding of one of her nieces."

"Who's she?" Wade asked.

"A Spanish *haciendada* who lives out of El Paso." Clem almost spit the words at him. She wished he would let her and Hadley have their discussion without interference. But he took no notice. His eyes were on the sheet of paper on which he wrote.

"She should be here pretty soon," Hadley finished.

"I don't see this as a problem," Clem said. "She makes a trip every year; we've never had any trouble."

"According to Ramson, she could be delivering valuable religious artifacts to the San Fernando Cathedral. Gold altar pieces inlaid with precious jewels that are several hundred years old and go back to the conquest period. Talk says they're worth several million."

Clem sighed. Perhaps this was going to be a bigger concern than she had thought. "Times are so bad, outlaws will loot and murder for hundreds, much less millions."

"That's what Elm and I thought about last night after Ramson and Hammond left. Trouble is brewing, Clem. Big trouble."

Her back was to Wade, but she felt his gaze on her. She was aware of him as she had never been aware of another individual before. It seemed to her that tension began to stretch tautly between them the minute he walked into the room. As surely as if he had spoken aloud, she felt his disapproval of her wearing the star.

"Let's not blow things out of perspective, Hadley. All we have so far are rumors. Let's just sit back and see what happens. By the way, let me repay you for the bounty you paid Ramson and Hammond."

"No need," he answered. "I got it from Arnold."

"You've already seen the mayor."

"Seen and *heard* the mayor. We just concluded a council meeting." He looked over her shoulder at Wade. "That's where I was."

"Oh!" This did not bode well. "Where did you meet and when? I saw no activity when I rode through town a while ago."

"You wouldn't have," Hadley answered. "We met at the mayor's house about six this morning. Lord, but it was bad. The worst meeting I've been to in years."

"Council meetings generally aren't fun, but I guess this one would be worse than usual," Clem agreed, a little ticked because she had not ridden the full length of the street. If she had, she would have noticed the horses and buggies tethered in front of the mayor's house. Of course, she really had no cause to be irritated. The townsfolk were not yet accustomed to her being the deputy sheriff. Surely if they were, they would have invited her.

Now, she turned and encountered Wade's candid gaze. His face, as well as his eyes, were emotionless.

"It's the first meeting in many years where the Sheriff hasn't been present," Clem said, and her palms felt clammy. "If you had called me, I would have been there."

"Fact of the matter is," Hadley said, "the council didn't want you there. That's why we met at Arnold's. Less chance of you spotting the horses and buggies, since his house is on the opposite side of town from you."

Clem slowly lowered her cup from her mouth without taking a swallow. "I take it, I was the center of discussion."

"Right."

"And?"

"And . . ." he turned to look out the window once more "here comes our good Mayor. I'll let him tell you. He's the one who loves giving speeches."

The door opened, and the mayor entered the office, a large gust of wind whipping the bottom of his greatcoat about his legs. "Morning, Clem."

"Arnold." Shivering from the draft created by the wind, she edged closer to the stove and refilled her cup with coffee. She watched in surprise as the door opened again, and two other council members entered the office. She nodded to the banker and hotel owner. "William. Emmett."

"Clem," they said together.

Slightly amused as well as curious, she watched as the three took off their hats, gloves, and coats, their movements almost synchronized. She listened as Hadley introduced them to Wade. They all shook hands and exchanged greetings.

"What's the occasion?" she asked, her question directed to any one of the three. "This is the first time all of you have been in the sheriff's office together, since the Sheriff refused to let the vigilantes lynch Tyland Burke for horse thieving last summer."

"Clem," the mayor said, "Mrs. Bedford and I want you to know how sorry we are about the death of your father. I would have come over to see you last night, but when I got to the house the lights were out, and I figured you were resting."

After Hadley and Wade left, Clem had blown out the lamps because she wanted solitude and privacy for her grief, but she had not been asleep . . . far from it.

"If there's anything we can do," he continued, "please let us know."

"Thanks, Arnold," Clem murmured, tears again burning her eyes. Barely able to contain her grief, she wondered if she would ever be dry-eyed again. Whatever the differences had been between her and the Sheriff and the mayor and council in the past, she knew that Arnold sincerely meant what he said.

"The same goes for me." The banker stepped forward, his watery blue eyes filled with compassion. William Pinely was tall and thin, his suit jacket hanging loosely over his prematurely stooped shoulders. He jabbed one hand deep into his trouser pocket; with the other he plucked at the frizzy brown beard that hid gaunt, skeletal features.

"Anything you need or want. Just name it," he continued. "Clement and I had our arguments in the past, but I respected him as sheriff. Mrs. Pinely will be sending some food over to the house later today."

"Thank you, William," Clem answered.

"The same goes for me, Clem," said Emmett Frazier, owner of the Lawful Hotel and Saloon. Thick auburn curls escaped the edge of the black derby hat he wore. Although his complexion was ordinarily ruddy, today it was redder because of the biting wind.

"Thank you all." Her gaze moved from one to the other of them. "You're so kind." Then no one seemed to know what to say or do. To break the uncomfortable silence, as well as to cover her sense of vulnerability, she asked, "How about a cup of coffee?"

"Just what I want in weather like this," the mayor said. "Yes, sir, that will hit the spot. It's mighty cold out there."

"Yep," Pinely murmured, "it sure is."

All of them hid their emotions behind mundane and repetitious conversation. Out of the corner of her eye, she saw the tenderfoot writing. Damn it! She would love to jerk that pencil out of his hands and break it into smithereens; then she would like to tar and feather him and ride him out of town on a rail. By sheer willpower, she swallowed her anger.

After Clem had poured all of them a cup of coffee and refilled Hadley's cup, she said in a voice she strove to keep steady, "Now, Arnold, what *really* brings you and William and Emmett over here?"

"Well, Clem . . . I guess Hadley told you that we — uh — we just had a meeting of the council."

"Yes."

The mayor cast a quick glance at the editor. "Did you tell her what we discussed?" When Hadley shook his head, Arnold sighed, his left hand running up and down the length of his gold watch chain — a sure sign he was nervous.

"Don't worry, Arnold," Clem assured him. "Lawful isn't going to be without a sheriff. Just before he died, Clement swore me in as Deputy Sheriff."

"Yes, that's—that's what Hadley told us," Arnold stammered, his face flushing. He glanced from William to Emmett, both of whom offered nothing to the conversation, but who seemed to be silently urging him to continue. Setting the cup on the edge of the desk, he fumbled in his pocket to extract finally a handkerchief that he swiped across his face. "And well, Clem, that's what we have to talk about."

"Nothing to talk about." Clem brushed her hand over the star. "I'm going to wear this badge with as much pride as my father."

"Clem," Arnold said, "this morning the council voted to appoint a male sheriff to fill the vacancy, until we can elect a new one."

Truly astounded, never having thought of this possibility, Clem removed her gaze from the mayor, and in turn looked around the semicircle of men who stood in her father's office. Although all of them appeared to be uncomfortable, they looked her straight in the eye. They were standing behind their decision, these good citizens of Lawful.

Then she looked at Wade Cameron. His eyes seemed to be softer, but that infuriated her more than his being emotionless. She did not want his pity. She remembered all he had said last night, and she had almost laughed in his face. She would not have believed the council would strip her of the star. How smug Cameron must feel, she thought, to be sitting here, listening to the council read her the riot act.

She turned her back on him, her gaze finally resting on the editor.

"That's right, Clem," Hadley said.

The editor's steadfast eyes were pinned to hers. In

them Clem saw grief; in the voice she heard apology; she heard sympathy she was ill-equipped to deal with at the moment. She could tolerate the dude's attitude better than she could anyone's sympathy. Arrogance and pity made her angry; they made her want to fight.

"The council voted, and while the majority felt like we needed a male sheriff, the vote was not unanimous. However, in defense of the council, I have to tell you, it was a tough decision for us to make. If it hadn't been for Ramson and Hammond having doubts about your being able to keep law and order, we probably would have given you a chance."

"You've let two bounty hunters influence your decision to allow me to be the deputy sheriff?"

"Now, Clem," Hadley said, "I know what you're thinking."

"No, you don't, damn it! As editor of the *Lawful Tribune,* you've been known to put words into other people's mouths, but don't think you can put thoughts into my head, or that you can read my mind. You have no idea what I'm thinking, and if you did, the four of you wouldn't be standing here in front of me."

Yesterday had been a terrible emotional drain on Clem, and today promised to be no better. Yesterday she had lost her father; today, in addition to her loss of him, she had lost the confidence of the council. To make matters worse, they were trying to strip her of her integrity in front of the Easterner.

"Please understand, Clem," Arnold said gently, "none of us voted against you. We voted the way we did, because we're *for* you, Clem. We're just worried about you — you being a woman and all. And look what you'd be facing, if those bounty hunters had decided to stay in town and to give us some trouble."

"Ramson and Hammond have never given us any trouble," Clem objected.

"But they *are* bounty hunters, professional gunmen, Clem," Arnold pointed out. "Most of them bring back their prey dead because it's easier. You know we never really approved of Clement's using them."

"He knew the chance he was running," Clem argued, "and they never failed him. They've always been respectful."

"I know they have, but you've got to remember circumstances have changed with your pa's death. He was the one who kept them in order, Clem, no one else. If these men should see Lawful as easy for the taking, they could become dangerous; they could become a magnet for others of their kind."

"He's right," Wade said.

Clem whipped around. "You stay out of this. This isn't your concern. This is between the council and me."

Wade grinned. "Yes, ma'am. I'm duly chastised; however, it does make sense."

The mocking words ringing in her ear, she turned back to the mayor. "I'm not worried about them, Arnold, but because the council is, I promise that after breakfast, if they're still in town, I'll run them out. I owe them no allegiance. Let me keep the badge."

Clem realized she was begging, but she had made a solemn promise to Papa. She had to keep it. He would have done the same for her. He was a man of his word.

"It's not only them," the mayor argued. "Think about the gunfighters that are gathering in El Paso."

Clem had known disappointment in her life—plenty of it—but nothing compared to what she was experiencing now. At the moment she felt as if she were being torn apart; her friends had become her enemies. In most cases love was not an emotion; it was a word to be bandied about. Deborah and Rand had proved that hypothesis to her. Now these upstanding council members, who were hiding behind the excuse of protecting the people and who were feeling sanctimonious and justified in their action, were proving it further.

"Can't you understand how I feel?" Clem argued. "Even if this were not my job, it's my responsibility. I promised the Sheriff."

"No." Arnold shook his head.

Clem could never remember Arnold being this adamant before. She looked from one of the men to the other and observed their closed expression.

"Clem," Emmett said, "you must remember you're a woman—"

She heard the chair grate behind her as it was dragged across the floor. Cameron. They were using the same argument he had used last night, the one she had waved aside.

"Pardon my skepticism," she said, "but somehow, Emmett, it's hard for me to believe that you're really worried about me because I'm a woman—seeing as how I've been a woman all twenty-one years of my life, and I've been helping Clement for the past three, without any objection from the council."

Deciding to call in some of the markers the councilmen owed her, she paused only for a breath. "Not once did any of you object to my being a woman when you needed help. Remember, Arnold, the day that I escorted you to Ft. Stockton so you could get the material your wife wanted for her new dress. Just think what that dress cost—the lives of three Indians and two guards. And you, William. How many times have I kept guard on the bank for you? Emmett, how many miles did I ride in an electrical storm to get the food stuff you needed for the saloon. During the drought I'm the one who brought water barrels in from the Pecos weekly. I drove for days in the blister-

81

ing heat in danger of Indian attack. No one insisted *that* was a man's job!"

She shook her head. "No, indeed, *gentlemen,* not one time did you remind me that I shouldn't be doing this, since I was a woman. But now, all of a sudden, my being a woman is so important."

"Now, Clem—" Arnold dabbed his forehead. "Don't go getting mad on us, and don't twist up everything we say. We do appreciate all you've done for us, and it won't go unrewarded, but we've voted, and that's the way it is. We're not going to change our minds. Fact of the matter, we've already sent a wire—"

"So you sent the message last night and had your council meeting this morning! All this behind my back. Congratulations on the fine, outstanding job you and the council are doing, Mayor. If I had some whiskey here, we'd toast the nobility of manhood."

Arnold fidgeted with his waistcoat and shifted his weight from one foot to the other. "We . . . uh . . . we didn't mean to hurt your feelings, Clem, but we had to know if we could get . . . uh . . . get someone to take the job and replace Clement."

"To replace me, you mean," she said, then added, "And will *he?*"

"Well, yes," Hadley drawled.

Silence hung heavy in the room, and sounds ordinarily never noticed—breathing, the shuffle of feet, the rustle of material as poses were changed—suddenly became a clamor.

"We'd like the badge," Arnold said.

The badge offered her a certain amount of immunity, but whether she had it or not, she could and would keep her promise to find Alarico Olviera. She thought about challenging the council and carrying her grievance to the people, but that went against the grain. While her father had done many unorthodox things during his terms as sheriff of Lawful, he had always obeyed the council. After all it was the elected, collective voice of the citizens, who had the right to make appointments to fill vacancies in city offices until an election could be held. She reached up to unpin the badge, the bottom of the shank catching in the soft material of her shirt.

As if this were a sign from Providence, she stilled her movements and looked at each of the council members one by one. "Who's going to be my replacement?"

Arnold lifted his hand and drew his thumb and index finger down either side of his mouth. "Rand," he mumbled.

"Who's he?" Wade asked, and Clem turned to see him leaning against the door, in much the same pose he had assumed last night at the doctor's office. His pencil was poised over his notebook.

"Rand McGaffney," Arnold said. "Clem's uncle."

Chapter Six

Wade shifted positions, and again Clem was made aware of his broad shoulders, of the hint of strength beneath his coat.

"Why do you think he's the one to replace the Sheriff?" Wade asked.

"Because he was trained by Clement," Arnold answered. "Him and Clement rode together for years. I'd put Rand up against anybody."

"Yep, I would, too." For the first time William Pinely spoke. "And I reckon Rand is probably the only man who can control Clem, now that her pa is dead."

Clem's fist came down on the table with a resounding thud. These men could condemn her for being a woman; they could fire her from the job, but they were not going to treat her as if she were chattel belonging to a *man!* And they were no longer going to humiliate her in front of this Easterner. Grateful for anger, because it acted like a dam to stem the flow of tears, she rose.

"No man controls me, and the sooner all of you get that through your heads, the better it'll be for all of you." She rubbed her palm across the badge still on her shirt. "Gentlemen, you have the authority to appoint an interim sheriff, but until he arrives, I am the

84

deputy sheriff of Lawful, Texas. Now, I'm going out for a little while, and I would appreciate it if none of you are in my office when I return." Moving from behind the desk, Clem crossed the room in long strides, yanked her jacket from the rack, and began to put it on.

"Clem, when you get over your anger, you'll realize that what we did is for the best."

"Arnold Bedford—" an arm in one sleeve, the other sleeve dragging the floor, she swung around to glare at the mayor, "angry or not, I'll never believe my giving up the badge is for the best for me or for Lawful. Don't treat me like a child or try to be my parent."

Clem jabbed her arm through the other sleeve and grabbed her hat, clamping it on her head. Three long strides carried her out the door, past Wade Cameron, past the tantalizing scent of his cologne. Equally long and angry strides carried her to the church. Opening the door, she walked into the sanctuary, where she stood in the vestibule and stared at the closed coffin sitting in the back of the building. Taking off her hat, she slowly walked down the aisle and stood in front of the altar. She ran her hand over the lid.

"Well, Sheriff, Rand's coming back. I really didn't think he'd have the nerve to show up, but he is. It looks like he'll be wearing the star, not me." She lapsed into silence, then took a deep breath and murmured, "I didn't give up the star though. I told the council that I was Lawful's peace officer until Rand gets here. Even if I wanted to, and I don't, I can't leave the people unprotected. With your death, the vultures will be swooping down on Lawful."

A long time later, Clem heard the door open, the sound echoing through the silent building, and cold air swirled around her. She turned to see Wade Cameron enter the church. When he closed the door, she asked, "Are you following me?"

85

"I am."

Unlike Hadley, Wade Cameron appeared to have rested well during the night. His black hair, long enough that it brushed the collar of his coat, was no longer wind-tossed; it was combed back from his face, a lock falling across his forehead to soften the otherwise hard, unyielding countenance. He began to walk toward her, his footsteps breaking the silence.

"I've thought about nothing but you since last night, and I'm sorry about what happened at your office this morning."

The words had a ring of sincerity to them.

"I'll bet," she said, trying to maintain her anger . . . at least, her irritation. Intuitively she knew that she had to keep her distance from Wade Cameron.

He took three more steps. "I want to do a story about you and your father. Would you mind?"

Clem donned her hat and walked toward him, meeting him halfway up the aisle. As tall as she was, even in her boots, she still had to look up at him. "I thought you said this was Hadley's story, not yours."

"I did. I want to write a different kind of story."

"I don't see how you'll have time to write one," Clem replied. "Aren't you leaving on the next stage?"

"That depends on you." The blue eyes stared directly into hers. "If you give me permission to write about the Sheriff, I'll stay here until the story is finished."

"Good-bye, Mr. Cameron."

"You don't mean that," he said softly.

"I don't want you to do a story on me or the Sheriff. I don't like newspapermen in general, and I don't like you in particular." She shoved past him, her shoulder brushing against his chest.

When she reached the vestibule, he said, "Elm and Hadley seem to think you're a tough woman, Clem, but I don't think you're nearly as tough as you want people to believe."

"You've a right to your own opinion." Clem did not turn.

"I say you're frightened."

"I am." Her hand curled around the handle, but she did not open the door. "I'm afraid for the citizens of Lawful now that the Sheriff is dead."

"I think you're afraid for yourself. You think if you give up that badge, you're going to be pushed aside and forgotten. Are you angry that your uncle is returning?"

Clem said nothing.

"What really happened between him and your father?"

"None of your business."

"Why don't you want to talk about it, Clem?" Once again Wade's footsteps echoed through the church as he closed the distance between them, and he spoke to her back. "With or without your help, I'm going to write the life story of Clement Jones."

Clem whirled around, a hand flying out to knock Wade's notebook from his hand. Papers scattered around their feet. Wade bent to retrieve them but not before Clem saw the sketches of her father.

"Who drew these? That artist who's traveling with you?"

Wade straightened. "My cousin."

She was so angry, her voice shook when she spoke. "He had no right to do this. I never gave him permission. My father's body isn't on display for every Tom, Dick, and Harry to view and draw at their pleasure."

"I asked him to," Wade replied. "I didn't think you'd mind."

"You bastard!" Clem drew her hand back to strike him, but Wade caught her wrist. "Pretending you wanted my permission to do an article on my father, and you'd already told that artist to draw him. You

87

scheming, conniving, low-down—"

"I apologize."

She twisted her arm, but couldn't prize it from his grasp.

"I didn't realize you would be offended by Prentice sketching your father's death face. Here," he released her hand "you may have them."

Clem grabbed the drawings from him.

"Now, Miss Jones, with or without your help, I'm going to write a story about your father. I'm an expert when it comes to figuring out what topics appeal to readers. They'll love this one: Gunslinger turns sheriff, but did he ever really turn from a life of crime? Will his daughter follow in his footsteps?"

Clem felt the blood drain from her face as she leaned against the door and braced her legs, forcing herself to stand straight and tall. "What do you mean?"

"I've been up since early morning over at Hadley's office, going through old newspapers and scrapbooks, listening to his typesetter talk about your father. I'm finding Clement Jones to be a most interesting character, and he's far from being a saint."

Clem took a deep breath. People around here understood and accepted her father for what he was; they knew the West bred its own particular brand of law and order, and there was a fine line of difference between the good citizen and the outlaw. She could imagine what kind of sordid story this stranger, this man from the East, probably born to a life of luxury, would weave about her father's life—about his young and restless years. She had been right to be apprehensive of Wade Cameron.

"Leave the Sheriff alone," she finally said—a hint of pleading in her tone. "Can't you let him die in peace?"

"I didn't choose the way he lived or died," Wade replied, a gentle undercurrent to his words. "He did.

But I can choose the way his story will read. It'll be to your advantage to work *with* rather than *against* me."

"If I work with you," Clem said, only now realizing to what lengths she would go to protect her father's past from the public, "what will you expect of me?"

"I want to see every piece of memorabilia you have of his, the photographs, old letters, journals, and scrapbooks. Any and everything. I even want to see his logs and reports since he was elected sheriff."

"What if I don't cooperate?" Clem asked.

"I'll get your uncle to help me."

Clem shook her head. "You wouldn't!"

Wade grinned, and Clem was astonished at the change in him. She almost considered him handsome—in a rugged sort of way. This, too, surprised her. He was an Eastern dude; he should not be rugged. He should be soft and effeminate and weak . . . most undesirable. And she definitely should not be attracted to him.

"I would elicit the help of anyone to get my story. I really would. Even with you helping me, I'll talk to your uncle."

"The hell you will," she whispered.

Wade's eyes narrowed, and he said softly, so softly she had to strain to hear, "The hell I will. But as long as you're working with me, you'll always know exactly what I'm writing and can correct any misunderstanding under which I might be laboring."

Wanting to be as far away from him as she could, not understanding the sudden, tingling awareness she had of him when she actually despised all that he stood for, Clem said, "Give me some time to think about it."

"All right, but not too long. I want an answer soon. I want to get started. And don't get any bright ideas. I saw how much material you have of your father's. I'll know if you're holding back on me."

Clem folded the sketches and slipped them into her jacket pocket. "Mr. Cameron, whether we work together or not, don't try to bluff me. The Sheriff taught me how to gamble when I was a little tyke, and I know a bluff when I see one. I give better than I take."

"Are you threatening me, Deputy?"

Standing in front of her now, extremely close, Wade's grin deepened. Clem looked into his eyes, and could imagine how women fell under his spell. His eyes were like sapphire pools. A woman — she — could easily drown in the velvety blue depths. She caught her breath, inhaling the fragrance of his cologne, and tingled anew.

"What are you really doing out here?" she asked.

"Right now I'm writing a story about Sheriff Clement Jones and his daughter."

"You're doing that," Clem agreed, "but that's not why you're out here. Your story on the Sheriff is an afterthought."

Wade braced a hand against the wall, his arm brushing against Clem's shoulder. She was virtually his prisoner, and had no desire at the moment to change the situation. He had shaved that morning; his face had no beard stubble, and it was deeply tanned. Odd, she thought, Easterners usually were pasty and white.

"You're right," Wade conceded. "If the stagecoach had not needed repairs, I wouldn't be here in Lawful at all. We would have made our stop and driven straight through to San Elizario and El Paso."

His close proximity restricted Clem's breath and caused the blood to rush through her veins. Wade Cameron was posing a problem with which she had to deal, the sooner the better. "Where were you headed? San Elizario or El Paso?"

"First one, then the other," he replied.

"You didn't come out here for your health or to view the scenery?"

"No. I'm looking for a man who disappeared thirty-five years ago. His older brother Nash Dillon has traced his whereabouts to El Paso."

"Who is the man?"

"Bryan Dillon," he said. "Ever heard of him?"

"No. Why are *you* looking for him?"

"Nash hired me. I'm good at solving old stories, so he figured I might have a good chance of finding Bryan, and if not Bryan, perhaps his heirs. Since the Dillons are one of the wealthiest families in New York, Bryan or the heirs stand to inherit a large fortune."

"What are you going to get out of this?"

"Money. Fame. Recognition. And gratification."

"In that order?"

"In that order. I've always preferred wealth to fame, recognition, or gratification."

He laughed softly. Clem liked the resonant sound that seemed to caress her; then he pushed away from the wall, away from Clem, and for a moment she felt bereft and a little disappointed with his confession. She wondered what kind of man he really was. At times he seemed so reminiscent of Papa, and again so different.

"If you haven't eaten," he said, "may I take you to breakfast."

"I'd like that, Mr. Cameron."

"Call me Wade."

"I'll think about that."

As they walked out of the church into the gray, dismal morning, the eastbound stagecoach splashed through the muddy ruts, coming to a halt in front of Frazier's Hotel and Saloon. Jumping to the ground, the guard waded through the mire. At the sidewalk, he picked up a long squat bench which he set below the stagecoach door. Then he moved back to the hotel and hoisted onto his shoulder a large plank that leaned against the wall.

Once the board extended from the sidewalk to the bench, he opened the door and assisted a woman from the coach. Covered in a black velvet cape that billowed in the wind, her face was hidden in the folds of the hood. By the time she stood on the sidewalk in front of the hotel door, the guard had dropped her luggage at her feet.

"Here you are, ma'am," he said. "Where do you want me to carry these?"

"Put them in the lobby of the hotel," she said, and turned in the direction from which Clem and Wade walked. A gust of wind blew the hood from her head. She lifted a gloved hand and brushed tendrils of hair from her face.

Clem gasped and stopped walking. She felt as if life itself had abandoned her; her breath caught in her lungs; her chest hurt. Her mother was here!

"Do you know that woman?" Wade asked again, shivering from the cold and raising his collar around his neck. He stuffed his hands into the pockets of his coat.

"Yes."

Wade recognized her to be the woman in the photograph.

"She's my mother."

The woman took a tentative step forward and looked as if she wanted to smile at Clem, but the gesture never quite made it to her lips. She lifted a gloved hand halfway up in the air, then dropped it. The wind flattened the black velvet cape against her body, and tendrils of brown curls escaped the elaborate chignon at the nape of her neck. The photograph had failed to capture the true essence of her beauty. Her hand went to her face, long, slender fingers brushing the hair out of her face.

"Clementina," Deborah called.

Wade looked down at the woman who stood at his side. She had faltered when she first saw her mother, but now her back was ramrod straight, her shoulders thrown back, her head high. Gone was the alluring, evocative woman whom he had glimpsed several times during the past few hours. In her place stood Deputy Sheriff Clem Jones—the woman who could ride, cuss, and shoot like a man! Her right hand rested on the stock of her revolver. As if she were assessing an opponent, Clem's face was expressionless, her eyes focused on the newcomer. Slowly she began to walk, Wade falling in step with her.

When they reached her, Deborah said, "Hello, Clementina."

Deborah was the first person Wade had heard call Clem by her given name, and she made it sound beautiful and musical. Her voice was deep and husky. Clem's would sound like that when she was older.

"Hello, Deborah." Clem's voice was colder than the north wind that howled down the street and around the buildings.

"I—suppose you're surprised to see me."

"Yes, I am," Clem answered.

"You should have known I would come," Deborah replied.

"Deborah," Clem stepped back "I'd like for you to meet Wade Cameron, a journalist and magazine publisher from New York. Wade, meet my mother Deborah Jones."

"Mr. Cameron." Deborah tipped her head slightly and smiled.

Wade stepped forward and smiled into the face of a woman who looked much too young to be the mother of a twenty-one-year-old daughter. "Mrs. Jones, it's a pleasure to meet you."

Deborah returned her attention to her daughter. "I'd like to see your father's—your father. Where is he?"

"At the church."

Deborah nodded, her chin quivering. "When's the funeral?"

"This afternoon," Clem answered, and turned to one of the children who darted into the hotel behind her. "Laban," she called out and dug into her pocket for a coin, "will you carry these bags to the Sheriff's house, please?"

The child caught the coin that Clem tossed him and stuffed it into his breeches' pocket. "Yes, ma'am," he said, "I sure will."

Then Clem looked at Wade. "If you'll excuse us, my mother and I would like to have some time to ourselves."

"Of course," Wade answered, then said to Deborah, "You're the woman in the photograph, aren't you?"

Deborah smiled—a sad smile that seemed to emanate from her eyes. "I could be, but I'm not sure what photograph you're talking about."

"At Clem's house last night I saw a photograph of the Sheriff and you and two other men. It looked as if it had been taken many—several years—"

"If it's the one I'm thinking about, it *was* taken many years ago, Mr. Cameron. Right after Clement and I were married," Deborah assured him. "Clementina wasn't born yet, and we were living in San Antonio. Rand . . ." Deborah paused, then said, "Rand—Clement's adopted brother—and one of Rand's close friends were visiting with us at the time. It was Rand's idea that we all have our photograph made together."

"You haven't changed much, if any," Wade said,

94

studying her face. "I'd have recognized you anywhere."

"No," Deborah said, a bitter edge to her voice, "many accuse me of being a woman blessed with eternal youth, Mr. Cameron, but I sometimes wonder if it hasn't been a curse rather than a blessing. Now, if you don't mind, I'd like to be alone with my daughter."

"Of course," Wade said. "Good day, Clem, Mrs. Jones." He turned and walked over to the sheriff's office, leaving the two women standing in front of the hotel.

"You're looking good, Clemen—"

"Don't call me Clementina." Clem was aware that she was curt, but was unable to help herself. She resented her mother's coming to town for her father's funeral. She had not been here for him when he was alive, and now he had no need of her. Clem took a step, but Deborah laid a detaining hand on her arm. Clem flinched away from the touch.

"You didn't intend to send me word about your father's death, did you?"

"No."

"How you must hate me."

Refusing to look at her mother, Clem gazed at the solemn sky. "No, I'm over that. I have no feelings for you whatsoever."

Her mother reached out and caught Clem's arm again. "No matter how you feel, I love you, and I did care about your father."

"I can tell," Clem said and looked into her mother's eyes. "You waited until he was dead to come back to him. Go peddle your story to someone else. I know the real reason why you're back."

"I'm here because of you," Deborah said. "I came as soon as I received word, because I wanted to be here with you. I knew how you must be suffering."

"I'm really touched," Clem said. "It's not exactly coincidence is it, that you're returning to Lawful at the same time that Rand's coming back."

Deborah's eyes opened in surprise, their color deepening with emotion. Her voice was lower, more husky when she spoke. "Rand is coming home?"

Oh, yes, Clem thought, her mother was still in love with Rand McGaffney. She laughed shortly. "Save the theatrics for someone else. I'm not a believer and not likely to be converted. I know what the two of you did to Papa."

"If you truly feel this way toward me," Deborah asked, "why are you letting me stay at the house with you?"

Now Clem's gaze strayed to the sheriff's office. The shade was up, and through the window she saw Wade sitting at the desk, going through papers. Already gathering information for his story, she thought.

"Because, Wade Cameron is a journalist. Specifically he's out here to find a missing person, but he's not really choosey about his story. If he can't find the one he's looking for, he'll create another. I don't intend for him to dig up Papa's past. While he's here, you and I are going to be civil to one another."

Deborah's eyes softened. "You don't have to protect your father, Clem. He was wild in his youth, that's true, but he has nothing in his background to be ashamed about."

"No?" Clem drawled sarcastically. "How about his wife and brother having an affair and running off together? How about the loving wife abandoning her husband and daughter for a younger man?"

"That's not the way it was, Clem. I tried to tell you years ago, but you wouldn't listen then—"

"I idolized you and Rand," Clem continued, the words refusing to be dammed up. "My mother and my uncle. How could you? How could you come back and resurrect all those painful memories?"

"I loved your father," Deborah said, "and I love you."

"But you weren't *in* love with him," Clem accused, unable to stop herself.

"No, I wasn't in love with him, but he knew that when he married me. I was foolish to have married him, but I was young and truly believed that through the years I would come to love him as much as he loved me."

"That gave you no right to fall in love with Rand."

"I don't know if anyone gives another the right to fall in love, Clem, but it's true I did fall in love with Rand, but it's also true that he and I never, *never* had an affair. We respected ourselves too much for that, although your father never credited either of us with honor or integrity. I was never unfaithful to your father. Any infidelity he suffered was purely imaginary and of his own making."

Not ready for her mother's defense, Clem wanted to be angry and to resent what Deborah was saying about her father, but she could not. Her mother could still touch her heartstrings. Clem wished it were different, because Deborah had hurt her and her father so deeply, but truth of the matter, she had never ceased loving her beautiful mother. But Clem refused to allow Deborah to hurt her again. She had to put some distance between them; she had to think.

"Deborah," she said, "you go on to the church and see Clement. I've already been. I'm going to get Rusty-Be-Dusty, and I'll meet you back at the house."

"Clemen—Clem—" Deborah clasped her gloved hands together and shivered against a blast of the wind. "Please come to the church with me. I don't want to go by myself."

Clem looked into her mother's face. The brown eyes, misty with tears, stared sadly at her. "All right," Clem conceded. "I'll meet you down there later. I

97

want to go by the office to clear out the Sheriff's and my things."

"And to see what Cameron is up to," Deborah added.

Clem nodded. Without uttering another word, the two women parted, Deborah going to the church, Clem to the sheriff's office. When she opened the door, Wade was still sitting at her father's desk, thumbing through a sheaf of papers. Hadley, standing behind, peered over his shoulder.

"Anything I can help you with?" Clem asked.

"Nope," Hadley said. "We were curious about the wanted posters and were looking to see if we could find anything on this fellow Wade is hunting. Thought he might be wanted by the law."

Clem grinned and drew a breath of relief. Wade was not going through her father's personal belongings.

"You two don't fool me. In particular, you and the council are worried about the gunslingers who are going to be headed this way when news of Clement's death gets out. Well, you'll have a little worry, but not much when they learn that Rand has been appointed to take his place. Now, if the two of you don't mind, I'd like to clear the desk out."

Wade laid aside the stack of posters through which he had been looking, pushed back the chair, and stood. "Are you still going to have breakfast with me?" he asked.

"Sorry, I promised Deborah I'd meet her at the church as soon as I packed the Sheriff's personal belongings."

"Since both of us missed it at the house this morning," Hadley said, "how about my joining you, Wade? Frazier is known for turning out the best food in town."

Wade laughed. "Why not, Hadley."

After the two men left, Clem sat down behind the desk and sorted through her father's possessions. She put them into a wooden box and slid it into a corner so she could pick it up later; then she walked to the church to find Deborah waiting in the vestibule. Both of them stood and looked down the long aisle at the opened casket. Then without speaking, they walked side by side to the back of the church. For a long minute they stared at the man who seemed to be sleeping so peacefully; then Deborah began to weep. After a moment's hesitation, Clem embraced her mother.

"I know you don't believe me," Deborah sobbed against Clem's chest, "but I cared for your father."

Clem drew her mother even closer as if to protect her. But care was not enough. Her father had needed and wanted love, and was too proud to accept less. She had needed and wanted a mother who left her.

Chapter Seven

Clem stood on the boardwalk in front of Frazier's Hotel and Saloon, her gaze moving up and down Main Street. The funeral was over and people had begun milling again. Proprietors were unlocking their doors and raising the shades. Business as usual, Clem thought. Instead of the Sheriff to patrol the streets and to keep law and order, it was his daughter.

Although she was sanguine about accepting the responsibility, it weighed heavily on her shoulders, now that she knew the council preferred a man to her, in particular that they preferred Rand to her. No matter what arguments they had presented, no matter how reasonable they sounded, she still smarted from her confrontation with them earlier in the day.

Turning, she pushed through the doors and walked into the dimly lit interior of the saloon. She was looking for Ramson and Hammond, who had stayed for the funeral. The council's warning still ringing in her ears, she wanted to make sure they left as quickly as possible.

Because it was early in the day, few were in there. In one corner at a table beneath a wall lamp, four men played cards. Several others sat at scattered tables throughout the room. The bounty hunters were not there, and she was relieved. Although she would have no compunction about asking them to leave Lawful, they had served her father well, and she had no desire to make enemies out of them.

The bartender waved and called to her, "Howdy, Deputy. Come on in and have a drink. I have your favorite. If not a drink, come in out of the cold."

"Believe I'll do both," she said. "How are things going?"

"Peaceful right now," he answered. "But they'll be picking up later in the day."

"Don't worry. The boys and I will be keeping an eye out. Just checking to see if Ramson and Hammond have left yet."

Grady shrugged. "Don't know. I haven't seen them since this morning."

Clem leaned against the bar, and glancing into the mirror, she saw a young man enter the saloon, his spurs jangling as he swaggered to the bar. He looked to be her age . . . if that old.

"How about a sarsaparilla?" Grady said.

Clem smiled. Ever since she had been a child, Grady had provided her with her favorite drink. "Believe I will."

The newcomer slapped his hand on the bar, and Clem turned to look at him. He flashed her a grin, his blatant gaze moving slowly from the top of her head to her feet and back up.

"Howdy," he said.

Clem nodded.

"Be with you in a minute," Grady said. When he set the carbonated drink in front of Clem, he grinned. "I can remember the time when I was sitting a glass of milk in front of you."

Clem smiled, memories rushing to mind. "Me, too, Grady."

"When you was knee high to a grasshopper, the Sheriff would hoist you on the bar."

"It's a mighty interesting story you're telling," the man said, "but if you don't mind, bartender. I'm thirsty. I've been riding a mighty long time. And, mind you, I don't want milk or sarsaparilla."

"Sure thing," Grady said. "What can I get you?"

"Whiskey."

"A glass of whiskey coming up."

The man shook his head and wagged his index finger in the air. "A whole bottle coming up."

While Clem finished off her sarsaparilla and talked with Grady, the man downed several glasses of whiskey in quick succession.

"Guess I better be shoving along," she said. "Hokie and Turbin wanted to meet with me this afternoon."

"I'm glad they gonna be the deputies right on. I'd be worried about you otherwise."

"Me, too," she agreed. "They served the Sheriff well, and I know they'll do the same for me."

"Check by later," Grady said. "I have the usual for you."

Clem smiled. Through the years Grady had always managed to give her a few bottles of sarsaparilla to take home with her. "Thanks, and I will."

Before she could turn, the young man moved closer to her. "I don't have the usual to give to you. I have something better."

"Not interested," Clem said.

"Maybe you could be if you'd let yourself. I'm Chester Powers. Who are you?"

"Clem Jones, Deputy Sheriff."

"Clem Jones," he murmured. "Daughter of Sheriff Jones."

"The same."

His gaze swept to her hips and lingered on the revolvers. "I hearsay you're good with them guns."

"I am."

"Well, Clem, as one good gun to another—" he smiled and waved his hand toward an empty table, "I'm inviting you to have a drink with me."

"No, thank you."

He stepped nearer to her, his whiskey breath blowing against her face. He clamped his hand around her wrist. "Aww, come on. One drink. I'm a lonesome cowboy in need of some female company."

Clem jerked her arm from his clasp. "I said no."

"Think you're too good to have a drink with me?" he sneered.

"I'm too busy," she replied and shoved past him to walk out of the saloon. She felt his gaze on her as she walked out, and she kept her head up, her shoulders squared, her back erect . . . just like her Papa had taught her to do. No one would know the fear she felt.

Having seen drifters like Chester Powers come and go in Lawful all her life, Clem quickly dismissed him from mind as she walked down the street toward the sheriff's office. One woman was as good to them as another. She was glad that Hokum Smith and Turbin Davis had agreed to serve as her deputies. She felt better knowing that she had someone to back her up, and she trusted these men.

At her office she met with the two deputies and outlined their duties for the week, then decided to call it a day. She was weary. So much had happened to her during the past two days. Remembering Grady's promise, she returned to the saloon.

On her way she saw Prentice Fairfax walk out of the newspaper office, and wondered if her cousin was there also. She hesitated, and for a second pondered the idea of going over. She had a good excuse. She was still on duty, patrolling the streets. Stopping by

103

Hadley's would be a natural thing for her to do.

She had been surprised to see Wade at the funeral, but quickly decided she should not have been. Everything he did was motivated by his desire to get a story, not because he admired her father or liked her. The admission brought about a tinge of disappointment, but it also reminded her why she did not like the man, why she did not trust him; it also prompted her to go home.

Remembering her sarsaparilla, she headed straight for the saloon. Unlike this morning, the room was filling up with people. Lamps were lit and burning all around. Horace Newman sat at the old piano that needed tuning and played light, airy tunes, his singing loud and off key. In the far corner of the room, Chester Powers sat by himself. On the table in front of him was one empty whiskey bottle; another was two-thirds filled.

"I'm glad you came back," Grady said. "I wondered if you'd forget."

"Not when it comes to my sarsaparilla," Clem answered.

"Is that the strongest drink you can handle?" Powers's voice sounded from behind her.

Clem slowly turned and looked into glazed, bloodshot eyes. "It's the strongest drink I want to handle."

"Been hearing people talk about you being the best shot around," Powers said.

Figuring the man was drunk and wanting to avoid trouble of any kind, Clem shrugged. "Good enough."

"How good?" he egged.

"Mr. Powers, why don't you call it a night? From the looks of the bottles on your table, I'd say you're drunk."

"I am, and no woman's gonna tell me how much I can drink."

"It's the deputy sheriff who's telling you to stop before you create a disturbance. It's time you left the saloon."

He said in a loud voice, "Are you giving me an order?"

"I am."

The pianist quit playing and singing; talking and gambling ceased; men slowly backed away from the bar to give Clem and Powers plenty of room. Grady moved to one end of the bar.

Powers laughed. "And what, Miss Deputy Sheriff, are you going to do if I disobey? Beat me with a crochet needle?"

"I don't crochet," Clem said.

The room grew still and quiet. Powers looked around nervously, but no one joined in his banter. He stepped away from the bar, straddled his legs slightly, and dropped his hands so they hovered about his revolvers. He was ready for a fight, a fight that Clem wanted to avoid at all costs if she could, but a fight she would not run from if reason failed.

"If you don't stop drinking and leave the saloon, I'll arrest you and let you sleep your drunk off in the jail."

"Never."

Clem's gaze never wavered from his. "I'm going to give you five minutes to get out of here."

He shook his head. "I'm not leaving, and you can't make me."

Clem pushed away from the bar and said quietly, "I figure you're drunk, and I don't want to take advantage of you, but you are leaving, one way or the other."

Clem heard a noise on the stairway behind her, and out of the corner or her eyes, she saw Ramson and Hammond. Another problem. But she could not think about that one until she resolved the present

105

one. She only hoped that the bounty hunters were still friendly toward her.

"I'm gonna count to three, Miss Deputy Sheriff," Powers said, "then I'm gonna draw. Been hearing a lot about how fast you are. I think I'll see for myself."

Murmuring among themselves, the people quickly shuffled about, getting out of the way. Ramson and Hammond walked down the stairs and stopped a few feet away from her.

"Need some help handling this cub?" Jeb asked.

"No, I can handle him. Thanks all the same." She saw the bartender reach for the sawed-off shotgun she knew he kept concealed beneath the counter. "Grady, I meant what I said to Jeb. I can handle this. Go get Hokie or Turbin for me."

"One," Powers counted.

Grady scrambled from behind the counter and raced out of the saloon.

"Two."

Clem was fast; she knew that, but she also knew that she had never faced another human in a face-to-face shoot-out in her life. Her heart pounded furiously; her blood seemed to roar through her head; her palms were clammy. For the first time in a long while, Clem knew she was afraid. Inside she was shaking so badly, she was uncertain whether she could aim her gun after she had drawn it.

Slow down, girl, she remembered the Sheriff saying. *Relax and breath deeply. Keep your head.*

"Three."

Powers's gun cleared leather, but not as quick as Clem's. She fired first, her bullet catching him in his gun hand. He screamed and his arm jerked, causing his shot to miss Clem. His revolver fell to the floor. Using his good hand, he clasped the other, blood dribbling through his fingers.

106

"You god-damned woman," he screamed. "Why didn't you kill me? I'll never be able to shoot a gun again. You've ruined my hand."

"But saved your life . . . this time." Hokie strode across the room to where Powers stood. "What do you want me to do with him, Clem?"

"Take him to Elm's office first and get his hand taken care of, then escort him out of town." Clem looked at Powers. "Don't come back to Lawful. I won't be lenient the next time."

Hokie pulled his battered hat lower over his forehead and grinned at Clem. "You can count on me, Deputy Sheriff. It's good as done."

As if nothing untoward had happened, the saloon came alive again. People gathered around her, clapping her on the back and congratulating her on doing such a fine job. Then Grady announced that the next round of drinks was on the house, and the crowd quickly shifted its attention from Clem to the host.

"You handled yourself well, Clem," Jeb Ramson said, "but you should have killed him. That boy's gonna hate you to his dying day, and maybe he'll be coming back one of these days to get you."

"I'll have to take my chances," she answered.

Jeb smiled. "You even sound like your pa."

"Thanks," she murmured. "Do you know Powers?"

The bounty hunter nodded his head. "He was building quite a reputation. I saw him a few days ago in El Paso."

"Are there quite a few like him gathering there?"

"Three including Powers, when Dulles and I left. Don't know if any more have joined them."

"Are you heading back that way?"

"Not us," Jeb said. "Figure we'll keep the skin on our back longer if we hunt down desperados. Fighting feuds ain't my kind of business."

"I supposed you and Hammond are on your way out of town," she said rather than asked.

He nodded. "We're on our way to San Antone. If ever you need help, you know how to reach us. We'll work for you, just like we did your pa. Same arrangement."

She nodded and watched as they walked out of the saloon. Then she moved to the bar and picked up her two bottles of sarsaparilla. These were probably the most expensive she would ever drink.

Shortly after the shooting, Elm, Hadley, and Wade, each one bundled up warmly, walked up Main Street to the livery stable. The dreary weather brought darkness of night sooner than ordinary. The wind was blowing, but not as strongly as it had been earlier. The sky was still overcast with rain never far away, the temperature low.

"I'm proud of Clem for standing up to Powers," Elm said. "People are gonna figure she's a strong Deputy Sheriff, and she is, mind you. But, let me warn you, this is the beginning of her reputation as a fast gun, and it concerns me. Also, I'm worried that Powers will try to get even. He was really ranting and raving while I was taking care of his wound. No telling what he'll do to her."

Like Elm, Wade was worried about Clem. Regardless of the consequences, she was determined to be the deputy sheriff. The story of her taking Chester Powers had already made the round in Lawful and would circulate like wild fire through the countryside. With each retelling it would be embellished, until neither Clem nor Powers would recognize it. It would compel other gunfighters to come and match their skill to hers.

108

"Maybe you're worried unnecessarily," Hadley said. "She shot his gun hand and splintered some of the bones. He'll never be able to use it again."

"Maybe not that hand," Wade pointed out, "but he's got another one he can learn to use."

"He could," Hadley conceded, "but it's doubtful."

"If his resolve is strong enough, he will," Wade said. "He won't be the first to do it."

"I don't think he poses a problem," Hadley iterated. "Even if he should, it'll be long after Rand has arrived. What happened today will serve to warn others to stay out of Lawful."

"One thing for sure, Cameron," Elm said, "you ought to pay that whipper-snapper artist you brought along with you real good. He's getting enough sketches of people out here to fill a museum. While I was doctoring Powers's hand, he was sitting there drawing and Powers was doing a lot of talking. He's a close friend of Ike Perry."

"Ike Perry." Almost against his will, the name slipped out of Wade's mouth.

"A gunslinger," Hadley said. "He and some more hired guns are in El Paso now. Jeb Ramson figures Borajo hired them."

Jeb Ramson! Wade had met him once. Dulles Hammond, he had only heard about! Was this homecoming week? Wade wondered. Prentice had described this trip as a fool's mission. He would be surprised to know how aptly his description fit.

"That boy's earning him some money, too," Elm said, referring to Prentice. "He did two drawings of Powers. He sold one to him and kept the other."

Having reached the livery stable, the three men stopped, and Elm pushed open the door. "Lester, have you got my buggy ready?"

"Sure do." The owner met them at the door. "Must

109

really be an emergency to get you out in weather like this, Elm. Who you going to see?"

"Clyde Mulebauer."

"Good thing for you that he don't live far from here," Lester said. "Else you'd be out 'til late tonight."

"Still might be." Elm followed Lester McLean to the buggy, and set his medical bag in the seat. "No telling how bad the old fool has hurt himself. Looks like he'd know he's too old to be breaking horses. I told him that last time he was thrown, but he won't listen to me."

Still standing at the door, Wade heard a noise at the back of the building. He turned to see two men saddling their horses. One he did not recognize; the other was Jeb Ramson. During the years that Wade had worked as a bounty hunter, he had crossed paths with Ramson once, then briefly and only in passing. He wondered if the man would recognize him. A part of him did not want to be recognized, but he had known this was a possibility when he came west.

Leading their horses up front, Jeb said, "We're mighty grateful to you for giving our horses such good care, Mr. McLean. We'll see you the next time we're through Lawful."

"Sure thing," Lester answered. "You and Mr. Hammond are welcome here any time."

Having reached the buggy, the two men saw Hadley and Elm.

"Well, gentlemen," Jeb said, "me and Dully are on our way to San Antone. We promised Clem that we'd be leaving as soon as Clement was buried. Also promised that if she needed us, we'd be by her side."

"Thanks for the offer," Hadley said, "but Hokum Smith and Turbin Davis have already agreed to be her deputies."

"She's going to do all right," Jeb said. "She's a mite

110

green, but that'll change after she's been at it for a while."

"Hear tell she handled Powers real good," Hadley said.

"She did right well," Jeb admitted, "but she made a big mistake. Instead of wounding the pup, she should have killed him. I told her so. If that kid learns to shoot with his left hand, he'll be back after her. Even if he doesn't come back, she better be looking over her shoulders from now on, to see if he is."

"Yeah," Hadley said, "that's what we were discussing on the way over here."

Ramson glanced over at Wade, but recognition did not register in his expression.

"Thanks again," Hadley said, "for bringing in Porter."

"Hadley," Wade said, "I'm going to the house. I'll see you later."

"Much later," Hadley replied. "I'm going by the office first."

Wade turned up the collar of his coat and hurried out of the building. His mind was awhirl with thoughts of Clem and Powers, of Ike Perry and Jeb Ramson. How ironic that his past and future had come together to create a situation that was likely to explode any moment.

Clem had been lucky that Chester Powers was not a seasoned gunman. Next time she might not be as fortunate. As much as Wade hated to admit it, Ramson was right. By shooting Powers in the hand, Clem had made an enemy out of him, especially since she was a woman and he a man. His pride would not allow him to live with that. According to the gunfighters' creed, she should have killed him. One less enemy to fear.

But Wade understood her motive and admired her for it. Having stood in that exact spot five years ago,

111

he imagined what her reasoning had been.

He looked toward the sheriff's office. The shade was up, and in the lamplight, he could see Clem pacing back and forth. Hurried steps carried him across the street, up the boardwalk. He opened the door and walked into the warm room.

"What are you doing here?" Clem asked.

"I heard about Powers," he said, his gaze going to the bottles of sarsaparilla that sat on her desk.

She rubbed a hand up and down an arm. "He provoked me," she said. "He gave me no choice."

She was still wound up. Wade knew. How many times had he stood in that exact spot? How many men had he faced? Of course, there was one major difference between him and Clem. He had been a bounty hunter; she was the deputy sheriff.

"No," he said, "you made the choice, Clem, when you decided to keep the badge. I told—"

"Don't come in here with your I-told-you-sos," Clem said.

"You could have been killed, Clem."

"Well, I wasn't. You'll get your story!"

"I'm not worried about the story; I'm worried about you. There'll be others coming," Wade promised. "Now that you've faced Powers, you'll have to face more."

"I'm the sheriff," she said. "It's my duty to protect the citizens from the likes of Chester Powers."

"Yes," he said slowly, "it is the sheriff's duty. Just remember, Clem, although you're wearing a badge, and what you're doing is called justice, you're setting yourself up to be an executioner. When you face a gunslinger, it's either kill or be killed."

Clem walked across the room and yanked her coat from the rack. "Thanks for the advice. I'll be going home now. I see Hokie on his way over."

Before the deputy arrived, Clem picked up her bottles of sarsaparilla and marched out of the room, slamming the door on Wade. He stood there for a long time, staring at her through the window until she disappeared into the dark. He remained at the sheriff's office a little longer and visited with Hokie. When he left, his mind was cluttered with the events of the day.

When Nash Dillon had hired him, Wade had known the assignment would be a tough one. If he had not desperately needed the money to save his journal, he might have turned Nash down. Again he might not. The story of Bryan Dillon's disappearance had always intrigued him.

By the time Wade arrived at Hadley's, it had begun to drizzle again, and the wind was blowing harder. It looked like another cold, wet night. Wade felt as if he were frozen solid. He smelled the aroma of food, and knew Hadley's housekeeper was preparing dinner. He stopped by the kitchen to announce his arrival.

"Glad you're in, Mr. Cameron," Philana said. "Right nasty weather out there. Dinner will be ready shortly."

Wanting some time to himself, Wade hurried to his room, glad that a fire was burning brightly and the room was warm. Again he thought of Clem facing Powers, and he was angry at her for taking on a man's job—and a dangerous one at that. Then he remembered how alluring she was in her nightdress. Still he could not erase from memory the thought of her being killed by a gunman.

After he slipped out of his coat, he picked up his luggage and set it on the bed. He opened it to lift out a flat, black leather box that he carried to the dresser. Setting it down, he unlocked and raised the lid to reveal in the lamplight two nickel-plated revolvers, lying

113

on burgundy velvet. Wade ran his index finger down the ornately carved barrel to the ivory inset on the stock.

For five years he had kept his promise to himself and not worn them. Yet he kept them cleaned and loaded and always carried them with him. His hand curled around the stock, and he lifted it from its velvet cushion. How perfectly it fit his hand; how natural it felt. His finger lightly caressed the trigger.

Returning the revolver to its case, Wade walked to the window, where rain ran in rivulets down the pane. He stared down the street. A pale light from the flickering lantern on the post in the yard reflected in the water that filled the deep wagon ruts.

His watch faintly chimed the hour, and his fingers curled around the delicate gold chain that lay against his brocade waistcoat. Extracting from his pocket the timepiece that Nash Dillon had given him as a gift, Wade held it in his palm and studied the daffodils, meticulously designed and etched into the cover. It was an exact replica of the watch Nash Dillon had worn for the past thirty-seven years.

Oh, yes, Nash Dillon knew exactly what strings to pull to get one to obey his summons, and regardless of the person, Nash was a man to pull them without hesitation, without conscience, as long as he obtained what he wanted.

Wade would not forget the day Nash had summoned him to the palatial Dillon House, located on the outskirts of New York City. Had it been five months? It seemed like it was only yesterday. The September afternoon had been mild, Wade recalled.

"I don't care where you have to go or how long it takes," Nash Dillon had said, "I want you to find my brother."

"Why me?" Wade had asked.

114

"I've always gotten the best, and you're the best. Also, you're the only man I trust."

"I'm no longer a bounty hunter," Wade said, closing his mind to bitter memories. "And have not been for the past five years."

"Being a bounty hunter is nothing to be ashamed of," Nash said. "You were the best. Not one time did you kill any of the criminals you captured."

No, Wade thought, he had not killed one, a record not many bounty hunters could attest to, nor would they want to. But Wade knew many of those whom he brought in hated him with a vengeance. They would rather have been killed than brought back to be put in prison.

"You always brought your man back for trial," Nash said. "You never failed to find a missing person, and you never botched one assignment."

"Your memory is failing. I know I failed on one. How many more I can only guess," Wade said bitterly, the vision of a sixteen-year-old dangling on the end of a rope swimming in front of his eyes.

Newby Perry had had a price on his head for robbery and murder. He was wanted dead or alive. Wade had found and brought him in. At the subsequent trial Perry was found guilty as charged and sentenced to hang. Wade would never forget the anguished cries of the boy's widowed mother. Days after the hanging, and only hours before Wade was leaving the Kansas town on another assignment, the sheriff learned that Newby Perry was innocent. Then Wade had gone after the real killer, whom he had found and brought in.

"You didn't botch that assignment, and that boy's death was not your fault," Nash said. "You can't be held to blame because the boy was falsely accused. You acted in good faith on the information you had

115

been given."

"But if I had not found and brought him in, he would have escaped and would be alive today. He would have had time for the real killer to show his hand."

"You got him, too."

"But too late to help the boy and his family. Somehow I fail to see the justice." Wade still had nightmares about his role in Newby Perry's hanging.

"Wade, you can't go through the rest of your life blaming yourself for the boy's death. You must accept that you're not guilty." Nash paused, looked directly into Wade's face, then asked, "Does his family have any idea that you're responsible for the allowance being paid to them each month?"

Wade stared silently at the older man. He did not know why he was surprised. Nash made it his business to know all that was going on in New York City finance.

"No," Wade answered slowly, "I set it up so that they would think it's the result of an insurance policy taken out by the father."

"Please—accept one last assignment as a bounty hunter. Go to West Texas and check this clue out."

Wade shook his head. "Nash, I'm tired of chasing people, shadows, and ghosts of the past. If your brother is alive and wants to be found, he knows how to contact his family. Thirty-five years of silence should tell you something."

"The man who brought the watch in to the jeweler in New Orleans asked for a new one to be crafted, Wade," Nash said. "A smaller one. One for a woman."

Wade said nothing.

"What if this watch is being made for a daughter?" said Nash softly and persuasively, one hunter to another. "What if I have a niece somewhere on the West

Texas frontier? Perhaps in El Paso."

The watch gently spun from the end of the chain, the gold glinting in the sunlight, the motion mesmeric.

"If you'll take the job," the older man continued softly, "I'll pay you one million dollars."

Wade raised his head. The amount was incredible.

"Money earned for an honest day's work," the low voice droned hypnotically. "Money without the Dillon name attached. More than enough money to save the *Journal*."

Wade agreed that the offer was tempting — the most tempting he had ever received. Slowly he drawled, "Do you realize what you've said?"

"I do."

"You'll pay me that much for *simply taking the job?*"

"For taking the job," Nash concurred. "I have the contract already drawn up, waiting for your signature." He opened the top drawer of his desk to withdraw a stiff sheet of white paper. He held out a check in Wade's name for the sum of one million dollars. "You may take this to my bank tomorrow. It's as good as cash. Yours to do with as you see fit, no matter what you report."

Wade never moved, but steely blue eyes studied the man before him. "I never figured you for a fool, Nash, but with this setup, I could take your money, do absolutely nothing, and come back with a false report. You'd never know the difference."

"I wouldn't," Nash had agreed quietly, "but you would."

And I would, Wade thought, returning to the present as he rubbed the condensation from the window pane with his palm. Lightning crawled the blackened sky, and in the brilliant flashes of illumination, Wade saw the scraggly tree across the road and someone — it

117

looked like a man — who hurried past it, his shoulders hunched against the wind. The tree was no more than a bush, yet it was tall and strong enough to be used for a hanging tree, its spindly, naked limbs waving through the air. The person, in front of the house now, his face revealed in the flickering lantern light, was only a boy who looked to be about eighteen, a mere child; yet, he was old enough to hang.

Newby Perry was only sixteen when he was hanged!

Odd how Wade could put thoughts of his bounty-hunting days out of his mind for long periods of time. Then unexpectedly, out of the blue, something would jar his memories, and names would begin to roll through his mind. Today he knew quite well who had jarred the memory that started the names to scrolling.

Melton Strouthers. Vern Ballard. Frank Franklin. Dac Washburn. These four were those he remembered the most vividly. Mean and vicious, they were the ones who swore to kill him if they ever got out of prison. And any one of them would, if given the opportunity. A shiver of apprehension ran his spine as he thought of them. He could only hope his path would never cross theirs.

Wade walked to the table and poured himself a glass of whiskey. Lying beside the decanter, he saw a note from his cousin. Prentice informed Wade that he was having dinner at the hotel with Emmett Frazier and his family, and was leaving some sketches for Wade to see.

Picking up the drawings, Wade sat down in the chair in front of the fireplace. As he sipped his whiskey, he slowly sorted through the stack, able to trace the events of the day by the people Prentice had drawn. The last one was a picture of Chester Powers. Not the defeated and hysterical man he had been when the doctor had treated his wounded hand, but

118

as Prentice had imagined him to look when he had challenged Clem.

Behind the last drawing was one of Prentice's doodle sheets. Wade was about to lay it beside the chair, when he noticed a name that Prentice had written many times, underlining it several.

Ike Perry. He would be twenty-four now. He was nineteen when his brother was hanged . . . for a crime he did not commit. Although Wade had chased down the culprit, he had always believed that Ike Perry was also involved, that Newby had died to protect his brother.

Wade looked at the sketch of Chester Powers again. Then he was seeing Ike Perry.

Wade had returned to the small Kansas cow town with the guilty man in tow. He knew this would be no consolation to the Perry family, but he had to do it for himself, to ease his conscience. Ike Perry had called him out, but Wade, knowing he was the better gun, knowing the youth had no chance against him, had refused the challenge. He turned and was walking to his horse, when someone shouted.

"Look out."

Wade spun around, drawing as he turned, and his bullet caught Ike in the right hand.

"You son-of-a-bitch," Ike yelled, gripping his wounded hand.

Returning his revolver to the holster, Wade said, "I could have killed you, Ike, but I didn't. I'm giving you a chance to live, a chance to turn your life around, so that you don't end up on the end of a rope like your brother."

Ike had glared at him with pure hatred in his eyes. "Don't think this is over, Cameron, and don't think I'll ever forget what you've done to me. You better kill me while you have the chance. If you don't, I'm going

119

to hunt you down and kill you. That's a promise."

Wade only hoped that Clem had not made a mistake in wounding Powers.

Chapter Eight

In her bedroom, the door ajar, Clem stood in front of the window, staring into the night and thinking about the events of the day. She was still weak kneed when she thought about her shoot-out with Powers. And this was only the beginning. She moved to the night table and picked up the badge. The Sheriff had always told her it cost a lot to be a peace officer, and the rewards were scarce. Now she more fully understood what he had been saying.

She heard footsteps in the hallway; then her mother called. "Clem, supper's ready."

"Go ahead and eat. I'm not hungry."

Already having had one long, heated discussion with Deborah about being the deputy sheriff, Clem had not told her about the shooting with Powers. She knew her mother would learn about it soon enough, but she was still smarting from Wade's blistering words and accusations. She did not want Deborah to start on her. Clem moved to the bed and picked up her father's saddlebags. She laid them in the box with his personal belongings that she had removed from the office, then bent to scoot it beneath her bed.

Had she listened to her head rather than her heart, she would have left her father's burial to the townspeople, and would have gone after Alarico Olviera the day he shot Clement. But, no matter what her duty was to law and order, her father came first, the badge second. Now she had lost them both. Still, that did not release her from her promise to find Olviera.

He had the advantage of a head start, but that had been his since the shooting. The rain had begun that night, quickly turning into ice. For even the most astute tracker, the ruts and tracks were quickly hidden or eradicated. For most, that was, but not for Peaceful. Tomorrow she would ride into the mountains to enlist his help. The old Mescalero warrior would be her eyes and ears.

For all Clem knew, Olviera could be and probably was in Mexico by now, especially if Father Borajo were guiding and deluding him with the lie that the gringos were trying to take the salt away from the Mexicanos. But nothing would stop Clem from finding Rico Olviera, not a priest, not a river, not a boundary. She would chase him until one or the other . . . possibly both . . . were dead.

But what have you gained if you kill Olviera? her conscience nagged. *He's only a pawn. The man you really want is Borajo. Listen to your father; find the evidence and expose him to his own people. Destroy the source of the evil.*

"Clem," Deborah called again, this time her voice nearer and more determined, "you have to eat something."

"I said I'm not hungry." She moved to the dresser and picked up the sketches that Prentice had drawn of her father and looked at them. Although she still resented Wade's having asked Prentice to draw them, she had to admit they were a good likeness.

Deborah knocked. "You haven't eaten a bite today. You must take care of yourself or you're going to be sick. Please, Clem."

Sighing, Clem knew her mother would not stop until she had eaten, and now that they were arguing the subject, she realized she was weak with hunger. And she needed strength to carry out her purpose. She opened the top drawer of the dresser and dropped the pictures into it. "I'll be there in a minute."

Last night had been rough, Clem thought, but nothing like tonight. The numbness that accompanied the shock of her father's death was wearing off, and she faced the cold reality that Clement was gone, that Deborah and Rand were reentering her life, and the badge no longer belonged to her. She wore it, but it was not truly hers. All of this was more than she wanted to think about, yet it kept pressing in on her. She was glad that she was leaving for the mountains early in the morning. This would get her away from Lawful and her sorrow for a little while; it would give her time to think, to decide what she was going to do with her life after she caught Olviera.

Lifting her head, she looked at her reflection in the mirror. Although her hair hung loose about her face, the muted glow of the lamplight could not disguise the signs of her grief. The skin around her eyes was dark, and her cheeks hollow. She touched the tip of her finger to her face. The evidence of her fatigue and sorrow would go away in time. Not so her features.

She gazed intently into green eyes that were unlike those of either parent. When she was growing up, she had continually searched for a resemblance to one of them, but had found none. Tonight was no different. Weary of examining her face, she straightened up and glanced over to the bed and saw one of Deborah's lace handkerchiefs.

All too well Clem recalled the day Deborah had left them. Clem did not take into account the rightness or wrongness of Deborah's actions; she simply remem-

123

bered the pain, the hurt, and loneliness that followed. She also remembered the nights that her father had prowled the house unable to sleep or eat. His life had seemed vacant after Deborah left, and his feelings had affected Clem. Now the two people whom Clement Jones blamed for having totally ruined his life, for destroying his family, were returning to play major roles in her life. Naturally she was concerned about the effect they would have on her.

Clem heard a soft knock on the front door and wondered who it was. No matter, she figured that in a few minutes Deborah would learn about the shootout. There was no way Clem could keep it secret from her for long. She slowly walked across the room into the hallway.

The knock came again; however, when she entered the parlor, Deborah had already answered the door, and her soft, husky voice drifted back to Clem.

"Mr. Cameron, what a nice surprise."

Not him again, Clem thought. Had he not forced himself on her enough for one day? She stopped in the doorway and stared at him. His hair was tousled, and the lamplight flickered golden shadows across his visage. Although he was a tenderfoot, he was different from those Clem had met in the past. He exuded an aura that — despite his sophistication — proclaimed him a part of the southwestern environment.

"I was worried about Clem," he said. "I wanted to make sure she was all right."

"As well as one can be, when they've recently lost a loved one," Deborah replied.

Clem's gaze shifted to her mother. Again she was reminded of Deborah's beauty. Her dark brown hair was braided and drawn into a sleek and elegant chignon at the nape of her neck. Both women were dressed casually, but unlike Clem who wore her dressing gown over her nightshirt, Deborah was dressed in a lovely hunter green housedress. Gone were the petticoats and bustles, and the soft material clung alluringly. Not a hair in that elegant chignon was out of place.

"I'm not talking about her father," he said. "I was worried about the shooting."

"Shooting!" Deborah turned to Clem.

Clem seethed. He had no right in the world to come to her house and rile Deborah up. "It wasn't anything."

"What happened?" Deborah demanded.

Clem related the events in a dull monotone to play down the danger; still her mother's face whitened with fear and shock.

"My God, Clem! What has your father done to you?"

"Leave Papa out of this! I'm responsible for my life."

"Clem," Deborah begged, "give that damned badge up."

"I've already made my decision," Clem said, "and I'm going to stick by it. Nothing you say or do will make me change my mind, so I don't want to hear any more lectures. Is that clear?"

Deborah opened her mouth, then closed it, and nodded her head. She turned to Wade.

"Mr. Cameron, won't you come in? This way we can close the door and shut out some of the cold."

"I'm not intruding, am I?"

"Yes," Clem began.

"No!" Deborah interrupted and gave her daughter a scathing look that dared her to say another word. "We would be delighted to have company this evening. We're about to eat dinner. Would you join us?"

Wade looked from Deborah to Clem, and she shrugged. At least, if he were visiting with them, her mother would be on her best behavior and would not be giving her any lectures.

"Since Clem and I didn't get to have breakfast together," he said, "I'd enjoy having dinner with you."

After Wade pulled off his coat and hung it on the rack, he and Clem followed Deborah into the kitchen. The two of them sat down while Deborah quickly added another place setting. For the most part, Deborah and Wade carried the conversation, each keeping it light and entertaining and away from Clement. None of them ate much, Wade less than any.

When they had finished their meal, Deborah walked to the stove to pick up the coffeepot and refill their cups. "Your assignment must be an exciting one to have brought you this far west."

"Not so exciting," Wade answered. "I'm looking for a man who disappeared over thirty-five years ago. A man named Bryan Dillon. Perhaps you've heard of him?"

"No." She filled the three cups. "I've never heard the name before, that I recall. Have you, Clem?"

"No, I told him that earlier today when he asked me."

"What makes you think he's out here?" Deborah asked.

Wade pulled out his watch, the one Nash Dillon had given to him. "This is a replica of a timepiece worn by the Dillon males. The work done on them drew high acclaim when the famed jeweler and artist Antoine Afrodille handcrafted *only* four of them in 1840. One belonged to Bryan's grandfather, one to his father, and one each to him and Nash. Each watch differed in only one aspect; each had the initials of its owner etched in the case."

"Daffodils?" Clem asked as she studied the watch, running the tip of her fingers over his initials.

126

"Afrodille's work always bore the daffodil flower motif," he answered, then added, "Six months ago a man appeared in a jewelry shop in New Orleans and produced a timepiece like this one, the only difference being the initials. Instead of mine, they were B.D."

"For Bryan Dillon," Clem said.

Again Wade nodded. "The man asked the jeweler to replicate it—only this one was to be smaller. It was to be a lady's watch. The jeweler immediately recognized the famous Afrodille watch and asked the man if he could keep it. The man said no. He suggested a wax mold be made. When that was completed, he took the timepiece, promising to pick up the new one in several weeks. The jeweler immediately called the New Orleans police, who sent an inspector to the hotel to question the man, but he was already gone. Evidently the jeweler's behavior frightened the man, and he never returned for the lady's watch."

"How did the jeweler know this was the Dillon watch?" Clem asked.

"The last letter Nash received from his brother came from New Orleans. Because the watch was such a distinguishing clue, Nash periodically sent detectives down to make the rounds to see if one had shown up. Also because Nash is wealthy, he's offered an enormous reward for clues to his brother's whereabouts."

"What led you to West Texas?" Deborah asked.

"In the man's vacant room, the inspector found a receipt from an El Paso hotel."

"How fascinating," Deborah said. "I hope you find him or some information on him, but probably you won't, unless he wants to be found. Men who come west have a habit of changing their names and leaving their pasts far behind. Of course, from what you've said, I can't understand why this man disappeared in the first place—seeing his family was quite wealthy

127

and he wasn't running away from anything."

"I don't know either," Wade mused, "and I've given it a lot of thought. I guess that's another reason why I'm intrigued with this assignment. There are so many unanswered questions."

Deborah rose and moved to the kitchen cabinet to fill a kettle with water. "Sometimes, it's better to leave the questions unanswered."

"Some people may feel that way," Wade said, "but not me. I want to know."

"Perhaps one of these days you'll find him or find out what happened to him," Deborah said. After she set the kettle on the stove, she returned to the table and began to clean scraps off the plates. "Take your coffee into the parlor," she suggested. "I'll clean up the kitchen."

"I don't mind doing the dishes," Clem said, uncomfortable with the idea of being alone with Wade. Today at the church she had experienced odd, although pleasurable, sensations all through her body, as she had stood alone with him in the vestibule. And tonight prior to his coming, she had been thinking about him. Mere thoughts of Wade Cameron affected her emotions, sending them from one extreme to another. One minute she disliked him intently; the next she was totally enthralled by him. She did not know whether she wanted to be in the close confines of the parlor with him . . . alone. She felt better, more in control, when she disliked him.

During dinner she had paid little heed to the conversation between Wade and Deborah; she had been thinking about the man. Although she was inexperienced when it came to intimate relationships between men and woman, she did understand she and he were physically attracted to one another.

"Leave the dishes," Deborah said, the words a wel-

128

come intrusion to Clem's troubled thoughts. She filled two plates to overflowing with food. "I promised Hokie and Turbin that I'd bring them some supper. As soon as I return, I'll do them."

"I'll do that," Clem said.

"No," Deborah answered. "I want you to rest. You've been through a lot these past two days. It won't take me long."

Reluctantly Clem agreed and led the way into the parlor, where the fire had died down and only embers glowed in the grate. She walked to the wood box to find it empty, then moved to the clothes rack on the wall next to the door. "I forgot to bring in some wood."

As her fingers curled over her jacket, she felt Wade's hand on hers. She turned her head to look into his face. He had moved so quickly and quietly, she was unaware he was close to her until she felt his hand over hers, until her face was only inches away from his, his warm breath blowing tendrils of hair against her cheek—so different from Powers's whiskey-smelling breath earlier in the day.

"I'll go get the wood," he said.

Although Clem heard what he was saying, only the tone registered. It was soft and reassuring, a gentle caress to her frayed emotions. She could feel only his touch and could smell only the fragrance of his cologne. She saw only the texture of his skin, the kindness in the depth of his eyes. Something, the same thing that had happened to her earlier today when she had stood next to him in the church, was happening all over again; something she knew about—something Maybelle had told her about—but something she did not fully understand. Wade's proximity and his touch were creating new sensations in her, sensations she had not learned how to handle. She was apprehensive because she had never experienced it before. Always

129

she had known how to deal with situations and people; if she had not, her father had.

In the distance — the far distance — she heard Deborah call good-bye, and the back door slammed shut. Clem wanted to call her mother back; she needed her mother; she needed someone to help her. She was no longer in control of herself, much less the situation. Her errant emotions replaced logic and reason; her only thoughts were of the man standing so close to her. She looked at the large, sun-browned hand that covered hers. The fingers were long and wellshaped, his nails clean and cut short. While they were not callused like a farmer's or rancher's hands, they were strong.

"It's too cold and wet for you to be out there," Wade said.

Clem did not know how to deal with his kindness or those special emotions he stirred up in her body. "Of course, it isn't," she said. "I've been doing this all my life. I'm not a child who has to be taken care of."

"No," he said, an unusual inflection in his voice, a smoldering warmth in his eyes, "you're no child, Clementina. You're a woman, a very brave woman. I want to do this because I care about you."

For the first time in her twenty-one years, Clem felt like Clementina Jones and a woman. She felt like a very special person. Tenderly Wade uncurled her fingers from the jacket, took her hands in his, and led her to the sofa. Clem loved the warmth of his touch, and at this very moment she needed and wanted the strength and protection that his clasp seemed to promise. Forgotten was her resolve to keep him at a distance, to let her anger and dislike shield her from him.

"You don't have to prove your mettle to me, Clementina."

Again he called her by her given name, and it sounded nice.

"Maybe the people of Lawful expect you to be the rough, tough gunslinging sheriff, but not me. I'll accept you for yourself."

The gentle voice, the sincere eyes were Clem's undoing. The lecturing would have driven her from him, but these words of care and concern tugged her closer to him; they bonded her to him. Ordinarily she would have been wary of a man like Wade, but tonight she wanted the gentleness he was giving to her; she wanted to hear the kind words. She felt the dam to her emotions give, and tears were not far away. A warning clamored in her brain; one she heeded. She jerked her hands, but his grip tightened. Although he refused to let her go, he did not hurt her.

"Go ahead and cry," he said, "It's not a sign of weakness."

"It is for me."

"Then cry for me."

He sat down on the sofa and drew her into his arms. When he pressed her face against his chest, she began to sob. Immediately she felt a sweet relief. He held her close, whispering words of comfort to her. Steady was his heartbeat, warm and secure his embrace.

"Right now, crying is a physical release from the grief you feel in losing your father. It's a release from the tension you've felt since you faced Powers. It's natural to feel this way. You know you won't be seeing your father again. You know you're going to have to face life and its problems by yourself. At the moment, you feel all alone and quite like a ship without a rudder."

"How do you know?" She sniffed and burrowed her face deeper into the soft, herbal-scented shirt he wore.

"I've been through it before," he answered. "My mother died from pneumonia when I was twelve, and my father died about five years ago. Also I fought in the War between the States, so I understand what it's like to have to kill another human being."

Clem knew she should not be snuggled up against Wade, but it felt right; it felt good. She made no effort to move from his embrace. She slid her palm up his chest and played with one of the buttons on his shirt. "Were you and your father close after your mother died?"

Settling back into the cushioned sofa and drawing her with him, Wade said, "Yes, we were. I suppose that comes with being an only child and with my mother having died when I was so young. It's sort of similar to what has happened to you."

"Umhum," she murmured.

He shifted positions again, the move bringing them even closer together. She enjoyed being close to his warmth and his strength. Her breasts rested against his chest, her legs against his, and she was convinced his body was made of iron, but he was real and alive. His fingers slid through her hair, his palm resting against her scalp. She tingled from the top of her head to the bottom of her feet. For a long time she lay in the circle of his arm, neither of them talking. Finally, however, his hands curled around her upper arms, and he gently set her aside. Wondering what was wrong, she looked up at him.

He nodded to the fireplace. "Nothing but ashes." His voice was thick, his eyes shadowed with an unfamiliar emotion. He reached for the afghan that hung over the back of the divan. Tucking it around her, he said, "All of us will freeze to death, if I don't get some wood." He grinned, and his voice sounded normal once again.

132

He was not angry or displeased with her, she thought, and laughed softly. Everything was all right. Contented and warm, she remained in a ball in the corner of the sofa, watching as he slipped into and buttoned up his jacket and tied the wool scarf around his neck. When he went outside, she snuggled deeper into the divan and closed her eyes, visions of Wade Cameron swimming in her mind. She had never known another man like him before, and never had a man stirred her emotions to such a degree as he did. The door opened, and he came back into the room, his arms loaded with wood.

"I'll have a fire going in a few minutes," he said. "You stay under the blanket where it's warm." He kicked the door shut, walked through the parlor to the wood box. Kneeling in front of the fireplace, he began to bank the fire. Clem watched the pull of material across his shoulders—broad shoulders—as he worked. She noticed the stretch of material across his flexed thighs as he knelt there; he had lean, powerful legs.

"We'll have this room warm in a little while now." He rose and brushed his hands off, then turned to smile at her as he took off his scarf and jacket and rehung them on the rack. Walking to one of the large wing-back chairs, he dragged it across the room and turned it so that it faced the fire; he did the same thing to the other one. Then he returned to the sofa, caught Clem's hands in his and pulled her to her feet. "Let's sit in front of the fire."

Again Clem was inundated with raw emotion. Simultaneously she was disappointed and relieved. A part of her—a part with which she was unfamiliar and had only recently begun to assert itself—wanted him to take her into his arms again and to hold her tightly and to stretch out on the sofa with her once again. Her body had never seemed so alive and demanding;

133

it felt as if it were something apart from her normal self.

But another part was glad that he had put distance between them. She had known when she first saw Wade that he would be trouble. She had not known at that moment the enormity of her prediction; then, she had thought he would hurt her father; now, her fear increased, for she knew he had the power to hurt her. It was up to her to see that he did not.

After she sat down in the chair and stretched her feet to the fire, she spoke in order to get her mind off her errant thoughts. "Are you really interested in doing a story about the Sheriff?"

His hands crossed over his stomach, his legs extended to the fire, Wade stared at the blaze for a long while before he said, "I'm more interested in doing a story about the two of you. The theme would be the father and daughter law enforcement team. I could title it 'The Sheriff and his Deputy.'"

"Not a team anymore. That's a thing of the past."

Leaning back against the leather upholstery, Wade rolled his head to the side and looked at her. "But I'm going to write a story to immortalize him, Clem."

"Even when you think he's been a gunslinger."

"I don't think he was a professional killer," Wade explained, a perceptive edge to his voice. "I think he was a product of the country that spawned him—the same as you—and I want to write his and your story. I want to write a story about the country."

Clem smiled as she gazed steadfastly into those dreamy blue eyes. "At first, I didn't want you to write Papa's story. Now I do. I want people to remember Clement Jones."

As they lapsed into silence, Clem turned her head to stare into the hypnotic dance of the flames.

After a while, Wade asked, "Clem, do you want to

tell me about your father and mother?"

"No." A long pause followed. "But I will. I'd rather you hear it from me than anyone else."

Chapter Nine

Clem began to talk about Deborah and her father and Rand, surprising herself that in the telling she remained composed. When she finished, she felt as if a weight had been lifted from her shoulders, and sorrow washed from her heart. She was not nearly as resentful of her mother and uncle as she had been earlier.

"Yesterday was the first time I saw my mother since she left five years ago," she said. "The first time that I've talked with her."

Then they slipped into a comfortable silence; words were not necessary between them. After a while, Wade rolled his head against the back of the chair and smiled at her.

"Do you mind if I look at your father's photographs?" he asked.

Clem hesitated before she said, "I'll get them."

For the second time in such a short while she surprised herself. First, she had told him about her past; now she was allowing him to look at her father's photographs. She could not imagine her opening up so completely to a stranger, especially to a journalist, but she was. She had changed her mind about Wade Cameron. She felt comfortable with him. She disappeared into her bedroom, returning in a few minutes with the album, which she set on the reading table. In the other hand she held up a bottle of whiskey.

"Papa's," she said. "We kept it for company."

"I'd rather be a friend than company," Wade said, "but if company gets that, then I'll settle on being company right now."

Clem did not answer because she could not. Happiness seemed to bubble up within her like an artesian well, and she was afraid any minute that something would happen to destroy this incredible time they were together. While Wade dragged the chairs to the table, she poured the whiskey; they sat down across the table from one another.

Finally they had gone through all of the photographs, and Wade leaned back to finish off his drink. The front door opened, and Deborah entered the house.

"It's getting colder," she announced, setting the food basket on the hall table and taking off her cape. "But it's stopped raining."

"How are Hokie and Turbin?" Clem asked.

"Doing fine. They told me to tell you not to worry. They have everything under control."

Wade began to sort through the photographs again. "I can't find the one with your mother, father, and several of their friends."

"That's strange," Clem said. "I'm sure it was here earlier."

Deborah joined them, standing behind Clem's chair.

"Here," Clem said. "Here it is."

Wade took the photograph. "This looks like it, Clem, but it's not the same. It's more faded than the one I saw last night."

"That has to be the one," Clem announced, her search completed.

Wade contemplated it longer, then sighed. "Somehow, I remembered it as being more than what it is."

"Probably your desire for it to be more, led to your imagining it was more." Clem laughed. "Perhaps, because I didn't want you to look at them the other night, made you think it was more."

Wade laughed with her. "You're probably right."

Clem leaned closer to him, and both of them gazed at the photograph. The most identifiable people were Deborah and Clement. The image of the man standing next to Clement was faded, yet his features could be made out; the features of the third man were totally undistinguishable. Yet through the blur of sienna, it was clear that the man was bigger and taller than either of the other two men.

"He's big," Wade said, thumping the photograph. "He makes me think of a locomotive—solid steel and power." He looked at Deborah and asked. "Who are these two men with you and Clement?"

"That one—" Deborah pointed to the man standing next to her husband, "is Rand, Clement's younger adopted brother. I'm not sure what the other one is named. We knew him only as the Blacksmith."

"Makes sense to me," Wade said. "He looks like one. Was that his occupation?"

"No," Deborah said thoughtfully and picked up the photograph to study it, "I don't think so, but I'm not really sure. He was too polished and debonair, his speech too refined for him to have been a smithy by trade. He never talked about his past, but I always figured he came from back East somewhere."

When she laid it down, Wade turned the photograph over and looked on the back. "Someone recorded the date but not the names. Were these fellows part of a young gang that Clement rode with?"

Clem laughed. "I hope this isn't an example of your being subtle."

"If it were a gang, Mr. Cameron," Deborah said quietly, "I certainly was not a part of it. Clement and

138

Rand rode together and occasionally other friends joined them. They created mischief, but were not professional gunmen. They never killed a man unless it was self-defense, and they never egged a shooting."

"Where is the Blacksmith now?"

"I don't know," Deborah said. "Once Clement became a lawman, the Blacksmith drifted on. I haven't seen or heard from him in years."

"Why are you so interested in him?" Clem asked.

Wade shrugged. "Just a gut feeling I have about him. Do you have a magnifying glass? I'd like to see if I can make out his features better. If only he were not a blur," he murmured.

"I think we have one somewhere." Clem rose and walked to the chest on the other side of the room.

Wade turned to Deborah. "You said he was Rand's friend. I suppose he was closer to Rand's age than Clement's?"

Deborah hesitated a long while before she said, "I never knew how old the Blacksmith was. I always had the feeling he was older than Rand, closer to Clement's age, but I simply don't know. He's the kind of man who will never show his age."

Wade nodded, then took out of his pocket a small notebook and pencil. "I'm going to do a story on Clement. Would you give me some background material on him?"

"What would you like to know?"

"Where did he come from? How long has he been out here? Why did he come?"

"He's from Louisiana originally," she answered. "I met him in New Orleans. My parents operated a shop on Front Street, and we were having trouble with criminals who wanted to extract protection money from us. My father went to the police, and Clement, who had recently returned after a long stay on the western frontier and was now a New Orleans policeman, was assigned to the case. Single-handed, he wiped out a gang that blackmailed shop owners along Front Street." Deborah's voice grew nostalgic. "He said he fell in love with me the minute he laid eyes on me, and I was infatuated with him. Although he was sixteen years older than I, he was a handsome man. Before I knew it, we were married."

She quickly added, "I can see the cogs in your mind turning. No need to do any quick arithmetic, Mr. Cameron. I'm thirty-nine years old now. I was sixteen when Clement and I married."

"How did you happen to move out here?"

Deborah paused a moment before she said, "Clement couldn't stand being confined to civilization, and after he and Rand killed part of the Lorenzo family — a father and two of his sons who headed up the gang in New Orleans — he began to receive threats in the mail from the remaining family members. He was afraid something would happen to me. Also, Clement was the kind of man who needed the freedom the West offered. Soon after Clementina's birth, we moved to El Paso and eventually to Lawful. Later it became clear to me that Clement wasn't married to me but to that . . . that badge. It was his life."

Clem laid the magnifying glass on the table. "Papa was dedicated to helping others. Ma—" she stopped when she almost called Deborah mama. "Deborah always referred to it as that infernal badge, but the Sheriff always called it the star."

"He revered it much like Christians revere the Star of Bethlehem," Deborah said, a bitter tinge to her voice. "Both he and Rand felt that way . . . evidently so does Clementina."

Clem moved closer to the table and saw Deborah staring at Rand's photograph, and stroking it gently with the tip of her fingers. Even now her mother thought more of Rand than she did of her husband.

140

Continuing to gaze at Rand's photograph, Deborah picked it up.

"Rand's father was a cheap crook and gambler in New Orleans," said Deborah. "He was killed twenty-eight years ago when he tried to fleece one of his customers. Clement was in New Orleans at the time and happened to be playing poker with them. He's the one who made the report to the police. When he learned that McGaffney had an eleven-year-old son, Clement brought the boy out west with him, and they became like brothers. When Rand was fifteen, they returned to New Orleans, both of them getting a job on the police force and working there until we all moved back to Texas."

"Hadley said there may be one person in town who might be able to tell me if Bryan or someone fitting his description was ever in these parts. Maybe you know her. A Mrs. Herschel?"

"Merica Herschel! Of course," Clem exclaimed, "I had forgotten about her. Hadley's right. If anyone knows about Bryan Dillon, she will. She knows everybody."

"Good! That's the person I want to see. Hadley promised to take me tomorrow," Wade answered, "and I figured since she was close to a hundred years old, I had better see her right now."

Clem nodded. "For the past year Miss Merica's health has been going down. She isn't lucid much of the time and lives in a world all her own. I guess that's one reason why I didn't think about her."

"Would you like to ride out there with us?" Wade asked. "You could tell me more about your father."

"I'm sure Clem has more pressing things to do," Deborah said.

Although Clem intended to decline Wade's invitation, she was irritated that Deborah had answered for her and that she had been so curt. Her mother had no

141

idea what she had planned for tomorrow. Clem was also puzzled by Deborah's behavior. Earlier she had seemed delighted to see Wade; now she seemed rather tense and nervous.

"Sorry," Clem said to Wade but gazed at her mother, "I've already made plans. I'm going into the mountains tomorrow. I want to let Peaceful know that Papa is dead."

Deborah pushed back from the table, the legs of the chair grating against the floor as she moved. "I wish you luck tomorrow, Mr. Cameron. I hope Miss Merica can give you the information you're looking for. Now, I think it's time for us to say good night. Clem and I are extremely exhausted."

"Of course," Wade said and rose. "How thoughtless of me."

Deborah's behavior was quickly driving Clem's irritation into anger. She laid a hand on Wade's arm. "Please don't go." Her eyes caught his. "I'm not ready for bed yet. I'd like for us to talk some more about Papa now . . . tonight. Go on to bed," said Clem softly to her mother, "I know you must be exhausted."

The two women stared at each other, as if in a silent battle of wills. Neither was weak-kneed, but finally Deborah nodded and walked across the room. Pausing in the doorway, she looked over her shoulder. "Be sure to lock up before you go to bed."

"I will." The words were barely civil. Clem hated being treated as if she were a child, especially in front of Wade. If anything, she wanted him to look upon her as an adult . . . *perhaps a woman,* a small, inner voice taunted.

After Deborah walked out of the room, Wade said, "We can talk tomorrow, Clem. You look as if you need to be in bed, too."

Not you, too, Clem thought, but only said, "In a little while."

The evening had been perfect, until she had seen Deborah pining over Rand and had been treated like a child by her mother. Clem did not want Wade to leave while she had this bitter taste in her mouth.

"Have you always been in publishing?" asked Clem.

"No." If he were surprised by the abruptness of the question, he never showed it. He smoothly followed suit by answering, "I didn't start writing until after I was discharged from the army."

"You said earlier that you fought during the War between the States?" Clem rose and moved across the room to stand in front of the fireplace, where she spread her hands over the blaze.

Wade dragged his chair and sat down in it. "Yes, and afterwards I stayed in the army and traveled west."

"Where were you stationed?" Clem asked.

"Fort Concho."

"You know how to use a gun?"

Wade looked at her, raising a brow quizzically. "I do."

"Are you good?"

Wade shrugged. "Passable, I suppose. I don't have much occasion to use a gun in New York."

"You told Maybelle that you were thirty-four years old?" she said more than asked, changing subjects as quickly as a jackrabbit flitted across an open field.

Now Wade laughed softly. "That's right."

Clem correctly interpreted the laughter and was a little embarrassed, but not enough to stop her questions. "You—aren't married?"

"No. Why?"

"Simple curiosity."

She was unwilling to let him know that she was personally interested in him, that of all the single men whom she had met in her life, he appealed to her. While she found it ironic that she was attracted to an

143

Easterner, she also understood her fascination with him.

She had either too much or too little respect for commitment to want to marry. She had seen what happened to her parents, and she did not want this for herself. Still, she was aware that her body was awakening to biological needs. Her physical reactions to Wade Cameron were evidence of this.

After Deborah left, Maybelle had taken Clem under wing and a few years ago had explained the sexual relationship that existed between a man and a woman after — *and only after* — they were married. Although Maybelle warned her that "the sexual experience was not altogether pleasant," she also cautioned Clem about protecting her innocence and "saving herself" for the man she married. If she did not, the older woman cautioned, no decent man would want to marry her. The lesson had ended on this ominous note. Clem had always supposed that her father had prompted Maybelle to play the role of mother.

So far Clem was finding the sexual experience to be pleasant, contrary to Maybelle's warning. The longer Clem was around Wade, the better she liked him. She wanted to know him better, and wanted him to teach her all about sexual relationships between a man and woman. Since she did not wish to marry, Wade Cameron was an excellent choice for a teacher. In a few days he would be moving on, and she would not see him again. While the thought should have been comforting to her, it was not; it brought a haunting sadness with it.

"Nothing more than curiosity."

Wade's words jolted Clem from her thoughts, and having forgotten what they were discussing, she turned to look into his probing eyes.

"Your interest in me, all of these questions," he prompted, "is nothing more than curiosity?"

144

Much more, she thought, but now was not the time to confess. "I like to know what makes people the way they are."

"Are you telling me this inquisition is a result of your training under the Sheriff?" Clearly he was unconvinced.

Clem walked to the sofa, and sitting down, she spread the afghan over her legs. "I guess it must be." Her questions answered, her curiosity appeased, she began to relax. Her eyes grew heavy. Wade had been correct earlier. She was exhausted. Now that she had admitted her attraction to him, now that she no longer warred within herself, she was content and ready to rest.

"Have you figured me out yet?" he asked lazily.

Clem's thought processes were slowing down. "No," she muttered, "but I will. Most men like their coffee black. I wonder why you like a spoon of sugar in yours. I haven't figured that out yet."

His soft laughter drifted over to her.

"I'm not going to tell you. You'll have to unravel that mystery for yourself."

Clem's breath grew deeper, her eyes heavier. From afar, it seemed, she heard Wade speak.

"Now that your uncle is going to be appointed sheriff, have you thought about letting him go after your father's killer?"

"No." Her answer was hardly more than a breath.

"When are you leaving?"

"Pretty soon, now that Hokie and Turbin have agreed to be my deputies." She was having difficulty translating words into coherent thought; she could hardly force her tongue and lips to form the words. "I couldn't have left the town — unprotected."

"No," Wade mused, "I don't suppose *you* could."

She roused enough to ask, "Are you being sarcastic?"

145

"No, I understand the code you live by."

He stood and walked to the fireplace, tossing several more sticks of wood on the fire. Through narrowly slit eyes, Clem gazed at the flames as they danced higher and higher, as her lids grew heavier and heavier. They closed; she yawned and was asleep.

Turning his back to the grate, Wade stood for a while longer in front of the fire and watched her sleep. He had been attracted to many women during his life, but had not felt a need to protect any of them as he did with Clem. Yet not one of these women had been as tough and strong as she, or seemingly as less in need of protecting than she. He moved closer to the sofa.

Clem lay on her side, a cheek resting against the pillowcase. Strands of hair curled around her face and dark lashes lay in a crescent on her cheeks. He smiled when he saw the faint splattering of freckles across the bridge of her nose. Somehow these made her seem extremely vulnerable and were not part of the attire of a deputy sheriff.

Many of his male friends had whiled away long hours with voluptuous beauties, but Wade had always been intrigued by tall, slender women. However, those whom he had known paled when compared to Clem. She was altogether lovely.

Leaving her, he walked down the hall and peered into the room where she had gone for the album. He could tell this was her room. It looked like her: the oak dresser, armoire, four-poster bed and night table. The round reading table and two matching chairs. The simple gauze curtains over the two windows. The room was friendly but not overly feminine. It was a direct reflection of its owner.

By lamplight Wade built a fire, then turned down the covers before he returned to the parlor. Again he stood over her. The firelight burnished her hair to a

146

high sheen and cast her in a golden nimbus. Thick lashes lay on creamy cheeks. Her lips, rosy and full, tilted in a tremulous smile. Gone was the deputy sheriff of Lawful, Texas. In her place was one of the most desirable women Wade had ever beheld . . . and he wanted her.

But she was an innocent! The thought struck Wade full force, and he almost staggered from the blow. Again he gazed at the splattering of freckles; she was so young. He was thirteen years her senior in years, eons older than her in experience. While he did not have a high opinion of women in general, and figured that most were out to snare a husband any way they could, he knew Clem deserved better than he intended to give. She was one of the few he had met who deserved to find a husband . . . if she wanted one.

Scooping Clem into his arms, he held her close for a moment. He savored the feel of her in his arms, the soft warmth against his chest, the sweet feminine smell. The skirt of her dressing gown brushed down his arm and legs. In her sleep she laid her palm against his chest and snuggled closer to him, her breasts rising and falling gently with her breathing. Quietly, so as not to awaken either her or Deborah, he carried Clem into the bedroom and laid her down.

After he tucked the covers about her, she stretched and breathed in deeply. Then she curled into a ball, murmuring in her sleep. Wade brushed the silken tangle of hair from her face.

"Good night, Clementina Jones. Sweet dreams."

He should hire a buggy, and despite the perils of traveling alone to El Paso, should leave Lawful and Clementina Jones in the morning. He should leave for good and never look back. He needed a clear head for the job ahead of him, and already he was becoming involved with a woman who was an innocent. Even if he did not care about breaking her heart or ruining her reputation, he had to consider that he would have to spend extensive time delicately building up to the moment when he would possess her.

He had an insatiable desire to refine Deputy Sheriff Clementina Jones, to take her back East with him and to make a beauty out of her. He would create a lady New York society would sit up and take notice of. But he knew himself well enough to know that she would be nothing more than a possession, something for him to show off, something to occupy his attention for a while. Generally a woman did not interest him for long, and he did not suspect Clementina would be any different. Once he had made her his, the challenge would be gone and interest would wane. For his sake . . . no, for her sake, he would leave Clem Jones alone.

Something—everything—about this woman unsettled Wade, and no matter how much he might try to convince himself otherwise, Clementina Jones was different from all other women he had ever met.

She was one woman he could not possess and leave.

Clem awakened early the next morning and stretched, shoving her feet down the length of the bed and gasping when her toes touched the chilled covers. She quickly drew up and returned to her cocoon of warmth, burrowing into a ball, in no hurry to get up and build a fire.

Last night had been enjoyable. Wade was different from what she had expected when she first met him. Not the kind of man she wanted in her life permanently, of course. She wanted a man who was stronger and tougher than she, a man like Papa. But Wade Cameron was a man who could teach her to be a woman.

He was not a Westerner, but he had other characteristics that qualified him for this role. One, he was not married. He was handsome and had a way with women. He had served in the army in the west and was a passable shot with a gun. He wasn't altogether a tenderfoot. She smiled as the thoughts skittered through her mind.

Then she remembered, she had gone to sleep in the parlor. She bolted up. She was no longer in the parlor; she was in her bed.

Wade had put her to bed!

Warmth seeped through Clem's body. Wondering if he had taken off her robe, she peeked beneath the covers. She breathed a sigh of relief when she saw she was wearing her robe over her nightshirt. But she was disappointed that she had not been awake to enjoy the pleasure of being in his arms.

She lay there a long time, trying to assess Wade Cameron, one minute liking him very much, the next minute wondering what he was really doing out here. Behind that bland passivity lay more than met the eye. Clem would swear to that. She had encountered men like him before—men who had something to hide. Naturally, because she was personally interested in him, she wanted to know what. But life in the West had taught her to be discreet in prying.

Oh, well, she thought. Whatever Wade Cameron had to hide in his life had no bearing on hers. As her father would say, she had things to do, places to go, and people to see today—cold as it might be.

Deeply inhaling, lightly coughing when her lungs completely filled with the frigid air, she flung the covers aside and hurriedly built the fires in the bedroom, the parlor, and the kitchen. Then before Deborah awakened, she bolted the back door—evidently the way Wade had exited through last night when he left. Shivering and hugging her arms around her chest, she dived back in the bed and stayed there until the house was warm enough for her to dress without her teeth chattering.

Moving to the armoire, she quickly donned heavy undergarments and selected a pair of dark brown wool trousers and one of her newest shirts—a winter plaid in various shades of green, yellow, and rust. She smiled at her reflection in the mirror when she tied the marigold bandanna around her neck. She was glad Anona Cuellar, Lawful's only seamstress, had convinced her to purchase it. It really did complement her outfit and highlight the color of her hair. Rather than pulling her hair into a coil on the crown of her head as she usually did, she clasped it at the neck with a tortoiseshell clip and let it hang in waves down her back. Stepping back, she took one last look at herself and smiled, pleased with the overall effect.

She was pouring a second cup of coffee when Deborah entered the kitchen, looking immaculate in her ivory-colored dressing gown, her hair hanging in a single braid down her back. Deborah laid a newspaper on the table and moved past to the kitchen cupboard.

"You're up early." She gave Clem a careful perusal, her gaze lingering on the loosened hair. "And dressed to go out."

"I'm going to see Peaceful."

Deborah only nodded, then turned to pour herself a cup of coffee. "You were leaving without telling me?"

"I told you last night."

"Only after I confronted you."

"Only after you presumed to answer for me. I would appreciate it if you wouldn't be that presumptuous again."

"Why didn't you tell me about the shoot-out?" Deborah asked.

"I knew you would be upset and would give me a

150

lecture. I did what I had to do, and I didn't want to be reprimanded like a child. I'm rather tired of people telling me what I can and can't do."

"I only have your best interest at heart," her mother replied.

"Please leave my interest to me. I want us to get along," Clem said, "but you're going to have to realize I'm all grown-up now. I'm a woman capable of making my own decisions."

"Yes," Deborah murmured, "I can see that. What's your real reason for going to see Peaceful? To get him to help you track down the man who shot your father?"

Clem did not answer.

"I thought so." Deborah pulled a chair from the table and sat across from Clem. "Don't go after him. That's a job for a — for someone tougher than you. Let Rand do it."

"Alarico Olviera belongs to me," Clem insisted. "Getting him is my job, because it's my father he shot, and I'm not going to let Rand get him. If the council wants Rand for their sheriff, then let them have him. It's his duty to stay here and protect them. It's my duty to find the man who shot my father. And, by god, I'm going to do it."

"And you made sure no one else would know who to go after, didn't you?" Brown eyes stared accusingly into Clem's.

"What do you mean?"

"I mean this article." Deborah thumped the newspaper with her hand. "Not once did Hadley mention the name of the man who shot Clement, and I can only conclude that you refused to tell because you're hell-bent on finding him yourself, or the two of you are working together on a dynamite story."

Although Deborah had been gone for five years, she still had the ability to disconcert Clem with her astuteness. "You've concluded right," Clem conceded, "but not for the right reasons. I do want to find Olviera myself, but I also want to stop some of these vigilante committee actions from taking place. You heard about the hanging in Botello last week, didn't you? Lionel Porter was guilty of cattle rustling. He probably would have been hanged anyway, but he deserved a trial and sentencing. I'm not going to allow that to happen to Olviera. And you know if people hereabout knew Olviera was the one who shot Clement, they would take matters into their own hands. You know how well loved and respected Clement was."

"I would rather a vigilante committee handled this than you, and don't try to fool me, Clem. I'm your mother and you're my child, no matter what you think, and I know why you're going after that boy. I know you."

"I'm that much like my father," Clem said.

"In this instance you're not like your father. He wore the star with pride, Clem, and he believed in what it stood for—the American system of justice."

"Are you saying I don't?"

"You say you want to save Rico Olviera from a vigilante committee, and that may be true. But deep down you want him for yourself—not to bring him back for a trial and sentencing—but to satisfy your need for revenge. At least the vigilantes claim to be working for justice, and in most cases they are. You're working for your own selfish reason."

Deborah rose abruptly, the chair toppling to the floor. She made no effort to pick it up. Clasping her hands together, she moved to the counter and stared out the window. "Three days ago your father was killed. Now I'm afraid that you're going to be killed, too. That shoot-out in the saloon! You're right: in many ways you are like your father. You think you're

152

the only one who can administer justice on the frontier." She whirled around. "You're all I have left."

Clem rose and embraced her mother. "Mama," she said, "I'm not going to die, but I am going to hunt down the man who shot Papa. No matter how much anger and bitterness I feel, I'm going to bring him back for trial."

As soon as the words slipped from her mouth, Clem knew they were true. She no longer harbored a desire to kill Olviera. She planned to use him to help her expose Antonio Borajo as a fraud.

"I'm not going to take justice into my own hands, I promise."

Deborah slipped her arms around Clem, holding her tightly. "Clemmy. My little Clemmy. I couldn't bear to lose you, darling."

"But you did."

"I couldn't stay, Clem, not with your father emotionally abusing me, not with him accusing and punishing me for infidelity, for something I had not done. I asked you to go with me, but you had already judged and found me guilty. You wanted to stay with your father."

"You never came to see me."

"That was wrong of me," Deborah confessed, "but I've never been strong like you and your father. I was the coward in the family. I wanted to come see you, many were the times, but I couldn't face you rejecting me again. I could never forget how quickly you believed I was having an affair with Rand. However, you were only sixteen at the time."

She was quiet for a moment, then moved away from Clem to refill her cup with hot coffee. "Besides, you never came to see me."

"No," Clem admitted, "I didn't."

While Clem still found it hard to believe her mother's confessions, she no longer condemned her out of hand. She loved her mother, no matter what she had done, or *if* she had done it. It would take a while for them to bridge the gap in their relationship made by the five-year separation, but in time they would. When Deborah left, Clem was still a child. Now she was a woman, and they would have to become adult friends.

"I'm going into the mountains to find Peaceful," Clem said.

"Since I can't talk you out of it, I want to warn you that before I left El Paso, I heard a group of renegade Mescaleros escaped the reservation in New Mexico."

"Diablo Negro," Clem murmured.

"Not only is he plundering and killing, Clem, he and his band could be carrying smallpox infection. It's not safe out there."

"You know I've been vaccinated."

"When will you be back?"

"Tomorrow sometime," Clem answered as she, too, stared out the window. "I figure that's all the time I have. Gunslingers are bound to hear about Clement's death and start drifting into town. They're going to think Lawful is an easy mark without a strong-armed sheriff."

"When will Rand be here?"

"Arnold said he was at Ft. Stockton the night Papa was killed," Clem answered. Again she felt a stab of bitterness. Always her mother thought about Rand. "Even with the bad weather, I reckon he'll be traveling pretty much day and night, so I'll give him a couple more days."

"Clem, I'm planning the barbecue for Doña Pera."

"Just like old times, huh?"

"I'd like for you to be back for that."

"I'll see about it."

"Do you mind if I invite her and Pilar to stay with us while they're in town? Doña Pera was very kind to me while I was living in El Paso."

"No," Clem said, "I don't mind, and I'll be back as soon as I can."

"Clem, you will be careful, won't you?"

"I will." She moved across the room, and her hand was on the doorknob when Deborah spoke again.

"Are you—going to see Wade Cameron?"

Clem's grip on the doorknob slackened. Something in Deborah's voice—that same tone Clem had heard last night—caught her attention. "Yes, he's asked me to help him do the story on Papa. Why do you ask?"

Her back to Clem, Deborah continued to stare out the window. "I would rather you didn't see him again."

"I resent what you're doing to me, walking back into this house and into my life as if you've never been gone. During the past five years, I've learned to take care of myself. I don't need you to tell me who I can or can't see."

"Clem, I can understand how you feel, but in this you must listen to me. I know so much more about life than you do. You're so young, so inexperienced. You don't know how easy it would be for a man like Wade to use you, and he's the kind of man who will use a woman."

An apprehensive shiver slid down Clem's body. She felt totally exposed and wondered if her mother were able to read her mind. "You didn't think about that when you left. Why now? Could it be that you're interested in Wade Cameron yourself?"

Deborah tensed. "Of course not! I'm only thinking of you."

Clem reached for the door handle and pulled. "Thanks, but save your concern for yourself. I'll think for myself. At least, the mistakes I make will be mine, and I won't be able to blame them on someone else."

As the door closed, Clem heard her mother say, "You may want to accept full responsibility for them,

Clem, but you can't. Some of the responsibility has to rest on your father's shoulders."

Clem paused and said over her shoulder, "If that's true, then some of it rests upon your shoulders."

"Yes," Deborah admitted, "it does."

The front door to Hadley Moore's house swung open, and Clem stared into Wade's surprised face.

"You said you wanted to visit with Miss Merica. I'll take you if you want to go this morning. She lives off the beaten track, and I'm afraid for you to go out there by yourself. Hadley—" her gaze dropped lower, and she saw a wedge of dark, crisp hair revealed at the neck of Wade's shirt. She caught her breath and raised her head to encounter those blue eyes. "He's busy with the paper, and no telling when he'll have time to take you. Besides he wouldn't be a good one for you to travel with. He—he couldn't protect you at all."

"Come inside out of the cold." Wade caught her hand in his, gently tugging her into the hallway. When the door closed, he asked, "How does your mother feel about you—"

"Let's get one thing straight right now," Clem interrupted, stung because he was treating her like a child. "I answer to no one but myself. Deborah gave up that right when she walked out on me. Now, I don't care if you go or not. I simply offered my assistance, because I thought you wanted to find this man. Evidently you don't want to go with me, so I'll say good-bye. Take your chances with Hadley. Wait around until he finds time to take you."

She turned; however, before she could open the door, Wade caught both shoulders and whirled her around to face him, jarring her so that the Stetson fell to the floor. His body flattened against hers, pressing

156

her back to the door. He bent his head, and his warm breath blew over her face and neck.

"Another thing we need to get straight—" a hand strayed to her face to brush a tendril of hair from her cheek, "is you must stop jumping to conclusions. Whether you can physically protect me or not, I'd much rather take my chances with you than with Hadley Moore."

Mesmerized, she stared into the blue eyes. How could she have ever thought they were steely?

"I want . . . to . . ." He paused.

"What?" Clem was fascinated by the way his eyes darkened.

"I want you to take me to see Miss Merica, Clem . . . Clementina."

Until Wade had uttered her name, Clem had never really liked it. Now it was a sweet caress. She liked the feel of his arms about her; they were strong and warm and protective. But she was uncertain she liked the way his touch seemed to arouse her emotions. She loved the heady feelings that his nearness and his touch evoked, but when it happened, she seemed to be at the mercy of her emotions. She could not afford to lose control of herself; that was the only way she could protect her heart.

"I think, Wade Cameron," she heard herself whisper, "that you want to kiss me."

"Yes," he answered, his voice ragged, "I do."

Clem's heart began to race. "Then do it, because I want you to."

She heard his swift intake of breath; she felt his chest rise and fall against hers.

"Have you ever been kissed before?"

"No." Although inexperienced, she raised her head and awaited the touch of his lips on hers. "I'd like for you to be the first."

First his warm, coffee-scented breath tickled her

157

lips; then his mouth touched hers in a delicate kiss. So fragile was the touch, yet she felt it all through her body. When she shivered, he drew her closer, and she seemed to melt into his strength and warmth.

"Oh, Wade—" she stammered as his lips brushed back and forth over hers, as his hard body firmly acquainted itself with hers to create delicious sensations, "this is wonderful."

Her words were stopped when his arms tightened around her, his hands pressed her even closer, and his lips claimed hers in a full kiss. His tongue gently stroked the indention of her closed lips, still she did not open her mouth; she did not know to. Lost in the beauty of such incredible feelings, she brushed her palms up Wade's chest, the fingertips of her right hand touching the wedge of black hair she had been looking at earlier. The texture of his skin was warm and moist, the hair crisp and thick.

As his tongue grew more insistent, and his hands began to rub her back, slipping below her belt line to touch her buttocks, she trembled anew and opened her mouth. Now her hands wound around his neck, her fingers tangling in the thick hair that brushed against his dressing gown collar. She clung to him, pressing her breasts into the hard muscles of his chest.

She never dreamed that something as glorious as this existed in the whole wide world and that it was hers for the taking.

Chapter Ten

The sensations Wade felt as he held and kissed Clem made him forget his resolve from the night before. He no longer thought about the thirteen years' difference in their ages. He brushed his hand through her hair, and barely lifting his mouth from hers, murmured, "I've wanted to kiss you from the minute I saw you in the doctor's office two nights ago."

"Even when I looked so—"

"Even then. You're one of the sweetest women I've ever kissed or held in my arms." He lifted his head higher and smiled at her. "Revolvers and all."

"I'll take them off," she offered.

Her eyes were bright, her cheeks flushed. Wade had seen the look many times before on the faces of women who were infatuated or in love with him. This time, however, the expectancy on Clem's face made him feel guilty. Clearly he had taken advantage of her youth and inexperience.

"No, don't do that." Reluctantly he removed his arms from around her and stepped away. How could he have done this? he asked himself. She was an innocent and did not know better; he did.

Clem asked, "Is something wrong?"

"Yes." The answer was abrupt. Too abrupt. He could see the bewilderment in her eyes. In a softer

159

tone he said, "I shouldn't have kissed you. I—"

"Why?" Her eyes rounded in surprise. "Didn't you enjoy it?"

Not having stood in this place for many a year, Wade was uncertain how to proceed. His nature compelled him to give her an honest answer, to explain that he did enjoy it, but that his attraction to her was purely physical; however, his heart did not want to see her hurt, not so soon after her father's death. Beneath that facade of rough, tough local sheriff was a delicate and fragile woman. A man of the world, he knew he had the ability to hurt her deeply.

"Yes," he answered, "I did, but—"

"Then nothing is wrong, because I enjoyed it, too. I'm glad you did it," Clem announced practically, as if this were an everyday experience for her.

She was extremely happy—no, he corrected himself as he looked at her more closely—she was extremely satisfied, and there was a fine line's difference between happiness and satisfaction. Her expression never changing, she added, "Thank you for putting me to bed last night. I was in such a deep sleep, I don't even remember you carrying me to my room. I hope I wasn't too heavy."

From most of the women with whom Wade was acquainted, he would have taken this to be feminine wiles at their best, but he was uncertain about Clem. He seemed to be getting cross signals from her and was glad she had not been privy to his lustful thoughts the first night he had met her, the night he had fantasized about melting the frost in her eyes, or last night as he stood in her bedroom holding her in his arms, feeling the firm rounded buttocks and the length of leg against his body and looking at the turned-down covers on the bed. The scene had been most provocative and tempting. He was hard pressed to remember when he had been tempted more.

"Clem —" He paused. She lifted her head and gazed candidly into his eyes. "Have you ever had a serious beau before?"

"No."

This was the answer he expected. He caught her hand in his and led her into the parlor to seat her in the chair in front of the fire. Not really knowing what to say, he looked into her expectant face. He had never envisioned himself in this position. Yet someone had to take her into hand.

"Did your father ever talk to you about —"

Exhibiting no embarrassment at all, Clem laughed softly and again shook her head. "No, are you?"

He was amusing her! More confused than ever and not a little irritated with her superior attitude, Wade shoved his hand through his hair and paced back and forth. Damn Clement Jones for putting him in this predicament! He was trying his hardest to do what was right toward her, and she was laughing at him. Not that he felt the least avuncular toward her. In fact, considering their kiss from a moment ago, he felt the opposite. He was lustful where she was concerned. Yet, out of nowhere, conscience reared its head — it was a powerful one — and he felt it was his responsibility to protect Clem's innocence. Talk about the horns of dilemma; they were goring him in two.

He stopped in front of her and looked down into those sparkling eyes, so different from the first time he had looked into them. She rose and closed the distance between them.

"Papa always said there was some things you didn't need to be told about, you just knew how to do them," she explained to him quietly in that wiser-than-thou voice she had assumed the night they met. Even then she had filled him with a feeling of vulnerability that was uncomfortable. It was no different today.

"Some things you just learn by doing," she explained. "Maybe that's the way it is with a man and a woman, Wade? I've always been curious about kissing. I knew what it was and how it was done, but I'd never practiced. There was nobody around here I wanted to practice with. Now that I've done it with you, I know what it's like, and I really enjoyed it."

Wade did not credit himself with hearing her correctly.

"Yes," she repeated, nodding her head, auburn curls dancing around her face, "I really liked it, although Maybelle said I wouldn't."

"Maybelle," he repeated, wondering if he sounded as insane to her as he did to himself.

Again Clem nodded and laughed quietly. "After Deborah left, Maybelle took me under wing. She told me about the sexual relationship between a man and a woman."

"Oh!" Wade had no idea what else to say. This was his first experience with conversation of this sort. Oddly, he had the feeling that he was the gauche one.

"Maybe," Clem continued, "we can do it some more later."

Dumbfounded, Wade could only stare at her. With a nonchalance he could not explain, she stooped, picked up the Stetson, and settled it on her head.

"You told me that I'd find you very much of a man, and I do, Wade Cameron."

When Wade had uttered those words to her, he never dreamed she would be tossing them back at him so casually.

"I'm sure glad the stagecoach broke down and you were forced to stay in Lawful. I think I'm going to learn a lot from you." She moved across the room to peer into a mirror as she fiddled with the scarf around her neck. "By the way, where's your cousin?"

The abrupt change in subject gave Wade pause. Prentice was the farthest thing from his mind. He had to stop and think. "Still in bed."

"Are you going to take him with us?"

How could she react to him and his kisses with such nonchalance? Wade wondered.

"No, Prentice isn't one to stray too far from comfort unless it's absolutely necessary, and I can't imagine there would be any reason for him to go to Miss Merica's."

"Since he's drawing pictures of everybody else in town, I figured you would want him to draw one of her. No telling what kind of stories you'll be able to write about her."

"If I find I want a portrait of her," Wade said, "I'll send Prentice after it."

"Well, if you want to go with me, you'd better change into some traveling clothes—warm ones—and let's be on our way. Also it might be a good idea if you would wear a revolver. It would make me feel a little easier about you."

Wade was confused with good reason. From a man who had been in total control of the situation—or who had thought himself to be in control—he had gone to a man being totally controlled. A few minutes ago, he thought he had swept Clementina Jones off her feet with his devastating kiss. Now he learned that she had not been swept anywhere. She was conducting an experiment, or better yet, she admitted to getting practice.

Maybe, Wade, a small inner voice said, *you're upset because she swept you off your feet. Maybe you're upset because the woman is totally unaffected by your kisses, by the kisses that other women find so devastating . . . and you're totally affected by her.* This, in itself, was a new experience for Wade. Pushing such disturbing thoughts from his mind, he allowed his frustration to mount. Clem Jones had no right to do this to him. While he had only been satisfying his curiosity, it galled him to no end to learn that she had been doing the same.

"You do still want to go, don't you?" Clem asked.

"Yes, let me get changed. I'll be with you in a few minutes."

"I'll be waiting out front."

Humming, Clem walked out of the house around to the barn, and while Wade dressed, she hitched the horses to Hadley's buckboard. All the while she basked in the afterglow of Wade's embrace and kisses. Perhaps Maybelle would have a different story to tell if she had ever met a man like Wade Cameron. Clem really had enjoyed being kissed by him; she liked him to touch and hold her. But she acknowledged she would have to be careful to keep from becoming involved with him. She was not quite the innocent her mother thought her to be.

Clem realized that she was not the kind of woman with whom Wade generally associated. Unlike her, they were soft and delicate; they were sophisticated and trained in the social graces. Clem believed Wade cared for her, but caring was a long way from loving. She was an interlude for him, and he would be leaving as soon as he had safe conveyance to El Paso. She must be careful where he was concerned; she did not want him to take anything of hers, more specifically her heart, with him.

She would have preferred Hadley's buggy, but the buckboard would have to suffice. Since Hadley had allowed Wade and Prentice free run of his house as long as they were in town, she figured he would not mind their using his transportation for the day. Furthermore, by not renting a horse or buckboard from the livery barn, no one would know that she was gone. Turbin could take care of things until she returned.

After she unsaddled Rusty-Be-Dusty and turned him loose in the small corral, Clem put her saddlebags, binoculars, and rifle on the seat of the buck-board. Climbing aboard and arching her shoulders against a blast of cold north wind, she drove to the front of the house. While she waited on Wade, she looked around. Things seemed to be quiet — a little too quiet for her peace of mind, but she wondered if she were getting jittery over nothing. A simple case of nerves now that she was the deputy sheriff of Lawful. Her gaze slowly traveled the horizon. She saw nothing more than a tiny spiral of smoke many miles to the east. That caught her attention.

She straightened, pushed her hat back, and reached down for the binoculars. Could be anything, but she felt it was an ominous sign. When she heard the front door open, she lowered the binoculars. Wade, dressed in an overcoat, pushed through the gate.

"Do you have any guns?" she asked.

"I don't wear them."

"I didn't ask that." She hopped to the ground. "But I guess if you don't wear them, you don't own any. Wait here. I'm going inside to borrow one of Hadley's rifles for you."

"Don't we have enough weapons, Clem," he asked. "Your rifle and two revolvers. Why don't we just get more ammunition?"

"I'll do that, but I also want another rifle." Her gaze returned to the small line of smoke. "Since I always expect trouble, I'm never surprised when it shows up, and always pleased when it doesn't."

Wade followed the line of her vision. "Indians?"

"Could be. May not be anything." She moved to-ward the house, raising her voice so that Wade could hear her. "Rumor has it that the Black Devil is on the loose and is in these parts. I think we ought to be pre-pared, in case we happen to come across him."

A step behind her, Wade asked, "Who's the Black Devil?"

"Diablo Negro, a Mescalero Apache chief. He left the reservation in New Mexico. I suppose some are worried that he's on the warpath, and he might be."

"You don't think so?" Wade asked.

Clem opened the door, moved down the hallway into Hadley's library, heading straight for the gun cabinet on the far wall. "No, I think he and his warriors are tired and homesick; they wanted to go home. But I want to be safe in case I'm wrong. My biggest fear is that he's carrying the smallpox infection. Elm sent to Ft. Stockton for medical supplies. I'm hoping we'll get them in time to start vaccinations. I hope you've been vaccinated."

"I have."

"Good. That's one less thing I have to worry about."

Wade snorted softly, and Clem turned from the cabinet to look at him.

"You know," he said, "despite what you think, I really am quite capable of taking care of myself."

"Yeah, I can see that." Her gaze moved down his immaculately clad body to the expensive leather shoes peering from the leg of his trousers. "How long has it been since you've used a gun?"

"Five years."

"You know," she said, looking him squarely in the face, "I can't quite figure you out, Wade, and I've been giving it a lot of thought."

"The teaspoon of sugar."

She ignored his teasing. "You don't look like the kind of person who would be out West looking for a missing person. Why didn't this rich fellow back East hire a bounty hunter or a private detective or someone who had a personal stake in finding his brother, or someone who understood the code of the West? Why you?"

"I do have a personal stake in finding Bryan Dillon. The money I earn for either finding him or finding out what happened to him will finance *Cameron's Journal*. The story will also be mine, and I'm going to earn even more from that." He moved to stand in front of her. "Clem, don't judge a man by the guns he does or does not wear. I understand the code you people out here live by, although I don't condone it. If we get into trouble, I won't let you down."

"Make sure you don't. We may not get a second chance to make it right."

She stared at him for another second, before she opened the cabinet door and selected one of the rifles. She had a lot to learn when it came to being a woman and pleasing a man, but she knew how to protect herself; she knew how to survive out here in the West. Bending, she opened the bottom drawer and picked up several boxes of ammunition which she stuffed into her jacket pockets.

"Come on. Let's go see Miss Merica. I don't have time to waste. After I bring you back to town, I have things to do."

"Such as going to see that Indian you were talking about last night." He matched his stride to hers.

"He's one of the best trackers hereabouts. When he was younger, he rode with the Sheriff all the time. As he got older, he rode only on the tougher assignments."

"Will he go with you to hunt Olviera?"

"I don't know." She never stopped walking and was at the gate by the time Wade locked the front door. "I guess I'm hoping he will. By now, Borajo will have put Rico in hiding. I don't know if even Peaceful could find him."

"Who's Borajo?" Wade called out, and Clem heard the click of his shoes against the boardwalk as he hurried to the wagon.

"A Mexican priest at the mission in San Elizario." Clem lay the rifle and ammunition in the buckboard, then climbed in. "He's one of the primary parties interested in a monopoly on all the salt lakes in the area. He claims he's working for the Mexican population around El Paso. The Sheriff figured the padre was manipulating them and their votes for purely selfish and personal gain. The Sheriff also believed Borajo has a gang of cutthroats to do his dirty work."

"And Rico was probably one of these?" In one smooth movement Wade was sitting on the seat next to her.

"That's what the Sheriff figured. When I catch Rico, I'll find out."

Wade pulled his scarf tighter about his neck when the wind renewed it force. "Do you have any evidence that the priest is involved in such unsavory activities?"

"Nope. The Sheriff was investigating, and I figure he was getting pretty close to something." She turned and began pilfering in the back of the wagon. "It's fearful cold today. I grabbed some blankets out of the barn. Figured we might want to wrap up. The ride to Miss Merica's is a long one." Once they were bundled up, Clem gave the command; the horses moved; the buckboard jolted forward.

"From what you said a minute ago, I take it you think Borajo had your father killed because he was close to exposing him?"

Clem knew the journalistic hound was sniffing out a story. "Could be," she said, "also could be the fact that the Sheriff was one of the few gringos who the Mexicans trusted and listened to. He had promised them that he would see that the rest of the salt lakes remained public domain, and they believed him. With him gone, they'll follow Borajo without any questions being asked."

"Surely not."

"The man is powerful, and people are afraid of him—Anglos as well as Mexicans."

"So, Deputy Sheriff, as I see it, your job is becoming a little more complex, circumstances changing your options. Maybe the fellow who fired the shot that killed your father really isn't the one responsible for your father's death."

"You've pretty well summed up the situation as I see it."

"Are you going to shoot this fellow, too?"

Although the question was asked tongue-in-cheek, Clem chose to treat it seriously. She gently slapped the reins across the horse's rump. "Not unless he forces me to. The Sheriff taught me the code of the West, Wade. He also taught me to respect and abide by it. And I do. Now, let's change the subject."

"Clem," Wade caught her hand and she turned to look at him, "please don't go after these men. I can understand how you feel about your uncle, considering what you think he and your mother did to your father, but he's the one the town council has appointed as interim sheriff. It's his responsibility to hunt down criminal elements, not yours."

"Someone shot my father. I'm going to find out who. Would you do any less for your father?"

"It's different—"

"Because you're a man and I'm a woman?"

"I guess I was thinking that, but the main reason is I personally don't want anything to happen to you." A slow smile traced his lips—lips that caught and held Clem's undivided attention. "I'd . . . like for you to be around so I can teach you more about kissing. You know the basics, but you really do need more practice. And then . . . there's more to learn than kissing . . . if you're willing."

"I am."

His words excited her. Leaning over, she pressed her mouth lightly against his, and although his lips were cold, they were firm and moved slightly to send a shiver of pleasure through her body.

She murmured, "I do need the practice, and I have a lot more to learn."

He brushed a gloved hand gently against her cheek. "Yes, you do. No telling how long it'll take me to teach you."

"The Sheriff always told me I was a fast learner."

"Speed may be good when it comes to drawing and shooting a gun," he murmured, "but kissing is best if it's slow and thorough. That way you can savor the pleasure. Like this, for example."

His arms slipped around her, and despite the bundling of coats and blankets, he pulled her close to him. Her eyes open, Clem stared at the texture of his skin, the firm chin, the mouth, then she looked into those blue eyes, that despite the cold were sultry and stirred a reciprocal passion in her.

"In loving," Wade said softly, "you get the most pleasure from giving pleasure."

His lips touched her forehead, brushed down her nose, finally to settle on her mouth. The kiss was tentative at first, then it deepened. Despite the cold north wind, warm pleasure coursed through Clem, and she dropped the reins, lifted her hand, and twined her fingers in the thick hair that met the collar of his coat. She responded to his kiss, hesitantly at first because of her inexperience, then gradually her lips moved against his, and she gave herself to the wondrous urges that flowed through her.

This time she immediately opened her mouth to receive the thrust of his tongue. She wished they were not on their way to Miss Merica's; she wished they were somewhere else with nothing between them. She wanted to press her body against him, to feel his strength once more. As his lips and tongue played havoc with her emotions, she trembled in wonderment. Under this man's tutelage, the mysteries of sensual pleasure were slowly unfolding. The reality of that pleasure mixed with desire was far more powerful than her imaginings had ever been.

Sitting in the buckboard, once again bundled warmly in blankets, Clem gave a last wave to the white-haired woman who stood on the front porch of the small house. Although the wind cruelly whipped her coat around her fragile frame, the wrinkled face was wreathed in a smile.

"Thanks for lunch, Miss Merica," Clem said.

"My pleasure." The old lady brushed wisps of hair from her face. "Glad you and your young man could visit with me, Clem. Don't wait so long before you come again. I only wish you could have stayed longer, and I could have helped him more."

"Maybe you didn't know anything about Bryan Dillon, Miss Merica," Wade called out graciously, "but you've given me more information than I can write about during a lifetime. I appreciate your talking with me. And lunch was truly delicious. What you served compares with the meals served in the best restaurants in New York City."

Although she waved a dismissing hand through the air, Miss Merica's smile widened even more. "I'm supposed to say, don't pull an old woman's leg, Wade Cameron, but I won't. I don't git much flattery, and I'm gonna enjoy what little I git. Now, Clem, I want to congratulate you on having the good sense to choose a fine young man like Wade Cameron. He's a green 'un all right, but he's a good 'un. You couldn't have done better."

"Thanks, Miss Merica." Having corrected the old woman's misconceptions several times already, Clem did not bother to do so again. If she had not understood . . . or accepted . . . the four previous explanations of who Wade was and what he was doing out here in West Texas, chances were she would not understand or accept it this time.

"And, Clem, give my condolences to your mother, and when you see Rand and Peaceful tell them hello for me."

"I will," Clem promised.

"Clem!" Miss Merica called a second time. "Be sure to let me know when you're going to git married."

"Yes, ma'am," Clem answered, then muttered, "If I didn't know Miss Merica better, I'd think she was doing this deliberately."

Wade chuckled softly and tucked the blankets more securely around their legs. "I'm not sure you do know Miss Merica. Despite all you and Hadley have told me, I don't believe she's senile."

"You can't be serious!"

He shook his head. "She's the only person out here who seems to know I'm a good man, despite my being a green 'un, and she didn't make fun of my having a teaspoon of sugar in my coffee."

"You can't just pick out the parts you like and leave the rest," Clem pointed out. "She also thinks you're my young man and that we're going to be married."

"Well" — Wade shrugged — "maybe she's not totally all there, but I really did like her. She may not know what's happening, but she sure knew what had happened."

"It was nice of you to let her think she had helped you."

"She has," he insisted, "but not with my most immediate concern. I suppose I was expecting her to produce a miracle. I was so sure Bryan Dillon was or had been out here, that I counted on her to have some information on him. I didn't figure the name would mean anything, but I thought she would recognize either Bryan's or Nash's photograph."

"You're so sure Bryan's alive?"

"No," answered Wade, "I'm not sure he's alive, but I do believe *someone* is alive who either knew him or knew about him."

"Simply because he had Dillon's watch?"

"Partly because of that and partly because of a hunch. I also believe a woman is involved. Could be a wife or a daughter."

"More than likely since the watch is only now being reproduced, it's a daughter or a granddaughter," Clem said. "How old did you say Bryan was?"

"He would be in his mid-sixties. He was about twenty-eight when he left, and he's been gone for thirty-five years."

"You really are looking for miracles."

"I've gone through all the wanted posters in the sheriff's office, and Bryan's picture wasn't among them. You don't happen to have another one of the Blacksmith, do you? One that is clearer."

"You've seen all the photographs I know anything about," Clem said. "Why do you keep harping back to him? Do you think he and Bryan Dillon are the same person?"

"I'm not sure what I think," Wade answered slowly, "but I have a hunch that the Blacksmith may be the key."

"You thought that about Miss Merica and were wrong."

"No," Wade clarified, "I thought she would be able to guide us to the key. Do you remember the Blacksmith at all?"

If anyone thought she was tenacious, Clem thought, they should meet Wade Cameron. When he got his teeth into something, he did not turn loose. "Vaguely, but not enough to tell you anything about him. Be patient. Rand will be in Lawful by the end of next week. I figure it'll take him about ten days to

173

make the trip, maybe a little longer considering the rain. When he gets here, you can question him to your heart's content. He can probably tell you the Blacksmith's real name and he may know where he is now."

They lapsed into silence, Clem concentrating on her driving, Wade retreating to the solitude of his thoughts. They had traveled about a quarter of a mile and were nearing a large hill, when they heard shooting.

"Someone's in trouble," she yelled.

Wade barely had time to grab the hand rail before the horses went into full gallop and the buckboard gained momentum.

"We've got to be careful and prepare for the worst. Could be Indians or outlaws." She tossed the reins to Wade, and not even taking the time to notice whether or not he had caught them, she turned in the seat and grabbed her rifle. She pulled her revolver from the holster and handed it to Wade. "Here. You may need this. Even if you don't, I might. So be prepared to shoot."

Wade flashed her a big grin. "Yes, ma'am."

"You won't think this is so funny if it's Indians or outlaws."

"No, ma'am," was his amused answer.

As they rounded the hill and the road straightened, Clem saw a rider. Turned in the saddle, so that his back was to her and Wade, he shot into a gang who chased him. Their faces were covered with white hoods.

"Damn vigilantes," Clem shouted above the shots ringing though the air. Although she knew she was too far away to hit anyone, Clem clamped the rifle to her shoulder and began to fire. She wanted to apprise the vigilantes of their presence.

"Do you know who the rider is?" Wade asked.

"No." Clem squinted her eyes, trying to make out the man. "But he's young. You can tell by the way he sits in the saddle. Can't make out the horse either. Looks like they're coming from the direction of Botello." She fired again, but the group of pursuers did not stop.

"Can't you go any faster?" Her bottom slid across the seat as the buckboard swayed from side to side.

"Yes, ma'am." Wade flicked the horses again, prodding them to an even faster pace.

After another flurry of shots, the lone rider fell to the ground. Closer now, Clem again fired her rifle, her bullet finding its target in one of the pursuers. He screamed out in pain, but, although wounded, remained astride his mount. As if realizing the presence of someone else for the first time, the gang halted; their shooting stopped. The vigilantes paused in their chase for a moment as if in conflict — wanting to make sure their quarry was dead, but also wanting to disappear. Wade pushed the horses faster, closing in on the fallen man.

"What are you going to do if they decide we're easy prey?"

"Show 'em we're not," Clem answered. "Anybody that hides behind a mask is a coward, and none of them want to be identified. They aren't going to take a chance on being captured. See there. Look at 'em. They're turning tail and running."

"You're pretty sure of yourself."

"Of myself and the people who live out here." Clem's gaze never left the vigilantes. "When you get even with the body, jump out and give him some help. I'll take the buckboard and chase the others. Maybe I can catch one. Maybe more."

"Or maybe they'll catch you. Maybe worse." His voice was edged with concern. "Let them go. You'll never catch them in the buckboard."

"I may not. But I'm going to follow them a ways to make sure they don't come back." Clem laid her rifle aside and grabbed the reins from Wade. She reached over and pushed him out of the wagon, calling as he tumbled to the ground, "I'll be back as soon as I can."

Clem laughed when she heard Wade's curses ringing through the air, but she did not slow down or look behind. Without his pointing it out to her, she knew she would not be able to catch up with the pursuers, but she wanted a closer look at them. Perhaps she could spot a horse with a distinguishing mark, but they separated and were soon lost in the cluster of foothills. Giving up the chase, she turned and headed back to where Wade knelt.

"Chest wound that's bleeding badly," Wade said. "We need to get him to a doctor immediately." Wade lifted the man in his arms and moved toward the buckboard. Hard blue eyes caught and held her gaze. "And don't you ever push me out of a moving vehicle again without warning me."

"Yes, sir." Grabbing the blankets, she clamored over the seat and quickly spread them out to make a bed. "Put him here."

The wounded man groaned, then murmured in a heavy Spanish accent, "Help . . . me . . . please. . . ."

"We are," Clem replied.

Wade leaped onto the buckboard seat, grabbed the reins, and headed for Lawful, as Clem separated the material of the wounded man's shirt and looked at his chest. Reaching into her pocket, she pulled out a handkerchief which she wadded up and pressed against the wound to stop the bleeding.

"It is bad, no?" he whispered.

"It's bad." She brushed thick black hair from his forehead. "We're going to take you to Lawful to the—" The words died on her lips, and her face blanched. "Olviera," she mumbled through numbed lips and

176

stared at the youth. In an instant her compassion turned into confusion. "Who were those men, and why were they chasing you?"

A bloody hand reached up to catch Clem's wrist; accusing eyes stared into her face. "You are asking me that, *Senorita?* Surely you jest."

"Who are those men?" Clem demanded.

"Your friends, *Senorita.*" As he spat the words at her, his face twisted in pain. "Gringo vigilantes who wanted to hang me for killing your father."

Gringo vigilantes! As Clem had feared, word had gotten out, and it had not come from her, and once Hadley gave his word she trusted him implicitly. Wade looked over his shoulder, his gaze catching Clem's. Correctly interpreting her silent question, he shook his head.

"I don't know who was chasing you," she said to Olviera. "I've told no one that you killed the Sheriff."

"Were you saving the pleasure of finding me for yourself?"

"I intended to find you," Clem admitted, but finding him had not brought the pleasure she had supposed it would. "You're sure the men chasing you were gringos?"

His eyes closing, dark lashes lying against pale almond cheeks, Rico Olviera breathed in deeply several times. His voice was weak when he spoke. "*Sí*. They came to my house to hang me for killing the Sheriff. The leader spoke English. He . . . told me that they weren't going to let a no-good Mexican like me kill the Sheriff and get away with it. I have told only Father Borajo, and he—he wouldn't tell anyone. Someone must have learned it from you, *Senorita.*"

Clem did not have as much confidence in Borajo as Rico did; but she also had no reason to suspect that the priest would tell anyone.

"Father Borajo is a good man who fights for the

177

rights of the Mexicanos." Rico rallied his strength and spoke emphatically. "Why cannot you Americanos understand this? We are only asking that the salt lakes remain common property, so that we may continue to use the salt as we have done in the past. Our people are uneducated, and we have need of a spokesman. Father Borajo is this man."

"Did Father Borajo send you to Chupedera Lakes the other day, when the Sheriff and I happened on you?" Clem asked.

One of the wheels bounced through a large hole in the road. Clem caught the side of the buckboard to keep from sliding into Rico. He groaned and clutched at his chest, his face twisting in pain.

"No." He caught his breath. "We were to stay away until he gave us instructions to return. When he learned that I had gone and that Sheriff Jones was dead, he was angry."

This contradicted what Clem had been thinking about the priest. She wondered if Olviera were lying to protect him, or perhaps the priest hid his true feelings from Olviera. "Who sent you?"

"No one. Although I knew Father would be angry, I went for myself and my family. We are poor, *Senorita,* and we are hungry. I knew I could earn some money, if I transported the salt to Mexico and sold it."

"I can't believe you would go against Borajo's orders."

"*Sí,* hunger will prompt one to do foolish things, *Senorita*. Now, I am paying for my sins. I am giving my life for the one I took."

"Not if I can help it," Wade called over his shoulder. "We'll be in Lawful directly."

"Perhaps," Rico murmured, his energy flagging as quickly as it had surged. He gasped with a spasm of pain and pressed his hand against the handkerchief. "Please, *Senorita,* take me to Father Borajo for confession and the last rites before it is too late for me." For a moment his eyes cleared, and purpose seemed to shield him from pain. "I . . . must . . . I must see him before I die."

"Lawful is closer, and you're in no condition to be traveling any farther than you have to," Clem said. "You'll only need a priest for confession and the last rites if we don't get you treated."

Olviera stared into Clem's face, then a crooked smile touched his whitened lips. His hand relaxed and fell to his side. "You do not hold life and death in your hands, *Senorita*. I think perhaps if you did, you would let me die. I am—guilty of killing your father, *Senorita*, but I did not do it on purpose. I would not have killed him, because he was one of the few gringos who were helping our people."

Clem lowered her head to look into ebony eyes, filled with sorrow as well as pain. He stopped talking and breathed deeply.

"When your men shot from behind, my horse bolted. My finger tightened on the trigger, and the gun fired. I'm so sorry, *Senorita*. I did not mean to do it."

Wanting to know the truth, obsessed with knowing it, Clem searched Olviera's face as if it were written there for her to read, but life was not that simple. "The Sheriff and I were alone. We had no men behind you. You and your people were the first to shoot."

Olviera shook his head. "We did not. We were waiting for the Sheriff to approach."

"Would the Sheriff have sent Hokie and Turbin without your knowing?" Wade asked, and Clem shook her head.

"Whoever shot, *Senorita*, shot one of my men in the back. He did not die immediately, but he died." The dark eyes filled with tears. "He was my younger brother, who had only recently celebrated his fifteenth

179

birthday. I understand how you feel about your father's death. If I live, my life, like yours, shall be dedicated to revenge. I shall spend it hunting down the man who killed Arturo. But I shall not live." His voice grew weary. He gasped, a shudder racked his body; then he grew still, and his eyes rolled back in his head.

Clem laid her fingers against the pulse point in Rico's neck. "He's dead," she announced.

Finding Alarico Olviera and punishing him for killing her father had been Clem's strongest hold on sanity. Now she felt the world slipping out from beneath her feet. Wade stopped the horses and turned around. She lifted her head and stared into Wade's eyes, only lowering hers when she saw his shadow with pity.

Chapter Eleven

"You believe Olviera's story about someone shooting him and his group from behind?" His arms crossed over his chest, Hokum leaned against the wall of the sheriff's office and gazed at Clem.

"He had no reason to lie." She slid a letter into one of the desk's pigeon holes.

"Where do we go from here?" the deputy asked. "It's evident there's more to this than we thought. Seems like someone really went out of their way to kill Clement, and now mebbe that someone has killed Olviera."

"That's what I've been thinking about ever since Olviera confessed," Clem said. "It also seems to me, Hokie, that whoever killed the Sheriff was disguising himself by riding with Olviera. It quite possible that his death had nothing to do with the salt. None of this is making any sense to me any more, Hokie."

"Just leave the thinking to me and Turbin for a while," Hokie said kindly. "Things are pretty quiet right now. Why don't you take a few days off and get some rest?"

"I think I will." She sighed. "I'd like to go see Peaceful. The way news travels, he probably already knows about Papa's death, but I'd like to talk to him."

"Need to tell him about Black Devil and the smallpox epidemic," Hokie said. "While you were gone to

Miss Merica's, a wire came from Ft. Stockton. They're sending us some vaccine. We should have it by the end of next week."

"Good. That alleviates one of my worries. Have you told Elm?" When Hokie nodded, she rose and picked up her hat. "I better get a move on. I'd like to be a far piece up the road by the time night sets in. While I'm gone, Hokie, I'll leave things here in Lawful with you and Turbin. If you need me, you can find me at Peaceful's village."

"Be careful, Clem," the deputy said. "Those vigilantes what killed Olviera are dangerous, and as I said before, I have my doubts about them being vigilantes of the real sort. Since nobody here knew Olviera shot the sheriff except you, Hadley and that reporter, and none of you said anything, the kid's killing had to be an inside job, done by men who knew he was not guilty. They killed the boy because they felt he had become a liability to them. If you get in their way, they won't hesitate to kill you."

"I know. I've been thinking about that, too." She shook her head. "There's so much I don't know, and what I do know doesn't fit."

She walked to the window and looked down the street. The buckboard was still parked in front of Elm's office. Then she shifted her gaze to the general store, where the door opened, and two women walked out. One of them was Maybelle, the other Odetta Albany.

"Odetta and Maybelle," Hokie said. "Two of the biggest gossips in town. What do you want to bet Maybelle's headed either for here or for Elm's office?"

"How about here?" Clem said, when Maybelle struck out across the street.

Both she and Hokie laughed.

Shortly Maybelle opened the door and walked in. "I knew something was wrong when you and that dude

182

drove that buckboard through town like you were running from the devil hisself, but I couldn't get over here. I had to finish filling Odetta Albany's grocery list. That woman isn't interested in anything but her flour and her coffee, and you can tell it by looking at her figure and smelling her breath." Her gaze came to rest on Clem. "What happened?"

"Alarico Olviera," Clem said.

"Dead?"

Clem nodded. "Vigilantes got him between here and Botello."

"Alarico Olviera." Maybelle paused. "Isn't he the Mexican boy who bumped heads a time or two with Clement over the salt lakes?"

"Yes, and he's also the man who shot the Sheriff."

"How do you know?"

"I saw him."

"But said nothing?"

Knowing her friend's insatiable curiosity and persistence, Clem explained, "I didn't say anything about it, because I wanted to be the one to find him, Maybelle. He shot my father."

"Now he's been shot. How did the vigilantes know he was the one who killed the Sheriff?" Not waiting for Clem to answer, she said, "Reckon he was bragging about it. Young guns always think they're immortal. Can't wait for the world to know they've killed somebody important."

Maybelle turned and moved toward the door. "Well, I guess I better go see if Elm wants me to bring him a burying suit for the young man. If he does, I need to look at him to get his size. At the rate you're bringing in bodies, Clem, I'm going to be out of suits soon."

"Seems kinda silly to me," Hokie said, "to buy new clothes to bury somebody who's already dead. Why not bury them in their old clothes and save the new ones for people who can wear them?"

183

"Hokie, I'd just as soon you kept your opinion to yourself," Maybelle said on quiet laughter. "You're not good for my business." She moved to the door. "Well, Clem, I'd better be going. I have lots to do, and I can't be away from the store for long. Reckon I need to rush an order to San Antonio for more black suits."

The door had no sooner closed behind her than Hokie said, "Well, Maybelle will make another sale, and news of Olviera's death will be spread all over town."

Clem heard a soft knock on the window and looked out to see Wade. Smiling, he motioned to her. She waved to him, then walked to the clothes rack to get her jacket. As she slipped into it, she said, "I'll be going, too, Hokie. I have quite a few miles to travel before the sun sets on this day."

When Clem stepped out of the building, the wind hit her full force to remind her of the inclement weather, to remind her of the long, hard ride ahead. Chilled despite the heavy clothing, she shivered, and for a moment wished she could retreat to the warmth of her house. By nightfall, the temperature would drop even further. Then she would be hampered by darkness as well as the cold. At the buckboard, Wade caught her by the waist and swung her into the passenger's seat.

"I'll drive," he said with a smile. "You can look at the horses on the street and see if you can identify any of the markings. Also, in case you need to draw your guns quickly, you won't have to worry about me or the buckboard and team. And, this time, if anyone needs a ride, *you* can hop out and help them."

"I won't be helping anyone for a while." Clem buried her hands in her pockets and ducked her head against a strong gust of wind. "I'm leaving here and going to the mountains to see Peaceful."

"How long will you be gone?"

His question sounded matter of fact, evincing only curiosity, no emotion. She turned to look at him, but he kept his eyes on the street, maneuvering the team around a large mud puddle.

"Several days." She paused. "Will you be here when I return?"

"I'd like to be," he said, "but I need to get to El Paso."

Talking ceased as they neared the house and Wade guided the buckboard into the barnyard. Soon he and Clem had the team unhitched and the horses rubbed down, fed, and secured in their stalls. As quickly Clem saddled the roan.

"Would you like to come in for a little while?" Wade asked. "The housekeeper has taken the day off, but we could rustle up something to eat, I'm sure."

"Thanks," Clem replied, "but I'll get something at the house."

For all her bravado, Clem was out of her depth with Wade Cameron. The kissing and cuddling had been wonderful, but she knew it would inevitably lead to something much more intimate. Wade had promised as much; she had asked for as much.

But face to face with the request, she realized she could not go through with her plans. She had not known Wade long, but already he was making inroads to her heart. This was unsettling.

Carefully balancing herself on the narrow planks that provided a narrow walkway from the barn to the house, she led Rusty-Be-Dusty through the muddy yard. When she was even with the water trough, her boot slipped over the edge, and her feet flew out from under her. She flailed her arms through the air but could not regain her balance. Wade reached for her. Before he could catch her, however, she landed in the trough, bottom first, legs and arms in the air.

Spitting and sputtering, she kicked as the icy water

surged around her, quickly penetrating the layers of clothes. Then her hands caught the sides and she began to pull herself up. Wade caught her shoulders and hauled her the rest of the way out and swung her into his arms. By this time, she was shivering and her teeth chattering.

"You'd better put me down," she said disjointedly. "I'm going to get you wet."

"It doesn't matter," he said, "I've got to get you into the house where it's warm. You're going to catch your death of a cold." His arms tightened about her, and she snuggled closer to his chest, thankful for the warmth of his body against hers.

"This . . . isn't an excuse . . . to get . . . me alone . . . with you?" Her teeth were chattering so badly she could hardly talk.

Smiling down at her, he held her more tightly against his chest. "I do take advantage of any opportunities that come my way."

Too cold to say more, Clem curled up against his body and let him worry with getting her in the house, which was not much warmer than the outside; however, the walls shielded them from the ferociousness of the wind. He walked past the parlor. When he began to climb the stairs, she pushed away from him.

"Where—where are you taking me?"

"To my room," he answered matter-of-factly. "There's plenty of wood in there, and it's small enough to warm quickly. Also I have some dry clothes you can put on."

And much more intimate! As much as the idea appealed to her, it also frightened her. Earlier in the day she had felt as if she were in control, but not now.

Opening the door, Wade walked into his bedroom and set her feet on the floor. He knelt in front of the hearth and built a fire; then he stood and turned to her. Clem felt as if her heart had stopped beating as

186

they stared at one another. Slowly he began to walk toward her, and her chest hurt. She was unable to draw air into her lungs.

When he stood inches in front of her, he said, "I'm going to close the door, so the room will warm quicker."

Clem nodded, breathing a sigh of relief when he walked past her, out of the room. She stood in front of the fire, and although she was still cold, she did not remove her clothing. The door opened and Wade returned, but she did not turn around. His footsteps echoed through the room. A drawer opened. More footsteps. He was behind her.

"Here's a pair of Prentice's trousers and one of my shirts, Clem. I know they'll be much too large for you, but at least they're dry."

She turned to see the garments spread across the bed—the white cambric shirt, the dark blue trousers and a pair of dry socks. In one hand he held a gray-checkered shirt and a pair of trousers for himself. He walked to the washstand and opened the bottom door to extract a large towel.

"I'll change clothes in the other bedroom while you dry off." He pointed to the bed. "Put those on, then call me when you're dressed."

Again she nodded, unable to remember a time when she had been this tongue-tied, but for the life of her she could not speak. She watched the long strides take him out of the room. For a few seconds after the door closed behind him, she remained in the center of the room where he had set her down. Eventually she stripped out of her wet clothes, dried off, and put on the trousers and shirt which smelled faintly of his herbal cologne. She was buttoning the shirt when he knocked.

"Come in," she called.

He entered the room, a tray balanced on one hand.

"I was going to brew us something hot like chocolate or coffee, but it would have taken too long to get another fire going. So I settled for second best — a bottle of whiskey." He closed the door. "I figured we needed every little bit of help we could to get warm."

She nodded her head.

Setting the tray on the night table, his gaze slowly ran the length of her body, and when his eyes made contact with hers again, they were dark.

"Papa always said this kind of weather called for a stiff drink."

Pretending a nonchalance she was far from feeling, Clem rolled up the sleeves of the shirt. She picked up her sodden scarf and wrung it out at the edge of the fireplace, the water sputtering against the heated stones. Then she draped it over the mantle so it could dry.

Wade poured two glasses of whiskey, but left them sitting on the tray. He moved to where she stood.

"Your hair," he said.

Before Clem quite realized what he was doing, he finger-combed the tangles from her hair, then led her to the fire.

"Here, sit down, and I'll brush it dry."

She never thought to protest.

He handed her the glass of whiskey and sat in the chair, guiding her between his legs. Relaxing as he brushed her hair, she sipped her drink, allowing the liquor to warm her insides as the fire warmed her flesh.

"I ought to spread my clothes out so they can be drying," she said, eyeing the pile of wet garments in the middle of the room.

"First things first." He continued to brush.

Clem wanted to remain where she was, but deep down she knew she must get away. "I really need to be —"

"There's no rush. You've waited this long; you can wait a few more hours."

That was true, but Clem wanted to allow nothing to take precedent over her mission, and she could easily allow her feelings for Wade to do so. If she changed her goals now, her life would have no definite meaning . . . or it would take on new meaning. She was uncertain whether she could handle the consequences of either option.

She pushed up on her knees and turned to find herself inches away from Wade—the same distance he had been while he was brushing her hair—only now they were facing each other. She was cradled between his legs. Her doubts melted away beneath the warmth of his gaze. Then he lowered his head.

Feeling the warmth of his penetrating gaze, she lowered her head. The shirt had slipped from one shoulder to reveal the top of her breast, and Wade was staring at it. He reached out, long fingers catching the material and lightly grazing her burning flesh as he pulled it over her shoulder once again. When he raised his head to look into her eyes, her blood seemed to boil through her veins and her pulse hammered at the base of her throat. She drew in a deep, steadying breath.

"Clem," Wade murmured, "you're beautiful. And I must get you out of here."

"Where would I go dressed like this?" She held up her arms, the sleeves of his shirt flapping through the air.

"If I don't get you out of here, I'm going to make love to you."

Excitement flowed through her body. For the second time in her life, she felt like a woman, and it was this man who had initiated the feeling both times. "Only if I allow you to."

Wade's gaze moved from her face to her arms back

189

to her face. They stared at each other for a long time before he stood and walked to the tray. Picking up the second glass, he quaffed the whiskey. He poured and drank another.

"Does drinking help?" Clem sat back, pulled her feet to her body, and wrapped her arms around her legs. He stared blankly at her. "Does drinking help curb the frustration a man and a woman feel when they are attracted to each other and don't do anything about it?"

He muttered under his breath and reached for his jacket.

"Where are you going?" she asked.

"I'm going to your house and get you some clothes," he said. "As wet as yours are, it'll take them a long time to dry."

Clem rose and walked to him. She pulled the jacket from his hands and dropped it to the floor. "Don't go. Stay here with me."

"I'd like nothing better," he said in a husky voice, his whiskey-scented breath touching her face, "but it's no good for either of us, Clem."

"Why?" she asked. "Earlier today the kissing seemed to be good for both of us. I thought we both enjoyed it."

"Clem, I'm thirteen years older than you."

"My father was sixteen years older than my mother."

"And look what happened to them," he said.

"We're not going to get married," Clem countered.

"What's going to happen to you when I'm gone?"

"That's my concern, not yours," she answered.

"Clem, two people can't make love without their sharing a certain amount of feeling between them. And generally a woman falls in love with the first man who makes love to her."

"That may be true generally," Clem conceded, "but

I don't think it's true for us. Knowing this and considering what you're teaching me, I'll guard against falling in love with you . . . if we *should* make love."

"Clem, I'm not going to take the responsibility for hurting you."

She reached up and touched his face, letting the tips of her fingers freely roam the rugged masculine terrain. "As you said, Wade Cameron, I'll take responsibility for my own hurt."

"Clem, I'm not the marrying kind."

His words stung.

"Even if you were," she said, "you wouldn't marry someone like me."

Wade stared at her for a second, then opened his mouth as if to protest her statement.

She hid her feelings behind a veneer of nonchalance. "I'm not like the ladies you're accustomed to, and you can't deny that."

Stooping, Clem picked up her glass, then she stepped around Wade. At the tray she picked up the bottle of whiskey and refilled her glass. After she had taken several sips, she held the glass out and looked at the amber liquid.

"Thanks for being truthful with me, Wade, and thanks for being concerned. Now, I'll be as honest with you, and in so doing set your mind at ease. I'm not looking for marriage, and especially not to you. I don't mean to be cruel, but when I marry, I want to marry my own kind."

Now that she had met Wade, now that she had experienced the joy that his touch generated, she wondered exactly what her own kind was.

Wade contemplated her for a moment, his expression turning from one of puzzlement into . . . surely not anger? Yet when he spoke, his voice seemed to be full of anger. "I'm not your kind?"

"No."

Clem was hard-pressed to understand Wade's abrupt change of mood. He was the one worried about her wanting marriage; she was simply setting his mind at ease.

"What is your kind of man, Clem?" A strange expression crossed his countenance, and his voice was harsh, like the planes and angles of his face. He did indeed seem to be a rugged product of the environment. His anger, his harshness, excited Clem.

"One who wears a Stetson, boots, and spurs. One who has two guns strapped around his waist, and a rifle in the holster on his horse." Wade spat out the words. "Revenge is his motive, and killing is the solution to his problems. Rough and tough are the adjectives that best describe him."

Before she could deny his accusations or say a word in her defense, he took the glass from her and returned it to the tray; then his arms went around her body, and he dragged her into his arms. As his head lowered to hers, he growled more than spoke his words, "Well, then if it's experience you want, I'll be glad to give it to you, no questions asked, no holds barred. Let's see if I can't be *your kind of man*."

Clem insinuated her hands between them, her palms against his chest and she shoved, but his strength was too much for her. His lips came closer, but she turned her face before they captured her mouth.

"No," she muttered, and freed one of her hands. Fear quickly chased away her excitement. "Not like this."

His hand slipped up to catch her chin and to hold her face still. As he contemplated her expression, the tension, the anger, seemed to melt out of his body. They both breathed deeply. Then reading this new response in his face, accepting the gentleness of his touch, Clem let herself lean into his body, her softness melding into his strength. His arm slipped around her, his embrace tightening. Clem felt his hardness against her.

Again she was surprised and puzzled by Wade Cameron. There was so much more to him that she did not know about. She looked up into his face, into the wonder of passion swirling darkly in his eyes. Now was not the time to know. Now was the time to experience all the wonderful feelings he could arouse in her. She could think later, when he was gone. They were going to kiss, and she welcomed it.

She lifted her face, and Wade eagerly accepted her lips as he crushed her closer in his arms. Clem quivered, slid her arms around his neck, and pushed her hands into the thick hair at the nape of his neck. She opened her mouth to receive him and moaned her desire through his warm lips. The hunger within her was so great, so intense, that when he lifted his lips from hers, she cried out.

"Clem, if we—if we—there'll be no turning back."

"There never was. Not from the moment we first met."

Chapter Twelve

"No," Wade murmured, "there has been no turning back, has there?" Fascinated by her hair, Wade pulled a strand through his fingers. "I've wanted to do this ever since the first time I saw your hair hanging down. It shimmered like silk in the firelight. In fact, I wanted and still want to touch you all over, to know and to claim every inch of your body."

He dropped the curl and began to trace the contour of her face, his fingers coming to rest on her chin. He had once thought her features gaunt, her eyes frosty, but not now. She was slender with gentle curves. Her eyes were soft and alluring. The chill gone, they were the color of the forest in the springtime.

"You're beautiful."

He touched the back of his hand to her mouth, lightly brushing the middle knuckle over the top lip. He felt her slight tremble, and her lips moved into that quiet, omniscient smile he had witnessed only once before, and that transformed her into a vision of loveliness. Again he caught his breath in surprise and admiration. Clem was wild, untamed, and spirited—a true product of her environment. He liked her. She excited him. His anticipation sent heat rushing through his body to settle in his groin.

Then, as if his passion embarrassed her, Clem lowered her lids, letting thick, curling lashes form a dark crescent on her cheeks. In others he would have considered this a coquettish ploy, but not with Clem. While she exhibited a wisdom and worldly knowledge that surprised him, she was also an innocent.

His hand dropped to the neck of the shirt—the color and texture reminiscent of her white cotton robe—and curled his fingers gently around her throat. He slowly lowered his head to brush his lips against her forehead and to trail them down her nose. Finally he pressed his mouth against hers in a whisper-soft kiss. Her lips were soft and warm beneath his.

Wade did not deepen the caress, rather he tantalized, but Clem moaned faintly; she was tired of the foreplay. Her lips claimed his, softly at first, then more firmly. As a flower opens itself to the morning dew, Clem's mouth opened to his. She leaned closer to him, her hands clutching his shoulders, her breasts pressing into his chest.

For a moment he seemed to be lost in time, his breath locked in his chest. Then he breathed—inhaling the essence of the woman standing in the circle of his arms. His embrace tightened, and he became the aggressor, his hands stroking her back as she welcomed his tongue into her mouth.

When he lifted his head from hers, he pushed his hands beneath the folds of the shirt to touch smooth skin.

"Am I—am I pleasing to you?" she asked.

"More than pleasing," Wade answered.

The material slipped from her shoulders to bundle around her feet. Their eyes caught and held, as one by one he undid the row of buttons down the front of his shirt. When she stood naked, his hands fell to his sides, and he stepped back. Only now did his gaze move from her face. Gone was the tough deputy sheriff. Before him was a woman, soft and utterly feminine.

Wade's stomach tightened as he looked at her; she was indeed lovely all over. The fluid lines and hollows of her throat led down to supple shoulders and rounded breasts. Her waist was slender, her hips gently rounded, the triangle at the pit of her stomach a riot of fiery red curls. His gaze lingered, then trailed the length of slender, shapely legs before returning to her face.

"How do I look?" Clem's eyes were wide and inquisitive.

"Perfect."

She blushed. "You've a handsome way with words, Wade. You make flattery sound like the truth. Are you as gifted a lover?"

"I do have a way with words," Wade admitted, "but I don't lie, Clem. If I say the words, you can guarantee they are the truth, not flattery." He stepped nearer and bent to kiss her forehead, his lips slowly moving all over her face, down the soft arch of her neck, back and forth over her collarbone. "And, yes, to your second question. I am a gifted lover."

"And a most conceited one, too."

"No, not conceited," he whispered, his lips tasting the skin that smelled so clean and fresh, that smelled faintly of his cologne, "only confident. I make love with women to whom I'm thoroughly attracted and who share a mutual attraction to me. In making love I always strive to give pleasure, and in so doing, little Clementina, I always receive the ultimate in pleasure."

"Always?" She breathed more than spoke.

"Always," he repeated.

"I feel all warm inside when you look at me."

"That's natural."

"What about the trembling?" she murmured. "Do women generally tremble when men touch them like you're touching me?"

196

Clem was so refreshing, her innocence so sweet and open, Wade could not contain his soft laughter. "Most do. It's the body's way of expressing its joy in being loved."

Experimentally she trailed her fingertips down his chest. "Do men tremble also?"

"Yes." Even to him his voice sounded thick.

He let his gaze fasten on her breasts, firm, round, and creamy. With his other hand he traced the nipple of one, and Clem inhaled deeply and dropped her hand; her stomach quivered. He lowered his head and leaned closer; Clem moaned softly as he took her nipple into his mouth. He dropped to his knees.

"What do I do, Wade?" But even as she uttered the words, her hands cupped the head that nuzzled the tender flesh of her stomach. "I'm quivering inside; I feel funny all over and don't know what to do."

Ceasing his caresses, he wrapped his arms around her and lay his cheek on her stomach. Although he was her teacher, he was also her lover, and wanted this time to be the most wonderful time of her entire life. He stood and stepped back from her to undress.

"You're so handsome," Clem murmured. Her gaze moved from his chest down his waist to settle on his erection. She moved closer to him, her hands skimming over his chest, around his nipples and down the swirl of chest hair to his pubic area. "You always looked muscular, but I—didn't expect you to be so strong."

They moved toward each other at the same time, melting into an embrace. Her fingers digging into his shoulders, she raised her head to receive his kiss. Again and again they kissed, each one deeper and more drugging. Finally Wade raised his head and lifted her into his arms.

Looking at her kiss-swollen lips, he whispered, "Are you sure, Clementina?"

"Yes."

He carried her across the room, laid her on the mattress, and slid onto the bed beside her. His mouth again claimed hers hungrily. His hand caressed her belly, then moved lower.

Writhing beneath his touch, Clem gasped, her hand catching his to still his movements.

"Let me make love to you," she whispered.

She placed light, feathery kisses against his neck and snuggled more securely against him. She rubbed her hand over his chest, up his arms, over his shoulders, and down his neck. She pulled her foot up the length of his leg. All the time she covered his face and neck with hot kisses.

"I think you forget who the teacher is."

He stopped her by leaning forward to cover the peak of her breast with his mouth. Exploring fingers parted her thighs and brushed up the pliant inner thighs to caress with light strokes, until he reached the triangle at their juncture.

His hand slid through the soft hair as he unerringly sought and found the place that would give her the greatest joy, the place he must prepare so she would know little pain when he made his initial entry. He felt Clem tremble anew as he traced the outline of her nether lips with a teasing finger. Little whimpers broke from her parted lips, and she arched her hips to meet his probing fingers; she welcomed the sweet invasion of his hand.

A long, drawn-out sigh escaped Clem when his fingers entered to explore her most intimate part. Her eyes closed, her body quivering, soft moans whispered through her lips, and her head rolled from side to side in pleasure.

Her delight was Wade's. Intent on giving her pleasure, his whole body joined in the amorous assault. As his hand probed, as his fingers moved inside her, his teeth teasingly grazed from the fullness of her breasts to the nipples and back again.

Clem writhed and cried aloud. Her hips began to undulate in that primeval dance as old as time itself. She arched her lower body, straining against Wade's hand. With all her incoherent love cries, with every motion of her body, she begged for release.

His manhood stiff and swollen, Wade's body also clamored for release. Yet he deliberately held back, fighting against losing himself in the lovemaking in order to give her ultimate pleasure. But his ache was turning from a dull throb of need to an acute wanting. He could restrain himself no longer, and she was ready for him.

His body hurting from the need for release, he moved so that she was beneath him, then eased his knee between her legs, opening them, spreading them apart. His hand slipped beneath her buttocks.

Clem's hand began to brush up and down the indentation of his spine, over his taut buttocks. His manhood tenderly probed into her femininity. He felt her tense, and her hands stilled their movement.

"Your first time will hurt a little," he said, "but never again. I'll be as gentle as I can." He felt her cheek brush against his chest as she nodded. His hands once again began to reassure her body, relaxing and soothing her, preparing her for entry.

Then her palms flattened against his chest, and she cried, "No."

Wade could not stop, not now. "Yes, my sweet." He locked his arms about her. "I told you that once we started there was no turning back. I can't, Clementina. I won't."

His lower body ceased moving as Clem became his prisoner.

"You'll enjoy it." His mouth hovered over hers, his whiskey-scented breath warmly touching her skin. His

199

lips captured hers. With consummate skill, he kissed and stroked her until all resistance fled. She caught his hand and guided it to her breast. Willingly, Wade caught the delicate flesh in his hand.

He was not aware that he had entered her until she gasped and the barrier yielded to him. He caught the muffled sob of pain in his kiss and gently ran his hands up and down the sides of her body.

"The pain is over with." He eased deeply within her, and the tension ebbed as she surrendered to him. "From now on, it's only pleasure."

Slowly he made love to her with deep, rhythmic strokes. Every touch gradually awakened her innocent woman's body to the pleasure he had promised her. Clem slowly, rhythmically moved her hips; her hands curled around Wade's shoulders, her legs embraced his back, and she arched upward to meet his thrusts. Now he was her prisoner.

"Oh, Wade," she cried out, and moved her body faster and harder against his, "I didn't know making love could be so wonderful."

"Just wait, sweetheart. There's even greater pleasure for you."

Wade lost himself in a magical world where nothing existed except him and the soft body beneath him. His thrusts were deeper, rapid, fierce, yet always tempered with care and restraint, lest he hurt Clem. Passion mounted higher and higher.

Clem tensed and cried out in ecstasy; she shuddered uncontrollably in his arms. Her moist softness pulsated around him; it clung with each instant of spasmodic contraction. Then she clung to him, catching his lips in a deep kiss of gratification.

Wade turned the kiss into one of deep passion, one of ultimate promise for himself. His hand tightened around her hips as he brought her closer to him, as he entered her deeply and fully. He shuddered in her arms as he reached a climax.

Lying side by side, covered with a light blanket, they basked in the beautiful world they had created with their love. Clem smiled and stretched; then she rested her cheek and palm on Wade's chest.

"I didn't know it could be so wonderful," she murmured.

Her voice was low as she ran the tips of her fingers through the hair on his chest. She propped up on one elbow and looked down at him. Strands of her hair trailed across his chest. He wrapped a curl around his index finger.

"I feel like my entire body is glowing," she confessed.

Wade laughed and dropped the curl so that he could cup her face with both hands. "You are glowing. You're more beautiful than ever."

Clem grinned down at him. "I suppose you're going to take the credit for that, Mr. Cameron?"

"I believe a small portion of the credit is due me." He pulled her face down to his for a sweet kiss. "Thank you, Clementina Jones, for having made love with me, and for allowing me to be the first man who made love to you."

"Thank you, for teaching me how to make love," she whispered. She lay down, pillowing her head on his shoulder. "I didn't realize it could be like this between a man and a woman. Maybelle had warned me that it would be unpleasant, something that a woman tolerated because her husband enjoyed it."

Wade chuckled softly, happy that he had satisfied her. "Maybelle was definitely wrong, my sweet. I promise you that it gets better and better. Practice makes perfect." His hand captured one of her breasts, and he leaned over to kiss it. "Shall I prove my point?"

"No," she whispered, her voice breathy, "I think perhaps I need to think of a way to get out of here before someone finds out I'm here."

Wade was not ready for her to leave. He wanted to keep her beside him. As many times as he had made love during his life, he had never enjoyed the experience as much as he had this time.

"I know you have to leave," he said, "but I wish we could stay here together indefinitely."

"Me, too."

She lowered her head and pressed kisses across his chest, moving from one nipple to the other, lower down the narrowing swirl of hair. Wade sucked in his breath when her lips touched the sensitive skin around his navel. His stomach tightened beneath her gentle ministrations of love. When her hand moved lower to touch him, he stilled her movement.

"If you keep this up, Clementina Jones, you won't be leaving this room any too soon."

Clem's laughter teased him, and he caught her into his arms, his lips settling on hers in a deep kiss. When he finally lifted his head, he propped up on an elbow and pressed his hand against her flushed cheek. As if he had never seen her before, he looked at her nakedness.

Slowly, leisurely he admired her beauty. His eyes traveled downward from her graceful neck and shoulders to her small breasts. He gently cupped one and touched the tip to see it harden with expectancy.

He raised his head and kissed her. As the kiss deepened, her hand moved up his chest. She pressed her body to his, and her taut nipples against him shot flames all the way to his manhood.

Tightening his arms around her, he released her mouth and showered kisses over her face, into her hair. Tracking the delicate curve of her ear with his tongue, he caught her earlobe tenderly between his teeth. She shuddered. With a slowness which belied the pounding fury of his heartbeat, he planted kisses in a trail down her neck and shoulders, over the fullness of her breasts, until he at last caught the nipple into his mouth.

Clem arched, and as Wade's hand lightly brushed down her body, over her hips and thighs, she caught her breath. When he shifted his body between her thighs, she slid her hand down his stomach and her fingers guided his manhood to its place. He would have entered her gently, but Clem would have no gentle coupling. She slipped her hands beneath his buttocks and pulled him tightly against her arched pelvis. She received him.

As his movements gained momentum, she met him thrust for thrust. Her arms clung to his shoulders; her fingers dug into the flexed muscles of his back; her eyes clenched tightly with passion.

Holding himself back until Clem had reached her climax, Wade now concentrated on his own pleasure. Two, three deep strokes and a cry of pained-pleasure, he released his seed within her. As the shuddering subsided, he rolled to her side and clasped her to him in a tender embrace. They lay together in blissful silence, their breathing and heartbeats returning to normalcy.

Eventually she sighed. "I really have to go."

"Home?" he asked, "or to the mountains?"

"Both." Her gaze swept to her wet garments still lying on the floor. "I have to change into dry clothes and take care of my guns."

He ran his hand down her back to cup her buttocks. "I like you this way much better."

"Thank you." She leaned down to kiss the tip of his nose. "I like your naked body, too."

Wade sat up, the blanket folding at his waist. "Clem, let Rand take care of finding your father's killer. Come to El Paso with me. Let's spend all the time together we can, before I return to New York."

"The offer is tempting, but I can't." She laid a finger over his mouth. "I won't."

She slid off the bed and quickly put on the borrowed clothes. Moving to the dresser, she brushed her hair with Wade's brush, then pinned it in a coil on the crown of her head.

"Do you have any regrets?" Wade asked.

Clem put both of Wade's socks on before she looked up to say, "Only one." Then she lowered her head and slipped her feet into her boots—the only piece of clothing she had that had not gotten soaked in the trough.

"That is?"

Standing, she picked up her wet clothes and gun belt. She walked to the door and said, "That I have to leave you so soon."

The house was empty and cold when Clem arrived, and although she would have welcomed a fire in the black wood stove in the kitchen, the aroma of food and coffee in the air, and a fire in the parlor, she was glad Deborah was not home. She could be alone with her thoughts and memories.

Hurrying to her bedroom, she built a fire, but long before the warmth chased the chill from the room, she shed her borrowed clothes and wrapped herself in a heavy dressing gown. After hanging her clothes on a line on the back porch, she returned to her bedroom, dragged a chair to the fireplace, and sat down.

She could hardly believe the drastic changes that had occurred in her life during the past three days. The man who had influenced her life the most was gone, but another had taken his place. One she loved, of the other she was uncertain—yet she knew he had also played an important role in her life, and she wanted his role to be even more important.

Clem did not know if she could afford to pay the price to have Wade Cameron in her life. She had been foolish to think she could dally so nonchalantly with human emotions. During her life, she had been attracted to men, and had wondered what it would be like to make love to them. But no man had stirred her like Wade Cameron.

Through half-closed eyes, she watched the flames dance through the air. Warmth infused her body; lethargy cloaked her. Beautiful thoughts drifted through her mind. She could easily see Wade Cameron, lying naked in the huge bed. He was hot, demanding flesh, and beneath a fine layer of dark hair and well-developed muscles, the skin of his arms and legs was tight and smooth.

She wanted to know again the sweet fierceness of his kiss; she fervently desired that he again possess every inch of her body. Even now that she was away from him, she was conscious of the stirring and demands of her body, stirring and demands she had not known about until Wade had awakened them in her. She had given herself to him eagerly, freely, holding nothing back. Under the spell of his hot kisses, she wanted him in a primal way that had nothing to do with thought . . . or reason . . . or justification.

When they had consummated their relationship, Clem realized the enormity of her actions. Only then did she truly understand what Wade had meant when he said there was no turning back. She would never be the same again. She felt totally out of control.

But at the time, she had not minded Wade's having control. As he promised, he gave her gentle loving, and his touch gave her pleasure she had never experienced before. In his arms she felt like a fragile treasure. She was beautiful and desirable.

How wonderful it would have been to have lain in his arms the remainder of the afternoon. He was so strong, his embrace so protective and reassuring. How easy it would be for Clem to allow Wade Cameron to become an integral part of her life.

The thought jolted her to her senses. Wade could not become a part of her life—integral or not—no more than she would allow herself to become a part of his. Wade Cameron did not want marriage, and there was no place in her life for marriage.

That is why she should be glad that Wade Cameron was her lover, Clem reasoned. She could give herself to him in abandon, knowing that in a few days he would ride away, and she would never see him again. Yet the mere thought of not seeing him again filled her with sadness.

Although she had been away from him no more than an hour, she already missed him—the sultry blue eyes, the deep resonant laughter, the husky voice that murmured endearments during their lovemaking. Her body remembered his kisses and wanted more.

Clem had spent all her life learning how to survive in a country that was no respecter of persons. The West Texas wilderness cared not if one were man or woman, adult or child. It was as harsh on the one as the other. Clem determined at an early age to be a survivor, and until today she had felt confident of her ability to survive . . . until she came face to face with her own femininity.

She rose and picked up her guns, dried and oiled them. The small porcelain clock on the mantel ticked away. The aftermath of lovemaking was fading, reality settling in. As emotions surely gave way to reason, Clem grew confused. She wanted to talk with someone, but Papa was gone.

She could not have talked with Papa about this anyway. He would not have understood. He had once told her that there were three kinds of women in the world: a whore, a mistress, and a wife. He had considered Deborah to be a whore. Clem wondered what her father would think of her now.

She thought about Maybelle, but knew she could not confide in her. Maybelle would not understand.

The front door opened and closed; footsteps moved into the kitchen, then through the parlor and down the hall. From the doorway to Clem's bedroom, Deborah spoke, "I went to get some groceries. Maybelle told me you brought in the man who shot your father."

"Yes," Clem murmured, laying her head against the cushioned back of the chair. She was glad to be rescued from her thoughts.

"Well, I'm thankful that's over. You don't know how worried I was about you this morning."

"You needn't have been," Clem said, visions of Wade Cameron once again spinning through her mind. "I can take care of myself. The Sheriff taught me how."

"I'm sure he did." Deborah walked into the room to stand in front of the fireplace. "But I worry nonetheless. How was your meeting with Miss Merica?"

"Interesting as usual." Clem's gaze never left the fire. "But it wasn't profitable for Wade. She knew nothing about Bryan Dillon."

"When will he be leaving for El Paso?"

"He never said," Clem answered, "but somehow I think he's going to wait around to talk with Rand. He wants to find out more about the Blacksmith. He thinks there's a connection between him and Bryan Dillon."

Deborah carefully folded her gloves. "Well," she finally said, "Rand will be here in a few days. Wade can question him about the Blacksmith to his heart's content. Then he can talk with Doña Pera when she arrives. She's lived in the area all her life. Maybe she knows something about the man."

Clem reluctantly stirred from her warm cocoon.

"Are you having the barbecue here at the house?" she asked.

"Yes, and by the way, I saw some material at Maybelle's today that would make lovely curtains for the parlor. I thought I would make some new ones, and—" As if she realized what she had said, she looked at Clem a little guiltily.

"I think it would be nice," Clem said. "Especially if Doña Pera stays with us. Pretty-up the house any way you want to. As you can see, Papa and I didn't have too much time to spend working around here."

"I didn't mean that," Deborah said.

"I didn't take it that way," Clem assured her mother with a smile.

Deborah returned the gesture. "What would you like for me to prepare for dinner tonight? I'd like to cook something special for us."

"Thanks for the thought, but I won't be here for supper." Clem extended her feet toward the fire, her gaze returning to the mantel clock. "I'll be leaving in a few minutes."

"Leaving," Deborah repeated. "But where are you going? The Olviera kid is dead."

Clem walked to the armoire to rummage for clean clothes. "I haven't been to the mountains to talk with Peaceful."

"You haven't changed your mind about going?"

"No."

Now that she had made love to Wade, Clem wanted the solitude the mountains offered more than ever. Maybelle had told her that her life would change if she ever gave up her innocence to a man, and although Clem's life was not changing in the way her friend had implied, her life had changed irrevocably. Clem needed time to come to grips with what was happening to her, and with what she wanted to happen to her.

On the one hand, she was the happiest woman in the world. She came alive in Wade's arms as she had never been alive before. But she was also saddened to think he had awakened such joy in her and would soon be leaving.

For all her talk, she did not want to lose him.

Deborah quietly left the room, and Clem dressed. By the time she was buttoning her shirt, her mother returned.

"Clem, are those your wet clothes hanging on the line on the back porch?"

"Yes," Clem answered, resenting the fact that Deborah's tone demanded an explanation, irritated because she so quickly supplied one. "When I was returning Hadley's buckboard, I stumbled and fell into the water trough."

"Oh, Clem," said Deborah, "you could catch your death of cold. Surely you can't—"

Clem held her hand up for silence. "Please, Deborah, don't start again."

"Is there always going to be this distance between us?"

"I don't know," Clem answered. "But it will be there for a while. It's going to take time for you and me to reacquaint ourselves. I'm having to accept you, and you're going to have to do the same with me. I'm no longer a child, and I don't appreciate being treated as one."

"You're right, and I apologize. I do want you to understand what *I* did and why I did it, but I was not willing to extend the same courtesy to you." Deborah walked to where Clem stood and lifted a hand to cup her daughter's cheek. She smiled tenderly. "Blame it on a mother wanting to recapture lost motherhood. I'll stand back and give you room to grow and to be an adult."

"Thanks," Clem murmured. Soon she would be able

to talk with her mother. Not now, but soon.

"Would it be presumptuous of me to offer you a glass of milk and a sandwich before you left?"

Clem laughed. "No, I'd like that."

Chapter Thirteen

Wade's journal was open on the desk in front of him, his pen lying beside it, but he had long since stopped writing to gaze out the window. There was little evidence of last week's storm. The sun was shining brightly, and it was warm enough to go without a jacket.

How appropriate the name Indian Summer would be!

Clem had been in the mountains with her Indian friend for three days. Three long days. Day after tomorrow the westbound stage would be coming through, and he would have to go, whether Clem had returned or not. He turned to look at his luggage. Most of it was packed and ready to go. But he was reluctant.

"I'm glad we're leaving," Prentice said from the door. "This town is getting on my nerves. I hope El Paso is more interesting."

"No more money to be made from drawing the townsfolk," Wade said. He closed his journal, and returned it and the pen to his writing case.

Grinning, Prentice walked to the bowl of nuts and fruit on the reading table. "My! My! My! But we have been testy for the past three days. As I say, to each his own. You had your diversion with the deputy sheriff; I with my portraits."

"And now that Doña Pera has arrived in town, you've begun sharing your artistic talents with her and her attendants."

Prentice laughed. "You're jealous! Don't be sarcastic simply because your diversion left you for a bunch of savages. Under normal circumstances I would call her your conquest, but this time, Wade, I don't think you conquered. You must be getting old."

"Must be," Wade agreed, not allowing his cousin to see how deeply Clem had affected him.

After a moment, Prentice said, "You can't become too involved with her, Wade. She's not the kind of woman you need beside you. You need someone—"

"Thanks, Prentice," Wade said. "I believe I can handle my own affairs."

"All right." Prentice held up both hands in mock surrender.

Wade was not at all sure that he could handle his affairs, or that he knew his own heart. He had been careful to explain to Clem that he was not a man to allow his emotions to become involved with a woman; definitely he was not the marrying kind. He remembered that condescending smile and the almost casual acceptance of his terms.

During the past three days, Wade had discovered that Clem had touched a tender chord in his heart, a chord of which he had been unaware. He missed her, all of her—the smiles, the laughter, the sunshine she brought with her. He hoped she returned to Lawful before he left on the stage.

He had contemplated staying until she returned, but his conscience would not allow that. Nash was paying him to trace down the last clue to Bryan's whereabouts, and Wade had done all he could in Lawful. He had to move on. The longer he stayed here the colder the trail became—and from the beginning it had not even been warm.

"Are you planning to go to the shindig Mrs. Jones has planned for the Doña?" Prentice asked, as he cracked two pecans together and began to dig out the pulp.

"I think so. I want to meet her. She may know something about Bryan."

The afternoon Clem left to go to the mountains, the matriarch of the Montelongo Hacienda and her entourage rode into Lawful. Doña Pera was an imposing woman, her numerous vaqueros resplendent in their uniforms.

"I thought maybe you'd forgotten about him," Prentice drawled sarcastically. "You've been so preoccupied with Clem lately."

Wade pushed back in the chair. "She's an enigma. Just when I think I have her figured out, I see another facet to her—another mystery to uncover."

"Oh, God," Prentice groaned, "here we go again. Only this time, old boy, I think you're the one who is caught. The deputy sheriff may be a bumpkin, but she's extremely smart. You better watch yourself or she's gonna hook you. Before you know what's happened, you'll be married and will live to regret it."

Prentice's words stung Wade. He shook his head. "No, I don't think so. Her parents' unsuccessful attempt at marriage has discouraged her from wanting matrimony. Her only goal in life is to be the peace officer of Lawful, Texas."

A loner, Wade had never needed people around him to be happy. That was one of the reasons why he had become a bounty hunter; he owed no one allegiance except himself. As long as he maintained his integrity, he had been happy.

Being a loner was also one of the reasons he had

never felt the urge to marry. He liked being with a woman and enjoyed her company, but he never wanted to feel any type of obligation to her. He wanted the freedom to come and go as he pleased. While some of his friends had that in their marriage, Wade did not believe in a double standard. It violated his principles for a man to shackle a woman into a marriage, simply to provide himself with a hostess for his home and a mother for his children.

Since Clem had been gone, Wade had been lonely — extremely lonely. He had been tempted to find someone who would take him to the mountains to find her; he had even passed by her house several times with the intent of stopping to talk with her mother, hoping that through the conversation he could learn more about Clem.

The last time he had done this, he realized he was behaving like a lovelorn schoolboy where Clementina Jones was concerned. This behavior startled him and caused him to examine his motives. Was lust prompting his loneliness and his actions, or was he infatuated with Clem?

The front door opened and closed, shattering Wade's thoughts.

Hadley ordered from downstairs, "Take him into the study, and lay him on the daybed. Oran, you go get Elm. Philana, get some water to heating on the stove. Elm's gonna need it."

Wade, followed by Prentice, hurried out of the room and downstairs into the parlor. "What's wrong?" he asked, his gaze settling on the elderly man who lay on the daybed.

"Sam Harper," Hadley said. "Went out to his place to question him about the Olviera incident. I found him unconscious."

Wade was close enough to see the wound in the

214

man's chest.

Harper flung an arm and groaned. "Got my . . . property," he moaned.

"Don't try to talk, Sam." Hadley knelt beside him. "Elm will be here in a minute to take care of you."

"Damn it, Hadley." The man said the words between grunts of pain. "They have a signed bill of sale for my property, and you tell me to shut up!"

"That's exactly what he's telling you, Sam Harper." Philana returned to the room with a basin of water and towels draped over her arm. "And you'll obey him, if you want to be alive to do something about it. Here, let me at him, Hadley. I'll clean him up a bit."

Sitting in a chair in the corner of the room, out of the way, Prentice propped his sketchbook in his lap and began to draw.

Philana took a pair of scissors out of her pocket and cut the fabric of Harper's shirt. Pulling it aside, she looked at the gaping wound. "It's a good thing you're an ornery ole cuss, Sam Harper. Otherwise you'd be dead."

He tried to chuckle, but coughed instead. "You've a wicked tongue, Philana."

"True." She now daubed a wet cloth gently around the wound. "How'd you get shot?"

"Gunslinger," he answered. "He's . . . been after me . . . and Thompson and Howard to sell our property around Chupedera Lakes, but I wouldn't. Yesterday he came riding up. I saw him in time to get my rifle. He had money and a bill of sale for me to sign. I refused and ordered him off my land. He left, but promised to come back, saying it would be worse for me the next time."

"Who is he?" Hadley asked. "Do you know?"

"Perry," Sam answered. "Ike Perry."

"Oh my God!" Hadley exclaimed, then asked,

215

"Who's buying the property, Sam? Him? Someone else? Do you know?"

"Some Mexican with a real common name. Don't recollect what it was."

Footsteps sounded on the porch, and the door opened.

Elm said. "Got here as soon as I could, Hadley. Where's the patient?" By this time he stood in the doorway.

"My place was the closest," Hadley explained, "and he's hit pretty bad."

Elm knelt beside the daybed, examining Harper's wound.

"I was afraid he was going to bleed to death, if he didn't die of the bullet," Hadley continued.

"You did right. Jostling him around in the buckboard, just to get him to my office, probably would have done him in," Elm grunted. "Philana, we're going to have to dig it out."

"That's what I figured. Got plenty of hot water and towels ready for you."

"What about whiskey?" Elm asked. "I figure I'm gonna need that more than I need hot water."

"I'll get it," Hadley said and moved to the liquor cabinet.

After Hadley handed the bottle to Elm, he and Wade walked onto the porch. Prentice remained where he was.

Hadley was going through the details of his finding Harper for the second time, when Hokie rode up. Conversation ceased. The deputy dismounted and tied his horse to the hitching rail.

"Maybelle's been saying for days that we're in for big trouble, Hadley. Well, I think it's a he, and *he's* here."

"Ike Perry," Hadley said. "One of the men Ramson

216

told us about. I guess they've already moved out of El Paso."

Hokie nodded. "Powers is with him. They say Sam Harper just sold his property at Chupedera Lakes. They figure Howard and Thompson will sell out next. They claim their price is high enough to make it worthwhile to 'em."

"I'll say it is." Hadley sighed and pushed his hand through his hair. "Sam's almost dead. Would have been, if I hadn't happened by."

"I'd better get Turbin." Hokie walked over to the window and peered into the parlor. "I'd sure feel better if Clement was here with us. God knows, me and Turbin ain't no match for Ike Perry when it comes to drawing and shooting."

Frowning, Hadley stood at the edge of the porch, his arms crossed over his chest, and stared into the distance. "I never realized how isolated we were until Clement died. Now, I feel like a kid who's lost his parents—alone and afraid."

"Yes," the deputy agreed solemnly, "that's the way most everybody's feeling."

"I wonder when Rand's going to get here? We sure could use him."

"Mr. Hokum!" A little girl ran down the road, her pigtails flying behind. "Mr. Hokum!"

Hadley stepped closer to the edge of the porch and shielded his eyes from the sun. "Why, that's Lucia McLean, Lester's granddaughter," he said. "What's happened now?"

She was winded by the time she reached the men. In between big breaths of air, she said, "Grandpa sent me to tell you they done shot Grady when he pulled his shotgun on 'em. They chased everybody out of the saloon but Laban."

Tears streamed down the child's face. "They got my

brother in there. My twin brother. He was sweeping the floor for Mr. Grady when they came in. Please, Mr. Hokum, get him out. They said if the deputy sheriff didn't show up by five o'clock today, they was gonna shoot him. Don't let 'em kill my brother."

"I better get back," Hokie said. "Someone's got to stand up to them. And with Clem gone, I'm the law and order here."

"I'll get my rifle," Hadley said, "and go with you."

"No!" Wade walked to the door. "I'll handle this, Hadley."

Hadley and deputy stared at him in amazement.

"You!" Hokie exclaimed. "Mr. Cameron, I don't mean no offense, but Ike Perry is a seasoned gunslinger. He's one of the worst of the lot. He has a reputation for killing women and children."

"I know who and what he is." Wade walked to the door. "And for the record, I'm an even more seasoned gunslinger."

Hadley's eyes glistened with curiosity, but he said nothing. Quietly Wade explained that he had been a bounty hunter.

Hokie shook his head. "Makes no difference, Mr. Cameron, I can't let you do this. I figure this is my job."

"If you want to save that boy's life," Wade said, "you'd better let me handle this. I'm the only one who can stand up to Ike Perry and come out alive."

Hokie opened his mouth to protest again, but Hadley laid his hand on the deputy's arm. "Listen to him," he said with a blind confidence that Wade appreciated at the moment. "He knows what he's doing."

Wade knew! He also knew that his integrity offered him no other choice. With determined steps he walked up the stairs, picked up one of his suitcases, and set it on the bed. Unbuckling the strap, he

218

opened it to pull out his boots. After he put them on, he returned to the bed and lifted the box out, raising the lid. He stared at his revolvers a second before he pulled them out with his holsters. He fastened the gun belt around his waist and tied the leather thongs about his thighs. He whipped his guns out of the holsters several times to get the feel of having them on again.

They felt natural. While it was reassuring, it also bothered him.

He walked to the dresser and picked up the marigold scarf that Clem had left the day they made love. He tied it about his neck. He was not ordinarily a superstitious man, but he always liked to have a good luck charm with him. In case he was facing the sun when he squared off with the gunslinger, he needed a hat to shield his eyes from the glare, to give him a better chance of survival. He would have to borrow one, because he had not brought one with him. He moved to stand in front of the cheval glass.

"It's been a long time since I saw you in those," Prentice said from the door. "How does it feel to have them on again?"

"Natural," Wade answered, "and if it weren't my best defense against Perry, I would be concerned. Looks like my past has finally caught up with me."

Prentice nodded. "I'm counting on you, Wade."

"Will you go into Hadley's bedroom and get me one of his hats. I figure we wear the same size."

When Prentice returned, Wade put it on and adjusted the brim.

"We all look alike, talk alike, and swagger alike, don't we?"

"Maybe so," Prentice agreed, his voice subdued, "but, thank God, you don't think alike. Don't be upset, Wade. It's something you have to do."

"I took them off because I was responsible for the death of one boy," Wade said. "Now I'm strapping them on again in hopes of saving another boy's life."

His hand swept down and closed over the revolver. He pulled it from the holster. The movement was smooth. He had not forgotten how. But was he fast enough? Could he face a man in a shoot-out? It had been five years since he had done so, five years that gave the edge to Perry. Wade was five years slower, five years older.

Ike Perry was young, only twenty-four. His reflexes would be better, his eyesight keener. Wade's heart thumped heavy and fast in his chest. His hands were clammy.

He had always been a peace-loving man. If he had ever brought a dead man in, it was because someone else shot him. Ever since he had hung up his gun, he dedicated his life to fighting for peace, arguing for, and writing about it. Peace was one of the themes of *Cameron's Journal*. Reasonable human beings, he had contended, could solve any problem without the use of violence.

Now he was going against his own beliefs . . . or was he?

The questions plaguing him, he walked out of the room, down the stairs, and out of the house. With resolute strides, he led the way to Frazier's Saloon. Following him were Prentice, Hadley, and Hokie, who held Lucia's hand. As they made their way down the street, people fell in behind them. All were amazed to see Wade wearing revolvers and in the lead. He heard the frenzied whispers and could imagine what they were saying.

Arnold Bedford, mopping his face with a handkerchief, came rushing out of the sheriff's office. His puzzled gaze bounced from Hokie to Hadley to Wade,

220

finally coming to rest on the deputy.

"What's the meaning of this?" he demanded. "That's a madman in there. This is no time for jesting."

"It's not a jest," Wade answered. "Can you swear me in as deputy sheriff?"

Arnold's gaze quickly swept down to the revolvers and back up again. "I can, but I don't reckon I will. I'd rather trust this to Clem than to you."

"You don't have that choice, Mr. Mayor," Wade said, and neither did he, although he knew it would hurt Clem to know what he was doing, "and the quicker you swear me in, the quicker I can take care of the dirty work for you. The quicker I can clean up the town and make it safe for you once again."

"Go ahead, Arnold," Hadley urged, again displaying his blind trust in Wade. "We don't have much time, and he knows what he's doing."

After Hokie nodded his head, Arnold swore Wade in. The deputy rushed across the street, returning with a badge that the major pinned on Wade.

Wade said to Hokie, "Go tell Perry to release the child. Let him know Deputy Sheriff Wade Cameron is waiting in the street for him."

Hokum nodded, tugged his hat, and walked away. When he reached the saloon, he called out Wade's message. In a few minutes Laban McLean came running out, not stopping until he was safe in his grandfather's arms. At the far end of the street, a rider approached. It was Clem. Ike Perry walked onto the boardwalk. Wade stepped into the middle of the street. The crowd moved back out of the way. The atmosphere was tense.

"Howdy, Cameron." Grinning, Ike lounged against the porch railing. "It's been a long time."

Powers came out and stood beside Ike. "Why, that's the dude I was telling you about. He's the one who's gonna do a story for one of them Eastern papers."

Ike laughed. "Hell, Chester, that ain't no dude. That there is Wade Cameron, bounty hunter, the man I've been looking for."

"I knew it," Maybelle said, and turned to see Clem dismounting from her horse. Beaming, she rushed up to her. "I knew I recognized him, Clem. I told you I don't ever forget a face. Wade Cameron's a bounty hunter. He used to work up Kansas way. I remember now. I read about him bringing in that Perry boy."

As Maybelle chattered, filling Clem in on what had happened during her absence, Clem listened with half an ear and stared at Wade, who stood alone facing the gunslinger. She had always sensed that there was so much more about him that she did not know. This is why at times she had the feeling that he, too, was a part of this environment. She had done a lot of thinking while she was in the mountains with Peaceful, first about the shooting of her father and Olviera, and then about herself and Wade.

She was terribly confused. Since she had allowed Wade to make love to her, she had changed. And the change was more than physical; it was more than the loss of her virginity. Before she had not thought beyond being deputy sheriff of Lawful, and while she still wanted to be that, she wanted more out of life.

What she was seeking was unclear, but it sufficed to know she was seeking new dimensions in her life. What had begun as a biological awakening of her body, was now an awakening of her entire being.

Ike Perry's mocking laughter jarred Clem out of her reverie.

"Wade Cameron is the man responsible for my baby brother dying," the gunslinger shouted. "Ain't

222

you, Wade?"

The man who was facing Ike Perry was the man who had helped to initiate this change of attitude and outlook. Right now she feared for his life. How good he had been made no difference. What counted was how good he was *now*, this day. Ike Perry's reputation was daunting, and she knew that if she were facing him, she would be scared. Was Wade? she wondered.

"You're responsible for an innocent boy of sixteen being hung for a crime he didn't commit," Perry taunted.

"I don't care who he is or what he done, Ike," Powers said. "He ain't the one who shot me. The woman did. The sheriff's daughter."

"I'll get the woman in due time, Chester," Ike promised. "Right now, I'm gonna have some fun with the bounty hunter. I've been hunting him for a long, long time."

Clem shoved through the crowd. This was her fight, not Wade's. She was the deputy sheriff, and even if she were not, Powers wanted her, not Wade. She had fought to keep her badge until Rand came, and she would not willingly give it to anyone else, Wade included.

"I wouldn't go out there." Hokum caught her by the shoulders. "Perry's already shot Sam Harper and Grady."

"Are they dead?" Clem asked, her gaze never leaving Ike Perry.

"Sam ain't. Don't know about Grady. He's in the saloon, and we ain't heard a peep out of him."

Clem pulled free from Hokum's clasp. "It's me they want, Hokie. I can't let Wade do my fighting for me. Until Rand gets here, I'm the deputy sheriff."

Hokie shook his head. "Not any more, Clem. Arnold just swore Wade in. He's the deputy sheriff of

Lawful now."

"I don't believe it."

About that time she moved, so that she saw the sunlight glinting off the star that was pinned to Wade's shirt.

"Lost track of you, Cameron," Perry said. "Couldn't find hide or hair of you after you left Dodge."

"I went back East," Wade answered, deliberately giving out information about himself. If he appeared to be easy prey, Perry would let down his guard. That would give him the edge he needed, the edge that five years had taken away from him.

"Scared?" Perry jeered.

Hell, yes, he was scared. Inside he felt like jelly.

"You know I regretted Newby's being hanged for a crime he didn't commit," Wade answered.

"All because of you."

"I thought that for a while," Wade answered, "but through the years, Ike, I realized that *you* were the one responsible for your brother's death. I've always suspected, Ike, that Newby died protecting you. It's too bad the other fellow who rode with you preferred being taken in dead rather than alive, or we might have learned exactly how involved you were in the holdup and murder."

"Just trying to soothe your conscience," Ike replied.

"How's the hand?" Wade asked. He hoped he struck a tender chord.

He had! A sneer of hatred on his face, Ike pushed away from the porch column. His facial features tightened; his lips thinned; and he flexed his left hand that hovered inches away from his gun.

"It took me a long time to learn to use the left hand." Slowly he walked down the steps into the

MORE PASSION AND ADVENTURE AWAIT... YOUR TRIP TO A BIG ADVENTUROUS WORLD BEGINS WHEN YOU ACCEPT YOUR FIRST 4 NOVELS ABSOLUTELY *FREE*
(AN $18.00 VALUE)

Accept your Free gift and start to experience more of the passion and adventure you like in a historical romance novel. Each Zebra novel is filled with proud men, spirited women and tempestuous love that you'll remember long after you turn the last page.

Zebra Historical Romances are the finest novels of their kind. They are written by authors who really know how to weave tales of romance and adventure in the historical settings you love. You'll feel like you've actually gone back in time with the thrilling stories that each Zebra novel offers.

GET YOUR FREE GIFT WITH THE START OF YOUR HOME SUBSCRIPTION

Our readers tell us that these books sell out very fast in book stores and often they miss the newest titles. So Zebra has made arrangements for you to receive the four newest novels published each month.

You'll be guaranteed that you'll never miss a title, and home delivery is so convenient. And to show you just how easy it is to get Zebra Historical Romances, we'll send you your first 4 books absolutely FREE! Our gift to you just for trying our home subscription service.

BIG SAVINGS AND FREE HOME DELIVERY

Each month, you'll receive the four newest titles as soon as they are published. You'll probably receive them even before the bookstores do. What's more, you may preview these exciting novels free for 10 days. If you like them as much as we think you will, just pay the low preferred subscriber's price of just $3.75 each. *You'll save $3.00 each month off the publisher's price.* AND, your savings are even greater because there are never any shipping, handling or other hidden charges—FREE Home Delivery. Of course you can return any shipment within 10 days for full credit, no questions asked. There is no minimum number of books you must buy.

4 FREE BOOKS

TO GET YOUR 4 FREE BOOKS WORTH $18.00 —MAIL IN THE FREE BOOK CERTIFICATE T O D A Y

Fill in the Free Book Certificate below, and we'll send your FREE BOOKS to you as soon as we receive it.

If the certificate is missing below, write to: Zebra Home Subscription Service, Inc., P.O. Box 5214, 120 Brighton Road, Clifton, New Jersey 07015-5214.

FREE BOOK CERTIFICATE

4 FREE BOOKS

ZEBRA HOME SUBSCRIPTION SERVICE, INC.

YES! Please start my subscription to Zebra Historical Romances and send me my first 4 books absolutely FREE. I understand that each month I may preview four new Zebra Historical Romances free for 10 days. If I'm not satisfied with them, I may return the four books within 10 days and owe nothing. Otherwise, I will pay the low preferred subscriber's price of just $3.75 each; a total of $15.00, *a savings off the publisher's price of $3.00.* I may return any shipment and I may cancel this subscription at any time. There is no obligation to buy any shipment and there are no shipping, handling or other hidden charges. Regardless of what I decide, the four free books are mine to keep.

NAME _____

ADDRESS _____ APT _____

CITY _____ STATE ZIP _____

(   )
TELEPHONE _____

SIGNATURE _____
(if under 18, parent or guardian must sign)

Terms, offer and prices subject to change without notice. Subscription subject to acceptance by Zebra Books. Zebra Books reserves the right to reject any order or cancel any subscription.   039102

GET
FOUR
FREE
BOOKS
(AN $18.00 VALUE)

ZEBRA HOME SUBSCRIPTION
SERVICE, INC.
P.O. Box 5214
120 BRIGHTON ROAD
CLIFTON, NEW JERSEY 07015-5214

street. "But I forced myself. Every day that I practiced, my target was you. I knew one of these days that I would meet you. I also knew it would be your loss, because I planned to kill you. But the more time passed, the more I figured I only wanted to cripple you up for life. That would be a greater punishment for you than death. Slowly, Cameron, limb by limb, I'm going to wound you. First your right hand, then your left. Your knees. Your elbows."

"Don't feel too confident, Ike, the best-laid plans sometimes go astray."

Ike's feet were planted firmly to the ground, his legs slightly parted. His gaze was steady, never wavering from Wade's.

"I think the party's over, old man. Time to get on with the business at hand." Ike laughed. "At hand really has a double meaning, don't it, Cameron?"

When Wade had faced Ike before, all the advantages had been on his side, not today. Ike was the younger, his reflexes sharper, his eye sight keener. He also had the afternoon sun to his back. Wade tipped the brim of Hadley's hat to shade out the glare as much as he could, without interfering with his vision. He rubbed his fingers against his clammy palm.

"How long has it been since you've been in a gunfight?" Ike asked.

"You're doing too much talking," Wade said. "Are you stalling for time? Maybe you're scared, huh?"

The crowd quieted, and even nature seemed to hush as Wade and Ike Perry faced each other. Wade's heart thumped loud and heavy; he wondered if Ike could hear it. For the first time in years, Wade was afraid. His eyes never moved from Ike's hand, from his left hand.

God, but he should have killed Ike when he had the chance!

225

In a split second Ike's hand moved, clasped the revolver, and pulled it from the holster. Instinctively Wade reacted, his shot sounding simultaneously with Ike's. He felt the impact when the bullet hit his shoulder and fire burned down his arm. He clamped his teeth together against the pain that seared his body and refused to drop his gun — no matter how badly he hurt.

"Told you," Ike shouted, "that I was gonna take you limb by limb. You're gonna die a slow death, Cameron."

Through pain-glazed eyes, Wade stared at Ike, wondering if he had missed him altogether. Had the years affected his eyesight or his aim that badly? Then he saw the stain as it began to color Ike's shirt.

Ike tottered; he staggered; he almost fell, but caught himself. He aimed the gun at Wade. His gun bellowed, the barrel wavered, going off into the dirt at Wade's boot.

"I'm . . . gonna . . ." Ike's voice trailed away, and he swayed. Slowly his knees buckled; he fell to the ground. He flung out his arm, his gun sliding across the street. A leg straightened. He was dead.

Wade walked to where Ike Perry lay. The crowd followed, making a tight circle around the two men. Exhausted, his arm hurting like hell, Wade dropped his gun into the holster and turned, pushing his way through the wall of people.

Prentice shoved through the spectators until he was at Wade's side. "Is the wound bad?" he asked.

Wade shook his head.

"Maybe now you've laid your past to rest."

"I wish that were true, Prenny, but I think I've just created a new one. It's going to start all over again." They walked toward the saloon. "Young guns are going to feel like they have to take on the one who got

226

Ike Perry. The only way this cycle ends is in death."

So much for his promise!

Behind him, Hadley said, "See if he's got the bill of sale on him."

Wade stopped on the boardwalk in front of the saloon. Hearing a horse gallop down the street, he looked up to see Powers making his getaway. He would make a report to the man he was working for, and only God knew what tomorrow would bring.

A hand touched his arm, and he turned to see Clem who had walked out of the saloon. They stared at each other for a long while. Her eyes were dark with disappointment and pain.

"Are you all right?" she asked—her voice was unnaturally calm. She touched the buttons on his shirt. "Let me see."

He caught her hands in his. "I'm fine."

He wanted to reassure her, but she pulled away from his clasp, from his touch. "You let me assume you were a tenderfoot. You let me make a fool out of myself."

"I didn't mean to embarrass you," he confessed, "but I saw no reason to tell you. Being a bounty hunter was part of my past."

"You were a bounty hunter," she said, "yet you faulted me for being a sheriff, for upholding the law. You accused me of being an executioner hiding behind a badge!"

Her voice throbbed with suppressed anger.

"I apologize," he said.

"Even if I were to accept your apology," she said, "it wouldn't erase the hurt or the humiliation."

"Clem, being a bounty hunter isn't something I'm proud of. Because of me an innocent sixteen-year-old boy was hanged! For the past five years I've had to live with that. After I found the man who was guilty of

227

the crime, I promised myself I'd never wear guns again." He paused, then said, "If it looked like you and I were thinking seriously about each other, I would have told you."

Clem sucked in her breath and nodded. After a moment, she said, "You should have known when you came out here, that you were likely to run into someone you knew back then."

God, but he was weary, and he had hurt her so badly he had no idea if she would ever forgive him . . . or forget. How easily it was to become entangled in the threads of your past; how binding they were.

"That's one of the reasons why I didn't want to come."

"But Nash Dillon offered you enough to tempt you."

"Enough to save my magazine," Wade replied and looked into accusing green eyes. "I told you when I first met you, Clem, I'm not the chivalrous kind. I'm quite pragmatic and materialistic."

"And hypocritical as I see it," Clem pronounced. "You told me you don't condone the code we live by out here, yet you used it for your benefit. At least I believe in it."

Too weary to argue further, really having no further argument, Wade was silent.

Eventually she said, "You need to have your arm looked at."

"I will. How's the bartender?"

"It's only a flesh wound. He was mostly frightened."

"Yeah," Wade drawled, "I guess we all were."

He faced Clem, and she stared at his chest, her hand rising to touch the badge he wore.

"It's not for good," he explained. He took it off and dropped it into his shirt pocket.

"It doesn't matter if it were for good or not," she said. "What matters is that you accepted it at all."

"It was for leverage only."

Never lifting her head, she nodded and unfastened the top buttons of his shirt to look at the shoulder where he was hit. Untying the bandanna from her neck, she folded and placed it over the wound.

"This does need attention," she said a second time.

"Elm's at Hadley's taking care of Sam."

"Then let's head over there, so he can take care of you."

"Clem, please try to understand. Right now, I need *you* more than anyone else in the world."

Clem wanted him to take her into his arms and assure her that everything was going to be all right, but she knew he would not, that he could not. She did not know all that had happened to precipitate the shoot-out, but she did know everything was not going to be all right for a long time, not for Lawful, not for her and Wade.

He only wanted and needed the physical release her body offered to him. His feelings for her were no deeper than lust. She could not retain her integrity and accept such shallow emotion from him. Wade's having made love to her marked a change in her thinking and outlook on life; the shoot-out marked a change in their relationship.

Wade put his arm around Clem, and they began walking toward Hadley's house.

"Clem!" Deborah called, running toward them.

Wade and Clem waited for her.

"Thank God, it wasn't you." Deborah's anxious gaze rushed over her daughter, as if to assure that she was all right.

"No," Clem said, "not this time. I just arrived back in town."

229

Deborah's gaze moved to Wade. "I wasn't aware that you knew much about guns."

Wade looked down at Clem, hesitated, then said, "I'm very familiar with them. For many years I earned my living with them. After I got out of the army, I lived on the frontier. I was a bounty hunter."

Deborah's hand went to her mouth in horror as she listened to Wade recount his story.

"Afterwards, I went back East and started working for newspapers as a detective of sorts," he concluded and wondered how many more times he would have to repeat the story. Probably he would not have to. Hadley would carry it as a first page story in the *Lawful Tribune*.

"Come on, Wade," Clem said. "Let's go see Elm. You need to get that shoulder taken care of."

"When will you be home?" Deborah asked Clem.

"I'm not sure. I'm going over to the office. I have a lot of work to do."

"I'm sure," Deborah said dryly, her gaze flicking between Wade and Clem.

"In case you haven't heard," Clem said impatiently, "Sam Harper has been badly wounded. He could be dead for all I know. Both Grady and Wade are wounded. I have a salt war on my hands, Deborah, and I have to do something about it."

"I'd like for you to come home as early as you can," her mother answered. She turned and pointed to the stately woman who stood across the street holding a little girl by the hand. "Doña Pera and Pilar arrived this morning, and have consented to be our house guests. Do you think you'll be home for supper?"

"I'll try," Clem said.

"Deborah," Maybelle called. "I have those lanterns you wanted for the barbecue tomorrow night. Do you want to come look at them?"

"I'll be right there," Deborah answered the store owner, then said to Clem, "I'd like you to help me plan the barbecue festivities. When you get home, we'll talk about it." Turning, she walked toward the general store.

Thoughts of Doña Pera, Pilar, and the barbecue slid into oblivion. None of them were important to Clem now. Her ego was bruised, and her heart ached. It would be a long time — if ever — before they were healed.

"I didn't want you to learn about me like this," Wade said.

"I would have rather it had been different," she answered, "but what's been done can't be undone." They had taken several steps when she said, "You're better than good with your guns, Wade."

"Am I?" He sighed. He did not like to hear Clem talk in this quiet, resolved tone. "Just because I killed a man today?"

"No, because you defended a town against an outlaw who was intent on doing them harm."

"I suppose I'm your kind of man now," he said.

Clem did not answer immediately. He was in too much pain, emotionally and physically, and would probably misinterpret anything she said. And to be honest, she was hurting, too. In her wildest imagination, she had never figured Wade to be a bounty hunter — a man who hunted other men for the reward. He had said he was materialistic, but she had not counted on this. While her father had used Ramson and Hammond, he had never respected their vocation. She could not visualize Wade in the same category as these two men; yet he had earned his living the same way — hunting down people.

And she had fallen in love with just such a man!

Whatever she might tell herself, however different

231

she might wish it to be, she loved Wade Cameron.

When they arrived at Hadley's home, Elm was walking down the stairs. "Philana had us move Sam up to the guest bedroom," he explained. "He's going to be needing round-the-clock care for a while, and she could do it better here."

The housekeeper followed Elm, her arms filled with soiled towels and Sam's clothing. "I hope you don't mind, Mr. Cameron, but this seemed the reasonable thing to do."

"No, it's fine," Wade replied. "It will actually work out quite well for me to move to the hotel, since I'll be leaving day after tomorrow. I'll have Prentice move my luggage later."

"If he can't," Philana said, "I'll get someone to do it for you."

Standing in front of Wade, Elm pushed his shirt aside and removed Clem's handkerchief. "Did you come out on the long end of the stick?"

Wade grimaced as the doctor's long fingers probed around the wound. "I'm not sure. He's dead, and I'm alive."

"Clean wound," Elm said. "It'll hurt for a while, but it's going to be okay. Let's go in the kitchen, so I can take care of it."

After Elm bandaged Wade's wound and put his arm in a sling, Philana brewed a pot of coffee and the four of them sat around the table, talking about what had happened. Later Hadley opened the door and walked into the room.

"Well, Clem," he said, and laid down the bill of sale on the table, "a Mexican by the name of Joseph Lorenzo bought — rather stole — Harper's property. No proof that Borajo is involved. From the way it looks, this Lorenzo fellow hired Powers and Perry, maybe more, to force Harper, Howard, and Thompson to

232

sale their property around the salt lakes."

Hadley poured himself a cup of coffee and sat down at the table. Looking at Clem, he asked, "Now, what are you going to do about it?" Before she could answer, he turned to Wade. "Or Deputy Sheriff Cameron, what are the two of you going to do about it?"

For the first time since Wade had taken the badge off and dropped it into his pocket, Clem remembered he had been duly sworn in as the deputy sheriff. Arnold had done for him what he refused to do for her. Clem understood Wade had wanted it for leverage, and she did not blame him. But she should have been here to do her duty, instead of visiting with Peaceful in the mountains. Had she been here Wade would not have needed to wear the star . . . her star.

She was also overly sensitive when it came to the badge. It had meant a lot to her father that she wear it; *it meant a lot to her.* He would not have liked the idea of a bounty hunter being deputy sheriff of Lawful, no matter what the reason. She could only wonder what her father's reaction would be if he knew her lover was a bounty hunter.

Wade pulled the badge out of his pocket and laid it on the table. "I'm not sure what the two of us are going to do," he answered. "Any questions you have in regards to this should be directed to Clem. She's the only deputy sheriff Lawful has. I just resigned."

Clem noticed that Wade was looking tired, and that he gently rubbed his arm as if he were in pain.

"I think you'd better get to the hotel, so you can rest," she said.

Hadley looked confused, and Philana quickly explained why Wade was leaving.

"Want me to drive you over there?" Hadley asked. "My buckboard is right out front, the team still hitched."

"No," Wade answered, "I'll walk."

"Yes, sir," Emmett said, waving his hand around the upstairs suite, a parlor and a bedroom, "you can have these rooms free of charge, Mr. Cameron. They're the best we have."

"I appreciate the gesture," Wade said, and walked to one of the large chairs and sat down.

His arm ached abominably, and he was tired. He wanted Frazier to leave so he could have some peace and quiet, so that he and Clem could be alone. At most he had little time left with her, and he did not want to share it with a third person. He had to get through this invisible wall she had built around herself since she returned to Lawful.

"Thanks, Emmett," Clem said and guided him to the door.

"Would you like for me to bring up some lunch?" he asked.

"That would be nice," Wade answered.

"Anything else I can do for you?"

Just leave, Wade thought, but only shook his head.

When the door closed behind Emmett, Clem walked into the bedroom and turned down the covers. Then she returned to the parlor.

"Why don't you lie down and rest?"

Wade wanted to protest, but the longer he sat, the more he realized he was weak and light-headed. He rose and walked into the other room. With one hand he began to unfasten his gun belt.

"Here, let me," Clem said, and moved so that she was in front of him. When she had unfastened the belt, she laid it on the dresser. After she removed the sling from his arm, she tugged the shirt from his trousers, unbuttoned and slid it from his shoulders, her

234

fingers grazing his flesh.

"Sit down," she said, "I'll take your boots off for you."

His boots and socks off, she knelt in front of him. He reached out and brushed tendrils of hair from her face. "My past makes a difference in the way you feel about me, doesn't it?"

"Yes. It's going to take some getting used to," she admitted. "I—bounty hunters aren't people whom I admire—admired."

"I never provoked a shooting, Clem."

Her dark gaze pinned on him.

"I killed only in self-defense, and I always brought my man in alive. I lived by the same code that you and your father live by."

"How you must have laughed at me," she mused.

"No," he assured her. "I found your concern endearing. I appreciated that you would go out of your way to take care of me."

She rose.

"I missed you, Clem. I'm glad you're back."

"Me, too," she said, in a cool, detached voice. As if she were his nurse rather than his lover, she said, "Now go to bed. You need to rest."

He nodded and grimaced as pain splintered through his arm and shoulder. "Will you stay with me?"

"No."

Chapter Fourteen

Clem did stay.

Sprawled across the bed on his back, Wade slept as Clem sat in the chair across the room from his bed. She watched his chest rise and fall. No longer tossing and turning, he rested easier now than when he had first lain down.

No matter how disappointed she might be, she could not leave him. A part of her wanted to despise and distrust him, because he had been a bounty hunter and because he had kept his past from her. Another part argued there had been no reason for him to confide in her. What she and Wade had shared, although intimate, had been nothing more than . . . lust.

She could hardly say the word. Still that was the impetus to their having made love. Wade had made no secret of desiring and wanting to make love to her, but his doing so did not come out of any feeling for Clem. He simply desired her body.

He had also warned her that women usually fall in love with their first lover. She had promised herself that she would not let her heart become involved. This was an affair; she would enjoy the moment and take the pleasure it offered. But Clem was quickly learning she was not casual about her feelings for herself or for others. Since she and Wade had made love, she felt differently toward him, and whether she wanted her heart involved or not, it was.

Before, when she thought about a man and a woman making love, she had been curious about it. Now, when she thought about the wonderful things Wade could do to her body, the excitement and passion his touch generated, she yearned for the same fulfillment, that same aliveness again and again. Now when she thought about a man and a woman making love, she thought about being married to Wade and of their spending their lives together. She could not imagine life without him. In such a short period of time, he had become a part of her.

Although she had been hurt and in a way angered today, by his having been sworn in as deputy sheriff and having disclosed that he was a bounty hunter, she still wanted him. She wanted him more now than before.

Wade rolled over, muttering in his sleep. Clem stood and walked to the bed, brushing his hair from his forehead. He felt fevered to the touch. Her hand strayed to his chest; the flesh there was also hot. Pouring water into the basin, she wet a cloth, then blotted his face and chest. Afterwards she folded it and laid it across his forehead. She stood for a long while gazing down at his body, the handsome sculpture of muscles ruined by the blood-stained bandage. Every ten or fifteen minutes, she would rinse the cloth and reapply it to his forehead.

She was sitting on the side of the bed when he opened his eyes. He looked at her, then around the room. He pushed up on his elbow, grimaced with pain, and collapsed on the pillows.

"For a minute," he said, "I forgot where I was."

"The hotel," she said. "How's your arm?"

"Hurting a little," he answered and moved gingerly, again wincing from pain. "How long have I been asleep?"

"A couple of hours. By the time lunch was brought up, you were asleep. Would you like something to eat?"

"I thought you weren't going to stay with me," he said, lifting his hand to brush tendrils of hair from her face.

"I couldn't leave. I was worried about you." She dropped the cloth into the basin and stood.

"Clem—"

Walking to the dresser, she picked up a bottle of medicine.

"Prentice and Elm came by.

"What did Prentice want?"

To warn me not to fall in love with you. To let me know that I'm not suitable for you.

"He wanted to check on you. He said he'd come by later."

His obviousness exaggerated by an unsuccessful attempt at subtlety, Prentice had pointed out that Wade was not the typical bounty hunter and should not be condemned out of hand. He had received his degree from Harvard; his mother had been a member of an old aristocratic New York family. Although they no longer had money, they were still a prestigious name. Wade moved in high society, and his fee for searching for Bryan Dillon made him a wealthy man again. Wade had his choice of women back East; women who would easily fit into his social circle.

"Elm left some medicine for you to take. He said it would help with the aches and pains. You're to mix a tablespoon of it in a glass of water every four hours. He said it will probably make you drowsy."

"Clem, at the moment I don't give a damn about

238

Prentice, Elm, or medicine. Please come sit down and let's talk." Wade sat up, moaned, and fell back on the mattress. "Oh, God!"

Clem ran to the bed and put her arms around him. "Wade, what's wrong?"

"Nothing, now that you're here with me."

She pulled back, but he caught her hand and held her.

"Guess I'm getting old, Clementina. I can't take getting shot up like I used to." He touched her face. "Thanks for staying with me."

"You're welcome," she murmured. "And whether you want it or not, it's time for your medicine." She rose, moved to the dresser where she mixed the medicine in water, and brought it back to him.

He drained the glass and made a face. "I don't know which is worse, the pain or the medicine."

"Elm said it was an Indian herb that would relax you and allow your body to heal itself. He also said you'd have lots of dreams tonight."

"I'd much rather do other things tonight than dream," he said.

As Clem gazed into his eyes, despite all her resolve, despite her lectures to herself, anticipation began to pulsate through her body, a rush of expectation she had never known before she met Wade.

"Right now," Clem said, her voice sounding husky to her own ears, "you'd better eat." She cleared off the night table; then she walked into the parlor, returning with the tray of food.

"You know we're going to have to talk sometimes, Clem," Wade said. "You can't run from it forever."

"We've talked," she said and lifted the covers from the dishes. "There's nothing more to say."

"What about us?"

"There's never been an us, Wade." She returned to

239

her chair. "There's been you and me. Each had his own reasons for doing—for doing what he did. I simply allowed myself to get caught up in passion, and you—"

"Yes." She felt Wade's dark gaze pinned to her. "And I what?"

"I was available," she answered, "and willing to make love to you. You were perfectly willing and happy to teach me the rudiments of making love. The only us that was involved was our desire not to get married."

"Clem," Wade swung his legs over the side of the bed, grimaced, then paused a moment to take a deep gulp of air. "I know we started this for those reasons, but I really do care about you."

Clem smiled. "I care about you; otherwise, I wouldn't be here to see that you eat and take your medicine. I've even ordered a bath to be sent up for you. While caring is wonderful in friendship, Wade, it's not the emotion upon which an *us* relationship is built. As inexperienced as I am, I know that. My mother cared for my father, but that was not enough to bond them together in a happy marriage."

Slowly he stood and walked to her. Placing his hand on her shoulder, he asked, "We never discussed the possibility of marriage."

"No," Clem said, "we didn't."

"Are you regretting what we shared?"

She shook her head. "No."

"When I leave for El Paso, will you come with me?"

"I gave it some thought, when I was in the mountains with Peaceful," she said.

"And?"

"No," she answered. "Now why don't you eat?"

He gazed at her darkly for a moment, then nodded and dropped his hand from her shoulder. "Only if you'll join me."

"I will. I'm rather hungry myself." She dragged her chair across the room, sitting across the night table from him.

"Did you enjoy your trip to the mountains?"

She nodded. "Everyone was warning me about the dangers of my trip, and nothing happened to me. Not so here. Ike Perry comes to town, nearly kills Sam Harper, forces him to sign a bill of sale for his property, and challenges you."

"He didn't challenge me," Wade said. "He challenged the deputy sheriff."

Munching on a piece of chicken, Clem leaned back in her chair. "Was that why Arnold gave you the badge?"

"Partly, but he also gave it to me, because I wasn't going out on that street and fight a duel of death with a man unless I had the law on my side. I had done enough of bounty hunting, Clem. I wasn't going out there as Wade Cameron, bounty hunter." He leaned across the table and caught her hand in his and squeezed. "I meant it when I said I didn't want your badge, Clem. I don't. It's yours to do with as you like."

Clem believed him; she felt his sincerity; she saw it in his eyes. "I'm going to keep it until Rand gets here, and I've decided to run for sheriff in the next election."

With a heavy heart, she knew that she and Wade had no future together. Their love was not fated to be. She had read about starcrossed lovers, and perhaps they were. Maybe the only star in her life was the badge.

She knew—whether they married or not—the only man for her was Wade.

Wade gazed solemnly at her and said nothing. She

saw the anger stir in his eyes . . .

"You disagree," she said.

"You say you want to be sheriff because you believe in justice, and because you want to protect the citizens of Lawful," he countered. "But if you become sheriff, you're putting the lives of the very people you're sworn to protect in danger. You know as well as I do that every gunslinger in the country is going to come by here to take on the fast-drawing, gun-toting woman sheriff. This town will attract riffraff like—"

"The Sheriff wanted me to expose Borajo, and I intend to do that," Clem interrupted, clearly regretting that she had invited Wade's opinion, when she knew it would be diametrically opposed to hers. And what did he know about her and her being a law enforcer? "I could do it without the badge, but unlike you, *when you were a bounty hunter*, I want to be on the side of the law when I do."

Wade glowered at her, but said nothing more. Clem lowered her head and took a bite of food that was absolutely tasteless.

Eventually Wade asked, "Do you ever think about marriage and a family of your own, Clem?"

"Yes," she answered. For the past three days, she had thought a great deal of having a husband and a family. But it would not be fair for her to admit that to Wade. He had made it clear to her that marriage was not one of his primary interests, and certainly was not on his immediate agenda. "But not right now. I have too many other things to do with my life. A husband and children will come later. When they do, I'll give them all my time and devotion."

"You could be pregnant even now."

He was worried about her conceiving, she thought. Well, she could set his mind at ease. "I could, but I don't think so. But I no longer have that worry. I had

242

the medicine woman give me some herbs that will keep me from conceiving."

Wade's fork clattered against the plate as it fell from his hands. He looked so astounded that Clem laughed.

"You look as if I've shocked you."

"I've never met a woman like you," he said.

"Thank you. I just wanted you to know that you don't have to feel guilty."

"Guilt has nothing to do with my feelings for you," he said.

When the medicine woman had given her the herbs, Clem had not known if she would take them or not. All the way back from the village, she had thought about giving birth to Wade's and her child. She found the thought most pleasing.

Now none of that would happen because she had thought about all Prentice had said, and she agreed with him, not that she would have listened to him if she had not believed the same things deep within her heart. She was not the kind of woman Wade would marry, when he did marry. She was merely a diversion while he was out here searching for Bryan Dillon, and she did not intend to be anyone's diversion.

They were looking at one another when a knock sounded through the room. Reluctantly Clem rose and went to answer the door.

"Hello, Prentice," she said.

"I thought I'd come by to see if Wade is awake," he said, his eyes not quite making contact with hers. "The townsfolk are concerned about him and would like to have a report."

"He just awakened," she answered. "I've given him his medicine, and he's eating a bite of lunch. Would you like to see him?"

Prentice followed her into the bedroom. "How's the

arm?"

"I won't be doing anything too strenuous for a good while," Wade answered.

"Hadley wants to do a story on you."

Prentice glanced uneasily at Clem, and she knew he was wondering if she had told Wade about their conversation earlier. She decided to let him squirm; that would serve him right for presuming to tell her who and what Wade needed in his wife.

"He told me to let him know when he could come by."

Wade laughed. "I figured that. If I'm feeling better later, I'll talk with him."

"I'm going to get to do the drawing that will accompany the feature," Prentice said, and reached over to pick up a drumstick. "I was wondering if this is going to make a difference in our catching the stage to El Paso day after tomorrow."

"Yes," Wade answered.

Prentice nodded. "You're not going to leave until you feel that this salt situation is under control?"

"That among other things. Remember, I want to talk with Doña Pera."

Prentice looked at Clem and scowled; then he looked back at Wade. "This isn't your battle. You did what you had to do today, but the problems these people are having with those damned salt lakes are theirs, not yours. You don't have to fight for them."

"He's right," Clem said.

"You could have gotten killed," Prentice pointed out. "Time has made a difference, Wade."

"Are you telling me that I'm too old for this kind of life?" Wade grinned at his cousin.

"You've been away from it for too long."

"Only this morning you seemed to be proud of what I was doing," Wade said.

244

"That's when you were fighting for yourself."

"Thanks for the concern, but it's my decision to make," Wade said.

"So we're staying," Prentice announced. "Can I get you anything?"

"Just make sure my luggage is moved over here," Wade answered. "I want to change clothes."

"I'm on my way to do that now," Prentice replied and rose. "Elm said to send for him if you needed him. Also I need to give the deputy a report. Lots of people are asking about you, Wade. You've become their hero. They think they have another Clement in you."

While the cousins talked, one of the hotel attendants came upstairs to light the fire in the parlor; then the tub of cold water and towels were brought up, with a promise to deliver the hot water in an hour.

After Prentice left, Clem said, "Wade, listen to him. This is our problem, not yours."

"It became mine today," he said. "We both know that whoever is behind this salt takeover isn't going to give in this easily. More gunfighters are reported to be in El Paso, and they'll be coming this way soon. It could be an even bigger fight than we first supposed."

"Still, it's my fight, Wade, not yours." She stacked the dishes on the tray.

"I'm not leaving you to face these men alone," he said. "Hokie and Turbin are good men, but they're not gunfighters. You need someone by your side who is as good if not better than you are, Clem. Surely your father taught you that."

He removed a dish from her, set it on the tray, and caught her hand. "Please look at me."

She did.

"Whether you want to admit it or not, I'm that man."

245

She looked down at the hand that held hers fast.

"Yes," she said softly, "you are that man."

He was the man who had awakened her to the yearnings of her body, the man she wanted beside her for the rest of her life, the man whom she wanted to father her children. He was the man who would soon be leaving her, returning to a life of which she would not be a part, a life of which she knew nothing.

"Let me straighten up the mess. One of the servants will be up shortly to get the tray."

With a sigh, he released her and pushed back into the pillows. She completed stacking the dishes and carried the tray into the parlor.

Returning to the room, she asked, "Would you like for me to go now?"

"No, I'd rather not be alone, if you don't mind. Facing Perry today brought back a lot of memories, memories that may have been better left hidden."

"It's better you came back and faced them, Wade."

She walked to the window and stared at the activity in the street. Only hours before a man had been killed. Now people were moving about, tending to their business as if nothing had happened. Another body lay in the undertaking room; Maybelle had another sale.

"Perry's out of your life permanently now, and you did it the right way."

"The only way," he said, then asked, "Were you surprised to find that the bill of sale was not in Borajo's name?"

"Yes, I was so sure it would be. I told Hokie the other day that we have so few pieces of this puzzle, and none of them fit together. It's hard to know what to do, when you don't even know who you're up against. The salt flats are not so important or lucrative that those gunslingers would want control of them."

She reached into her shirt pocket and pulled out the crumpled up bill of sale. Reading it, she said, "Joseph Lorenzo. The name is familiar, but that may be because it's a common name around here."

"I don't know one way or the other," Wade answered, "but you have to realize, Clem, I haven't been keeping up with what's going on out here. There's going to be lots of names that I don't recognize."

She returned the paper to her pocket. "I'd better get going," she said. "I told Deborah I'd be home for dinner tonight. She wants me to help her with the barbecue tomorrow."

He held out his arm and beckoned to her. "Would you tell me goodbye?"

"Good-bye," she said.

He patted the mattress.

"No." She walked to the door.

"Clem, will you have dinner with me tonight?"

"No, I promised Deborah that I'd spend the evening with her and Doña Pera."

Clem and six-year-old Pilar sat on the floor of the parlor, watching as Doña Pera pulled one beautiful dress after another out of the large trunk. But Clem's thoughts were not on the clothing.

"I know that you prefer to wear the trousers, Clem," the doña said, her brown eyes twinkling, "but it is time that you also wore dresses. I am sure that you can find several in here that will fit you nicely, and if they don't, you may alter them."

"Thank you for the offer," Clem said, reluctantly dragging her thoughts from Wade and looking at the growing pile of dresses beside Doña Pera, "but I couldn't take any of these dresses. I'll buy some mate-

247

rial at the store and have Anona make me some."

"Even a seamstress with a reputation as widespread as Anona Cuellar would not be able to sew you a dress for the barbecue tomorrow."

"I'll have a dress to wear the next time you come," Clem promised.

"I want you to wear one tomorrow," Doña Pera said.

Truth of the matter, for one of the few times in her life, Clem did also. She wanted Wade to see her in a dress. She knew that she could not begin to compete with the women in Wade's life in terms of sophistication, but she could show him that she was feminine when the occasion called for it. Simply because she was from the West did not mean she had no class or culture.

"You'll have to choose one of these," the doña continued. "As you well know, I travel with many suitcases. I buy plenty for my nieces and nephews. There is enough in here for you to take several, without anyone missing them."

Although the trunk was almost as deep as Pilar was tall, the child eagerly dug through the clothing, yanking out dresses and tossing them to the side. Finally she found one that pleased her. She lifted it out of the trunk, then straightened, her thick black braids falling over her shoulders. Her brown eyes, flecked with green and unusually beautiful, glistened.

"Here, Clem," she said, holding the dress up by the shoulders. "Look at this one. It's my favorite."

Clem took the green gingham from the child.

"It's beautiful," Deborah said.

The material was bright as spring.

"You want it," Doña Pera said, "take it. Go into the bedroom and try it on. Let's see how it fits you."

Clem looked at her mother, who nodded.

"Try it on."

Without a second bidding, Clem rose and moved into her bedroom, stripping out of her clothes. She slipped the dress on and twirled around in front of the cheval glass. It fit snugly and in all the right places; she filled it out. She ran her hand over her breasts and down her rib cage. She clasped her hands at her waist. She felt beautiful and feminine.

"Clem," Deborah called, "let us see."

She returned to the parlor and stood in the door, looking from Doña Pilar to her mother. For a second neither said a word; they stared. For a woman who was sanguine with her role in life as a peace officer, complete with guns, trousers, and boots, Clem began to doubt her ability to be feminine. Maybe she only felt beautiful to herself.

Pilar leapt up from the floor, clapping her hands, dancing, and chanting, "Clementina, you are beautiful."

Deborah rose, walking to her daughter, their gazes locked together. Clem had not realized how important it was for her to have her mother's approval. Her lungs seemed to have stopped working; her heart thundered against her breasts.

Deborah touched Clem's shoulder to smooth a wrinkle. Her voice when she spoke was teary. "You are beautiful, Daughter. Even in your trousers and shirts, you were beautiful. Tall and slender and majestic."

Clem sucked long-needed oxygen into her lungs, and she smiled—a smile that began in the depths of her soul and colored her eyes and her lips.

"You're still that same woman, but in a dress, you're softer."

"Yes, Deborah," Doña Pera said, "she is a beautiful blending of you and Clement. From what I've observed, she has inherited the strongest traits in both of you."

Never in her life had anyone compared Clem to her parents. This thrilled her. "Do you really think so?"

The old woman tilted her silver head and smiled. "Yes, my child, I do, or I wouldn't have said it. Now get down there and select two or three more dresses."

"I'll only need this one for the barbecue," Clem reminded her.

"But you will soon have a beau," Doña Pera said, and again the brown eyes glistened, "and you will want a few dresses to wear for him. It's good to let them see that you are strong, but it's also wise to let them know you're a woman. As your mother has said, in a dress a woman can look softer and more vulnerable." She waved an index finger through the air. "Now, mind you, that doesn't *make* you softer and more vulnerable. It simply gives you the advantage at times because you appear so."

Clem leaned over the trunk again and began to sort through the dresses. The women laughed together as they talked and jested and exchanged women's talk. This was another first for Clem, and she truly enjoyed the conversation.

But underlying her happiness was the thought that the beau she had chosen for herself would soon be leaving, and he did not return her feelings.

With her mother's help, Clem selected two more gowns, a blue cambric housedress and a rose-colored ball gown. She had changed out of her green dress and was hanging her new things in her armoire, when Deborah walked into the room.

"You're going to look lovely tomorrow," her mother said. "Green is a beautiful color for you. You're going to be the center of attention, and will have to fight the single men from around you."

"Perhaps," Clem murmured.

250

She wanted the attention only of one man, and while she had it for the moment, he would soon be gone. She knew in her heart of hearts that she would never love another man. She did not rule out that she would someday get married and have children, but she would never love another man as she loved Wade.

"Is something wrong?" Deborah asked.

"No."

"It's Wade Cameron, isn't it?" Deborah said. She walked to the armoire and ran her hands over the fabric of the dresses. "You're infatuated with him, aren't you?"

"Yes." Her back to her mother, Clem moved to the chest of drawers. She did not turn around; she could not. She knew that her emotions would be written on her face and in her eyes for her mother to read. She could admit to her feelings and make her admission sound more objective. But if her mother saw her face, if she read her heart, she would know how deeply involved she was with Wade.

"How does he feel about you?"

Drawing in several deep breaths, masking her emotions, Clem put on her brightest smile and turned. "He likes me, but that's all. He mostly wants to be around me so that he can get material to write the story about Papa."

As Clem had known she would, Deborah searched her face for an inkling to her deepest feelings for Wade. Finally she said, "That's not true, Clem. Wade Cameron is infatuated with you. I can tell it by the way he looks at you."

Clem said nothing.

"What's going to happen when he leaves?"

"He's asked me to go with him."

"He wants to marry you?" Deborah asked.

"No."

Nonplused, Deborah stared at Clem. "Are you going with him?"

"No." *But I want to. Knowing how he feels about me, knowing there can be no future for us, I still want to go.*

Chapter Fifteen

"Wade, are you up yet?" Prentice knocked on the parlor door at the same time that he called out.

"Stop the pounding," Wade shouted back, using his good arm to push out of bed. He stood a moment flexing his shoulders and his arms, especially the wounded one. It was still stiff and painful, but manageable. He flexed his hand several times to limber the fingers. They were almost as good as if he were not hurt.

Standing, he tugged the top sheet and wrapped it around his waist, part of it trailing behind as he walked to the other room. After he unlocked and opened the door, he said, "I would have expected anyone but you."

Prentice scowled and pushed by his cousin to march into the room. Over his shoulder, he said, "Clementina Jones, maybe . . . hopefully? I have a feeling she's the reason you were glad to be moved over here. Now you and your visitors can have a privacy that was denied you and them at Hadley's."

"Do I hear censure in your voice?" Wade asked.

"Yes, you do," Prentice answered. "Nash Dillon isn't paying you a million dollars to fight for those salt lakes or to dally with the deputy sheriff. You're jeopardizing our trip."

"You're here with me because I invited you along," Wade said, "but you're not my conscience. Nash is paying me to search for Bryan Dillon, and I'll do it my way in my own time. Now, if you don't like the way I'm doing it, buy a ticket on the next eastbound stage and head for home."

"I didn't mean to upset you," Prentice said, "but, Wade, you got yourself all shot up yesterday, and that was okay because this was something personal for you, but, damn it, you're not personally interested in the Chupedera Salt Flats."

"Prentice—" Anger surged through Wade in such proportions he had to restrain himself from jerking his cousin up by the lapels and throwing him out of the room. "Shut up. I don't want to hear another word about my staying in Lawful, about the salt lakes, or *about Clementina!*"

Prentice nervously brushed his hand through his hair and gazed at Wade. Finally he lowered his head and mumbled, "I thought maybe you'd be up and ready for breakfast. Afterwards we could go to the sheriff's house, so you could talk with Doña Pera about Bryan."

Although Wade was furious at his cousin for interfering with his life, he also felt guilty. It had been a long time since he had given Bryan Dillon more than a cursory thought. Most of his thoughts were reserved for Clem; surely all his feelings and emotions were.

"Give me a few minutes," he said and turned toward his bedroom, "and I'll get dressed."

"Wade," Prentice said, "I apologize. I didn't mean to make you angry."

Wade lightly slapped his cousin on the shoulder. "No offense taken," he said.

Wade strode back into the bedroom, moving to the window to raise the shade to allow early morning sunlight to spill into the room.

"By the way, I ordered breakfast while I was downstairs, and asked that they bring it to your room. I hope you don't mind," Prentice called.

"Fine time to ask me. Just make sure I don't have to pay for it."

"No worry, Wade, you're a local hero. You're not going to have to pay for a thing. Around here, they venerate you almost as much as they do Clement Jones. Right now, if I've figured it right, you and Rand McGaffney are running a close second. Another shoot-out or two, especially one between the two of you, and we'll know who's first."

"Is that meant to be sarcastic?"

"No," his cousin answered, "it's just a simple statement that reflects the way life is out here . . . so it seems."

Deciding his arm felt well enough so that he did not have to wear the sling today, Wade dressed quickly, donning trousers, shirt, and socks. Then, with no hesitation, he slipped into his boots. Now that his reputation was revealed, there was no sense hiding his expertise with a gun, and if something untoward happened, Clem would need him and need him right then, not later. As quickly he fastened his gun belt around his waist and picked up Hadley's hat. Shortly after breakfast was delivered to the suite, he stepped into the parlor.

Prentice, sitting at the table in front of the window with his mouth full of pancakes and sausage, gave Wade the once-over. He leaned back and dabbed his mouth with the linen napkin. He said nothing, but he did not have to. His gaze spoke volumes; it was full of disapproval.

Prentice waved his hand over the table. "Join me. I've ordered enough for both of us."

Placing the hat on the table beneath an ornate wall mirror, Wade eyed the fried eggs and potatoes, mounds of grits, and pancakes and syrup. Then he spied the pot of coffee. "It looks good, but after taking that concoction Elm gave me, my stomach isn't up to this. I'll just have a cup of coffee."

"How many do you figure will be coming, Wade?" Prentice asked.

"To the barbecue?"

"Gunmen." He talked between bites of food. "Last night I listened to Hokie and Turbin talk in the saloon. They said it wouldn't stop with Perry. In fact, they think Perry's death will bring them in droves."

"They're probably right," Wade conceded. Coffee in hand, he wandered over to the window and gazed into the street. "That's one of the reasons why I have to stay, Prentice. I can't leave Clem here to face them alone. I just hope Rand gets here soon. We sure need his gun."

"You know she's in love with you," Prentice said.

His back to his cousin, Wade asked, "What makes you say that?"

"While you were sleeping yesterday, she and I visited together."

Wade turned, his anger tempered with curiosity. Just what had Clem said to Prentice? "And she confessed her love for me?"

"No, but I could tell. She asked me about your life in New York, and I described it to her." His gaze never wavering from Wade's, he said, "I know you were angry at me a minute ago for interfering with your life, Wade, but Clem has a right to know. If you care about her, you can't keep leading her on. If you're thinking about taking her back to New York with you, you're not being fair to either one of you. What's going to happen when you tire of her? When you meet the next amour."

Wade wanted to be angry at Prentice; he wanted to lash out at him, but this time he could not. Every-

256

thing his cousin said was true. Throughout his adult life he had flitted from one casual relationship to another. Yet Clem was more than any of these relationships had been. His feelings for her were deeper; he truly admired and respected her.

As old and trite as the expression was, Clem brought brightness to his life. When he was with her, he saw life through her eyes. He was teaching her to love, or was he merely teaching her the skills with which to make love? She was teaching him more; she was teaching him to laugh again and to care . . . and to love.

Yesterday after she had left him, after she had refused to kiss him good-bye, he had felt lonely and rejected—a first for him where women were concerned. Intermittently through the afternoon, he had toyed with the idea of taking her back to New York with him, but he kept telling himself she would not fit. He was not sure that she would want to.

A crowd had already gathered at the Joneses when Wade arrived. As he moved through the crowd, the people greeted him with smiles and congratulated him on the way he handled Ike Perry. They talked with him and asked his opinion on various and sundry matters that were part of their everyday lives. In a matter of hours, they had forgotten he was a reporter from back East. Now he was one of them. In fact, he was learning that, since he was an expert in handling a gun, he was considered to be an expert period—bar no subject.

In the backyard he worked with the men and women getting the barbecue pits ready. Wagons lumbered up, loaded with the beef, pork, and chicken; he supervised the unloading. Soon the meat was on spits, that were rotated during the day until the meat was done. He would have joined in the games, but his shoulder was too sore for strenuous activities. Besides, he needed to use the time to visit with Doña Pera.

He slowly made his way to the front of the house to find the Mexican *haciendada* sitting in the shade of a large tree. She cooled herself with an ornate fan, decorated in gold and ivory.

"Doña Pera," he said, walking up to her. "I'm Wade Cameron, a journalist from New York. If it wouldn't be an inconvenience, I would like to talk with you for a few minutes."

"I always find it an honor when a handsome young man wants to talk with me," she said. "What do you wish to speak about?"

"I'm searching for a man by the name of Bryan Dillon who may have been in or around El Paso."

Doña Pera folded the fan and laid it in her lap. Gazing into Wade's face, she said, "You think I should know something about this man?"

Wade sat down at her feet. "I hope you do. Clem and her mother told me that you have lived in the El Paso vicinity all your life."

She nodded her head.

"It seems logical to me," Wade continued, "that if this man indeed had been out here, you would have heard about him, at least."

"I don't recognize him by name," she said, "but tell me something about him."

While Wade told her all he knew about Bryan Dillon, Clem—wearing shirt and trousers—joined them, also sitting at the doña's feet. She quietly listened.

When Wade was through telling her the entire story, Doña Pera said, "All you have of him is knowledge of his watch showing up in New Orleans? The watch with the daffodil engravings?"

Wade nodded and pulled his watch from his pocket. He handed it to her. She studied it intently.

"The original one," Wade repeated himself, "the one that was given to Bryan when he was a young man, ended up at a jeweler's in New Orleans. From it a mold was made so that a lady's timepiece could be crafted. The man who ordered it never returned to pick it up."

"You know this to be a fact?" the doña asked.

Wade nodded.

She turned the watch over several times, looking closely at the daffodil engravings. "It is a beautiful watch, *Senor*, and an interesting story, but I have never heard of a man called Bryan Dillon." She returned the watch to him. "Why is this man being sought for after all these years?"

"He has a brother who is alive and who wants to find him or his heirs. They are an extremely wealthy family, *Senora*, but Nash and his wife have no children. If Bryan is alive or if he has heirs, he—and or they—would inherit the Dillon estate."

"I'm sorry," she murmured, picking up her fan and gently swinging it back and forth in front of her face. "I cannot help you, *Senor* Cameron."

Wade returned the watch to his pocket. "Perhaps you know of a man called the Blacksmith?"

She stopped fanning again to gaze pensively into his face. She opened her mouth, and when she spoke, she seemed to be groping through her thoughts. "Do you think this man is somehow connected with Bryan Dillon?"

"Most of the time I don't know," Wade confessed, "but other times I think he is. Judging from what people have told me about him, and from his photographs, he's not the run-of-the-mill cowboy."

"No," Doña Pera said, "the Blacksmith is truly a unique if not mysterious man. He and Clement rode together when they were younger men, and before Clement became sheriff of Lawful. The one called the

Blacksmith rode farther west. Some years ago he returned to El Paso, and the last I heard of him he was
living in Mexico."

"Do you know what town?" Wade asked. "I'm curious about him, and would like to talk with him to set
my mind at ease."

"I know the town," the matriarch said, "but sometimes, *Senor*, one's past is best kept secret if one is trying to make a future for himself. I'm sure the
Blacksmith would not want me to talk about him."
The brown eyes settled on the revolvers Wade wore.
She rose. "Now, if you will excuse me, I am an old
woman who gets stiff if she sits too long. I will walk
around and meet the guests."

Although Wade knew she had revealed all she intended to, he rose with her. "Doña Pera, please, tell
me where he is. A man is looking for his brother, and
this is one of three leads I have to him."

The old woman turned and looked at Wade. Finally
she said, "He lives in the mountains of Mexico, in a
small village not many miles south of El Paso. Stop at
the mission in San Miguel; the padre will show you
how to reach him." Then she swept off, her black skirt
trailing behind.

"Well," Clem said quietly, "you have a definite lead.
You know that the Blacksmith is alive, and where he
is."

Wade nodded his head, but he could not feel happy
yet. Somehow he had the feeling that the closer he
was to one of the leads, the farther and farther Bryan
was slipping into obscurity. And really the Blacksmith
was not a clue to Bryan; he was a mystery that Wade
wanted to solve for himself.

More significantly, Wade felt that the closer he was
to finding Bryan, the shorter his time with Clem. Perhaps Prentice was right in his assessment. Maybe
Wade was deliberately postponing his search so that

he could stay with Clem. The mere thought of leaving her tore at his heart.

Clem stretched out on the patch of grass. "Perhaps you'll soon have your mystery solved."

"Whether I find him or not, I'm close. I can feel it in my bones." But Wade did not want to waste this precious time together, talking about Bryan. He looked at her and, lowering his voice to a whisper, said, "That's not all I'm feeling, Miss Clementina Jones."

"What do you think of the gala event? I don't suppose it compares to the parties you attend in New York?"

"Deliberately changing the subject?" he teased.

"Yes."

She was still hurting from yesterday, he thought. "You have quite a crowd."

"It's going to grow," she said. "By nightfall, it'll be twice this big. After supper, we'll have music and dancing. The lanterns will be glowing, and the sky will be lit up with millions of stars."

"Can you dance?"

"I can, but not too well. Deborah taught me before she left, but I haven't had much practice."

"Promise me all the dances."

"No," she replied. "If you want one, you'll have to sign my card."

"You little vixen." He touched her face, intending to run his fingers over the sprinkling of freckles, but she pulled away from him. "You're guaranteeing that I'll be here and be here on time."

"No," she answered. "I don't care if you come or not. If you want a dance with me, you'll have to get in line with the rest of the men."

Wade did not know if he liked this new aspect of Clementina Jones. If she had been one of his New York socialites, he would have accused her of being coquettish, but not Clem. She was being her usual forthright self.

"I assume your shoulder is better today, since you're not wearing your sling," she said.

Again he noticed that Clem avoided intimacy of any kind with him. A result of her conversation with Prentice. Although he was still slightly annoyed with his interfering cousin, he really could not fault him. But he was annoyed with Clem. He preferred having women fling themselves at him.

"Much better. I guess that stuff Elm gave me really works."

"Any dreams last night?"

"Yes," he murmured, stretching out and lying beside her. "I dreamed of an auburn-headed temptress who made love to me all night."

"I would rather you didn't talk like that in public," she said. "It's rather embarrassing."

"What would you do if I leaned over and kissed you?" he asked, laughing when her cheeks flamed.

She stared straight into his eyes. "I'd yell that you were taking unfair advantage of my person."

"Oh, God!" He seemed to growl the words. "It's all I can do to keep my hands off you. I'd love to take advantage of your person."

"That you'll not have the chance to do," she said, and rolled away from him. "I have to go. I promised Deborah I'd help her set up the jam and preserve table."

Wade laughed softly, ironically. "Things are pretty bad, Clementina, when I can't compete with jam and jellies."

"Supply wagon's coming in from the fort!" Six-year-old Laban McLean shouted as he ran down the road to Clem's house. "Mr. Smith spotted it down the road and said at the speed it was traveling, it should be here in about twenty minutes."

Eager for the mail and news from Ft. Stockton and back East, many of the people began to rush toward town to wait for the wagon. Among them were Clem and Wade. They stood in front of the sheriff's office when the wagon rolled at breakneck speed around the corner.

"Indians," the driver yelled at the top of his voice. "We was attacked by Indians. Get the doctor. We have people hurt."

Darting across the street, Wade and Clem reached the wagon at the same time that it lurched to a halt. By the time the wounded driver had climbed down, a woman jumped out of the rear, falling down in the street on her hands and knees. Two little girls hopped out behind her.

"My children," she screamed hysterically, waving her hands in the air and drawing her two children close around her, "help me and my babies. Those savages killed my husband; they've hurt me and my daughters. Please, someone, help us!"

Deborah also raced down the street, and despite her beautiful gown, she knelt in the dirt and helped the woman to her feet. She placed her arm around the woman's shoulder.

"We'll help you," she said soothingly. "Come on. Let's get out of the street. You're going to be fine now."

Emmett Frazier stood at the entrance of the hotel, the door thrown open. Grady had already raced out and was helping Wade at the wagon.

"Bring 'em in here," Emmett shouted. "I'll take care of them," he called. "It's closer than the doctor's office."

Deborah led the woman and children into the hotel, while Wade and Clem turned their attention to the driver.

"You're wounded," Clem said.

"Don't worry about me none, ma'am," he said. "Just a graze. I'll be all right. Take care of them two in the wagon. They's the ones who are hurt the worst."

Clem climbed up on the seat and peered into the bed of the wagon, to see Wade examining two bodies. Unable to see around him, she asked, "Are they alive?"

"Two dead, and another one seems pretty bad," he answered and unbuttoned one of the men's coats to examine him better. "I hope the doctor gets here soon."

"He's here," Elm panted, pulling Clem back so that he could climb into the wagon, "but it's too crowded in here for me to do anything for him. Let's take Emmett up on his offer. Hey," he yelled to two of the onlookers, "help us move this man into the saloon."

Elm looked over at Wade. "I can see that it didn't do me any good to tell you to keep your arm in that sling for a day or two."

"It felt better this morning," Wade replied, but as he worked with the casualties, he felt the bite of pain and fatigue.

Backing away so they could move the man and remove the bodies, Clem turned to the driver, who hung onto the side of the wagon with one hand. The other he clamped over the blood-sodden coat that covered his chest.

"What happened?" she asked.

"Indians," he said, lowering his head and spitting. "We knew they was around. The captain at the fort warned us about Diablo, but I figured for sure they wouldn't attack. Not in weather like we was having." He jerked his thumb in the direction of the wagon. "The kid. He didn't have no chance. Those Indians seemed to come out of nowhere about twenty miles from here. If it hadn't been for him—" he tipped his head in the direction of the wounded man who was being carried across the street into the doctor's office, "we wouldn't have made it. I ain't never seen a man who can shoot a gun like him."

"When did they attack?" Clem asked.

"Yesterday afternoon."

"Did they take anyone captive?" Clem questioned as the two of them began to follow Wade across the street. If they had, immediate pursuit was necessary. Even then finding the Indians and rescuing the captives was not assured.

"Nope, not nary one," he answered. "Like I said, we was lucky to have this feller traveling with us."

"I'll get some of the men, and we'll go after them," she said.

"Ain't no need," the man said. "We met a scouting party out from the fort, and they took out after 'em. Reckon if anybody can find 'em, them soldiers can."

When Clem reached the sidewalk, she heard her mother scream and rushed into the hotel lobby to see Wade holding Deborah in his arms.

"The man," he said to Clem. "It's—"

"Rand," Deborah said, her face ashen. She pushed out of Wade's arms and walked toward Clem. Her eyes were dark with concern. "What am I going to do if he dies?" she cried. "I can't lose him, too."

"He won't die," Clem promised.

"Deborah, Clem, one of you get in here," Elm shouted from the downstairs bedroom. "I'm going to be needing some help. Can't take care of things by myself."

Clem followed her mother into the bedroom and gazed at the unconscious man who lay on the bed. Rand McGaffney Jones, Clem thought. He had changed during the five years, but not much. He was older, a little more worn. His hair was thinner than she remembered, and he was heavier.

"Are you up to this?" Elm asked Deborah, as he removed the instruments and medicine out of his black bag and laid them on the night table.

"Yes. The rest of you get out of here," Deborah ordered in a quiet but authoritative voice. "I'll help Elm with this. Clem, you'd better help the woman and children. She's in shock and shouldn't be by herself."

Clem soothed the woman and little girls, then turned them over to the care of Odetta Albany. When she walked out of the front door onto the boardwalk, she found Wade talking to the gathering crowd. Although they were quiet, there was an undercurrent of tension. They were anxious, almost angry. It would take little for them to become riled up.

"There's cause to be concerned, but no cause to get hysterical." He turned to the driver. "Cornbeef, do you know for sure this was Diablo Negro?"

"No, sir, sure don't, but since we heard tell he's carrying the smallpox plague, I figure we got a problem on our hands. Word has it, he's a renegade on the warpath."

Again a murmur of anxiety raced through the crow. Clem held her hand up to silence the crowd. "If you read your paper, you would have seen the column Hadley wrote informing you of the rumor of a smallpox epidemic. He also told you to get into town and get vaccinated. We have the medicine at Elm's office for those of you who need it."

Maybelle came bustling out of the general store. "While Elm's tending Rand, I'll get everyone ready for the vaccinations. Just go down the street and form a line in front of Elm's office."

"Do you reckon we need to form a posse and go hunt Diablo?" Turbin asked. "Even if he don't have smallpox, he's attacking the settlers, and he's gonna be trouble."

"I don't think Diablo Negro is responsible for this

266

attack," Clem said. "And even if he were, I don't need a posse. I know where he's headed. If he's here, I'll be able to find him anytime I choose."

"He's headed for home," Turbin said, and looked toward the mountains in the distance. "He wasn't there when you were, was he?"

"No," Clem answered, "but Peaceful is getting old and tired. He's seeking the Happy Hunting Ground. I believe he somehow relayed the message to Diablo Negro."

"Did the old man know when Diablo would be home?"

Clem nodded.

"What are you going to do?" Wade asked.

"In the morning I'll head back to the mountains," she answered. "I should arrive there about the time Diablo Negro does."

"You're protective of him," Wade said. "Why?"

"From hearing Papa and Rand talk about him, and when I was very small, I saw him a time or two. When he was a young boy, he used to ride with the Sheriff and Rand. Mostly, I know him through Peaceful."

Ironically, with her father's death, Clem's entire life was changing. While some of the changes were for the better, others were sad. She was losing many of her childhood friends. There was a certain glory and wisdom that came with womanhood, but with it also came grief and sorrow, as an old life gave way to a new one. She could cope with the old one; she did not know about the new one.

"You like him?"

"Yes, and I trust him. I hope I'm not too late with the vaccine."

"Will Elm travel with you?"

She shook her head. "No, they won't allow another medicine man in the village. Since they'll accept me

267

without question, he's taught me what to do. I'll give the inoculations."

"I'm going with you," Wade said. "I don't want you out there by yourself."

Clem did not resent Wade's wanting to go with her, but she did resent his proprietary tone. "I've already been out there by myself," she reminded him.

"I didn't like it then, and I like it less now. The situation is worse. So, I'm going."

Clem was glad to have someone want to be with her to take care of her, but she did not trust herself alone with Wade. She could hardly maintain a distance from him now, and they were surrounded by people. If she were alone with him, she was afraid she would succumb to his charm.

"We'll see," she said, and noticed that Wade's eyes narrowed and his mouth thinned in disapproval.

"When are you leaving?" he asked.

"Depends," she replied.

"You go on back to the barbecue," he said, "I'll tell Elm to get the vaccine packed for you."

Clem nodded and began to walk in the direction of her house.

She heard Wade call, "Remember, I'm the only one who is going to dance with you."

"We'll see," she called back.

She wanted to turn to see what effect her words had on him, but she did not. She certainly did not want to let him know how much she cared.

"He's not hurt nearly as bad as it looked." Elm gently patted Deborah on the shoulder. "A pretty hard lick knocked him unconscious, but he'll be up and around in a little while. Good as new. Do I need to send someone over here to stay with Rand?"

"No."

268

After Elm closed the door, Deborah sat on the side of the bed and looked at Rand. Tears ran down her cheeks. Tears of relief; tears of joy. It had been five long years since she had seen him, but he had not changed. Straight brown hair framed a face that was as rugged as the West Texas terrain, and dark lashes lay against his sun-browned skin.

With a damp cloth she cleaned his face and chest, and she sat there waiting — something she was good at doing. She had been waiting for him for five years. She brushed hair from his face. Time had been good to him.

The door opened, and she turned to see Clem enter.

"How is he?" she asked.

"Elm said he would be fine. Mostly bruises and a bad bump to the head. He should be regaining consciousness any minute now."

"Do you want me to stay with him," Clem asked, "so you can get back to the barbecue?"

Deborah wrung her hands together. "No, I'd rather stay here. I want to be here when he awakens. Do you mind supervising the barbecue?"

"No."

Clem tensed, and Deborah could imagine what was going through her daughter's mind. While it mattered to her, this was not the time to discuss it. She wanted Clem to understand her feelings for Rand, but whether she did or not, Deborah was going to make her bid for happiness with him. If he turned her down, if he no longer loved her, she would have tried.

Although she and Rand had never shared any kind of intimacy, other than holding hands, and had only spoken of their feelings for each other on one occasion, she loved him. She was saddened by Clement's death, but she hoped it would not stand in the way of her and Rand finding happiness together . . . if Rand should still want it.

Clem asked, "Is there anything in particular I should do?" She listened as Deborah gave her instructions for carrying off the events of the day. Then she slipped out of the room.

Once again Deborah was alone with Rand. She sat quietly, changing the cool compress on his forehead every fifteen or twenty minutes, and brushing her fingers through his hair. Finally he stirred and moaned softly.

"Where am I?"

"In Lawful," Deborah answered, her voice teary. "At Emmett Frazier's Hotel."

He pushed up and looked around wildly. "The Stoddards?" he asked. "Are they all right?"

"The mother and children are. The husband was killed."

"Indians," he muttered, his eyes closed. "Comanches."

"Yes," she answered. "Now, lie back down and rest."

Rand lay there for a few seconds; then he opened his eyes again and blinked several times, as if trying to focus his vision, as if he were trying to place something or someone. "Deborah," he murmured, "is that you?"

"Yes," she whispered.

He rubbed his eyes, then focused on her again. This time he smiled. "Yes, I can see you." He lifted a hand and touched her cheek softly, delicately, as if he were afraid he would hurt her, as if he expected her to disappear. "You're more beautiful than I remember. I'm glad you're here."

"Oh, Rand," she cried and laid her head on his chest. "I don't know what I would have done if you were killed. First Clement. Now you. Maybe Clementina."

He circled his arms around her and held her close

270

to him. "Don't cry," he soothed, and rubbed the back of her head. "Let's put the past behind us and look toward the future."

"I can't stand that damned star, Rand. It's almost destroyed my life."

Rand pushed himself up and squirmed so that he held Deborah in his arms. "It's not the badge," he explained. "It was Clement's outlook on life. He's the one who made it more important than it should have been."

"Yet you came back to wear it," she said.

"I was on my way home before I learned Clement was dead," he said. He opened his mouth as if he were about to tell her something; then he shook his head. Finally he said, "I had to try one more time to convince him that you and I—that—"

Deborah nodded her head against his chest.

"I didn't make it," he finished.

"I think Clem understands," Deborah told him.

"I only hope Clement does."

"He does."

"I still love you," Rand said.

The words she so desperately wanted and needed to hear. Words she had imagined him saying to her over and over through the years. Imagined words that had saved her sanity, that had given her the strength to go on when Clement had accused her of infidelity and had turned her daughter against her.

She said, "I love you."

For a long time they lay there, quietly in each other's arms. They did not talk because they had no need for words; at the moment they had no need of passion. They needed the comfort and protection of each other's love, the assurance that they were there together, the promise that they might have a future together.

Then later, at almost the same time, both of them

began to talk, the words tumbling out as each filled the other in on the five years of their lives the other had missed. A little later, Rand gently removed Deborah from his arms. She gazed into his face, making no attempt to hide her longing.

He groaned and captured her mouth with his. The kiss was soft and sweet, and filled with years of wanting and waiting. Deborah knew that she had come home after a distant and lonely journey. She had found her mate. Their mouths parted, but he held her tightly.

"Deborah, when the time is right, will you marry me?"

"Yes."

For a while longer they lay there, safe in the haven of each other's arms. This time it was Deborah who pushed away.

"I need to get back to the house," she said. "We're having a barbecue for Doña Pera Montelongo. I'll be back later to visit with you."

"No need for that," he said. "I'm going to be up and about in a matter of minutes. First, I'd like to take a bath and change clothes. Then I want to see Clem. After that, the city council."

"I'll tell the desk clerk to bring your bath as I'm going out. You'll find Clem at the house."

Rand slipped off the bed and walked to where Deborah stood to press a light kiss to her lips, one devoid of passion but one full of promise.

"Don't give me up. I'll be there."

"I'll be waiting," she said.

The afternoon had flown by as Clem organized the barbecue, putting Hadley over the men's games, Odetta over the jam and preserve competition, and Laban and Lucia McLean over the younger children's games. Supervising the cooking herself, Clem had time to think about her mother and Rand.

When she had walked into the room and had seen Deborah sitting on the edge of the bed beside him, she has been angry that her mother was here for Rand, but had not been here for her father. As quickly as it came, the feeling left. She had come to the realization in the past few days, that her father had pushed her mother away. When she had needed him, he had not been there for her. In the end, Clement Jones's pride had been his downfall. Unable to forgive his wife, he had allowed his pride to chase her away.

Now that Clem loved Wade, she could better understand her mother's feelings for Rand.

She looked up from the spit where she was turning a piece of beef, and saw Rand walking toward her. She moved away from the fire, waving the smoke out of her face and brushing hair from her face. The years seemed to fade away, and she was the little girl joyously waiting for her favorite uncle.

"Hello, Clem," he said when he was standing in front of her.

"Hello, Rand."

"I was on my way home to see Clement, when I heard the news about his death. It came over the wire at Ft. Stockton."

Not knowing what to say, she said nothing.

"I'm sorry about Clement," Rand continued. "I loved him, Clem, just like a brother."

"I know," she whispered and held open her arms. "Uncle Rand, I know."

He stroked the back of her head. "About Deborah and me —" he began.

"You don't have to say anything." She pulled back and looked into his face. "Deborah's told me, and I believe her. I'm glad you're home. I've missed you."

"Me, too," Rand said gruffly.

"Well, Rand," the mayor called from across the yard and walked toward them, "I'm glad to see that you're no worse for wear."

"Arnold." Rand turned and shook hands with the mayor. "I'm not an easy one to get. I was taught by the best."

Arnold bobbed his head. "You sure were. I'm glad to see you. We sure need your help. You want to tell him, Clem, or shall I?"

"I will," Clem answered, knowing how Arnold liked to embellish stories.

Rand stood quietly as Clem told him what had happened during the past few days. When she was finished, Rand asked her questions about the men gathering in El Paso, and she answered. She took off the badge and handed it to the mayor.

"I told you I'd wear it until Rand got here."

"Rand, I hope you're ready to take on the responsibility of this badge," Arnold said.

Rand shook his head, much to Clem's surprise, much to the surprise of everyone who stood around them.

"No, Arnold, if Clement wanted her to have it, and if she wants it, I'm not going to be the one who takes it from her. I'll gladly work as her deputy, just as I did for her father."

Arnold looked crestfallen. "But you said you would in your telegram."

"You didn't tell me that Clem was wearing the star or that she wanted it."

Having already decided that she wanted to be with Wade more than she wanted to wear the badge, that she wanted to be free to travel to El Paso with him or wherever he should ask her to go, Clem moved to where her uncle stood. She took the badge from Arnold.

Pinning it to Rand's shirt, she said, "It never really belonged to me, Rand. Had you been here, Papa would have wanted you to have it. It's rightfully yours."

Rand gazed into her eyes. "Are you sure, Clem?"

She nodded. Never had she been surer of anything in her life. "I'm glad that you're up and better. I'm going to get the vaccine and go up into the mountains. It's rumored that—"

Rand nodded. "I heard about it. Do you want me to travel with you?"

No, she thought, she really wanted Wade to go with her, but that was not wise.

"If I need someone, I'll get Hokie or Turbin."

"When are you going to leave?" he asked.

"In the morning. Wade's having Elm pack the vaccine now. I'll go pick it up later, so I'll be ready to leave before dawn."

"Who's Wade?" he asked.

Clem smiled. How avuncular he sounded, but she did not take exception. She figured she would have to deal with this from him and Deborah for a while, at least. Also she found it nice to have people around her who cared.

Before she could answer Rand, Arnold said, "I think you're taking a chance waiting this long to leave. If it were me, I'd—"

"If you think so, Arnold, why don't you take it to him," she said, turning to walk away.

"Well, I never—" Arnold blustered.

"No, but she knows what she's doing," Rand said. "Now, Arnold, if you'll excuse me, I want to talk with Clem."

Overhearing Rand, Clem waited for him to catch up with her.

"Now, young lady, who's Wade?" he asked.

Before dark, Clem slipped away from the crowd and went into the house to bathe. Excitement tingled throughout her entire body. She could hardly wait for Wade to see her in the new dress. She laughed to herself. She could hardly wait for him to see her in a dress period. He had seen her in her robe, but a dress — the green gingham dress — was different.

After the bath, she took her time dressing. She put on the clean chemise her mother had provided for her. Then she dropped the green gingham over her head, leaving the top button of her bodice undone. The material was soft and felt good against her skin.

Moving to stand in front of the cheval glass, she thoroughly enjoyed her moment of femininity. She ran her hand down the midriff, liking the way her body molded the dress to give it form and shape. It was such a contrast to the shirt and trousers she wore everyday. Listening to the music, she hummed and spun around, the skirt of the dress twirling around with her.

Still humming and imagining the look on Wade's face when he saw her, she combed her hair dry and pulled it to the nape of her neck, clasping it with a tortoiseshell clip. She pulled a strand of hair through her fingers. Wade thought it was pretty and liked her to let it hang loose.

She put on the shoes that she had purchased this morning from the general store. She had taken only a few steps when she realized they were uncomfortable. She would have a miserable time this evening if she wore them. She looked at her boots, then she looked down at the dainty button-up patent leather shoes on her feet.

What would it matter if she wore the boots? she thought. They would be hidden by her dress. She laughed softly. Becoming a lady was harder than she had supposed. She could learn to wear dresses quicker than she could the shoes. She was going to have to practice longer with them.

Finally she decided to wear the shoes, as long as she could tolerate the discomfort. When it became unbearable, she promised herself she would put on her boots. Tingling with excitement, she walked through the darkened house. As she glanced through the window into the yard, brightly lit from the many lanterns that hung from the trees, she smiled. She could hardly wait to show Wade her new dress or to tell him that she was going to El Paso with him.

She opened the door and walked onto the veranda, into the yard. She was standing beneath one of the lanterns when she turned and saw Wade walking up to her.

"Clem!" he said, as if he could not believe his eyes. "What a wonderful surprise!"

"Doña Pera gave it to me," she said, "and Deborah altered it. Do you like it?"

"For a woman who can outdraw, outcuss, and outshoot any man, you're lovely." He lowered his voice to a seductive level. "Desirable and kissable. So very kissable."

He leaned down to kiss her, but Clem drew back. She almost laughed aloud at his astonishment.

"As pretty as one of your New York lady friends?" she asked, her voice breathless.

"More so," he answered.

For one of the first times in her life, Clem felt utterly feminine. The music swelled into the air, and Wade caught her by the waist to swing her onto the dancing square. Giving herself to the flow of the music, she dipped and swayed. She smiled and spoke to those who danced around her; she listened as Wade murmured endearments in her ears. She even batted her eyes and flirted with him. She was thoroughly pleased when she saw his eyes darken and his face set in scowling lines.

She inhaled into her nostrils the clean, brisk masculine fragrance that she associated only with him. His cheeks were smooth and shaven, his hair brushed back from his face. He wore a clean shirt and trousers. Gone were his revolvers.

Clem's eyes rested on the opened vee of his shirt, and she stared at the crisp, dark crop of chest hair. Although they had so recently made love, desire once again slid down her insides to nestle in the lower part of her stomach. She felt the warmth first, then the fire as the embers burst into a flame of wanting, of intense wanting.

What was she going to do when he left her to return East? How empty her life would be.

"Clem," he said, "I heard about you giving the badge to Rand. Will you change your mind about going to El Paso with me?"

"No," she answered, deciding to let him worry a little. "I've got to let the people know that I'm going to run for sheriff in the next election."

"So you're going to begin your campaigning?" He seemed to grate the words.

"Yes, I suppose so."

The lantern light spilled down on them as Wade looked into her face. His eyes were dark.

"You're an enigma, Clementina Jones, and I'm not going to turn you loose until I figure you out."

Clem laughed softly. "You had better be careful with your promises, Wade Cameron. That could be a mighty long time."

He swung her around, her skirt billowing about her ankles. About that time, Hokie tapped Wade on the shoulder.

"I figure you've had her to yourself long enough, Mr. Cameron. I'd like to dance with the belle of the

278

ball."

Wade scowled, but Clem continued to smile.

Moving into the deputy's arm, she said, "I'd love to, Hokie."

Clem enjoyed the evening, and she truly felt like the belle of the ball. Bachelors whom she had never met before singled her out for dances; her friends all asked for one. She danced until her feet felt as if they were going to fall off. She was tired but happy. She received perverse satisfaction in seeing Wade stand at a distance to watch her. She felt as if his face would forever be etched in a frown of displeasure.

Chapter Sixteen

During the night the temperatures dropped, and a cold front had blown in by the time Clem left the next morning. The pack mule behind slowed her pace, but she moved steadily, making few stops. Thoughts of Wade filled her mind. When she reached the mountains and began to climb, the journey become arduous as well as slow. Now she moved up a narrow pass, her head bowed, her collar turned up around her neck for protection against the weather. The higher she traveled, the colder it became. The temperature dropped drastically, and a cold wind blew, chilling her to the bone.

She had stopped to rest and to look around, when she thought she heard someone behind her. Quietly she nudged the gelding forward and moved behind a clump of rocks. She dismounted, tethered Rusty-Be-Dusty, and pulled her revolver as she inched forward so that she had a good view of the trail.

In the quietness—the heavy quietness—she heard nothing. She pressed herself against the rock, hardly daring to breathe. Still she heard nothing; she saw no one. Perhaps it was her imagination. After a few more minutes she straightened up, keeping her eyes trained on the path. Then she breathed easier and turned to see Wade standing behind her.

"What the hell do you think you're doing sneaking off without me?" He spat the words at her.

"What the hell do you think you're doing sneaking up on me?" she returned, her legs trembling so badly she thought she would fall to the ground. She had been so preoccupied with him that she had been careless. She had allowed him to get the drop on her.

"I told you I was going to travel with you. It's dangerous for a person to be out here alone."

"Don't you mean a woman?" she exclaimed, not caring that she did not sound too logical. "Don't you mean me?"

"I mean a person in general. I meant you in particular," he said. "I've been worried sick about you."

"Thanks, but I'm not your concern," she said and started to walk past him. "Now, if you'll—"

"If I'll *what?*" He caught her by the shoulders and dragged her into his arms, the movement knocking her hat off.

His lips came down on hers in a hard kiss. Still angry because he had frightened her, she kept her lips clamped together and insinuated her arms between them, pushing against his chest. His arms were strong vises that bound her to him. She wondered why she had ever thought him a tenderfoot. Then his lips softened, and they began to play with hers, arousing her.

She twisted her face from his. "Turn me loose," she demanded.

"You don't mean it," he said. "You're enjoying this. Admit it."

She did enjoy his kisses, but his arrogance drove her fury even higher. Pulling in her leg, she kicked him in the shin as hard as she could. When he yelped, she broke out of his embrace and stood back, breathing deeply and glaring at him.

"Somebody needs to take you under his wing," he said. "And I think I'm just the man to do it."

"Don't overestimate your charm or your ability," Clem said. "Now get out of my way. I've got to get moving, or I'm not going to get to shelter by dark. You had better go on back to Lawful. The weather and the trail are going to get worse before they get better."

"I'm staying with you," he said.

"Suit yourself."

"I usually do," he grated.

Riding single file, Clem led the way, neither of them speaking as they traveled. By dusk they reached the top of the pass. Clem urged Rusty-Be-Dusty into a trot, not stopping until they were in a shallow cave on the other side of the mountain.

Sliding out of the saddle, she said, "We'll spend the night here. It's an old Indian camp."

"How much farther?" Wade asked.

"About ten slow, winding miles straight through the mountains," she said, the wind whipping her clothes against her body. "That's why we're stopping now. If the weather gets worse, we wouldn't have a place to make camp."

Above the yowl of the wind, Wade called, "You take care of the horses, and I'll gather some wood."

Clem stared at him and for a minute she wanted to throw his words into his face, but she knew he was right. She had to control her emotions better than this. She refused to let him see how much his presence affected her.

"It feels like it's going to get a lot colder before morning," he continued.

She nodded.

282

After Wade disappeared into the night, Clem took care of the horses, then spread the blankets, making their pallets. She moved Wade's saddlebags over, the flap on one of them opening. Papers slid out across the floor of the cave. One by one Clem retrieved them, noticing that in the upper right-hand margin they were numbered. Sighing, she moved closer to the fire in order to see, and began to put them in numerical order.

Soon the words on the page caught her attention, and she read. Although the writing was rough, many words scratched out, others written illegibly above them, Clem enjoyed reading the story about her father. At times she laughed, other times she cried, but through it all she was proud. Wade had captured the essence of the man, showing that he was a product of the country he loved so much, that he believed in justice and wore the star with pride.

Wade pushed the branches aside and entered the cave, laying the wood down. Clem watched him toss several pieces on the fire; then he noticed that she held his manuscript.

"It fell out," she explained lamely and handed it to him. "I wasn't going through your things."

"What do you think?" he asked, returning the papers to his saddlebags.

"So far I like it."

Later, after they piled branches across the opening of the cave to block out the wind, they built a fire and ate their meal. No matter how closely Clem hovered to the blaze, she was cold. She tucked her chin into her collar, then felt Wade's arms around her. She stiffened and would have pulled away, but he held her tightly.

"I'm just going to keep us warm," he said, and

pulled the covers from the second pallet around them.

Then he poured each of them a cup of hot coffee. Bundled together close to the fire, they drank their coffee, but still did little talking.

"Now, that I know that the Blacksmith is living in Mexico, I may have to travel there," Wade said.

"Yes."

"I won't be leaving until things are settled in Lawful," he said, and set his cup down close to the fire. "I figure you and Rand will be needing all the help you can get."

"Thanks," she murmured, clutching the cup in her hands.

She had not wanted Wade to accompany her because she was afraid of intimacy with him; she feared her lack of resolve where he was concerned, and she had reason to be concerned. Already her body was remembering the magic of his touch.

"Did you get time to talk with him about Papa last night?"

"Not much. He was a busy man last night."

Clem turned her head about that time, their gaze locking together. He had never been more handsome or more desirable. The flames of the camp fire danced golden shadows across his visage; they burnished his hair to a sheen. His face came closer to hers, and she suddenly moved.

She tossed the dregs out of her cup and set it on the rocks surrounding the fire. Then she began untangling the blankets, separating his from hers. "We have to be up early in the morning," she said. "We had better get to bed."

He rose, his hands closing over hers to still her movements. "As cold as it is, don't you think we ought to sleep together?"

She laughed dryly. "A ploy to get me into your bed?"

His eyes flashed, and she knew she had touched a tender chord. "I don't have to resort to ploys to get women in bed with me. I was thinking about your health. But, if you don't want to, that's fine with me."

He jerked his blankets from her hands and quickly remade his pallet. Without another word, he lay down, his back to her, and drew his cover over his shoulders.

Clem straightened her blankets and lay down also, but she could not sleep . . . not with him so close. After a while, she rose and banked the fire, then she stretched out again. The wind began to blow harder, and Clem shivered. She rolled over, getting closer to the fire. She should have listened to him. She moved again.

"Damn it, Clem," Wade said, "you'll drive a man insane."

Before she knew what was happening, he had moved his blankets and was wrapping his body and his blankets around her. She tried to move away from him, but he clamped his arm around her waist.

"Don't say a word, and don't wiggle again," he warned. "I won't get an ounce of sleep with you twisting and turning like you've been doing for the past hour. Besides, you know what will happen to me if you keep squirming against me."

Quietly they lay there for a long time; Clem was not sure exactly how long. Still she could not sleep. She was warm in the cocoon Wade had created for them, but she was much too aware of the man who held her in his arms. Her back rested against his chest; her buttocks were curved against his stomach and thighs. She remembered his delicious threat.

"You still can't sleep?" he murmured.

"No."

"You're not still cold, are you?"

"No."

"What's wrong?"

He raised up to peer over her shoulder. She looked up, and in the firelight she saw the desire on his face. He was as aware of her as she was of him. He wanted her. She made no attempt to keep the wanting from her gaze. With a groan, he pulled her closer to him.

"I didn't mean for this to happen," he said.

"I know."

Without really contemplating what she was doing, she moved to raise her face to his. His lips eagerly took hers. She opened her mouth to accept him. The hunger in her was as great, as intense as it had been previously. If anything, perhaps it was more intense. She opened her mouth wider, holding him against her tightly, wishing they were not bundled in so many clothes. Clem kissed him, liking the feel of his tongue trailing the edges of her teeth, the sensation of his mouth caressing hers. When their lips finally parted, his breath spilled over her cheeks and throat, his tongue exploring the delicate shell of her ear.

She forgot her reasons for being angry at him. She forgot her resolve to keep him at a distance. She wanted him; she needed him, and that was the paramount thought in her mind. Her hand slipped up his chest to touch his uninjured shoulder. Gently his lips whispered over hers, moving back and forth before they settled into a sweet kiss with inexpressible longing. Then, the kiss that had begun so tenderly, deepened until both were drinking of the other's soul.

Finally he lifted his mouth from hers. "Clem, I didn't know what life was before I met you. I don't think I had a life. I merely existed."

He lifted a hand, touching her chin and the smooth curve of her cheek. He outlined the arched brows, the delicate nose. He traced her mouth. Clem pulled away from him to look into his fire-shadowed face. She stroked her hands through the thick tousled waves, dropping her hands to scratch her nails over his whisker stubble.

"When you're deputy sheriff, it serves your purpose to have your hair balled up on the top of your head, but when you're with me, I like to see it hanging loose."

He pulled the pins from her chignon, allowing her hair to tumble about her shoulders. He spread his fingers through it, softening it around her face. "I've never needed a woman before, Clem, but I really do need you."

"Want me, you mean," she said.

"No. I said what I mean." His hand slid down her throat beneath the collar of her coat, his fingers gently closing over the soft flesh.

"I understand what you were talking about the other night, when you tried to persuade me not to accept the badge. Yesterday, when I saw you facing off with Ike Perry, I was worried sick."

Clasping her shoulder with his hand, he tenderly pressured her closer to him, pressing her face into his uninjured shoulder.

"I couldn't have stood it if you died."

"Why?" he asked.

Because I love you, she wanted to say.

"You would have been dying for me," she answered, which was partly the truth. "You were taking my place."

She raised her head, and lifting a hand, rubbed it against his cheeks again. Her lips parted, she guided his mouth to hers. Gently they touched one another, almost a virgin touch, as if they were discovering the taste and feel of each other for the first time.

Through the bundling she felt a tremor ripple Wade's body. His lips again touched hers, and she allowed him to lead her into the deepness of passion. Desperation spurred her into urgency. He was leaving soon, and she wanted to know him as completely as she could. In time memories would be all she had of Wade Cameron. Compelled by the throbbing needs of her body that he had so recently introduced her to, Clem had to touch him; she had to hold on to him.

"Oh, Wade," she murmured, burying her face against his jacket, "with you, I feel alive, really alive for the first time in my life."

She did not know how it happened and did not care, all that mattered was they were under the blankets, divested of their clothing. Outside the wind wailed through the trees, the lonesome sound echoing through the cave, but they were together. They knew no fear for their future; they knew no loneliness. They had this moment and they took it.

The caresses Wade and Clem shared were as wild and primitive as the land about them. Wade's lips parted and his tongue plundered deep within her mouth. His hands rubbed against the length of her back, moved down her spine to grip her buttocks and press her against the hard, burgeoning evidence of his own desire.

"Take me, Wade," she cried. "Right now."

No soft words passed between them, no gentle caresses. They needed neither tonight. They were akin to the late winter storm that raged outside their magical bower of love. Time and again they proved the dual nature of fury and bliss as their bodies locked together in the age-old battle of love, as they moved to the frenzied rhythm of the wind. Each demanded from the other; each received.

Clem climaxed first, but even as she shuddered against him, she felt his own answering shudders. They clung together letting their hearts still, letting their breathing return to normal. For Clem there was no outside world, no plagues, no salt wars, no past.

She had no promise of a future with Wade. There was only now. As she lay wrapped in Wade's arms, she was unwilling to let go of the binding rapture they shared. She determined to make each moment last as long as she could.

A noise outside the cave awakened Clem, but she was not ready to get up yet. She burrowed further beneath the blankets into the warm curve of Wade's body. How wonderful it was to have his body pressed against hers throughout the night. When she felt him harden against her, wonderful memories stirred the smoldering passion within. She turned in his arms, her hand sweeping up his chest to his face. She scraped her fingertips over the black shadow of his whiskered cheek. She explored in minute detail the texture of his face and lips.

"Good morning," she murmured as she pressed kisses against his face. How wonderful it was to awaken with him beside her. "Time to get up."

"I wish we didn't have to," he said with a sigh and

held her tightly against him, "but we must."

Giving her a last hug and kiss, he dressed beneath the covers, both of them laughing as he squirmed around arranging his clothes. Then he was up, throwing several pieces of wood on the glowing embers. Clem was content to remain where she was and let him tend the chores. Golden light soon cast out the night shadows.

Moving back to the pallet, he leaned over her and whispered, "I'm going out for a while. You can fix a pot of coffee while I'm gone."

Clem smiled and stretched. Her body still glowed from their lovemaking. She touched his face with the tips of her fingers. "I'd rather not get out of here at all."

"But we have to, if we're going to get the vaccine to the village."

"Hurry back," she said.

After Wade left, Clem dressed and soon had a pot of coffee on the fire. While she waited for it to boil and for Wade to return, she repacked their bedding. Then she sat down close to the fire and poured herself a cup of coffee.

She heard a horse whinny and turned her head. Setting the cup down, she inched to a covered spot near the opening of the cave. Her hand hovering over her revolver, she crouched and she waited.

"From the smell of the coffee—" a masculine voice called, "I'm hoping for friendly faces."

"What's your name, partner?" Clem called out, cautious not to reveal herself.

"Eddy," he answered, and the horse and rider came fully into view in front of the cave.

He had no accent, but he was a vaquero. Revolvers strapped to his thighs protruded from the hem of the heavy poncho he wore. Smiling, he pushed off his sombrero so that it hung down his back suspended on the string, and she could see his face. A thick black moustache, the same color as his hair, drooped around his mouth. He was young, about her age, she would guess.

"I'm Eddy Gonzalez from San Elizario."

The stranger's face was open, his broad smile flashing white teeth; still Clem was uneasy and questioned his friendliness. It was too calculated to be genuine. Lone travelers were inclined to be distrustful, suspicious. That way they lived longer.

She slowly straightened, her hand continuing to hover over her gun, her gaze remaining on his face. He slipped from the saddle, tethered his horse, and—making sure his hands were quite visible and away from his guns—walked to stand several feet in front of her.

"Move the branches," Clem ordered.

He complied.

"Aren't you afraid to be traveling in this country by yourself?" His command of English was good.

Covertly Clem looked at the two Colt .45's the stranger wore. These were no ordinary guns; he was no ordinary cowboy. He may be one of the gunfighters who was in El Paso; maybe he was on his way to Lawful. She tensed. If only she knew where Wade was and what he was doing, she would know what to do.

She hoped this man was alone. As long as she was alert and had her guns, she could handle him, but she had a big problem on her hands if more were riding with him. If there were, they could have slipped up unawares on Wade; he could be their prisoner. Worse, he could be dead. And he had been gone a long time.

"It's not safe for a woman to be traveling by herself in this country," Eddy said. "There are many enemies. Indians, Comancheros, the land itself."

"Are you traveling by yourself?" Clem asked.

He nodded.

"Aren't you afraid? Aren't you facing the same enemies?"

He laughed. "No, but I'm a man, and you're a woman."

"What has gender to do with it?"

"Everything, *senorita* . . ." Ebony eyes openly skimmed the features of her face, admiration as blatant as the gaze. "There is a difference between a man and a woman."

Despite the anger that rushed through her body, Clem forced her lips into a smile. "I agree there is a difference between a man and a woman, but that difference doesn't dictate where I travel, or with whom I do or do not travel."

The broad smile never faltered, but the eyes narrowed. "I meant no offense."

"None taken."

After a lengthy pause, he said, "To set your mind at ease—"

"Don't presume to read my mind." Her gaze never strayed from his face.

Eddy's lips tightened, and he held the smile. But he could not disguise the irritation that flashed in the ebony eyes. "There is no reason for us to be distrustful of one another, *senorita*."

He waited, but she said nothing else.

"I smelled your coffee quite a ways back. I sure could use a cup right now."

Clem's gaze traveled to the camp fire. "I suppose I

can spare you a cup. Where you headed?"

"Lawful."

"I don't even know your name, *senorita*."

"Clem Jones."

"Any relation to Sheriff Jones?"

"His daughter," she answered.

Now Eddy's full attention turned to her revolvers.
"Go ahead and get some coffee," Clem said.
"There's the pot and cups."

Again she thought of Wade and wondered about
his fate. That he was a prisoner or wounded was
hard to bear; that he could be dead sent an unbearable wave of pain through her. Her mind was so
muddled with worry, she found it difficult to think.
Yet at the moment Wade's safety and hers depended
on her keeping a cool, clear head.

As Eddy moved to the fire, she asked, "What's
your business in Lawful?"

"Cattle. I work for the Bar-W out of El Paso," he
answered smoothly. "*El Patron* sent me to look over
Senora Fitzmeyer's herd, to see if we want to buy. Her
husband died several months ago, and she wants to
take the children and return to their home in Geor-
gia. She's selling out. But I suppose you know that."
He lifted the cup and drank greedily. "Word's out
that your father was killed at the Chupedera Salt
Flats."

The casualness with which he slipped the comment
into the conversation alerted Clem. "He was."

"Know who did it?"

"Alarico Olviera of San Elizario."

She watched the vapor from the coffee turn into a
white wispy spiral as it touched the cold mountain
air. Chilled—whether from the weather or out of apprehension of Eddy Gonzales—she did not know—

She pulled her jacket tighter.

"You wouldn't happen to know him, would you?"

"*Sí.*" He took several swallows before he spoke again. "Are you looking for Alarico, *senorita.*"

"No, I've already found him." She paused significantly, then said, "So did the vigilantes. They killed him."

Yet she had a gut feeling that she was not importing news to Eddy Gonzales. Eddy Gonzales could easily be one of the hooded riders who had chased Olviera. His expression remained blank.

"They shot him outside Botello," Clem continued. "Second death they have to account for during the past few weeks. They hanged Lionel Porter for cattle thieving."

"I heard." He sipped his coffee. "You know Olviera's younger brother was killed at the salt flats, *senorita?* Shot in the back only weeks before his fifteenth birthday."

Clem said nothing. Not sure what the man's purpose was in talking with her, she had to be careful not to reveal too much knowledge about Olviera.

"Rumor has it that it was the Sheriff's men who were laying a trap for the Mexicans."

"Rumor's wrong," Clem said.

He finished off the coffee and set the cup on the ground next to the fire. "Thank you, *senorita.*" He flashed her the brilliant smile she was quickly coming to dislike. "Pardon me for asking, but what are you doing out here?"

The innocent drifter role did not fool Clem. She had studied people all her life and recognized a professional gunman when she saw one. She had observed the way Eddy walked and held his hands; the way he wore his guns; and most of all, she was aware of the alertness of his eyes. They had taken in everything in the cave in a matter of seconds; as he drank the coffee, he had taken the time to study her and the surroundings. She could not allow herself to be off guard for one second.

"Taking vaccine to the Indians. Word from Ft. Stockton says we may have a smallpox epidemic on our hands. Diablo Negro has left the reservation in New Mexico and returned to Texas."

"So the Mescalero returns," Eddy muttered, and caressed the butt of his gun.

Again apprehension ran through her. Possibly this man was a cowboy, working at the Bar-W, but she did not think so. Again she thought of the possibility of his being one of the vigilantes who killed Olviera. Or he could be a professional gunman hired by the man who wanted the salt lake property, or a member of the Olviera family who, having heard by now of Alarico's death, was embarking on a vendetta. The many possibilities staggered Clem.

Although short, Eddy Gonzales looked as if he had whipcord strength, and Clem was alone with him. As long as she had her guns, she was not afraid and believed she could hold her own with him. Without weapons, Eddy would have a decided advantage. Either way she had cause to be concerned, and her concern for Wade's safety was greater than that for her own. Not knowing his fate, she had to be careful and bide her time.

"Who is the deputy sheriff of Lawful now that your father is dead?" he asked. "You?"

"No," she answered, "the council appointed Rand McGaffney. He was sworn in yesterday."

Eddy whistled.

"You've heard of him?"

295

"He's one tough gringo."

"And he'll even be tougher with the Sheriff dead," Clem added, and deciding that she had nothing to lose, asked, "Have you heard anything about professional guns gathering in El Paso?"

He nodded. "Not only heard about them. I saw some of them. Soloman Wise, Ike Perry, and Chester Powers. They brazenly ride the streets." He pointed to Wade's horse. "Perhaps the person traveling with you is another woman who is hiding, someone whom you are protecting?"

Clem smiled to herself. His curiosity had gotten the best of him.

"The person with whom she is traveling is a man," Wade answered, and both Eddy and Clem turned to see him step from behind a boulder. "He's hiding because he is distrustful and apprehensive. He wanted to know more about you before he revealed himself."

"He wanted to make sure I was alone," Eddy said.

"He did," Wade answered.

"That is smart of you, *senor.*"

"I thought so myself."

Clem breathed a sigh of relief to know Wade was all right, to know that he was here with her, that he had been all along. Long strides brought him to her side.

"Who are you, *senor?*"

"Wade Cameron from New York. Reporter and publisher," he answered. "I'm out here to do a story."

Eddy's gaze contemptuously raked over Wade. "You talk courageously, *senor,* but you seem to offer the *senorita* very little protection."

Wade chuckled. "I'd like to think I was protecting Clem, but it would be a mistake on my part to do so. She doesn't need protecting. She can take care of herself. As for me . . . looks can be deceiving. Ike Perry discovered his mistake the hard way."

"You are the man who shot him?"

"I am."

"Eduardo!" The short, heavy-set vaquero rose from the fire and, shielding his eyes against the mid-morning sun, moved to the edge of the clearing, his wool poncho billowing behind. Speaking in Spanish, he said, "I was worried, *mi amigo*. I thought something had happened to you. We were getting ready to return to camp to tell Giuseppe."

Talk of the Italian rubbed Eddy the wrong way. He disliked the New Orleans dandy, and worked for and tolerated him only because he needed the money. Soon he would have enough so that he would no longer need him; then he could do away with Giuseppe Lorenzo and his grandiose dreams of owning and ruling an outlaw town. Eddy could visualize himself as *El Patron* of Lawful, Texas.

He laughed aloud and lifted his face to the warmth of the sun. His dreams made him happy. "Sancho, my old friend, how long have we ridden together?"

"Since you were a small child at your father's hacienda," the grizzled vaquero answered and laughed fondly. "I taught you all you know about being a vaquero."

"And despite my education and intelligence, I would have never been more than a vaquero on my father's ranch," Eddy said bitterly. "My older brother inherited it all."

Eddy balled his hand into a fist as he thought about his father, who had seen to it that he was educated at one of the finest schools in Mexico City and

297

spoke English as fluently as Spanish, Yet his father had always been partial to his oldest son. One of these days, Eddy promised himself, he would kill both his father and his brother, one of these days when he had enough vaqueros himself to storm the ranch. Until then he could wait patiently.

"Mi hijo," Sancho said softly, "you cannot allow yourself to think about that. You are too high strung and will become angry and cannot control yourself. That is the one weakness you must guard against."

"No," Eddy said, "I cannot agree with you, my friend. My conscience was my greatest weakness, and I have done away with it. I know when to cut my losses. I answer to no one but myself."

Eddy's father and brother had accused him of being insane, but he was not. His father said he was subject to abrupt mood changes, jumping to conclusions and chomping at the bit, but that, too, was untrue. Eddy knew what he wanted out of life, and what he must do to get it. He was willing and able to make any sacrifice for his cause, even that of betraying a friend. Always he identified his goal and moved directly toward it, allowing nothing or no one to stand in his way.

"You have always been like a son to me," Sancho said. "That is why I worry about you, Eduardito."

"You should know better by now, Sancho. *La Dama De Suerte* is always with me and especially today." The spurs jingled softly as he and Sancho walked to the fire and joined five other men. Four of them were his trusted vaqueros; the fifth was Pedro Salvidar, Giuseppe's distant relative. Eddy disliked the man intently.

"I do not trust *La Dama*," Sancho said, and pulled at his scraggly, gray beard. "She has a fickle heart,

298

mi hijo."

"Today she has been true," Eddy assured the old man and moved closer to the fire. He was picking up a tortilla when he saw a pair of scuffed boots planted firmly in front of him.

"You have learned about Rico?"

"*Sí,* Pedro."

Eddy wrapped a piece of meat in the tortilla and took a bite. Resenting the vaquero's attitude and intrusion—having always resented him—he would let him squirm in curiosity for a while. Despite the boy's being related to the Lorenzos, Eddy did not like or trust the seventeen-year-old. He had only tolerated him up to this time because he had use for him. Now he figured that need no longer existed.

Sancho could be right, Eddy thought. He and Pedro were too much alike to ever like each other, and perhaps he was fearful of the younger man. One rose to the top of this profession by killing those who stood in the way. The fastest gun was always the one who remained alive. So far Eddy had been the fastest, but Pedro was getting better every day. If Sancho agreed with his plan, Eddy would kill Pedro today. That would be one less worry.

"Well?" Pedro prompted impatiently.

Eddy poured a cup of coffee and washed down the dry meat and tortilla. "Rico is dead."

"You know this for a fact?" the youngest vaquero demanded.

"I know it for a fact."

"You know who killed Ike Perry?"

"*Sí,* I know." Eddy's hand curled around the butt of his gun. He despised being put through an inquisition, especially by one of his underlings.

"No, *hijo.*" Sancho spoke softly and laid a gloved

299

hand over Eddy's. He looked up at Pedro. "If Eduardo says Rico is dead, Rico is dead. If he says he knows who killed Ike Perry, he knows." Now Sancho looked at Eddy; never raising his voice, he said, "Tell him who shot Perry."

"A *pistolero* by the name of Wade Cameron."

"Who is sheriff there now? The daughter? Or the brother?"

Eddy took a deep breath. He must be patient; now was not the time to react to this impudent idiot. But when the time did come, he would take great pleasure in killing him.

"Both are there, Pedro. The brother has become the sheriff, but the daughter still resides in the town. Since she is traveling with the *pistolero* Wade Cameron, I have reason to believe he is working with her, and that Giuseppe will find it difficult to take over the town."

Pedro's eyes narrowed, his gaze swinging from the old man to Eddy. "Then we must return to camp immediately and tell Giuseppe. He is eager to know."

"*Sí*, Pedro," Eddy answered, "we will leave as soon as I have eaten. Now, may I have some privacy."

Pedro cast him a defiant glance but walked away.

Eddy rose and laid his arm around the old man's shoulders. Moving away from the others, he said in a low voice, "I have more news—better news. I met Clem Jones this morning."

Sancho blinked puzzled eyes at Eddy. "What is so good about that? Everyone knows Clem Jones lives in Lawful; it's only natural you would meet her."

Eddy's voice lowered. "I did not have to go into town, Sancho. As I told you, *La Dama de Suerte* was with me today. Clem Jones and Wade Cameron are traveling through the mountains by themselves. We

300

could easily capture them."

Sancho glanced nervously over his shoulders at Pedro. His fear of the young man was evident. "I do not like this, *hijo*. Giuseppe has not given the word."

Eddy shook his head. "Why must we wait for the Italian? The opportunity has presented itself to us. Let us take it."

"No! I do not like this game, Eddy. You give and take your loyalty too easily. One minute you swear you are working only for Father Borajo; the next you are swearing the same allegiance to Giuseppe Lorenzo. Then you are turning them against one another; you are working against each of them. You have betrayed the padre by having us disguise ourselves as vigilantes and killing Rico for the Lorenzos; now you are suggesting we betray Giuseppe."

"Always, Sancho, I am loyal to us. To you and me. Giuseppe Lorenzo owes me. I owe him nothing, not even allegiance. Besides, my friend, we do not need him or the padre. Either would kill us in a second if we were no longer of use to them."

"I am afraid of the Lorenzos," Sancho said. "They are *loco*, Eduardo. Besides, what are we going to do with Pedro. He spies for them, no? He would tell them of our plan."

"Not if he's dead," Eddy said. "He's the only one of the vaqueros who are not loyal to us. And I can handle the Lorenzos. Think what pleasure it will be for us to capture Clem Jones. Why let those crazy Italians have all the pleasure of taking her body? Why let them get the money for selling her to a bordello in Mexico, when you and I are the ones who will be taking the risks? We'll be the ones taking her to Mexico. Why then, Sancho, shouldn't we also take the pleasure of her body and the pleasure of the

301

money—all of it can belong to you and to me! We can get away from here. We can buy that ranch you've always wanted, and settle down to become respectable people."

The mere thought of stripping the clothes from Clem's body set Eddy's tingling. He promised he would not take the Lorenzos' leavings. He would have his fill of Clem before he relinquished her to them. When he was through with her, he did not care what they did to or with her.

Sancho scratched his head, knocking his sombrero forward on his face. "How are you planning to do this? If you mess up Giuseppe's plans, he will kill you."

"I have been thinking about it all morning. Giuseppe wants Clem Jones desperately. Not only is punishing her part of his vendetta against the Joneses for having killed most of his family so many years ago in New Orleans, but he must have her in order to keep Giovanni in line."

"The *senorita* is for the young one?" Sancho asked, his brows rising in amazement. "I thought his desires were unnatural."

"They are, my friend. If Vonny gets Clem Jones, I have my doubts that she will ever grace the interior of a Mexican bordello, since his pleasure comes from inflicting pain on others. Still, Giuseppe crossed Vonny when he had Sheriff Jones shot. Now he must give something in replacement."

"That's the *senorita?*"

Eddy nodded. "We can capture her, then let Giuseppe know we have her and how much we want for her. I shall send Theodoro with the news. He can take with him an item—perhaps a note written in her own hand and a piece of her clothing—that con-

302

vinces him we have her. After he is gone, we shall take her to a place that he does not know, to our cabin."

"I shall take the message to Giuseppe," Sancho said.

Eddy squeezed the old man's shoulder. "Not this time, *mi amigo*. I do not trust Giuseppe. He knows how fond we are of each other, and he would take you prisoner, beat you for information, then kill you. I do not care what they do to Theodoro; he is expendable. We will not let him know where we are keeping her; therefore, he can not betray us. They will have to wait until I contact them."

After a long and thoughtful moment, Sancho nodded his head. "*Sí*," he said, "that's the way it must be. After you kill Pedro, we shall let the men know what we are doing, *sí?*"

Eddy nodded his head. "Until Giuseppe gives me the money—the full amount that I shall demand—I will not lead him to Clem Jones."

Again the old man nodded and lapsed into silence, finally to say, "You and I are going to take our pleasure with her?" Sancho scratched his chin, his fingers rasping against the beard stubble. "What happens when Giuseppe and Giovanni Lorenzo learn that you have betrayed them?"

Eddy laughed. "By the time they learn, you and I will be long gone. I shall lead them to the cabin where Clem Jones will be sitting, tied up and gagged, on the porch. You and the men will be in hiding to protect me. It's really quite simple."

"*Sí*, that's what concerns me. You are young, *mi hijo*, and I fear you're making a grave mistake by underestimating your adversary."

Eddy truly loved Sancho like a father, but resented

it when the old man began to act like one. "Just who am I underestimating, old man? Giuseppe Lorenzo or Clem Jones?"

"Both. What are we going to do with the *pistolero* who is traveling with the *senorita*?"

"Kill him," Eddy answered, "and make it look like Indians. Everyone will blame Diablo Negro."

"*Si*, he has returned." Sancho pushed to his feet, kicking the stiffness out of his legs. A gust of wind picked up the tail of his poncho furling it through the air. "Signs are all around."

"Perhaps he will get rid of Giuseppe and Giovanni?"

"Or us. You and I, we know these mountains, but Diablo Negro knows them better."

The old vaquero turned to squint into the distance, the wind howling about him, blowing his poncho around his legs.

"Let's kill Pedro and get the deed over with, Eduardo. The sooner we can get out of these mountains, the happier I will be."

Chapter Seventeen

The day was overcast, the blanket of black clouds hanging low. Clem could smell rain in the air. Her jacket was little protection against the harsh wind.

"How much farther is the village?" Wade asked, shifting in the saddle and looking around.

"Over the next mountain," she answered. "Why?"

"I've been worried ever since Gonzales left this morning."

"Me, too." She reached into her pocket and pulled out her father's timepiece. "We should be there by mid-afternoon. We might make it before the rain comes."

"Or before we run into Gonzales again. He's itching for a fight, Clem."

She nodded, and repeated a question she had asked herself and Wade several times already. "I wonder what he was doing on the trail to Lawful, and who he's working for?"

Since these were questions both had voiced before and that neither could answer, they lapsed into silence, once more riding in single file. For several more hours Clem led the way through the narrow and treacherous mountain passes. Finally they reached the bottom and emerged into a small clearing, where Clem waited for Wade to move to her side. She unfastened the canteen and took a long swallow before she handed it to Wade.

"Not much farther," she said and pointed. "Just over the rise."

Wade lowered the canteen, recapped and handed it to her. She had looped it on her saddle when she heard a movement. She turned, her hand moving to her revolver, but she was not quick enough.

"I'm so sorry, *senorita*, but I'm afraid this is as far as the two of you will be traveling." From a cluster of rocks behind them, Eddy spoke.

"Damn it!" Clem swore as both she and Wade tore out for the boulder ahead of them. Shots rang out, stopping them. Both drew their revolvers, again seeking escape.

"There is no way out, *senorita*. My men and I have you surrounded. Please drop your guns."

More shots pierced the air, coming close to both of them. Clem and Wade looked at each other, then dropped their revolvers to the ground.

"While I would rather not wound you, *senorita*, I will." His revolver drawn and aimed at them, Eddy on his steed rounded a large boulder. "Following you has been easy. I would have expected better from you."

"You were making a trip to Lawful to see *me?*" Clem asked.

"No, I came to find out if the rumors about Olviera's death were true. Finding you has been my added good fortune."

"I suppose you want to add another name to your growing list."

"A gunfight with the female deputy sheriff?" Eddy laughed. "Oh, no, *senorita*, no matter how appealing the idea may be, I do not want a gunfight. I want you." His eyes suggestively ran over her figure, and beneath the thick layer of clothes she felt her flesh crawl.

"What about him?" Clem asked.

Eddy smiled. "I have no use for him at all."

"Who are you working for?" Clem asked.

"I shall keep that secret a little longer, *senorita*."

Eddy laughed, his white teeth flashing through the moustache. "*Senor* Jones, you wear a handsome set of guns." He urged his mount closer to Wade and lowered his gaze to contemplate the nickel-plated revolvers. "I shall take them. I also want your gun belt, *senor*. I have never seen one so beautiful."

"No," Wade said. They were a gift to him from Nash. Eddy cocked the hammer on his gun and pressed it against Clem's arm. "I told you the truth, *senor*. I want her alive, and I shall have her that way. But I don't mind wounding her, if I have to. The choice is yours."

"He's bluffing, Wade." Clem's eyes never left Eddy's face.

"No, *senorita*, I am not."

The other vaqueros rode out, letting Clem and Wade know they were clearly outnumbered.

Slowly Wade's hand went to his buckle.

"I am sorry we must travel in such bad weather," Eddy said, looking over his shoulder at Clem, who was tied to the horse he led. Behind them rode Sancho and the four other vaqueros. "But I want to put as many miles between us and Lawful as I can, while the rain can wash away my tracks. I am going to take you to a safe place. No one will be able to find you there."

307

"Rain or not, Rand will find your trail and come after you," Clem promised. "He'll find me if he has to turn the world topsy-turvy. But not, Wade," she muttered to herself, tears running down her cheeks, mingling with the raindrops. "He's dead or soon will be."

Eddy shouted, "Yes, we're counting on Rand coming after you."

But he won't find you in time to keep me from taking you, Eddy thought gleefully. *Eddy,* an inner voice whispered, *what is Giuseppe going to think about you making love to the woman he wants for Vonny? Do you really think you can outsmart him?*

As if Giuseppe were speaking to him, Eddy looked around fearfully. He saw no one but the woman and his men. Still he felt as if he were being watched. He could see eyes peering at him in the dark. Damn Sancho! It was the old man's fault, talking about Diablo Negro. Besides, he thought, what he did with Clem Jones was none of Giuseppe's business. He straightened his back and shoulders. He no longer worked for either Giuseppe or Borajo.

But you did work for the Italian, and you know it's his plan to punish the woman. He won't like what you're doing. He's going to get angry. And Sancho is right, both the Lorenzo brothers are loco. They'll come get you.

Fear filled Eddy. He had witnessed Giuseppe's anger, and he did not want to be on the receiving end of it. Still, he could not relinquish Clem Jones. He so wanted to make love to her, and he would. He was a faster gun than either Giuseppe or Giovanni. He would not allow them to tell him what he could or could not do.

A burden lifted, he laughed. Nothing mattered. This was his day. Although the skies were dark with storm clouds, rain pelting down in sheets so thick he could not see a foot ahead, and the north wind assailed, he was extraordinarily happy. He threw back his head, letting the rain wash his face, and laughed and laughed. He, Eddy Gonzales, had found Clem Jones, and no one knew he had her. She was his to do with as he wished.

When they found the remains of the *pistolero,* they would assume Indians had caught them. A surge of power ran through Eddy. Now he was the one in control, not Father Borajo, not Giuseppe or Giovanni, but he, Eddy Gonzales, was the leader.

And he wanted to possess this woman. She was not the most attractive woman he had ever seen, but she was exciting to look at. He liked his women small and petite, with dark features, but he would take this Anglo with her light complexion and reddish brown hair. He had been fantasizing about her body ever since he had seen her at the cave earlier. He could only imagine all the beautiful female delicacies awaiting his touch. It was all his.

Later, he reached beneath his poncho and extracted a watch — the one he had found on the *pistolero*. Protecting it from the rain, he clicked open the lid and listened as it softly chimed the hour. The song was in French, but it was beautiful. If ever he needed money, he could sell the watch, but right now he wanted to enjoy it. He slipped it back into his pocket.

Only fifteen minutes had passed since he last checked the time. He needed to put more distance between himself and Lawful. He looked over his shoulder. Clem was sitting straight; her posture was almost defiant. Eddy grinned to himself. He knew she had to be tired; they had traveled many miles in the cold rain. But she was a spirited one, and he liked that. He jabbed his spurs into the sides of his horse and urged it faster, regardless of the rain and the mud-slick pathways.

"Do not worry, *senorita,* soon we will be warm and dry."

"I'm not worried, and I'm fine just like I am," Clem shouted. "I've been through worse than this during my life."

"You are lying, *senorita,* but I like your spirit." Again he laughed. This was the happiest he could remember being in his twenty-two years. He felt as if he controlled the whole world. "We will be there by nightfall."

Even if Clem did not, Eddy longed for the warmth of the cabin, for shelter from the rain, and for a drink of whiskey, for the soft bed. The soft bed on which he would conquer this Clem . . .

"Your name, *senorita,* it is just Clem?" When she did not answer, he said, "No, I know it is not. I heard Father Borajo call it one time, but I cannot remember. Perhaps in English you call yourself Clementine or is it Clementina? I think I shall choose the Spanish pronunciation. It is so much more romantic than Clem or Clementine."

Yes, he would drink his whiskey and make love to Clementina Jones on the soft bed. He would sleep; then awaken and make love to her again . . . and again.

He was a man.

Wearing nothing but his trousers and shirt, both sodden from the continuous drizzle, the shirt unbuttoned and his chest bared to the inclement weather,

310

Wade lay spread-eagle, staked to the side of the mountain. A fine mist of rain peppered his cold, chafed skin; the north wind cruelly blew against his body, already numbed with cold. His brain was also slowing down. A few more hours, and he would be dead.

Clem. He had to save Clem. He fought through the wintry fog that was stripping him of coherent thought. Eddy's intent was obvious. Wade shivered, not from the cold, but from the vision of what Eddy Gonzales planned for Clem.

With another surge of strength, Wade twisted his arms and feet, but the thongs, now thoroughly wet, were swollen and bit into his flesh. He screamed his frustration and pain.

He had to get free. A gust of wind tore his shirt from his body, and the mist turned into a heavy downpour, large drops of water stinging his skin. Blending into the rivulets of water that ran down the sides of his face were his tears.

Minutes . . . precious minutes passed. He opened his eyes, but the rain, beating down upon them, forced his lids shut. He cursed the rain, the cold, the world. He cursed his helplessness . . . but to no avail.

Then he yelled for help until his throat was hoarse and no sound would come. The frustration, the premature darkness, the cold, all combined against him, and he gave a cry of desperation. His mind wavered between Clem and the void. Despite the hammering of the rain and the blasting of the wind, he forced open his eyes and saw only the thick blanket of black clouds that seemed to be dropping lower and lower to suffocate him.

Then they fell on top of him.

Wade was aware of callused but gentle fingers probing his chest. He still felt the rain and the wind against his body, but he was not nearly as cold. Then he saw that he was wearing an Indian jacket and moccasins; he was lying on a travois. Someone was prepared to move him.

He looked up into the eyes of a grizzled old man, his face wrinkled and lined from the weather as much as from age. His black hair was liberally streaked with white, a heavy fringe hanging across his forehead in bangs; the remainder hung in a heavy, straight curtain around his face.

"White man."

Wade heard the soft words and focused his eyes on the Indian's face. Obsidian eyes, the most gentle eyes Wade had ever encountered, centered on him.

"Why were you staked out to die?"

"Outlaw," Wade croaked, and cringed at the pain in his throat. His head spinning so much he could hardly think. His body aching all over, he spoke disjointedly, "He — kid — napped — my woman. Must get her."

"Who is your woman?"

"Clem," Wade answered. "Clem Jones."

"We go with you."

"Clem — we — I must get her." His throat was much better; still it hurt. "We don't have any time to spare."

"We have no time at all. That belongs to the Great Spirit. Outlaw took your woman and your gun." The old man's words, a statement not a question, were derisive. "How you going to get her back?" He laughed, the sound not much more than a cackle.

"My horse."

"Outlaw no take horse, but I keep for rescuing

you."

"Damn the horse!" Wade exclaimed. "You can have it, but you've got to let me use him to find Clem."

The old man rose, and two young warriors helped Wade to his feet. Another led his horse to him.

"We will show you the way," the old man said, his obsidian eyes fastening to Wade's face. "We help you find Clementina Jones."

"Peaceful," Wade said.

The old man nodded. "I knew she was coming to see me. The Great Spirit told me. I have been troubled for her, but I thought it was the grief she suffered after her father's death. Do not worry, she is safe. My warriors will help you find her and bring both of you to the safety of my camp."

"Peaceful," Wade called as the Indian disappeared into the night, "take me to her."

"I will do that, *senor*. My grandfather is too old for the trip."

Wade turned to encounter another Indian about the same age as he, who had ridden up so quietly that Wade was not aware of his presence until he spoke. Over his shoulders were Wade's saddlebags.

In his native tongue, the Indian leader gave a command, and the Indians began to move down the trail in a single file. Wade mounted and followed them.

They had traveled for a good while when Wade said, "Can't we move any faster? We're going to lose the trail."

"We shall find your woman," he said. "But you must trust us. At best the mountain trails are dangerous; during a storm like this they are treacherous. We must travel slowly. Besides, we Mescaleros know these mountains better than anyone else. Once our scouts have located her, they will send word back to us. Then we will take a shorter route to get where she is."

Believing the man, Wade finally asked, "Who are you?"

"I'm not sure. I have been asking myself that question for many years. I'm as far away from an answer today, as I was when I first started the quest."

"Perhaps I should frame the question differently," Wade said. "I really wasn't prepared for a philosophical dissertation. What is your name?"

The Indian laughed softly. "In your language, I am called the Black Devil; otherwise, I'm known as Diablo Negro."

"Somehow I thought so," Wade murmured.

"Since we are introducing ourselves," the Mescalero said, "what is your name?"

"Wade. Wade Cameron. What are you doing here? You're supposed to be on your reservation in New Mexico. San Carlos or Cold Spring or something or the other."

"Something-or-the-other describes the place where we were herded," the Indian repeated. "Like San Carlos and Warm Springs, it too was in New Mexico. But it is not my home, *senor*. This is where Diablo Negro belongs, and this is where he is going to live and die."

He was quiet for a moment, then said, "The white man has stolen our land and has put us in reservations much like prison camps. He claims we will be safe there, but we are not. White men steal our food, our cattle, and our horses. They kill our women and children. The leader of the horse thieves killed my sister who was carrying a baby. He spoke in a foreign language that sounded like Italian. I am

314

going to find and punish him; I'll get our horses."

Again he lapsed into silence; finally he asked, "What are you doing out here?"

"Clem and I were bringing smallpox vaccine to your village."

"To stop an epidemic before it hit the white man, I suppose," the Mescalero said.

"No, she wanted to save your people."

"And what are we being saved for? To herd on a reservation like animals? Still, her thought and deed were noble. When I asked the question, I did not mean my village. What are you doing in West Texas? You are not one of us?"

"How do you know?"

"Your clothes," Diablo Negro answered. "They do not come from any of the general stores in this area."

"I'm from New York," Wade answered. "I'm looking for a man who disappeared years ago."

"Many men come west, Wade Cameron, to get lost. I doubt that you will find him, unless he desires to be found."

"My sentiments exactly," Wade replied, "but I promised his brother that I would try."

They rode many miles in silence, then Diablo Negro said, "I had hoped, Wade Cameron, I could come home and live out my life in peace, but it is not to be. The white man is not satisfied with my land; he wants my integrity. He wants me to be subservient to him. He has sent out word that I'm on the warpath, and that I'm carrying the smallpox plague."

"Are you?"

"I'm tired of fighting," Diablo Negro replied. "I want peace so that I can love my family and see my children grow into men and woman. I want to teach

315

them to love this land that has belonged to our fathers for hundreds of years. I want to grow into an old man with grandchildren around his feet. At night around the campfire, I will tell them stories about my exploits when I was a Mescalero warrior. I will tell them stories of the bygone days."

"How about the smallpox?"

"I have been vaccinated," he replied, and twisted a bracelet from his upper arm so that Wade could see the ugly scar.

"You're an educated man," Wade mused, "and I don't mean self-educated. You've been to school."

Diablo Negro's lips lifted slightly at the corners. "You forget, the white men love to teach the Indians. I have been exposed to missionary schools since I was a small lad."

The wind howled, and the rain hammered down.

"Tell me, Wade Cameron, how did you lose your woman and your guns?"

Quickly Wade recounted the story.

"Clem Jones is what life has made her," he said. "Just as you and I are. I haven't seen her since she was a little girl, and I worked for her father and uncle."

"You didn't happen to know another man who rode with them?" Wade asked. "A man named The Blacksmith?"

Eventually the Indian said, "Many men rode with Clement and Rand through the years."

Once more they lapsed into silence. Again it was Diablo Negro who spoke first, "I went through your saddlebags. You are a writer and an artist?"

"No, only a writer. My cousin drew the pictures."

"He is talented. I would like for him to draw my people, especially my grandfather. He is an old man, and I would like to have his likeness after he is gone."

"I believe I could persuade Prentice to do that for you."

"While my grandfather was bringing you to consciousness, I read what you have written, and I like it. You are a good writer. I would like for you to tell my story."

"What kind of story?"

"The story of my people."

A loud wailing sound broke out, and Wade started.

"Do not worry," Diablo Negro said. "That is my grandfather. He will ride part of the way with us. He is asking the Great Spirit to guide his warriors. One-who-is-at-Peace-with-the-Universe has a special vision; he has eye of the Great Spirit. Soon you will see your woman. And she will be unharmed."

Although he was usually the skeptic, Wade believed the man.

Clem cringed and blinked back the tears as she thought about Wade staked to the side of the mountain, wearing nothing more than his trousers and shirt. Eddy had taken his boots and coat and revolvers and the beautiful watch, all of which he would sell for a tidy profit.

For the hundredth time she wondered what he ultimately was going to do with her. She knew he would rape her, but what was her fate after that? She also wondered who he was working for. A while back they had stopped, and the vaqueros had grouped together for a long parley—one from which she had been excluded. Afterwards the group had separated. She, her captor, and five of the vaqueros had continued in one direction, a lone rider had gone in another.

She had to escape. Wade would soon be dead from exposure. If he did not die from that, a wild animal would get him. Clem had to return; she had to save him.

Was it only last night that she and Wade had made love? It seemed as if it were thousands of years ago. A soft bed, a warm fire, and Wade . . . and Wade, that's what Clem wished for. She heard another peal of maniacal laughter and shivered in the saddle. Eddy Gonzales frightened her, and his friend, the old vaquero named Sancho, had little influence with him.

"Around the next bend, *senorita,*" he called over his shoulder. "The cabin is around the next bend. Our journey is almost over; we shall soon be warm and dry."

Clem wanted the journey to end. Having been tied to her horse for hours, she was sore and stiff. She was so cold, she ached all over. But she also dreaded the moment when they arrived at their destination.

She did not have to exercise her imagination at all to know what Eddy planned for the night. The thought of his hands touching her body—touching her as only Wade had done—filled her with revulsion. She had to protect herself, but how? He had taken her guns along with Wade's.

Then her troubled thoughts ceased; they were in front of a small cabin. Eddy leaped down from his mount and ran back to Rusty-Be-Dusty. Eager to free her from the horse, he pulled out his knife and cut the ropes rather than work the knots loose. He did not loosen the ropes that bound her arms and hobbled her legs. Exhausted and stiff, unable to hold herself on the horse, she slid off. When her feet touched the ground, she cried out in pain. A thousand needles shot through her.

"Sancho, take care of the horses," Eddy shouted. Then he caught her into his arms and carried her into the cabin, laying her on the bed. He tied her securely to the metal frame. He struck a match, the small flame for one moment illuminating the entire room.

Locating the lamp, Eddy moved to the table and took off the smoke-darkened chimney. He lit the second match and touched the wick. It sputtered to life, and soft light filtered through the room.

Mumbling to himself, laughing ever so often, he closed the front door. All the while Clem worked with the ropes that bound her, but she could not untie them. As soon as Eddy had a fire going, he walked to the cabinet and opened the doors. Smiling, he held up a bottle of whiskey.

"Are you planning on celebrating by yourself?" Clem asked.

"No, *senorita*."

"May I have a glass of that?"

His gaze went to the bottle, then back to her. "You like whiskey, *senorita?*"

"I've never really drank that much," she answered, "but I'm cold and stiff. I could do with some right now."

Smiling, Eddy turned and opened another door, taking out two glasses which he set on the table. "I will give you some. We will have a good time tonight."

He shed his poncho and, reaching into his pocket, took out the watch to lay it beside the glasses.

"Where did the other men go?"

"It's not for you to worry about, *senorita*."

The entrance door opened and closed, cold wind gushing through the room as Sancho entered. *"Hijo!"*

He spoke in Spanish, glancing furtively at Clem. While she was not a fluent speaker of the language, she did understand enough to know what he was saying. She pretended an indifference.

"Something is wrong. I can feel it in my bones. We are being watched."

Eddy's face tightened, and he walked to the window, peering into the evening shadows, darker than usual because of the storm. Raindrops rolled down the window pane.

"Who do you think it is?"

"I do not know, Eduardo, but I am afraid. Very afraid. Are you sure Theodoro does not know about this cabin?"

"They are in there."

Diablo Negro pointed, and through the fine mist Wade saw the cabin, light filtering through the window. Eddy Gonzales and another man were talking; Clem was lying on the bed, her hands and feet tied.

"They have posted their guards and are ready for the night," the Mescalero continued. "Two are on guard; one is asleep in the hut where they keep the animals; the other two are in the house."

"There was another one," Wade said.

"According to my scouts, many miles back he split from them and headed toward San Elizario or Botello."

To get whom? Wade wondered. The priest. The man he worked for. Perhaps both. Perhaps one and the same.

"I want to get Clem out of there before that man abuses her worse," Wade said. "Have your men take care of the guards and the man asleep in the hut. I want Eddy Gonzales for myself."

"You would kill for this woman?"

"I would," Wade answered, "but I don't plan to kill Gonzales unless I have to. I need some answers, and he's the one who has them."

Wade dismounted and tethered his horse in a cluster of rocks. "I need a weapon. Would you loan me a knife? Gonzales took mine when he stole my boots."

Diablo Negro reached into the sheath at his waistline. "This knife was given to me many years ago by a man whom I respected greatly. I shall make you a gift of it. It has strong medicine, because it first belonged to a brave man. Clement Jones. Now use it to free his daughter."

Diablo slid off his mount. "I shall go with you. Two of us shall meet with two of them. I shall tell you when the men outside have been taken care of. My warriors will let me know."

Sancho paced nervously in the cabin. He heard the chirruping again, unfamiliar chirruping. He reached up and wiped beads of sweat from his upper lips.

"There, Eduardo," he said. "Did you not hear it?"

Eddy laughed and downed another glass of whiskey. "No, *mi amigo,* I did not. You are hearing things. Now, leave the house and let me have my pleasure. When I am finished, I will call you."

Sancho cast his gaze on Clem. "What if something went wrong?" he said. "What if Theodoro knew that we were betraying Giuseppe?"

Eddy rose and walked to Sancho, laying an arm across his shoulder. "We have nothing to worry about. Pedro is dead, and Theodoro can tell nothing more than what he saw. He knows we have Clementina, but he has no idea where we are. I assure you, he does not know about the cabin."

Again Sancho mopped his face with his hand. "You are sure you have thought of everything, Eduardo?"

"Sí."

"Then I will go outside and sleep for a while." He looked at Clem again. "You will call me when it's my time with the woman?"

Guiding Sancho to the door, Eddy laughed and clapped him on the back. "I promise."

Wade, standing in the shadows, saw Sancho leaving the cabin. He had only walked a few paces when Diablo slipped up behind him, clapping his hand over the Mexican's mouth and cracking his neck. With a thick sigh, the dead man slid to the ground with a dull thud.

"Now," the Mescalero said, "you have only the one inside the building."

Through the window Wade saw Eddy tie Clem spread-eagle on the bed and run his hand down her body. He cringed, hatred like molten lead burning through his body. His only thought to rescue her, Wade hurried to the door and threw it open, taking the Mexican by surprise.

"Wade!" Clem screamed. "You're alive."

"I never thought to see you again." Eddy whipped out his revolver, but Wade drew back his hand, the knife Diablo Negro had given him went singing through the air. It sliced through the gunslinger's upper arm. Yelling obscenities, he dropped his gun, jerked the blade from his flesh, and lunged at Clem.

Not concerned with his wounded shoulder, thinking only of Clem, Wade instantly met Eddy's challenge. He charged across the room, their bodies immediately locking in combat as fierce and deadly as that of any wild animal fighting for life itself; they *were* fighting for life itself.

Eddy was smaller and lighter than Wade; he was the youngest and the swiftest. But Wade had the advantage. He was fighting for the woman he loved. Locked together in mortal combat, they scratched and clawed for the gun. They pounded each other in the face with their fists. They rolled and tumbled. Finally Eddy grasped the gun. Wade, with the speed and agility of 'a much younger man, slapped the weapon from Eddy's hand. The gun slid across the floor, spinning around on its cylinder.

"Damn you!" the Mexican muttered, "I'll get you yet."

The agony in Wade's shoulder was so bad, he was not sure he could continue to hold Eddy down. The pain was unbearable. He gulped in needed air; then Eddy broke free, springing to his feet, giving Wade a punishing blow in the abdomen. Wade doubled in sheer agony. Eddy drew back his leg and kicked Wade in the ribs; when he fell to the floor, the youth stomped his back. The spurs bit into Wade's flesh.

Wade gritted his teeth together, refusing to let the Mexican know how badly he was hurt. If he did, Eddy would win. Eddy raced to the revolver. Picking it up, he aimed the weapon at Wade's heart. Wade groped for and found the knife. His hand closed around it, the adrenalin flowing, fear streaming through his being, giving him the strength to go beyond his natural abilities. With one last surge of energy, he pushed up on his knees. At the same time that Eddy fired, Wade sent the knife flying through the air. It plunged through Eddy's heart.

He stood for a moment, wide-eyed and disbelieving, staring at Wade. He clutched the knife with both hands and jerked it from his body. He took a step. Blood flowed from the wound. He staggered. He swayed. Then he fell.

Wade picked up the knife that lay at Eddy's feet, wiped the blood on his trousers, and moved to the bed. He cut the ropes that bound Clem and caught her in his arms, holding her tightly, never wanting to turn her loose.

Pain forgotten, he reveled in the joy of victory, in the joy of knowing that he had rescued Clem. Then his hands began a thorough examination of her body.

"Did he hurt you?" he asked.

"No," she answered. She pulled back and ran her hands through his hair, over his face and down his chest. "How are you? I thought sure you would die."

"I would have, had it not been for your friend Diablo Negro."

She looked around Wade at the warrior. "Hello," she said.

The Mescalero warrior smiled. "Hello, little Clemmy. It has been a long time since I saw you."

Her eyes twinkling, she said, "Long enough that I'm no longer called little Clemmy."

Diablo laughed. Then he walked to the door, and speaking in his native language, ordered his men to remove Eddy's body and to bring in Wade's and Clem's saddlebags.

"I wish I could have taken him alive," Wade said. "I think maybe he would have given us some answers that we need. Are the others dead?"

Diablo nodded.

"Not all of them," Clem said. "There was one who separated from the group long before we arrived at the cabin. I don't know where he went."

"Would you recognize him again if you saw him?" Wade asked.

"Yes."

Diablo looked out the window. "I think perhaps we should spend the night here. The weather is much too bad for us to be traveling. The storm will have passed by morning."

Wade and Clem agreed. When the numbness left her arms and legs, and she could stand again, Clem slipped off the bed and went to the cupboard. Soon she had a pot of cornmeal mush cooking and coffee boiling. At Diablo's request, Wade had taken out his writing portfolio, the two of them talking about the Mescalero Indians and their history as they looked at the sketches Prentice had drawn.

After they had eaten, Diablo said good night, rose, and walked out the door. He stopped and returned to the room. "I know the man called Blacksmith," he said.

Wade felt like a man who has been underwater, deprived of oxygen until he thought he would surely die. Although his first gasp when his head is above the water gives him the promise of life, it is painful. Wade's chest hurt from sheer anticipation and joy.

"Will you tell me about him?" Wade asked.

The Indian shook his head. "His story belongs to him. If he wants you to know, he will tell you. I will take you to him, if you wish. It is not far from here.

We can make the journey in two days."

"What about the smallpox vaccine?" Clem asked.

For the second time Diablo pulled the gold bracelet from his upper arm, then turned so she could see the horrible scar. "My warriors and I do not carry the disease. We have been vaccinated. I shall send one of my braves with the vaccine you have brought to my grandfather for safe keeping. When we make our return trip, you may stop in the village and vaccinate those who wish to have it." He looked at Wade. "Do you wish to make the journey?"

"Yes," Wade answered, "I do."

He felt as if he had slid the key into the lock and was about to open the door to unravel his mystery.

Chapter Eighteen

The storm and cold front had passed as quickly as it came, leaving an oppressive heat in its wake. The warmth of the day pressed in on Rand, who stood in the alley behind the sheriff's office and watched the Mescalero brave disappear into the distance. He had sneaked into town to deliver a message from Clem and Wade. Although Rand had read through it once already, he reread it. They had no need to fear a smallpox epidemic caused by Diablo Negro and his band, Wade reassured them. The Mescaleros had been vaccinated prior to leaving the reservation. Succinctly but graphically, Wade had sketched in the details of their ordeal, giving them the names of the men who had captured them. He also told Rand about Diablo Negro and his men pursuing a horse thief, who might be Italian or who spoke Italian.

The last sentence sent fear up Rand's spine. Ordinarily a man's nationality did not play into his crimes where Rand was concerned, but this time it did, because it affected him personally. He was unusually sensitive when it came to Italians. Before leaving San Antonio, he had heard that gunslingers were gathering in El Paso, and two of the names bandied around were Giuseppe and Giovanni Lorenzo.

He wondered if Diablo's horse thief could be one of them. Although they had been boys when he, Clement, and the Blacksmith had killed their father and older brothers, they had promised retribution, and Rand had no doubt that they would either fulfill their promise or die trying.

When Rand thought about the Lorenzos and their vendetta, he became angry with Clement all over again. Rand loved his foster brother and would forever be grateful that Clement had taken him under wing when his father had died in the gambling incident, but Rand recognized that Clement was not perfect, and now one of his biggest mistakes, certainly his deadliest, had placed a shadow over his family through the years, and now might be about to overtake them. Rand only hoped he was strong enough to protect Deborah and Clem.

At times, he needed to talk about it, but he couldn't burden Deborah. She had enough on her shoulders worrying about Clem. So he kept it to himself.

Rand was surprised at Wade's interest in the Blacksmith, but he supposed what he accepted as a part of life was something the Eastern reader would find exciting, especially if Wade exaggerated the events at all. Rand was glad to know what Wade and Clem were doing and where they were headed, but he had to let Deborah know what had befallen them on their trip to the village. She would be worried, even more so when she learned they were traveling on to Mexico, even more so when . . . if she learned about the Lorenzos.

The night when he was at Ft. Stockton, when the telegram arrived announcing Clement's death and asking him to wear the badge, Rand had sent word to the Blacksmith asking him to join him in Lawful.

Now, more than ever, Rand wanted the Blacksmith by his side. He needed his gun; he needed his friendship and support. Rand could not remember the last time he prayed, but today he was praying — praying fervently that he could locate the Blacksmith, praying that the Blacksmith would join him in Lawful.

When Rand walked into the office, Turbin said, "I'm glad that Indian had the good sense to sneak into town. It sure wouldn't have done for the people to see him. It musta been something important to bring him in."

"Yes," Rand answered, "very important. It was a message from Wade and Clem. They found Diablo."

With the exclusion of Clem's capture by Eddy Gonzales, Rand repeated to Turbin the information as written by Clem and Wade.

"So they're going on into Mexico to see if they can find that man Cameron is hunting," Turbin said. "I guess Cameron has gone back to being a reporter. Only this time he's toting his guns. For the life of me, I can't figure a man who knows how to use 'em, knows the importance of 'em out here, and who wouldn't be wearing 'em."

"Yeah," Rand said, listening with only half an ear, his mind really on other matters. "I'm going to Deborah's. I want to let her know Clem's all right. I'll be back as soon as I can."

"No rush," the deputy said. "Things seemed to have quieted down, since Clem took care of Powers and Wade killed Perry. Reckon we've established ourselves as having peace officers what count. Nobody's gonna want to tangle with the likes of you and Clem . . . and Cameron."

"I hope so," Rand said, "but I wouldn't put too much confidence in it. In fact, I'm a little worried, because it's too quiet. I just hope Thompson and Howard don't stray too far from town. I don't want to find them hurt or dead, and their property forcefully bought from them."

Turbin laughed. "After what happened to Sam, I don't think we have to worry about that. Thompson and Howard are staying mighty close. You go on home, and don't worry none."

Walking out of the office, Rand mounted the grey and rode down the street. Lawful had changed little during the time he had been gone. There were a few new stores and faces; others were gone. Because the line of civilization had not yet moved this far, and probably would not for many years because of the desert-like conditions, the town was still stranded on the frontier and easy prey for desperados.

Turbin's words did little to reassure Rand that all was well. Hired guns were in El Paso, and all of them had been linked to Ike Perry. Since Rand had been here, no one had mentioned the Lorenzos, and because of Deborah—and her fear of them—neither had he. He wondered if they had any connection with the horse thief.

Whoever was behind the salt property take-over had evidently hired an entire army of gunslingers. One of these days, when the people least expected them, they would come riding into town, leaving utter destruction in their wake.

By the time Rand tied his horse to the hitching post, Deborah was on the porch, a smile tipping her lips. If she had aged any during the past years, he could not tell it. If she had, he would not have cared. Her beauty was not just in her outward appearance; it was a reflection of her soul. She was a loving, giving person.

Every time he saw her, she was more beautiful.

Although he had been in love with her for many years, there was a glow about her now that he had never noticed before. Her eyes were brighter; her laughter more melodious; her spirit lighter. Rand was happy to see and feel her joy. The last year she had lived with Clement, she had been sad and withdrawn.

"What a pleasant surprise," she said, her eyes twinkling.

She was wearing a pretty blue gown. He hoped she had dressed up for him. He had begun taking his meals with her.

"But lunch isn't quite ready," she continued.

Rand returned her smile. "I didn't come to eat," he said.

"How about a cup of coffee?"

"I'd like that." Following her through the house to the kitchen, he said, "I wanted to talk with you about Clem."

"She's all right, isn't she?" Deborah asked, her voice heavy with concern.

"She's fine," he hastily assured her.

Breathing a sigh of relief, Deborah took two cups from the cabinet and set them on the table. Moving to the stove, she picked up the coffeepot.

"One of Diablo's braves rode into town today and brought a note from her and Wade."

"May I see it?" she asked.

He reached into his pocket, and as his fingers brushed the tip of the paper, he remembered Wade's mentioning the Italian horse thief. He did not want Deborah to see that. Like him, she might suspect the Lorenzos, and that would only add to her anxieties. He withdrew his hand without the note.

"I must have left it at the office. I'll bring it by later."

Quietly he told her the content of the remainder of the note, as Deborah poured them coffee and sat down at the table across from him.

"What does it mean?" she asked. "Who is this Eddy Gonzales? Why would he kidnap her? What's going on, Rand?"

"To answer all your questions, I don't know. I just plain don't know." He took several swallows of his coffee, then set the cup down. "They're going into Mexico with Diablo to find the Blacksmith."

"Wade has been quite curious about him ever since he looked through Clement's photographs," she remarked. "Finding and talking with him has almost become an obsession."

"The brave had orders to catch up with Diablo, so I sent word to the Blacksmith. I've asked him to come help me."

Rand sighed and rubbed the back of his neck. He walked to the back door and gazed into the distance, always looking for something, always expecting something, never quite sure what. Maybe trouble. He took several swallows of his coffee.

"I wanted to send word to Wade and Clem for them to hurry back, because I have the feeling I'm going to be needing them, but I couldn't. No matter what happens here, I don't want to put Clem in danger, and this isn't Wade's war." He paused and sighed heavily before he said, "I may have to send a wire to Ramson and Hammond, and ask them to come work with me as deputies."

"Those bounty hunters!" Deborah exclaimed. "My God, Rand! Have you lost your senses. Even Clement would have balked at deputizing them."

"Their profession is guns. Fighting is second nature to them; surviving is first. Better them, than someone I don't know." He paced the floor. "Hokie

332

and Turbin are good men, but they can't stand up to men like Soloman Wise and Ike Perry. If I'm going to defend the people of Lawful and those damned salt lakes, I'm going to have to have me some guns, and good ones."

Rising, Deborah walked to him and laid her hand on his arm. "I'm sorry I exploded. You know what's best. If it's hiring them, then do it. All of us trust your judgment. That's why the council wanted you to be sheriff. They knew you would do what's right."

Deborah's soft voice played with Rand's emotions; she set wanting loose in him so bad he could hardly stand it. He looked down at the creamy hand that lay against his dark brown shirt. He felt the heat of her touch through the fabric. He wanted her, had wanted her ever since he returned, and the wanting had turned into an agonizing yearning.

At night when he lay awake on his narrow cot in the office, he thought about Deborah. He wondered what it would be like to hold her in his arms all during the night, to slowly make love to her, to awaken in the morning with her beside him. He could not be around her without wanting more than casual touches. He looked into her eyes; they were intense. Her desire for him equaled his for her.

"Deb," he murmured.

"No one ever called me that but you," she murmured.

"My little Deb."

He had asked her to marry him at the proper time, but he could not wait that long. God, but he had begun to think there was no proper time. He would not wait. He swept her into his arms and strode toward her bedroom. He knew he should not make love to her, but he could not help himself. He had wanted to love her for so long, to show her how strong, yet how tender, his love could be. How satisfying it could be. He had wanted her to love him as long. The longing was too much for him today. He had to sate his . . . and her . . . needs.

"I'm glad you came," she whispered. "I've been so lonesome for you. It's all I could do not to come to the office at night. I've thought about you lying in that bed all alone."

Deborah slipped her arms about his neck and pressed her lips to his cheek. As she touched her tongue to his skin, her body trembled against him. His quick intake of breath did not go unnoticed by her. She unbuttoned his shirt and slid her hand beneath the fabric. Her fingers through the thick covering of chest hair felt his muscles tighten.

"Deborah," he whispered hoarsely, "I've wanted you for so long, and I thought I'd never have you. I despaired of ever giving or receiving love."

"I know how you felt, my darling, because I felt the same way," she whispered also, blinking back the tears. "But I shall give you love, all my love."

He set her down in her bedroom, and she lifted her face, looking into his eyes, allowing her passion and her love to shine in hers.

Neither knew shame, because love knows it not.

When he lowered his mouth over hers, she welcomed him, opening her mouth to his kiss. Her hand drifted upward to caress his cheeks and to brush through his hair. He held her tightly.

He broke the kiss and straightened; he simply looked at her. Both of them were breathing deeply. Her gaze never leaving his face, she backed away from him and began to unbutton her dress. Rand watched her movements, his eyes dark with passion.

Following her lead, he, too, unbuttoned his shirt. Warm pleasure flowed through her body as she watched him slowly open the material to reveal his broad chest, swirls of dark hair descending to the waist of his trousers . . . below his waistline.

Inundated with passion, she bent, picked up the hem of her dress and pulled it over her head. She tossed it aside. Her undergarments followed. At last their clothes lay scattered about their feet. Both of them were naked.

He was handsome, made up of long, sleek lines of hard muscle. She moved toward him. She wanted to be held by him, kissed by him, loved by him. Her entire being throbbed for him.

"Deborah," he folded her into his arms, "I know we should wait, but, God forgive me, if this isn't the proper time, then I can't wait for it." His lips moved to hers, their breaths mingling, their souls uniting.

Pulling away from him, she held his face in both hands and looked into those dark gray eyes to see his need. "This is the proper time."

His fingers burned against her skin as he caressed her breasts. Pleasure rippled through her body, and she arched her back. His lips loved the fullness first, then touched a nipple, his tongue moving in tantalizing circles.

Deborah found his touch searing, more searing than any she had ever experienced. It seemed to burn through her body to settle in her pelvis. As surely as she was his, he was hers. She gave herself to him with utter abandon, an abandonment she had never felt with Clement, an abandonment she had never been allowed to share with him. He had always treated her like a porcelain doll, not like a woman.

Rand must have sensed her urgency, because he too became urgent. Showing no mercy, he loved her, all of her. He caressed her breasts, moving from one to the other and back again; slowly his lips moved

335

down her rib cage, his tongue titillating the sensitive area around her navel. All the while he kneaded her buttocks, pulling her tightly against his hardness.

He lifted his head to recapture her lips, lips that were bruised and swollen from his kisses. Yet she wanted more. She knew she was wanton, but did not care. She was wild with need; she was desperate for love.

When he lifted her into his arms and carried her to the bed, her body was moistly hot, ready to receive him. She parted her thighs to his touch. She wanted no more foreplay; she wanted him within her. She met his lips with hers, as he gently lowered himself into her.

So many years their emotions had been wed; so long they had loved each other — loved at a distance. Now, for the first time, their bodies were joined together. As far as she was concerned, the marriage ceremony was complete with this coupling.

"Before God," she murmured, "I take this man to be my lawfully wedded husband to love, to honor, to cherish until death do us part."

His lips covered hers, the essence of her vow becoming a part of their kiss. His thrusts quickened; her softness received and held him; it pulsated around him. Their passion mounted until they climaxed together.

For a long while, they lay together quietly, simply holding each other.

"Thank you," she murmured. "You were wonderful."

"Was I?" he asked.

She heard the uncertainty in his voice and knew what he was really asking her, what he really wanted to know.

"You were better than Clement," she said. "I always cared for him, but I never loved him. I could satisfy him, but he was unable to satisfy me. Sometimes, I don't think he really tried. When it came to lovemaking, his satisfaction was of primary importance. I didn't seem to count."

Rand held her tighter, consoling her with his protective embrace.

"That's why he was so quick to believe that you and I were having an affair." She sighed. "I was able to bear the frustration until I fell in love with you. Even after that I would have stayed with him, but he began to play with me. I—I—"

Rand laid a finger over her lips. "You don't have to talk about it anymore, in fact, never again," he whispered. "Although I loved Clement, I knew him. I understood him. I also know what you went through. Never again, my darling." He sealed her lips with a kiss of promise.

Later he asked, "What will Clem think about our getting married?"

"I don't know," Deborah answered. "You know how close she was to Clement, how quick she was to believe the worst about you and me."

"As soon as she returns," Rand said, "we have to tell her."

"Yes."

He pushed up on an elbow and leaned down to press quick kisses down her neck and across her breasts. "I wish I could stay longer, but I need to get back."

"You could stay and have lunch with me."

"I promised Turbin he could leave early today. He and Hokie have some surveying to do."

Deborah remained in bed as he dressed.

"What do you think about Wade Cameron?" she asked.

Rand shrugged. "He seems to be okay to me. Why?"

"Clem's in love with him. She wouldn't have given up the badge if she weren't."

"Maybe we'll have a double wedding."

"She hasn't said anything about marriage," Deborah said.

She rose and gathered up her clothes to lay them across the foot of the bed. Still naked, she moved to the washstand to fill the basin with water.

He came to stand behind her, his hands gently cupping her shoulders. "You're her mother, and I know you're worried about her, but she's a woman, Deb. You've got to let her live her life. Give her space to grow. It's painful at times, but you've got to do it, if you want to keep her love and respect."

Deborah leaned back against him. "I don't want him to hurt her."

"He won't," Rand said. "Don't underestimate your daughter. She's made of strong material, like her mother."

"I hope she's stronger than her mother," she murmured. Then, looking at his reflection in the mirror, she asked, "Are you coming back later for lunch?"

He laid a hand over her shoulder to trail his fingers over the upper swell of her breasts. "I couldn't eat a thing. I've already had dessert." Then he pressed warm kisses into the hollow of her neck and shoulders. "Now, love, I must be going. I am sheriff of Lawful and have a job to do."

When he was at the door, Deborah said, "Rand, do you think the Blacksmith will come?"

He shrugged. "I don't know. This is the second message I've sent to him. Maybe he didn't get the first one. I mailed it before I left San Antonio, and sent it to his last known address. I told him about the Lorenzos—"

Deborah spun around. "The Lorenzos! You mean, *the Lorenzos,* the ones from New Orleans? The two younger brothers?"

Rand looked miserable; Deborah knew it had been a slip of the tongue. He had not intended to tell her. He twirled his hat in his hands.

"I've heard they're in El Paso," he said, "but I don't know if it's true or not. You know how rumors are."

"That's why you were coming back. You knew Clement was too old to stand up to them alone." She wrung her hands together. "Dear God, Rand, what are they doing out here? Have they come for us?"

"I don't know." Clearly he was as much at a loss for an explanation as she was.

"What are we going to do?" she demanded.

Tossing his hat onto a nearby table, he strode to her and embraced her. "Don't worry unnecessarily, honey. We don't know they're there. Even if they are, we don't know that they've come out here to carry out their vendetta. Let's take it a day at a time, all right?"

"Could that Eddy Gonzales and Clem's kidnapping be a part of this?" she asked. "Could he be working for the Lorenzos?"

"Again, baby, I don't know. It's possible, and to tell the truth, I've been thinking about it."

"Send to Ft. Stockton for help," she said.

"I have," he replied. "They have no troops to spare. The ones they have are out looking for the Indians that attacked the supply wagon and the Stoddards. God only knows why. By now those Comanches are in Mexico, hiding until the next time."

"Now I know why you were talking about hiring the bounty hunters. Maybe you should, Rand." She paused, then said, her voice stronger, more em-

339

phatic, "Hire them, Rand, and send them after the Lorenzos. Give them a third more than the posted reward for bringing them in dead."

"You fool!" Antonio Borajo shook his fist in Giuseppe Lorenzo's face. "You stupid fool! You have ruined everything for us. I don't have enough problems over the salt flats out of El Paso, but what you create more over the Chupedera Lakes!"

Giuseppe had never liked Antonio, and he liked him even less now. However, this was a time for solidarity, not division. They had mutual interests that were better served by their working together. Later, when he had what he wanted, Giuseppe thought, he would take care of his *dear cousin*.

"For you, perhaps," he said, "but not for me."

In the room above the cantina in Botello, the priest paced angrily back and forth. "The whole town is alerted now, and Rand is back. We could have handled Clement, because he was getting old and slow. But, no, you had to kill him. Now we have both his brother and his daughter to contend with. And this other man, the one named Wade Cameron, the one who killed Ike Perry. Had you waited, Giuseppe, we would have been in control of the salt flats and town by the time Rand got there, and both Clement and his daughter would have been dead. Lawful would have been your domain, and the Chupedera Salt Lakes would have belonged to me. Soon we'll have to fight the Texas Rangers!"

Giuseppe was not concerned about the priest's problems over the Guadalupe Salt Lakes out of El Paso; his concern was the Joneses and Lawful. He walked to the window and stared at the sleepy village. Theodoro, one of Eduardo's vaqueros, had paid

340

him a visit several nights ago, and had informed him that Eddy Gonzales had Clem and would tell him where she was when he received the money he wanted for her. The amount was staggering. Giuseppe was beginning to worry because he had received no other word, and Giovanni was getting restless.

A knock sounded, and a man's voice called, "Padre, it is Marco. I have something to tell you. It's important."

Borajo moved to open the door. A small man in white trousers and shirt held his sombrero in both hands in front of his chest. "Eduardo and Sancho are dead."

"Dead!" Borajo exclaimed. "I cannot believe that in such a short time all of this is happening! One by one, my men are being killed, and for what?"

Giuseppe started and hurried to where the two men stood.

Marco nodded his head. "I think you should come see."

Long strides carried Giuseppe and the priest outside to the wagon. Marco removed the blanket, and the two men stared at the dead bodies. Although they had already begun to decompose, Giuseppe had no difficulty identifying Eddy. The color drained from his face, Borajo jerked the blanket back over the corpses. He moved away from the wagon.

If Eddy was dead, Giuseppe wondered, where was Clem? How much did she know?

"Where did you find him?" the priest asked Marco.

"A vendor found them in the mountains at a deserted cabin. He brought them here in hopes they were outlaws and there was a reward for them."

"Damn," Borajo swore. Then: "Bury them."

"But, Padre, what about—"

"Just do as I say," the priest shouted. "I'll take care of the rites later."

"I was not worried about that," the man said. "I just wondered if there *is* a reward for these men."

"Go bury the men as I said, Marco," the priest shouted. "If there is a reward, I'll let you know later. Right now, I'm busy."

"*Sí*, Padre." The man slunk back from the angry priest.

Leaving the Mexican with the cart full of corpses, Borajo moved back into the cantina and the upstairs room. He prowled the room, alternately muttering and swearing. He poured himself a glass of whiskey and downed it in several large swallows.

"Eduardo was a problem," Borajo said. "I knew that I would have to get rid of him soon, but I wasn't quite ready. I'm just wondering what he was involved in that caused his death, and with whom?"

Giuseppe poured himself a drink, then sat slowly sipping on it. He felt it was time to confess his part in Clem's abduction. His need for Borajo was growing by the seconds. "I had Eddy and the vaqueros kill Olviera, and I sent Eddy to Lawful to make sure the kid was dead."

"You killed Olviera?" Borajo's words were dull. "Your men—my men—were the vigilantes?"

"Yes," Giuseppe admitted. "He had become a liability we could ill afford. Clem Jones interfered with our work, and we were unsure Alarico died immediately after we shot him, or whether he had lived long enough to talk."

Borajo drank a second glass of whiskey.

"Alarico did not know enough to tell, Giuseppe." The priest bowed his shoulders. "You should have left him up to me, as I asked you to. Both he and we would have been safer had he been allowed to go to Mexico as I ordered. If only Eduardo had listened to me instead of you." '

Giuseppe hated to admit it, but his cousin was right. This infuriated him, and he was determined to get rid of Borajo as quickly as possible. He despised being made a fool of. Of course, the death would have to look like an accident.

"Evidently, Eddy found and captured Clem Jones and the man who killed Ike Perry," Giuseppe said. "Eddy killed the man, making it look like the Indians had done it; he has—or had—Clem in hiding. He'd offered to sell her to me."

Giuseppe drew the note from his pocket and handed it to Borajo, who after reading it, crumpled it in his fist.

"When did you receive this?"

"Several days ago."

"By whom?" the priest asked.

"Theodoro."

Borajo laughed. "Of course, Eduardo would have sent his imbecile to you. Have you questioned him?"

"He says he knows nothing."

"He doesn't, I warrant. Eduardo was brilliant; he wouldn't have sent you a man he didn't think was expendable, and one who knew nothing, therefore, could tell you nothing." Borajo again paced the floor, his hands clasped behind him, his head bowed in thought. Finally he said, "It's safe to presume someone rescued Clem Jones. I doubt a woman could do this much damage."

"It's also safe to presume Eddy talked before he died."

The priest nodded. "Do you have someone whom you trust that you could send to Lawful to find out what is going on? Someone," he added sarcastically, "who can remain inconspicuous and live long enough to get information back to us."

"I will find someone," Giuseppe said.

"Good. Then, it is in our best interest if we sit back and wait. I shall return to the mission, you to Botello. Let us see what will happen." He paused thoughtfully, then said, "If Clem Jones is alive, she will return home shortly."

"The longer we wait," Giuseppe warned him, "the more time we give them to build their defenses."

Borajo nodded his head. "I wish you had thought of that sooner, before we lost so many of our best gunmen. Now it is time for me to return to the church."

As Borajo pulled on the door handle, Giuseppe confessed his greatest fear: "I don't know how much longer I can control Vonny. His one obsession is the vendetta against the Joneses."

Antonio Borajo stared coldly at Giuseppe. "Kill him if you have to. Too much is at stake to let a lunatic like him ruin it for us."

Giuseppe did not care if his hatred for the priest burned in his eyes or not. Rather than kill Vonny, he would kill Borajo.

Rand was standing by himself in front of the saloon when he saw the large cloud of dust in the distance. Riders were moving up from the south. Tense, apprehensive, he pushed away from the building. He hoped this was not a visit of the Lorenzos or any other gunmen. If it were, he was in trouble. Both Hokie and Turbin were gone today, completing a survey assignment.

Prentice walked out of the saloon, his gaze swinging up and down the street before it settled on the

344

riders. "Who do you think they are?" he asked.

Squinting against the glare of the afternoon sun, Rand shook his head. Slowly he walked down the street, Prentice by his side. People gathered behind him, curiosity buzzing through the crowd as they moved, all staring at the cloud of dust that came nearer and nearer.

Grady came to stand by Rand, his shotgun in hand. "I can't do much," he said, "but I'll do whatever I can to help you."

Barney Joiner came galloping into town, a mail pack slung over his shoulder.

"Cavalry's coming," he called out. "They've been trailing the Indians who attacked the supply wagon. They even caught one of 'em. They're headed back to the fort."

The promise of troops excited and relaxed the people. Everyone soon dispersed, leaving only Rand and Prentice on the street. The soldiers, when they arrived, were tired, their clothes dirty. With them they had a prisoner, an Indian brave who was bound to his horse.

"Hello, I'm Lt. Frederick." The officer dismounted and shook hands with Rand. "We've been chasing the Indians that attacked the supply wagon last week. We're mighty tired."

Rand smiled. "We'd love to have you as our guests, Lieutenant."

"Yes, sir," Emmett Frazier seconded, "be our guests. Come inside, and I'll give all of you a drink on the house."

"Thanks," the officer said, then turned to Rand. "We'd like for you to lock this buck up. He's the only one we caught, but we want to take him back to the fort for interrogation. He's running with a renegade bunch. We think he's one of Black Devil's braves, but

345

we can't get him to talk."

Rand looked at the cuts and bruises on the Indian's body. His gaze caught and locked with obsidian eyes that were void of any emotion. "Looks like you tried."

"Gave him a bit of his own medicine," the young officer said. "But he's a stubborn one. He would have died before he talked." He paused, then said reflectively, "He would have died singing."

Rand nodded. "His death chant."

"Well, these Indians are a strange lot. I can't imagine anybody singing in the face of death."

"I don't think this one was involved with the attack," Rand said. "They were Comanche."

"How do you know?" the officer demanded.

"I was there, and I know Comanches from the Apaches. I can tell by the way they ride and dress, by their weaponry. I know for sure they were not Mescaleros."

"Oh, well," the officer sloughed off Rand's words, "an Indian's an Indian."

"You're not concerned that you may have an innocent man?"

The officer shook his head. "The way I look at it, no Indian is innocent. This one may not be guilty of attacking the supply wagon, but he's guilty of something. And we're ridding civilization of a menace. At least, we're not returning to the fort empty-handed. We have something to show for our work."

"How long have you been out here?" Rand asked.

Frederick grinned sheepishly. "About four months."

"You've got a lot to learn, Lieutenant, and I sure hope you learn it soon, or you'll be a dead man. Now, you go on into the hotel, and I'll take care of your prisoner."

"Sir," Prentice said to the officer, "do you mind if I

draw pictures of you and your men?"

"Of courses not," the officer answered, immediately reaching up to brush dust from his shoulders.

Rand smiled as the artist introduced himself to the soldiers. He caught the reins and led the horse and brave down the street, stopping in front of the jail. The prisoner refused to dismount, and Rand had to pull him to the ground.

"You're making it rough on yourself," he said. "I'm not like the soldiers, but you are going to obey me."

In a heated contest Laban and Lucia McLean rolled barrel hoops down the middle of the street. Other children, cheering them on, ran beside them.

"Laban," Rand called, "when the race is over, go get the doctor for me. Tell him I need some help over at the jail."

By the time Elm arrived, Rand had locked the prisoner in a cell. Through the bars Indian and doctor glared at each other.

"I think I have a hostile patient on my hands, Rand. Don't figure he's going to take to my doctoring him."

"He may," Rand answered, and pointed to the Indian's forearm. "Take a close look."

"Well, I do declare, he's been vaccinated."

Leaning against the wall, his arms folded over his chest, his leg crossed at the ankles, Rand said, "I have a feeling that he's one of Black Devil's braves."

"Why do you think that?" Elm asked. "We just sent a passel of vaccine to his grandfather's village."

Rand unlocked the cell, and Elm entered the cubicle. As Elm examined the man who sat on the narrow cot, Rand repeated the information in the note Clem sent, careful to state where Diablo Negro was, what he was doing, and with whom he was doing it. He was doing this as much for the brave as for Elm.

347

"Clem told me that Diablo Negro and his band had trailed the horse thieves to Texas. They were on their way to intercept them when they found Wade, who had been staked out on the mountain and left to die."

"So why did the Mescaleros attack the supply wagon and the Stoddards?" Elm dabbed some ointment on the cuts.

Standing at the door, Rand gazed pensively at the warrior. "They didn't. It was Comanches."

For the first time, the brave's eyes flashed. Rand knew he had his attention. Elm recapped his medicine bottles and dropped them into his satchel. Shutting it, he walked out of the cell. Rand moved in and looked directly into the obsidian eyes.

"I'm Rand McGaffney, brother to Clement Jones. I've ridden with Peaceful, Diablo Negro's grandfather and with Diablo Negro himself. We are friends. I wouldn't be alive today if I didn't know a lot about the Indians out here. I certainly know the difference between Comanche and Mescalero."

The Indian continued to stare.

"If you'll talk with me, I can help you. Maybe get you back to your people."

"Why are you interested in the Mescalero?"

The Indian spoke in stilted English, a clear indication to Rand that he had been educated in a mission school.

"I'm the sheriff here," Rand said. "I'm interested in seeing that justice is carried out."

"I do not believe in white man's justice."

"Maybe not," Rand said, "but you better believe in me if you want your freedom." Moving out of the cell, he closed and locked the door. "You're a scout for Diablo Negro, aren't you?"

"He's not going to talk, Rand," Elm said. "You

might as well let the soldiers take him back to the fort. He'll be lucky if they hang him. If they don't, they'll put him in prison."

"White man's justice!" he exclaimed bitterly and leaped to his feet. "I have done nothing but follow thieves who stole our horses."

Wade's words echoed in Rand's mind. He nodded his head. "I thought so. Where are they?"

"Why do you ask this?"

Again the words in Clem's and Wade's note echoed through Rand's mind. The horse thief may be Italian. "Perhaps you and I are looking for the same men. I want to know where their camp is, so I can see how large a number the enemy commands. I'll help you escape, if you'll show me."

The Indian's lips moved so that he almost smiled. "It's in a valley in the mountains close to Botello."

"Not good enough," Rand said. "You'll have to show me."

"I don't believe you can help me escape. Even I know the soldiers are more powerful than you."

"But even soldiers are afraid of plagues." Rand looked at Elm and grinned. "Do you have some of those berries left? The ones that Laban and Lucia got a hold of on the day of the barbecue?"

Throwing back his head, Elm laughed. "If I don't, I believe I could get the younguns to rustle up some more." He peered through the iron bars at the captive. "Rand is suggesting I give you some berries that will cause you to break out in a rash and fever. If you eat them, you'll be mighty sick for several days. Mighty sick with a high fever. You figure if you don't die from the fever, you'll scratch yourself to death. But, mind you, you won't die." He chuckled. "For a while you might wish you could."

"The soldiers will believe you are," Rand said.

"I know of such berries. Are your soldiers that foolish?"

"No," Rand answered, "they just haven't been out here that long. They don't really know anything about the country or the people out here."

"Even if they were old-timers," Elm said, "it's a mighty convincing sight. I thought sure those two younguns were gonna die. Been out here a mighty long time myself, and I knew the berries weren't edible. But this was my first time to see the reaction to them."

"We'll give them to you on the day the soldiers are preparing to leave," Rand said.

"How do you know you can trust me to lead you to this camp?" the Indian asked.

"How do you know you can trust me?" Rand answered his question with a question.

"I'll be getting back to the office," Elm said. "Let me know if you'll be needing my services any more and when."

"I am Mountain Cat," the brave said. "You know where Diablo Negro is?"

"He's on his way to Mexico to find the man called the Blacksmith."

Mountain Cat nodded his head. "I will take you to the camp."

"Good." Rand locked the cell and moved to the door.

"But not before Diablo Negro arrives," the brave added. "If he is your friend, as you have said, he will join us."

350

Chapter Nineteen

The sun had begun its ascent, golden rays of light chasing away the last of the night shadows. The trip had been fast, with few stops and little rest, but it was worth it. At the top of the mountain, standing between Diablo and Wade, Clem gazed at the tiny village that was nestled into a crook of the stream that wound its way through a valley floor, bursting with the first signs of coming spring. From her vantage point, the village had a fairy-tale beauty about it; the most prominent structure the church, its bells gently tolling.

"This is the village of San Miguel," Diablo Negro said, a certain reverence in his voice. "The man called Blacksmith lives here."

Wade caught Clem's hand and squeezed it tightly. "I can't remember a time when I've been this excited about interviewing someone," he confessed. "I feel as if I'm almost home after a long, hard journey."

"You think the Blacksmith and Bryan Dillon are the same person, don't you?" Clem asked, her gaze shifting from the scene below to the man beside her. Always in her heart of hearts, there was a sadness that shadowed her joy in loving Wade, in their being together. The nearer he came to the end of his search, the closer she was to losing him.

351

Wade did not answer immediately, but finally said, "I don't know how to explain the way I feel so that you'll understand. But I know—somehow I know—I'm going to find something really great here. I'm not sure that it's connected with Bryan, and I don't really care. Finding Bryan or something about him is my assignment; I'm paid to do that. Finding the Blacksmith has gone beyond this. It's more like . . . a . . . mission. My personal mission."

As if to accent his words, the soft tones of the bells echoed through the valley again. As if they were saying it was time to awaken, roosters began to crow. The village stirred to life, men and women moving in and out of adobe buildings; children running to-and-fro on the main street.

For a moment Clem wanted to hold her arms out, embrace the dawn, and draw all its beauty into her arms. What a wonderful way to begin a day.

"It doesn't seem real, does it?" she said. "I keep thinking it's an illusion, and it's going to disappear."

"No," Diablo said in that hushed voice, "San Miguel is not going to disappear, and we are only a few hours away. Since the weather has permitted us to travel night and day and we have not slept many hours, we can make camp now, or we can rest after we have arrived."

He looked from Wade to Clem; Wade looked at her. She was exhausted and would have liked to rest, but she knew Wade wanted to finish the journey now. When she saw the pleading look on his face, she knew what her answer would be.

"Let's rest after we get there."

Diablo nodded and motioned to his warriors. "Let's begin our descent. We will be able to move faster, and should be there before the noon meal."

Again traveling single file down the narrow trail

that wound around the mountain, Clem followed Diablo Negro, while Wade rode behind her. They stopped only once to refresh themselves and rest the horses; then they began to travel again. By the time they entered the valley, the sun was high in the sky. The day was warm and gloriously beautiful.

Diablo Negro led them to the fountain in the town square. He addressed the villagers in Spanish, and they laughed and talked with him. Moving their earthen jars aside, they allowed their guests to water their horses.

"Perhaps you would like to rest and take a bath before you meet the Blacksmith," Diablo said.

Both Clem and Wade nodded; they had been traveling in the same clothing for two days and a night. Diablo pointed to the cantina.

"You will find rooms over there. They will also serve you meals and stable your horses. I will come for you in three hours."

Clem did not argue with him. She was so exhausted, she felt as if she would drop any moment. She and Wade draped their saddlebags over their shoulders, and as they walked to the cantina, Clem wished she had brought other clothes with her besides her shirt and trousers. She would like to have her green gingham dress to wear today.

As they walked into the cantina, they were greeted by a small woman who stood behind the bar. Her black hair was pulled back on her neck and coiled into a thick chignon. Large gold earrings brushed against her cheeks.

"How may I help you?" she asked in broken English.

"We would like rooms, baths, and lunch," Wade said.

She motioned for them to follow her and led them

up the stairs. Opening the door, she waved to the room, then stepped back. "This one will do, no?"

The room had two large windows, the shutters of both open so that sunlight poured in. Birds chirruped, and a cool breeze stirred the gauze curtains. The furniture—a double bed, chest, washstand, dresser, and two chairs—was rustic but inviting. The brightly colored blankets and pillow coverings were a beautiful contrast to the whitewashed adobe walls.

"Oh, yes." Clem sighed. It looked like heaven to her. All she wanted was to lie down and sleep for a long, long time.

"Yes," Wade said, "this will do fine."

The door shut, closing Clem in the room with Wade. Suddenly her exhaustion fled as she experienced an intimacy that she had never shared before with Wade. They had made love in his room at Hadley's, at the hotel and in the cave, but this was the first time they had shared a room together for the night—their room.

"Is something wrong?" Wade dropped his saddlebags on the bed.

"No," Clem whispered thickly, her voice sounding unnatural to her ears.

Wade took her saddlebags from her shoulder and tossed them on top of his. He caught her chin with the tips of his fingers and lifted her face to his.

"Is it bothering you to stay in the room with me?"

"No."

"I'm glad, because I don't want to be separated from you." His lips captured hers in a sweet and wonderful kiss. When he lifted his mouth from hers, he smiled. "I forgot how innocent you are."

"Not anymore," she denied.

"Very much so," he said. "My having made love to you has made some physical changes in your body,

354

but you are still an innocent, Clem. You are amazing and so refreshing. You're the kind of woman a man can't forget."

Clem managed to smile. How, she was not sure. Her heart was heavy. Wade spoke so easily of making love to her, and the changes it had brought about in her life, but he never spoke of loving her. He continued to remind her that she was not a permanent part of his life.

But he had never promised more.

Concerned that her sadness would show in her eyes, she moved to the bed and opened her saddlebags to spill her clothes over the bed. The longer she looked at the shirt and trousers, the more she wanted a dress. She could only wonder why all of a sudden a dress was so important to her. Was she trying to prove to Wade that she could be as lovely and as sophisticated as the women he knew in New York?

Silly woman, she chided herself. Clothing cannot give you what you do not have. *You're a country woman, Clem, and you'll never be anything else.* Wade finds you attractive, because you're one of the few single women he has met since he has been in West Texas. You are a diversion for him, nothing more.

She had to be something more. She loved Wade and wanted him to love her. When he made love to her, she felt that he did love her.

Somehow this little village was getting to her. She felt as if she had stepped out of time. She felt as if anything were possible. She could make Wade love her. She could!

Wade moved to the window, placing a hand on either facing. He turned when she walked to the door.

"Where are you going?"

"Downstairs," she answered.

"Why?" He looked troubled.

"I want to see if I can buy a dress."

"All right," he murmured, but Clem could tell that he was puzzled by her behavior.

"I'll be back in a moment." Hurrying downstairs, she located the landlady.

After Clem made her request, the woman thought a second, then smiled, and nodded her head. She stepped from behind the counter and studied Clem; she turned her around several times.

She smiled. "I will bring you one. What color?"

"I don't care as long as it's bright and pretty," Clem said. "One that is happy."

When she returned to the room, Wade was stretched out on the bed, his hands behind his head. Sitting down at the dresser, she unpinned her hair, letting it tumble about her shoulders. In the mirror she could see him watching her, and she wondered what it would be like to live with him, to know that he would be there to go to bed with her at night and to wake up with every morning. He would hold her tightly when she was lonesome or afraid. To know that he loved her.

But he did not want marriage.

Unable to look at his reflection any longer, she rose and walked to the window to gaze down on the dusty street. She listened to the gurgle of the water fountain in the plaza.

"You've been acting strange ever since we arrived," Wade said. "Is something bothering you?"

She shook her head, not willing to share her troubled thoughts with him. Then, to keep him from probing, she said, "Yes, I guess so. I guess I'm nervous about meeting with the Blacksmith. All my life he has only been a photograph. He's been a man that my parents have talked little about. Now, at last,

I'm going to meet him."

"I understand how you feel," he said. "I'm quite excited about it, too."

A knock sounded in the room. In answer Clem opened the door to allow two serving boys to enter with an exceptionally large elongated tub.

When she questioned them about its size, they replied, "*Senora* does not have a tub for the cantina, so she went to the padre. He loaned her his. We made this one for him. He is a big man who needs a big tub."

The boys moved in and out, delivering kettles of water until the tub was full. Next to it they laid towels, washcloths, and soap on the floor. Last, they brought in a basket filled with dried flowers. As they crushed them into the water, a wonderful fragrance filled the room.

"You may bathe first," Wade said. He pushed up from the bed. "Shall I undress you?" he asked.

"No," she murmured, "I'll undress myself."

Slowly—deliberately so—she removed her clothing piece by piece until she stood naked before him.

Although Wade had seen her naked before, he could not quell his pleasure in seeing her nude again. Astonishingly, she made him feel innocent; she made each experience new.

Naked, her entire body was haloed by the soft, golden rays of mid-afternoon sun. Her hair, autumn rich, hung in a thick curtain down her back, tendrils wisping around her face, silken strands falling over the beautiful swell of her breasts.

Unable to help himself, not really wanting to, Wade rose. Pleased now with the oversize tub, he quickly divested himself of his clothes and walked to her.

"Let's bathe together." His breathing heightened;

his pulse accelerated.

He stepped into the tub, and both of them sank into the water, causing it to splash over the sides. Their hands moved over each other's bodies as they washed, as they caressed. Exhaustion was forgotten; passion awakened.

Clem turned on her back in the water; he lay on top of her. Their lips met in a long, passionate kiss. With the tips of his fingers he touched her eyebrows, nose, cheek, and mouth. He felt her tremble beneath his whisper-soft strokes.

He caught her wrist and held it against his lips as he kissed each fingertip. His mouth moved down her index finger to her palm, where he planted more kisses. When she sucked in her breath, his lips traveled to her inner wrist. He brushed his chin around and around the sensitive skin, until he knew she could stand the torment no longer. Again she quivered beneath his touch, and his arms circled her body. His fingers cupped her buttocks to draw her closer to his arousal.

Clem lifted her hand and caught the back of his head, forwarding his lips to hers. She opened her mouth and received him. As his tongue teased and stroked her mouth, his hand strayed to the soft mat of hair between her thighs; gently he spread her legs and his fingers worked their magic on her. Again he heightened her desires and prepared her for his loving.

He angled over her and gently sank his shaft into her warm cavity. He murmured endearments in her ears; his hands spoke love to her. His lips caught hers, and she gave herself to the kiss, relaxing as he began to move within her. Deeper went his stroke; harder were his thrusts.

The water was their cushion, its warmth lapping

358

about them, creating an erotica of its own.

Her arms locked about his neck, Clem rose to meet him. Her hands slipped down his back to spread across his buttocks, to press him deeper within herself. She kneaded and drew designs on them. She traced the indentation.

Then she shuddered in his arms and gasped her pleasure. She relaxed and breathed deeply. Then Wade tensed; he lunged deeply into her; he gasped and shuddered convulsively. To meet and to sheath him fully, she arched her hips. They held him, then rotated to caress him as he climaxed. They clung together, letting the gentle lap of the water soothe them as their passion ebbed into ultimate satisfaction.

Later, dried off, they lay quietly on the bed.

Clem went to sleep almost immediately, but Wade was lost in thought. His lovemaking experiences were varied, and he had always found women who gave him satisfaction, women whom he admired and whose company he enjoyed. But since he had met Clem, he found that his sexual encounters to this point had been nothing but release. He had soon forgotten his partner; her face lost in a blur, soon replaced by the next woman.

Not so with Clem. The more he made love to her, the more he wanted to make love to her. Every time they came together, the experience was better, more satisfying. He knew that no matter how many lovers he would have in the years to come, he would never forget Clem . . . Clementina Jones. Through their lovemaking, a girl had blossomed into womanhood.

She had created a longing in Wade that he had not experienced before, that gnawed at him. Their lovemaking demanded more than lust; it demanded commitment. Although he was leery of marriage, he did not want to lose Clem. She was quickly becoming an essential part of his life.

The knock on the door awakened Clem from a deep and sound sleep, but she did not move. She smiled when Wade covered her with the blanket, then rose to pull on his trousers. He answered the door.

"I brought the *Senora* her dress."

Feeling her cheeks warm with a mixture of pleasure and embarrassment when the woman addressed her as Wade's wife, Clem shoved up on the bed. The woman held up a white dress with orange and yellow flower appliques.

"It is beautiful, no?"

"It is beautiful, yes," Wade answered.

"Also, *Senor,* I brought these." She held up some undergarments and a pair of slippers. "Boots would not look pretty with the dress."

Wade laughed softly, taking both the clothes and the slippers. "How much do we owe you?"

She answered, and as soon as Wade paid her, she disappeared and he shut the door. Clem slipped out of bed, and as she dressed, so did Wade. When she was through, she stood in front of the dresser and looked at herself.

Twirling around, she asked, "What do you think?"

"You're beautiful," he said.

She grinned at him. "The dress?"

"It's beautiful, too."

Hand in hand, they walked downstairs and ate their lunch, their conversation centered on the coming meeting with the Blacksmith. Later, after they had topped their meal with one of the landlady's delicious Mexican pastries, they strolled through the plaza. They came across Diablo Negro who lounged beneath one of the trees.

"I'm glad you rested," he said. "Both of you look refreshed."

Clem felt her cheeks warm beneath his scrutiny, but she did not avoid his gaze. "When can we meet with the Blacksmith?"

The Mescalero rose. "Now, if you like. He is waiting for you."

Clem could hardly contain her excitement as she and Wade followed the Indian across the plaza, down the dusty street to a small adobe building. As they drew near, Clem heard children calling out the alphabet in unison in Spanish.

Then a bell rang; the schoolmaster said something; ten or eleven children spilled out of the building. Following Diablo Negro, she and Wade entered the schoolroom. The priest had his back to them.

"Father Michael," Diablo Negro said, "here are the people who have come to meet the Blacksmith."

The priest turned, and in a low but vibrant voice asked, "Hello, how may I help you?"

"I'm Wade Cameron. I asked Diablo Negro to bring us here because we're looking for a man named Blacksmith. We'd like for you to help us find him."

"Why are you looking for him?"

He was an older man who exuded an aura of power. He dwarfed both Diablo Negro and Wade. His physique reminded Clem of a locomotive — solid steel. Clem felt as if the gray eyes that regarded them so solemnly were omniscient. She easily recognized him.

Wade finally stepped forward, gaping. "You're a priest!"

The man laughed quietly. "Yes, I am. I'm Father Michael Murphy."

"Who would have believed that you would become a priest?"

"I was hoping that no one would," Father Michael confessed. The warm gray eyes settled on Clem.

She felt as if she knew him. "Hello," she said, "I'm Clem . . . Clementina Jones."

His gaze raked her face, as if he could not believe what he was seeing. "Clement's and Deborah's baby?"

"Their daughter."

Again he laughed, the sound warm and gentle. "I did not realize how many years it had been. How are they?"

"My father is dead," she replied. "He was killed at the Chupedera Salt Flats."

"I have heard about the controversy over the salt, and I fear it is far from over," he said, "but I did not know Clement was dead. Word comes slowly to San Miguel, since we are off the beaten path. I'm truly sorry. Clement and I worked together in New Orleans. What about Rand and your mother?"

"They're in Lawful," Clem answered. "Rand's the sheriff now."

"He will make a good one." He moved to his desk and straightened a stack of books. "Shall we go to the house? There we can talk without being disturbed."

Clem was in a daze, as was Wade, when they walked out of the schoolroom. Father Michael dismissed the children for the day, and amid laughter and shouting, they scurried off.

"And Vicente," the priest laid an arm around the Mescalero's shoulders, "how are things going for you?"

Diablo Negro actually laughed and said to Wade and Clem, "No one but the Father calls me by my baptismal name."

362

"That's because I gave it to him."

Clem turned her head quickly and looked at the priest in surprise.

Diablo Negro explained, "When he was teaching me to read and write. He refused to let me be called the Devil."

"Can you imagine any pastor allowing one of his children to be called Devil?" Father Michael asked.

Clem listened as student and teacher teased one another by sharing memories together. It was evident the two men respected each other.

"Why have you left the reservation in New Mexico?"

"Because the white men pillaged our land, stealing our possessions, raping and killing our women and children. They killed my sister, who was with child."

The priest was quiet for a second before he asked, "You know who did this?"

"I know. I have followed him to a camp in the mountains to the south of Botello."

"My son," the priest said, "you must not follow the path of vengeance. You must leave things like this in the hands of God."

"God's hands are my hands, Father," Diablo Negro said. "Therefore I shall punish them."

"That's a hard path to travel," Father Michael advised.

"It is the one I have chosen."

When they arrived at the rectory, the priest led them through the house to the patio, covered with thick vines that formed a canopy and provided shade. After pouring them a glass of wine, he sat down.

Directing his remark to Wade, he said, "Earlier I asked you why you wanted to meet the Blacksmith, and you never answered me."

"I suppose Diablo Negro told you I'm a newspaperman?"

The priest nodded.

"I came out here to search for Bryan Dillon. The closest living relative he has, a brother, sent me to find him or to find out what happened to him."

Wade handed the daguerreotype of Bryan and the watch to the priest, who studied them as he listened to Wade recount his story.

"It is while I was looking through the Sheriff's personal belongings that I saw a photograph of you," Wade said. "A group photograph of you and—"

"I remember it well," Father Michael said, and returned the daguerreotype and watch to Wade.

"When Deborah talked about you, there were so many similarities between you and the man I was looking for, that I thought perhaps you were he. And if not he, perhaps you knew him."

He shook his head. "No, I'm not Bryan Dillon. I'm truly Michael Murphy, and there's not much about my life that is a great mystery. Some perhaps, but it does not concern anyone but God and me." He rose and walked to the edge of the arbor. His back to them, he said, "At an early age, I wanted to be a priest. I was educated to become one; however, before I took my vows, I fell in love. I turned my back on my calling and married."

He paused. "I never regretted having met Annie and having married. She was the love of my life. She bore our child—a boy. A little boy who looked so like his mother."

Michael stopped talking. When he spoke again, his voice was thick. "We had moved to New Orleans and bought a shop. It was not long until a group of Italian criminals, lead by one family, began to pressure us to buy their protection. I refused. In the

364

course of time, they killed Annie and little Michael. He died in my arms.

He paused to compose himself. "I promised myself that I would repay them in kind, and I did. Several years later, I joined Clement, and we killed all of the male family members but two small boys. I drifted west and became a professional gunman. Somehow along the way I picked up the name of the Blacksmith, and it suited my purposes for people to call me that. But being a gunman was not the life for me. In a manner of speaking, the Blacksmith died, and it was well. He left behind many sorrows and regret."

Michael's sandaled feet moved quietly across the tile floor. He came to sit by Wade. "The Blacksmith died the same night that another gunslinger died, probably your Bryan Dillon. He looked like the image on the daguerreotype and owned an unusual French watch."

Wade leaned to the edge of his seat. "You knew him?"

Father Michael paused. "Not in the true sense of knowing someone. Running from Texas Rangers, he and I both sought the safety of Mexico, but really found none. He went to work for a wealthy Mexican rancher, who betrayed him. I helped him escape prison, but before we could get to the border, we were attacked by Mexican vaqueros and badly beaten; then our bodies were pumped full of lead. Both of us were left for dead. The one you call Bryan died, but some peasants from San Miguel found and brought me here."

"Do you know where Bryan's watch is?"

"I think so. I would tell you, but I cannot," Michael said. "I would be betraying my vows as a priest. Things that are told to me in confession are

365

confidential."

"Damn it!" Wade swore.

"I said I couldn't tell you," Michael said, "but I shall contact the person who has the watch, and tell that person of your interest. Perhaps this person will contact you. That is all I can do."

Clearly disappointed, Wade nodded. "Will you tell me about yourself?"

Michael shrugged. "There's not much to tell, and what there is, is not that interesting. After I recuperated, I returned to the church, did penance, and served time in prison for my crimes. I spent the next years of my life convincing the church fathers of my repentance, my sincerity, and my devotion to God and the church."

He paused thoughtfully. "Finally, I became a priest. I have dedicated my life to the people of San Miguel, who know me only as Father Michael. I am still haunted by the death of my wife and son, and at times I must pray diligently to overcome my hatred for the men who did this. I have even harbored hatred and wanted revenge on the two Lorenzo brothers who are alive."

"The Lorenzo brothers!" Clem exclaimed and turned excitedly to Wade. "That's why the name on that bill of sale was so familiar. What were they named?"

"Giovanni and Giuseppe, I believe."

Clem leaned to the edge of her chair. "Would either of those names be translated to Joseph in English?"

"Yes," the priest answered. "Giuseppe is a form of Joseph. Why do you ask?"

"I believe one, if not both, of the brothers is in Texas," she answered. "And just maybe the Lorenzos are the reason why my father is dead."

"They promised revenge," Father Michael said, "and they come from a family who believe in and who honor their vendettas."

"Now it begins to make sense," Clem said. "The men shooting behind Olviera, his death. It was a trap to kill Papa."

"And perhaps you," the priest softly pointed out. "You are a Jones."

Clem nodded. "It's beginning to fit together."

Before his guests left, Michael promised a long interview with Wade on the following morning, prior to his officiating at a wedding for two of the villagers. He gave him permission to print the story of the Blacksmith, but asked that the Blacksmith be given a proper burial. Now by himself once more, the priest poured himself another glass of wine and walked through the house. This visit by these people had brought back memories he had spent years fasting and praying to forget. His past now loomed in front of him, coloring his future in dismal colors.

Clement was dead! Possibly killed by the Lorenzos.

Damn! He clenched his hand into a fist. Would he never be free from these men? Would they forever haunt him?

He closed his eyes, visions of Annie and little Michael swimming through his mind. He had owed it to them . . . or so he thought.

Would Rand, Deborah, and Clem pay for Clement's mistake?

He heard the knock and went to the door. Diablo Negro stood there, a note in his hand.

"I did not mean to disturb you, Father."

"You never disturb me, my son. I always look for-

367

ward to your visits. They bring me much joy."

"I sent one of my braves to let Rand know I was bringing Clem and Wade here to see you. He sent a note to you."

Michael read Rand's plea. He dropped his hand and crushed the paper in his fist. His friend needed him. Long, resolute strides carried him from the house to the church. He walked to the altar and stared at the cross on the white adobe wall. An hour passed, but he found no solace in his prayers.

A door opened and closed. Soft footsteps echoed through the building. Michael did not turn around.

"Father," Diablo Negro stood behind him, "you have been a friend to me and have helped me many times. You have always loved me as your son. Can I help you now?"

Michael turned, his brown robe swishing about his feet. "No, my son," he answered, and laid his hand on the Mescalero warrior's shoulder, "this is a decision I must make. A friend of mine needs me. He's all alone in his fight against injustice, against vengeance, and a hatred that has festered in the hearts of his enemies for nearly twenty years. If I don't go, he will possibly — probably — be killed. If I go, I will surely die, not literally but spiritually."

"Before you can make peace with your God, you must make it with yourself," Diablo Negro said. "Now you are fighting another kind of war. You are fighting illiteracy and poverty. You are teaching the children to read and write, so they can take care of themselves. You are making their lives better. San Miguel needs Father Michael more than Rand needs the Blacksmith."

"What will happen to Rand?" Michael asked.

"I will go fight with him. I am a man of war, at peace with myself now that I have chosen to come home."

That decision possibly resolved, Michael continued to stare at the crucifix. He had another to make that would entail the resurrecting of more memories that he and others had thought were laid to rest.

He must prepare for the journey.

The next morning Clem slept late, but Wade was up early, ready to meet Father Michael at the appointed time. Although he was not pleased that Bryan Dillon was deceased, he was glad to know that he was dead and the search for him could end; he was glad he could tell Nash. Wade was also pleased that he was going to get a detailed story of the Blacksmith's life. Readers would love it; it would sell his journal. True to his promise to the priest, the Blacksmith would die his fictional death, and no mention would be made of Father Murphy. As soon as the interview was over, they would be returning to Lawful.

He would wait a while to see if the person who had the watch would contact him, then, no matter what happened, he would head back East. He loved the frontier, but his home was New York, his vocation, *Cameron's Journal.*

Wade looked at Clem, who slept soundly. He felt increasingly guilty about his relationship with her. He had even thought about asking Clem to return to New York with him, but he could not imagine her there. As much as he was a product of civilization, she was a product of the West. She would wither and die if she had to live closed in.

She murmured in her sleep and brushed a tendril of hair from her face, before she snuggled under the cover once again. He had thought himself infatuated with Clem, but he had been infatuated with other

369

women before, and his feelings had never been this intense. His feelings for Clem far exceeded mere infatuation. He loved her.

The revelation startled him. It weighed heavily on his shoulders. Now that he had admitted it, what was he going to do about it?

The question still ringing in his ears, he picked up his writing kit and headed for the rectory.

As Father Michael talked, Wade sat in front of an English secretary and took notes, relying on the codes he had taught himself through the years for speed and efficiency. By the end of the hour, he had filled several pages front and back with details of the Blacksmith's life.

"Any more questions?" the priest asked.

Wade scanned his notes, then shook his head. "No, I think we've covered it thoroughly. I don't know how I can repay you for all your trouble."

"Send me a copy of the magazine with the story," he said with a twinkle in his eyes. "I would like to read about the Blacksmith."

"I will," Wade said.

Laying his pen down, he recapped the inkwell and tucked it into the reservoir in his writing kit. "Thank you for telling me about those articles in the New Orleans paper. At my first opportunity, I'll write a friend of mine and have him check through the archives to see if he can find copies of them."

Father Michael thought a moment, then said, "Being the vain man he was, the Blacksmith kept all those clippings about himself. If you'll promise to return them to me, I'll let you use them."

As he spoke, he moved to the desk and pulled out an old portfolio, brown with age and fraying around the edges. He untied the ribbon and began to thumb through the material. He pulled out a handful of papers, several sheets fluttering to the desk.

Thinking it to be one of the articles for which the priest searched, Wade picked it up and began to read. As quickly he lifted his head. "This is a police report," he said.

Father Michael rubbed his palm down his robe. "Yes."

"Clement Jones was under investigation by the New Orleans police, for being a part of the Lorenzo gang!" Wade exclaimed incredulously.

"Yes, and because of my friendship with Rand, I pulled the records when I left the force," the priest answered, and laid the portfolio down. "You may read them, and when you do, you'll see that they had no concrete evidence on him. All the Lorenzos and the investigating officers who could have testified against Clement were killed in the raid."

As Wade read the reports, Father Michael said, "Rand and I never knew that Clement, although an officer of the law in New Orleans, was also a member of the Lorenzo gang. He had amassed a small fortune in blackmail money. When he felt he wasn't getting his share of the goods, and when he learned that he was being investigated himself, he turned on them. He used Rand and me."

Father Michael idly thumbed through the reports. "I make no excuses for myself, because I needed no coaxing from Clement. I hated the Lorenzos for what they had done to my family, but I have always regretted that Clement used Rand. It was not until several years later, when Clement began to get threatening letters from the younger two Lorenzo boys, that Rand and I learned the truth. By this time Rand was in love with Deborah and wanted to protect her. I pulled the records, and we all migrated west."

371

"Why did you keep them all these years?" Wade asked.

"All of us have some innocent, little quirk that eventually gets us into trouble. At first, I kept these mementoes because they were part of my life. Later, I simply kept them. They reminded me where I came from and where, except for the grace of God, I would still be."

"May I borrow them?" Wade asked.

"You can the newspaper clippings about me," the priest answered. "But you can't have the records on Clement. He's dead; let his past die with him. He changed after he became the sheriff of Lawful."

Wearing her trousers and shirt, Clem waited outside the rectory for Wade. Her heart growing increasingly heavy, she watched the villagers as they prepared for the wedding celebration. Although they lived simply, they laughed a great deal and radiated happiness that was contagious.

Neither she nor Wade had ever made a declaration of love to each other, nor had either discussed marriage as an option. In the beginning she was curious and had simply wanted to know what lovemaking was about. She had not wanted marriage. Now she thought differently. Her dreams and goals had changed. She did want marriage, and she did want children — Wade's children.

She gazed longingly at those who darted about, playing tag. A little girl, a toddler in particular, caught Clem's attention. She sat at the edge of the street playing with a ball.

One of the older boys came running by to kick the ball from the child. As children will do, he laughed and continued to tap the ball farther and farther away from the girl. Wanting her toy, she rose and toddled down the road, her little legs shaky and unable to carry her as fast as the boy ran. She stubbed her toe on a tree root that grew across the road. She tottered, then fell, hitting her head on the edge of the water fountain. Her cry of anguish—or perhaps frustration—pierced the air.

Before anyone else could reach the child, Clem had scooped her up and was examining her. She checked her head to see that she was not badly hurt; she kissed the bump that had quickly risen on her forehead.

"It's going to be all right," she murmured in her broken Spanish, holding the toddler close to her breast.

The little girl hushed her crying, pulled back from Clem, and with brilliant black eyes, stared curiously in her face. A dirty little hand lifted to touch Clem's cheek and to pat her hair. She giggled.

"Rosita," an old woman said, giving Clem a snaggletoothed smile. "Her name is Rosita. She is my granddaughter."

"She is beautiful," Clem murmured, again conversing in Spanish.

The child smiled slowly, then kissed Clem on the cheek. Pulling back, she held her hands over her mouth and giggled again. Clem hugged her tightly. Rosita laid her head on Clem's chest and wrapped her tiny arms around her shoulders. A surge of maternal love flowed through Clem; it was different from the love that she felt for Wade or that his love generated in her, but it was altogether as powerful. It filled her with a longing to have her own child.

"Do you want me to take her?" the woman asked.

"No," Clem said, "if you don't mind, I'll carry her. Where shall I take her?"

"I'll show you."

Following the old woman, Clem was even with the rectory when out walked the priest and Wade, talking and laughing together. When Wade saw Clem, when he saw the child in her arms, he stopped in mid-sentence and stared at her. He moved toward her.

"She fell," Clem said, "and hurt her head."

"I've never seen you with children before," Wade said.

It was evident he was astonished.

Clem felt a little self-conscious. "I—she needed someone to help her."

Suddenly Rosita pushed away from Clem. She gurgled happily and squirmed to be put down. As soon as her little feet hit the ground, she toddled away.

"It's time to go," Wade said.

Wistfully Clem stared after the child. "I wish we could stay," she murmured. "I've loved being here."

"Maybe we can come back someday."

Clem heard sadness in Wade's voice.

"Yes, we can come back," she said, "but it's this moment I want, Wade, and we can never have it again."

"Then we must make more."

He embraced her tightly, and she clung to him. Something was wrong with Wade; she could feel it.

Chapter Twenty

Preoccupied with thoughts of Clem, Wade rode behind her as they moved single file through the mountains away from San Miguel. He still carried with him the image of her holding the child to her breast, and with the image came a swell of pride and love.

It was difficult for him to consciously reconcile the many facets of the woman he loved, and yes, he loved Clem. She was a mixture of many wonderful qualities. Parading through his mind were varied recollections of her. The daughter who loved her father. The no-nonsense deputy sheriff who fought to keep her badge in the face of opposition and bias, and who faced a reputed gunslinger in a shoot-out to protect her town. The doctor who would ride miles to inoculate Indians to protect them from the ravages of disease.

Foremost in his mind's eyes was the vision of the woman who was soft and alluring, who was tantalizing. The woman who soothed the hurting child and who could be a mother — the mother of his children.

This thought — as so many others he was having in regards to Clementina lately — was startling. Wade had envisioned himself a confirmed bachelor, a man never to be ensnared by marriage. But more and more frequently, the word was cropping up, and with it a longing to settle down. He was beginning to realize that marriage was only an entrapment to the man who did not wish the responsibility of loving. Once a man has made a commitment—the commitment to love—marriage no longer was a trap. Rather, it is the natural outgrowth of love.

The most difficult task for Wade had been to recognize the fine line's difference between love and infatuation, and he did. When he had admitted he loved Clementina, he had made his commitment to her. Now it followed that he wanted all the wonderful pleasures and the responsibilities that came with marriage to her.

Looking at her as she rode in front of him Wade remembered the seductress. Trousers stretched tightly against her body to outline clearly her long, slender legs, the round buttocks, the small waist.

He smiled as he thought about Clem's recent preoccupation with dresses; this was a way she had of demonstrating her desire to please him, to make a commitment of love to him.

Clem invigorated him; loving her made him want to do for her. No matter what they had done together, they were happy. No matter how mundane the activity, Clem brought an enthusiasm to it that made it an altogether new and exciting adventure for him.

Marriage to her would never be boring; it would be an adventure for life. In fact, the more he thought about it, the more excited he became with the idea.

But there were several obstacles to their getting married. Relocation was one of them. And only hours ago he would have thought it the biggest. Now, after talking with Father Michael, he saw another even larger one looming, because he intended to incorporate what he had learned from the priest into his story on Clement Jones. He would be glad when they camped for the night; he needed to talk with Clem.

376

Because of Clem's love for her father, and because of Wade's promise to her in the beginning—to let her know what he was writing—he wanted to let her read the latest text. He would rather take the coward's way out, but that was not his style. Furthermore, he loved Clem too much to deceive her. He also trusted her to understand his devotion to his work and to allow him to write the whole—and the true—story of Clement Jones's life. Surely she could see that Clement was a composite of all these traits.

Late in the afternoon, they stopped in a small clearing. Diablo circled back to where Wade and Clem waited.

"The path forks here," he said to them, "one way back to my grandfather's village, the other going to El Paso. I have been thinking it would be quicker, if the two of you returned to Lawful through El Paso. Rand may need you now."

Wade agreed with him.

"What about the vaccinations?" Clem asked.

"I know how to give them. The agency provided the vaccine, but no one wanted to risk their lives to give an Indian the shots. I have learned how to do many things," Diablo answered. "After I visit with my grandfather, I will join you in Lawful. Tell Rand for me."

Wade said, "Thank you for taking us to San Miguel, and for introducing us to Father Michael."

"I'm glad he was able to answer your questions for you."

Clem watched Diablo move to the head of the line, he and his braves silently disappearing as they blended into nature.

"I'm going to miss him," she murmured.

"Both of us are," Wade said.

She moved to mount again, but Wade caught her hand. "I'd like to talk to you before we start traveling."

Gazing at him curiously, Clem followed him to a small boulder and sat beside him. He caught her hands in his, then he simply returned her gaze. He wanted to be eloquent, but he found himself tongue-tied for one of the few times in his life. He wanted to confess to her, but he found that wanting to tell the truth was easier than telling it.

"What's wrong?" Clem asked anxiously.

"I love you," he said. He wanted there to be no misunderstanding on this point. "You're the first one I've ever loved, and the first to whom I've spoken these words."

Slowly her lips curved into a beautiful smile, and her eyes sparkled. She threw herself into his arms. "Oh, Wade, I wondered if you would ever say this to me. I love you so much."

Tears stung Wade's eyes as he closed his arms about her and held her close. Clementina Jones was the most precious thing in his life. He had risked life and limb for her; he would gladly do so again and again.

"I knew San Miguel was a magical place."

Would she think that when he talked to her about Clement's involvement with crime in New Orleans?

"Clem, will you marry me?"

"Oh, Wade," she squealed with delight. "Yes! Yes! Yes!"

He caught her arms and gently removed her from his embrace.

"But first we must talk."

"What's wrong?" she asked a second time, her gaze anxiously studying his face. "Are you worried about my not wanting to move to New York?"

"That's one of my concerns," he answered, almost glad that she had not forced him to the main issue.

"I'm willing to. Have you given any thought to my living there?"

Puzzled and momentarily sidetracked by her questions, he said, "I don't understand what you mean."

"I may embarrass you while I'm learning to be a lady."

He smiled. He could always trust Clem to look at a subject from an entirely new and different point of view. "I'm not sure what a lady is, and even if I were, I wouldn't necessarily want you to be one. I want you to be you; that's what I've fallen in love with. Let me assure you, my darling, you'll never embarrass me. I'm marrying you because you're you."

"Out here that's all right," Clem said, "but it won't be once we're there. Here I'm in my element; there I'll be out of it. At times, I'll even be unsure of myself. I can cope with it, but I'm not sure a successful businessman can. I don't want your friends or your business associates and acquaintances laughing at you, because of your bumbling wife."

"Clem, you'll be the toast of New York. Your honesty will bowl people over. My friends will love, understand, and admire you. What others think I don't give a damn."

She laughed softly. "And what are your friends going to think, when I slip into my bedroom and change from shoes into boots because my feet hurt. What are they going to think when I put on my trousers to go horseback riding? I give you fair warning, I won't be wearing those bloomer thingamabobs."

Wade laughed with her. "If that's what you want to do, you do it. However, I think perhaps we can get you shoes that will fit comfortably. And I have a country home where you can ride anytime you wish without giving thought to anyone else—but me."

"That suits me fine," she replied, snuggling up to him and kissing him lightly on the chin. "I think I'd like to work with you, too."

Wade chuckled. "Now, that I will have to give some thought to."

Clem pulled back and stared at him somberly. "You will?"

"No, my darling, I was teasing. I'll love having you work with me."

"I'd like to be married before we leave," Clem said. "I want my mother and Rand at the wedding. She'll plan it with me, and I'd like to ask Rand if he'll give me away. I just wish Papa had lived long enough—"

Again Wade crushed her in his arms. The mention of her father's name brought back unpleasant memories of his interview with Father Michael.

"You don't mind our being married before we leave?"

"No," he said, "I insist on it, because I don't intend for us to be separated on the long trip home. I've slept by myself as long as I intend to."

"I'll have to talk with Deb—with mama about it," Clem said. "We need to pick a date. I want to give her time enough for us to plan a big celebration, and I want to invite Doña Pera."

"And Miss Merica," Wade reminded.

"And her," Clem agreed.

She lifted her face to Wade, and he kissed her, a warm wonderful kiss that sealed their commitment of love. He held her against his body, loving the feel of her in his arms, loving the thought of their being together for the remainder of their lives.

She was his love, and he wanted to protect her from all harm. He decided now was not the time to talk to her about her father. Perhaps he was taking the coward's way out after all, but he did not want to destroy all the magic of the trip for her, nor for himself.

"We've been making good time," Clem said, as the two of them rode into El Paso in the early afternoon.

"We ought to," Wade grumbled good-naturedly. "We

haven't stopped to relieve ourselves, much less to sleep since we left San Miguel. We can afford to spend one night in here and sleep in a bed. Both of us need it."

Clem grinned at him. "Both of us need what?"

Wade chuckled. "You're becoming quite a tart."

"Yes," she admitted, "I really enjoy it, and so do you. If you don't, blame yourself."

"Oh, no, my darling Clementina, you cannot blame your sauciness on me."

Clem had been lighthearted since they had parted from Diablo and Wade had declared his love to her. She had chattered the miles away, planning their wedding and honeymoon, their entire lives. She continued to make plans until they reached the El Paso Hotel. By the time Wade returned from putting their horses in the livery barn, Clem had them a room. The bathroom was at the end of the hall, but neither minded as long as they could wash the trail dust from themselves and put on clean clothes.

Several hours later, they were rested and refreshed. They went downstairs and ate a late lunch in the dining room, capping their meal with a large slice of apple pie each. Before they left for a day of shopping, Wade made reservations for dinner that evening.

Clem was bubbling over with excitement when they entered the El Paso General Store. The saleslady—she introduced herself as Mrs. Irwin—led them to the section of the store where she had a rack of dresses in different sizes. One of the seamstresses in town, Mrs. Irwin explained, supplied the store with dresses that clients refused for one reason or another. She guaranteed that the dresses were not damaged in any manner. If Clem found a dress she wanted, the woman went on to say, the seamstress would alter it to fit.

Clem had no trouble finding one. Her hand immediately fastened to the sleeve of a yellow calico dress. "This one," she said.

She and the woman went into the back room for her to try it on. Wade waited in the store, idly moving up and down the aisles. All the while his gaze would swing back to the closed door.

It opened, and Clem walked out. Twirling around as she had done with the green dress that she wore to the barbecue, she said, "Do you like it?"

He nodded.

"May I wear it now?"

Again he nodded.

"I shall wear it to dinner tonight also. And there's a hairdresser in town, Wade. Mrs. Irwin said she will comb my hair for me. And there's another shop down the street where I can buy ornaments for my hair, and I can get some ribbons and—"

Clem's excitement rubbed off on Wade. Ordinarily he did not like shopping and avoided it at all costs, but today he thoroughly enjoyed it. They went through shop after shop buying her undergarments, shoes, stockings, and combs for her hair.

In the millinery shop, she came running to where he stood looking at the "creations," as the owner of the shop referred to hats she had personally designed and crafted. At the moment he was rather happy that Clem preferred a Stetson to one of them.

"Look, Wade," she called and strolled toward him, her head cocked to the side. She wore an outlandish hair ornament made of many ostrich feathers, one of which dangled over her face.

"Clem—" Wade began to protest, then he saw the mischievous smile that curved her lips and knew she was teasing him.

The afternoon passed entirely too quickly for him. Soon it was time for her to have her hair combed and styled. Having gotten directions to the hairdresser's shop from Mrs. Irwin, Clem and Wade caught a hackney coach and rode over.

Theodoro Gualterio pushed the cart of stinking chamber pots down the alley to the dumping area. He was bitter and angry. Since the death of Eduardo Gonzales, he was no longer a vaquero. Giuseppe and Giovanni Lorenzo had laughed at him; they had called him stupid and forced him out of their camp. To earn money he had been forced to take lowly jobs that paid only a peso a week. At times he felt it would have been better for him if he had died with Eduardo and the others. He would not be humiliated by having to empty and clean other people's chamber pots.

After he emptied the refuse, he washed the pots and reloaded them on the wagon, then began his slow, tedious return journey. When he reached an intersection on Main Street, he stopped to wait for the passing carriage. He hated wealthy people; they were the ones who did not empty their own pots, but had others do it for them.

The carriage stopped in front of the building directly across from him. The door opened, and two passengers disembarked. When the carriage rolled away, Theodoro had a good view of the man and woman. He gave them a cursory glance; then he looked again. He thought he recognized them; he did!

It was the man and woman they had kidnapped in the mountains. Both of them were alive!

Theodoro's heart began to pound fast in his chest. His thoughts began to run together so quickly they became jumbled. He turned the wagon loose. He heard it rolling down the street behind him, finally to crash into something. But he did not care. Here was his chance to find favor with the Lorenzos again. If he could lead Giuseppe to the couple, perhaps they would let him join them once more.

Hiding in the shadows, he waited.

383

"It is finished." *Senora* Mendez carefully fastened the last curl into the cluster on top of Clem's head and slipped the decorative comb into place. She lightly touched the brush to the curls that framed Clem's face. Then she stood back, hands on ample hips, to survey her masterpiece. "Do you like it, *Senora?*"

Clem was awestruck. She marveled at the miracle the hairdresser had produced. Her hair, which she had washed when she bathed earlier in the day, was drawn into a chignon of curls on the crown of her head. The severity of the style was broken by ringlets that wisped around her cheeks. The woman had done even more for Clem. Makeup added soft color to her face and enhanced the color of her eyes.

She could hardly wait for Wade to see her. Standing, moving away from the dresser, Clem walked out of the bedroom into the small parlor where Wade awaited her. On hearing her enter, he glanced at her.

He, too, was awestruck. Finally he said, "Clem, you are absolutely stunning."

She held her hands out to him; he caught them in his and pulled her to him. Lightly he kissed her on the lips.

"It's well worth the cost, my darling."

"Will you think that two or three years from now," she asked, "when I have my hair dressed and coiffed every day?"

"I'll always think you're worth it," he promised. "Now let's be on our way. We have a dinner engagement tonight, Miss Jones."

Much later that night, after Clem was asleep, Wade rose and dressed. Troubled about what the priest had told him, troubled because he had not yet told Clem, he picked up his writing case and walked downstairs to the lobby. Finding a desk in a secluded corner, he sat down and read through the notes he had taken yesterday when he had talked with Father Michael.

Taking out clean sheets of paper, he dipped his pen in the inkwell and began to write. First, he drafted a letter to a friend in New Orleans. He gave him the years that Clement had lived in the crescent city and ask him to find all the information he could find on the Lorenzos. Once it was sealed, he carried it to the night clerk for the morning postal pickup. The second letter he wrote to his home office, letting them know that he would be sending in several articles about the West; Prentice would furnish the illustrations.

Returning to the desk, he began to transcribe his notes before he forgot any of the pertinent details.

Theodoro ran all the way to the house where the Lorenzos stayed when they were in town. He hoped they were here tonight.

A servant opened the door.

"I must speak to *Senor* Giuseppe," Theodoro gasped. "I have news for him. Is he here?"

"No," the man said curtly and began to close the door.

"Wait!" Theodoro shoved his foot inside the casement. "I must see him. I have news about the sheriff woman. Where is he? When will he return?"

From the interior of the house, Giovanni said, "Let him in. I'll talk with him."

Holding his sombrero in both hands, Theodoro entered the house and walked into the large parlor, where Giovanni stood in his lounging robe.

"Hello, Theodoro. So you have news for us about the woman sheriff?"

Theodoro could tell that Giovanni did not believe

him. He nodded his head. "I saw her today. She is here in El Paso."

"Where?"

Did they think he was so stupid?

"If I tell you," Theodoro said, "will you let me ride with you again? Can I be one of your vaqueros?"

Giovanni moved silently across the carpeted floor. "Of course, you can be one of my vaqueros. Just tell me where she is."

Theodoro smiled. They had laughed at him and called him stupid. Yet he was the one who found the woman for them.

"They're together."

"Who's with her?" Giovanni asked.

"The *pistolero* who killed Ike Perry. The newspaperman."

"Ah, yes." Giovanni smiled. "The newspaperman."

Puzzled, Theodoro stared at the Italian. "Are you not interested in the woman?"

"Of course," Giovanni snapped. "Where is she?"

"They are staying at the El Paso Hotel."

"Thank you, Theodoro," Giovanni said. He walked to a table and opened the drawer. He beckoned. "Come. I would like to thank you for what you've done for me."

Money, Theodoro thought. He was going to be rewarded with money. He hastened to Giovanni's side. Giovanni cupped the back of Theodoro's head and pulled him closer.

"Look at what I have for you," he said. Then he drew back his other hand. Only then did Theodoro see the knife. "This is how I pay for stupidity."

"No," he screamed.

"Do something with the body," Giovanni instructed the servant as he wiped his knife clean.

He walked into his bedroom and changed clothes. Settling the black hat low over his eyes, he looked at himself in the cheval mirror. He loved to dress in black. It was most dramatic and suited his personality.

He would tell no one where he was going. He did not want Giuseppe to know, because he would stop him. He would deny him his pleasure. After all, Giuseppe had killed Clement without telling him. Clem Jones would be his without Giuseppe knowing. How proud his brother would be when he eliminated her, Giovanni thought.

Thinking about her excited him. Of course, in the end he would have to kill the *pistolero*. But he wondered if Clem Jones really knew her father? Did she know that he had been a member of the Lorenzo "family" at one time? Of course, there was no way he and Giuseppe could prove it. If they could have, they would have ruined Clement Jones and Rand McGaffney. Clement Jones had made sure that all those who could have identified him as a corrupt police officer were slaughtered.

But Giovanni decided that he would make sure he told her before he killed her; that would make her death all the more pleasurable. He walked to the dresser and opened the top drawer to pull out his leather case of knives. They were sharp, ready for him to use.

Now he must bide his time.

When Clem awakened the next morning, she was surprised to see Wade fully dressed sitting at the desk in front of the window. She pushed up on her elbows. "What are you writing?" she asked.

"Your father's story," he answered. Laying his pen down, he filled a second cup with coffee and carried it to her.

"I thought you were finished with it." She fully sat up and accepted the cup from him.

"I learned more information from Father Michael that I incorporated into it."

After she swallowed her coffee, she said, "You didn't tell me about it."

"No, we were so busy with other things yesterday. I couldn't sleep last night, so I worked on it."

"May I see it?" she asked.

Wade picked up several sheets of paper and brought them to her. Setting the cup on the night table, she took the manuscript and began to read. She could not believe what she was reading. She climbed out of the bed, the voluminous nightgown billowing as she walked toward him.

"You can't print this!"

"I am," Wade said.

"These are lies!" she insisted, slapping the papers against her hand. "My father was not a member of the Lorenzo gang. How dare you accuse him of this!"

"Your father was a member," Wade answered and walked to his writing case to extract a sheet of paper. "Look at this police report."

Clem took it and read it. "Where did you get this?"

"From Father Michael. When he left the New Orleans Police force, he stole these records."

"Well, this is what I think of these." Clem held the sheets of paper in both hands and twisted them, tearing them into pieces, letting the shreds flutter to the floor.

"I don't care what that man told you, my father believed in justice. He wore the star with pride, and I'm not going to let you desecrate his memory with these lies. I was right about you the first time I saw you. You're only out for a story. You'll write anything to gain sensationalism."

Although deep down Clem did not believe some of

her accusations, she was too angry and too hurt to be reasonable. She wanted to lash out, and Wade was the only one at whom she could do this.

"I write only the truth," Wade said.

"You can write the truth about the Sheriff without saying all of this. None of this is necessary," she pointed out. "I told you the West breeds its own particular brand of law and order, and there's a fine line difference between the good citizen and the outlaw. You promised me you weren't going to write a sordid story about my father."

"And if you remember," Wade pointed out, "I told you I didn't choose the way he lived or died. If the story is sordid, it's because his life is. I'm simply writing the story as he lived it."

Clem clenched her hands into fists. "How dare you stand in judgment of my father!"

"I'm not," he said.

"Even if this were the truth," she said, a little calmer now, "I'm asking you not to print it . . . for my sake, as well as the Sheriff's."

"I've thought about that," Wade said slowly, "but it's a story I want for my journal, Clem. It will sell issues."

"Selling issues is the bottom line for you."

"That's the way I earn my living."

"You can get other stories," she insisted. "You don't need this particular one. You have the million dollars Nash is paying you."

"I want the story for the journal, Clem, and when you get over your initial reaction to it, you'll realize it's not as bad as you think."

"It's worse than what I think," she snapped.

Wade moved toward her, but Clem stepped back.

"If you love me, Wade, please don't print that story."

"I love you, Clem," he said, "more than I've ever loved anyone else in my entire life, and I want to marry you. But I have a career and a job to do. You've got to understand this is part of my livelihood."

"You earn your living by digging up dirt on people and spreading it, no matter how it might hurt the living!"

Wade stared at her a second, his eyes darkening, his visage setting into angry lines. "Clem, the first time you spoke those words to me, I excused you because you didn't know me. Now you do, and I take umbrage. If you love me, you'll understand I must publish this story."

"From the very beginning," Clem said, "my family and I have been nothing but a story to you. That's all you really see in people, isn't it? In the coming months what will you be writing about? Your country bumpkin who moves to New York, delighting your readers with her bumbling ways? Or do you propose to write dime novels about the woman deputy? How many ways can you earn a living off of us?"

"Clem, you're being unreasonable."

"Perhaps," she conceded, "but I don't want to see my father's good name smeared in your magazine in the name of journalism. Let him die in peace, Wade."

Wade rode behind Clem as she led him through the mountains to a cave where they could spend the night. She did no more talking than was absolutely necessary. She was still angry at him.

"You didn't tell me there was no trail to this place," Wade said as he followed her through the narrow passageways. He kept a sharp lookout; the rocks were formed in such a precarious way, they were ready for an immediate avalanche.

"You didn't ask," she answered over her shoulder from her position as lead rider.

"Is this a way to punish me?" he asked.

"Nope," she said curtly. "This is the only path. That's why it has remained a secret. The Mescaleros did not let anyone know it existed, or it would have been ruined."

Several hours and only a few miles later, Wade said, "We're being followed, and have been for quite a ways."

Clem nodded. "Whoever it is, it's not an Indian," she said. "They're too clumsy. It could be a Mexican trader."

"It could be," Wade said, "but I don't think so."

"Neither do I."

"You continue riding," he told her, sliding out of the saddle and throwing the reins to her. "It will be easier for me to double back on foot to find out who it is."

"I'll do it," she said. "I'm probably better at it than you are."

"I'll take my chances," he said dryly.

His progress was impeded by the rocky terrain; yet it was also his protection, because it hid him from the pursuer. Finally he reached an elevated plateau where he could see the trail behind without revealing himself.

A lone rider, a cowboy dressed entirely in black, followed them. Quite possibly a gunslinger, Wade thought. But why would he be following them? Could it be someone who saw them in El Paso and recognized them? The thought was farfetched; yet there was a reason why the man followed. And he was following. He stopped to listen; he searched through the rocks for evidence of their passage.

Yes, Wade thought, they were being followed.

Although the going was rough, Wade made good time and gained on the man. He was closing in on him when the ledge he was walking on crumbled; he slipped into a large crack. He could find nothing to dig his fingers into; they slid down the smooth surface of the rock.

Fear nearly choked him. He was trapped, and Clem was alone.

He kept clawing, pressing himself flat against the wall, stretching as high as he could go. Finally he found a crevice. His entire body hanging by the tips of his fingers, he began to push himself up. The weight of his body was too much; his fingers slipped off, and he fell down. Again he climbed up and gripped his hands into the crevice. Pain racked every cell of his body; his fingers felt as if they were being torn from him. He strained until he thought the blood vessels in his face and throat would break.

Quietly, so as not to alarm the man and woman, Giovanni followed them into the clearing. He could not see them, but he saw their horses.

He had thought about bringing his men with him, but had decided against it. One could follow undetected more easily than a group. Besides, he had no doubt that he could handle both the man and the woman.

He slid off his mount, hobbled him, and crept forward until he saw the cave entrance. That is where they probably were.

Last night as he stood outside the hotel, he had imagined the man and woman making love. At first he had been furious to know that he would not have her virginity; then as the hours passed, he devised other ways to possess her that would be more pleasing to him.

Later, he had gone into the lobby, and he had seen the man writing a letter. For a few cents, the night clerk had informed him of Cameron's dispatch to New Orleans. He had even shown Giovanni a copy of the letter.

From her hiding place in the rocks, Clem could see the man clearly. In fact, he turned in her direction and she found herself staring directly into his face. She thought surely she was looking at Satan himself. The black eyes, although focusing on no one, were filled with comtempt and hatred.

The man crept forward, and when he crouched in front of the cave, his gun drawn, Clem leaped from behind, her boots crunching on the rocks when she landed.

"Drop it."

He stood absolutely still for a moment. The gun fell from his hands, and he slowly straightened and turned to fasten that contemptuous gaze on her.

"Who are you?" she asked, "And what do you want?"

"Ask your father, but—you cannot, can you? Your father is dead. Then ask your mother, and if she does not know, your uncle will."

"The Lorenzos," she whispered, and fear constricted her heart. "Which one? Giovanni or Giuseppe?"

"Good. You already know us," he said, evidently pleased. "What are you going to do with me?"

"Answer me, damn it," Clem shouted. "Which one are you?"

Immediately Clem regretted her impassioned outburst. She was betraying her emotional anxiety to the man. The worst mistake she could make. But she was worried, not only about Giovanni, but about Wade. True, she was angry with him, but she did not want something terrible to befall him. What was keeping him? He should have been here by now . . . if he were coming. If Giovanni had not gotten to him first.

"I'm Giovanni," he replied, "the youngest of the Lorenzos. I'm most curious. How did you learn of us?

Your parents? Or Rand?"

"You killed my father," Clem charged.

Giovanni shook his head. "No, Clementina Jones, I did not. I wanted to, because your father was responsible for the death of my father and older brothers, but my brother Giuseppe had him killed. The killer in this case was Eduardo Gonzales, but alas, there's nothing you can do to or for him. He's dead."

He was quiet for a second, then said, "Did you know your father was a member of the Lorenzo family?"

"You're lying!" Clem shouted. How many more were going to crawl out from behind the rocks to accuse her father?

"You wish I were," he said. "He was about to be exposed. That's why he turned against us and killed my family. He couldn't take the chance that they would—"

"You're lying!" she shouted again, not wanting to hear these kinds of horrible accusations about her father. He had loved justice; he had lived for it. The star was his life.

"Perhaps I am," Giovanni said, "but, again, Clem, why should I be? I have nothing to gain by lying. Furthermore, you can check it out with Wade Cameron. He dispatched a message to New Orleans last night. He instructed a man there to begin an investigation on your father."

The man was lying, Clem told herself. She tried to swallow the fear knotted in her throat. Fear caused her to shake uncontrollably.

"What are you going to do with me?" he asked again.

"Take you in for questioning," she answered.

"You'd better shoot me," he said and began to walk toward her, "and make sure you hit me in a vital spot because as long as I have breath in my body, my sole

394

purpose is to kill you." He laughed. "I don't think you have what it takes to shoot a man without a weapon."

"She may not," Wade said from behind Clem, "but I do!"

Relief washed through her. Never had Wade been more welcome; never had his voice sounded so lovely.

Giovanni stopped. "This is not your fight."

His revolver in hand and aimed, Wade walked to stand beside Clem. "You've made it mine. Get the rope," he said to her.

Her back was turned as she walked to Rusty-Be-Dusty. She heard a crunch as someone ran, and turned to see Giovanni rolling on the ground, his gun in hand. Shots whizzed through the air. The Italian grunted, sprawled on his back, his arms and legs flung out. Blood stained his shirt darkly.

Wade walked to where he lay. He tapped the body with the tip of his boot; then he knelt and touched the pulse point at the base of his neck.

"He's dead."

"Now there is only Giuseppe," she said. Then: "We need to bury him."

"I'd like to do that," Wade said, "but we better carry him to Lawful. I want us to have proof that Giovanni is dead. I want there to be no doubt in Giuseppe's mind when he hears the news."

The conversation was terse between them as they tightly wrapped Giovanni's body in his blankets. Afterwards they took care of the horses for the night. Moving inside the cave, Clem laid out their provisions while Wade built the fire. Together they laid the pallets for the night.

Still numb from her encounter with Giovanni, Clem had said little. Thinking about the Italian's accusations, she turned to Wade.

"Was he lying about the letter you sent to New Orleans?"

"No."

Clem stood and walked to the opening of the cave. "If you print that article," she said, "twenty good years of my father's life will be wiped out, obliterated."

Wade walked up behind her and placed his hands on her shoulders, but she twisted away from him.

"For the past twenty years, Clem, your father was all the law and order Lawful had. He stood between that town and criminal elements. He made a bad mistake, but the good he's done shouldn't be played down because of that mistake. When you've had time to sort this out, you'll find that I'm telling the truth. Please trust me."

"I'll always wonder if the story is the most important thing to you, Wade." She walked to the edge of the pool and began to undress. "I'm tired. I'm going to take a bath and go to sleep."

"Although it's warm," Wade said, "don't you think it's too chilly for bathing?"

"These are warm springs," she informed him. "The Mescaleros bathe here during the wintertime."

When she was clad only in her underwear, she sank beneath the water, glad for its bubbling warmth. She thought she would never feel depression as great as she had felt it the day her father died, but she was that heavy now. She felt as if Wade had betrayed her.

"Clem," Wade had shed his clothes and swam to where she was, "please listen to me."

"I love it here," she said, ignoring him. "It's been my hideaway since I was a small child, when Peaceful brought me, Papa, and Mama up here."

She swam away from him, waded ashore, and dried off. After she dressed, she sat on the side of the pool and watched the sun set. Wade left her alone with her thoughts and prepared their supper. Finally she moved to the entrance of the cave.

The hush of the evening descended, bringing a serenity and reverence to the beauty of the pool. Outside the cave, moonlight painted everything silver and softened the rugged terrain. She stood beneath a heaven of bright stars. Inside a fire blazed and joined the aroma of coffee and food to fill the cave with a warm coziness.

Wearing her new dress and her hair hanging about her shoulders, Clem knelt beside the fire, slicing the bread. She felt Wade's gaze on her back. She set the knife down and turned around. His eyes slowly touched her hair, her face, her breasts. As his gaze lingered, Clem's body responded to the visual caress, and beneath her dress she felt her breasts swell; her stomach tensed.

No matter how disappointed she might be with Wade, no matter how angry, he had the ability to arouse her passions. She wanted him with an ever-growing intensity, but she was not going to be weak. She would not allow him to use her, then make love to her.

"Clem," he said, "I love you, and I fully intend for us to be married."

She said nothing. She filled her plate with food and moved to her pallet to eat. Out of the corner of her eye, she saw Wade studying her, but he said no more. He filled his plate, and sitting across the cave from her ate also. Silence hung heavy over them.

Without speaking, she cleaned her dishes; Wade cleaned his. She prepared a pot of coffee for the morning and banked the fire. When she was finished, she moved her pallet across the fire. Without saying a word, Wade rose and picked up the covers bringing them back to his.

"I'm not sleeping with you," she said.

"Oh, yes, you are. We're not going to let a silly

quarrel separate us. You might as well learn right now, Clementina, that although we might disagree on many things during our marriage—"

"I think you ought to know I'm reconsidering our marriage," she interrupted.

"We might disagree on many things," he continued as if she had never spoken, "but you will not sulk and sleep in a different bed."

"I'm not sulking," she exclaimed, "and I'm not married to you, and I'll sleep anywhere I choose."

"Then you better choose to sleep on the pallet beside me," he said.

Clem was so angry at him, she marched to the cave entrance and stood there for a long time. She heard his boots crunching against the rocks as he moved toward her.

"We're going to have to be up early in the morning, Clem. Come on to bed."

"I'm going to sit up awhile longer," she said.

"No," Wade said, "you're not."

He swooped her into his arms and carried her to the interior of the cave, depositing her on the pallet. She bounded up, but he caught her. "It's going to get cold tonight, Clem, and you're going to need the warmth I can provide."

"I don't want anything you can provide," she said. "I can get along just fine without you."

"You want nothing I can provide," he said. "Let's see about that, Clementina Jones."

He reached out and caught her, dragging her into his arms. His head lowered, and his lips possessed her. She pressed her hands against his chest; she pushed against him, but she was fighting sheer muscle and strength. Traitor she was, she was also fighting herself.

"You don't need anything I can provide?" he taunted.

His hands clasping her waist eased up to cup her breasts. Then he caught her hand in his and slid it down between his legs. She felt his arousal, and her flailing ceased. She rubbed his hardness, and her body communicated a reciprocal need to Wade. She moaned softly.

"Say it, Clem," he egged, his voice husky.

His hands continued to caress her breasts, swollen and straining at the material of her dress.

"Say you want me to stop, and I will."

"Please," she mumbled,

"Please what?"

"Please make love to me," she cried.

Wade began to pull her dress off with the same urgency that she unbuttoned his shirt and trousers. Clumsy in their rush, each pulled away and quickly shed their clothes. When they were naked, they came together, sinking on one of the pallets, unmindful of the rocky cave floor.

Their coming together was primitive and earth-shattering; it was gentleness edged with violence; it was rough, devoid of prolonged foreplay, yet it was an expression of utmost tenderness. Wade's lips settled on Clem's mouth and moved against hers. As he stretched out, half over her, Clem's mouth slackened invitingly beneath his, and she responded with uninhibited warmth. His body, pressing her into the ground, was weightless. His giving and his loving was the warmth of life itself.

The deep driving hunger melded them together. Her arms circled his body; her fingers clutched his shoulders; they carried each other to an explosive climax.

Both shared the warmth, the tenderness, the oneness. In the wee hours of the morning, they fell asleep in each other's arms.

At break of day, Clem awakened. To keep from disturbing Wade, she eased off the pallet and slipped into her clothes. She walked to the entrance of the cave and stood, breathing deeply of the brisk morning air and enjoying the beauty of dawn.

The idyllic days were gone. They would arrive in Lawful today and would have to face the problems that awaited them—namely Giuseppe.

And she would have to face the truth about her father.

Chapter Twenty-one

Leading Giovanni's horse behind them, the body secured to it, Clem and Wade rode into Lawful. The townsfolk, glad to see them, also curious about their cargo, followed them down the street. By the time they stopped at the sheriff's office, a crowd had gathered. Opening the door, Rand and Hokie stepped onto the boardwalk.

"Who is it?" Rand asked the same question the crowd had called as they ran behind Wade and Clem.

"Giovanni Lorenzo." The same answer Wade had given. He slid out of the saddle.

Clem dismounted also. "He tried to kill me."

"Clem!" Breathless, Deborah shoved through the people. "I saw you riding in. I—are you all right?"

Clem embraced her mother, and they hugged tightly.

"I'm so glad you're home," Deborah said, pulling away to look at her. As if to make sure she were all right, that she were real, Deborah ran her hand over Clem's face. "I've been so worried."

"I'm fine," Clem assured her, then looked down at her dusty shirt and trousers. "Tired and in need of a bath."

"Who's this Giovanni Lorenzo?" Maybelle asked.

The owner of the general store walked around the horse of burden. "Another one of those gunfighters?"

Rand nodded his head.

A rumble went through the crowd; they were frightened.

William Pinely rubbed his gaunt cheek. "You know me, Rand. I don't say too much. I believe in letting a fellow do his job, but I have to tell you, I'm getting mighty worried about this, both as a citizen and as Lawful's banker," he said. Tension gave his voice a hard, almost unreasonable edge. "What are you going to do about it? You're supposed to be keeping law and order around here. You're supposed to be protecting us."

"That's right," another piped up and another.

Others nodded their heads in agreement all peered intently, awaiting an answer.

Deborah pushed away from Clem and stepped closer to Rand; she placed her hand on his lower arm, thus giving him her support publicly. Only weeks ago Clem would have been hurt and angered by her mother's actions, but not so today. Her love for Wade gave her a new understanding.

Rand laid his hand over hers, but never took his attention from Pinely. "I'm doing the best I can with what I've got, William. Now, all of you, please return to whatever you were doing, and leave the worrying up to me. After all, that's what you're paying me for."

Since the death of her father, Clem had seen the behavior of the city council in a different light, first through their reaction to her keeping the badge as voiced by Arnold. While he had always been blustery, he had never been forceful. Now she saw the same response in William. The usually meek-tempered man had become demanding. Fear!

"No," Pinely said, "I don't reckon that's so, Rand. We pay you for results. If worrying gets results, then worry. If it doesn't, then quit worrying and do something else."

Although Clem understood how the townsfolk felt, although she knew people had difficulty accepting the blame for choices they made, she resented their aiming these fears at Rand.

"William!" Coming to her uncle's defense, she stepped forward.

Rand interrupted. "Let me take care of this, Clem. William, I know you're upset, so I'm going to overlook what you're saying."

His gaze moved slowly through the crowd as he made visual contact with each person that stood in front of him. Some stared back defiantly; others lowered their eyes.

"Now, I'm not going to tell you a second time. Go back to work, and let me do my job. Let me be tense and do the worrying."

Murmurs could still be heard, rippling through the group; they looked at Rand, at one another, at the body draped over the horse, but eventually dispersed, only to congregate in small groups up and down the street.

Maybelle remained to say, "All of this can't be over the salt flats, Rand."

"No," he answered.

"Don't reckon you want to talk about it?" said she.

Rand smiled at her. "Not right now. I have all the pieces, but I haven't put the puzzle together yet. Give me some time."

"Of course."

Yes, Clem thought, all the pieces of the puzzle were beginning to fall together in their proper place to complete the picture. The only link missing was the one that would connect Antonio Borajo to them, and given time she would find that link. Giuseppe may have been the man who ordered her father's murder, but the priest was involved in the crime, by association if nothing else.

Pushing away from the porch column, Hokie took the reins to Giovanni's horse from Wade. "We're mighty glad to have y'all home. Now that the fuss is over, why don't you and Cameron go on in the office and sit a spell. I'll take the body over to Elm's."

"Guess I'll mosey on down to Elm's with Hokie. I reckon he's going to be needing me." Raising her hand to her face to shield her eyes from the glare of the mid-morning sun, Maybelle said, "Rand, I reckon you handled yourself and the crowd well this time, but it's not over. Just want you to know that I'm standing behind you."

"Thanks, Maybelle."

She and Turbin walked down the dusty street, leading the horse to the doctor's office.

"I'm scared," Deborah said. "They're determined to kill us."

Rand put his arm around her shoulder and hugged her to him. His hands circled her upper back in soothing motion. "They haven't succeeded, sweetheart. That's what counts. Why don't you come in here and stay with me for a while?"

Tears sparkling in her eyes, Deborah looked from Rand to Clem. "Both of you are going to fight to the bloody end, aren't you?"

Both nodded their heads.

"We have to," Rand said.

Deborah wiped her eyes. "I suppose so."

"Come on in with us," Clem said. "I have something I want to discuss with both of you."

Deborah shook her head. "We'll talk later. I need

404

to get back to the house now. I have food on the stove."

"This is important," Clem said. "It can't wait."

"All right," Deborah said, and moved into the sheriff's office with them.

The door was barely closed before Clem asked, "Do either of you know anything about Clement's involvement with the Lorenzos in New Orleans?"

"Of course," Deborah said rather impatiently. "Your father and I have told you the story many times."

"Not that story," Clem said, "the other one."

"Which other one?" Deborah murmured.

Rand crossed his arms over his chest and gazed down at the toe of his boots.

"Rand?" Clem asked.

"Why are you asking?" he wanted to know.

"Giovanni told her Clement was a member of the Lorenzo 'family,' " Wade said. "And when I was interviewing Father Michael Murphy, some police reports fell out of an old portfolio. I read them."

"And you asked questions. When you received the answers, you started putting two and two together," Rand said.

Wade nodded.

"He sent a letter to a friend of his in New Orleans," Clem said, "and he's asked him to investigate Clement and the Lorenzos."

Rand walked over to the stove, picked up the coffeepot, and filled a cup. "Clement was involved with them," he said. "When he learned that he was being investigated, he turned against them, using me and the Blacksmith. We thought we were going to arrest them and let the law take over, but before we knew what was happening, Clement had killed them."

Numb, Clem stood there, looking at her uncle;

405

Deborah pressed her hand over her mouth.

"All this time," Clem murmured, "you knew this."

"I knew Clement's killing them was unnecessary," Rand said. "I didn't know Clement was a member of their gang until many years later, when he received the first threat from them." Rand smiled weakly and looked from Clem to Deborah. "By then, we had you and Clem to think about. That's when we decided to move west, where no one knew us."

"Somehow," Wade said, "your past always manages to overtake you."

"Clem," Rand said, "you can't let this affect you."

Clem laughed bitterly. "But it does. The foundation of my life is gone; it was Clement Jones."

"No," Wade said, "he laid the foundation for you, but he's not the foundation. You're hurt right now, because you idolized him, Clem. Soon you'll forgive him, and when you can do that, you'll find that things are not nearly as black as you think them to be."

"I'd . . . better get back to my cooking," Deborah said, her voice hollow. "I'll—I'll expect all of you for lunch."

"I can't answer for them," Wade said, "but after the provisions Clem and I have been eating lately, I can tell you I'll be there."

"We'll be there," Rand promised.

Clem, walking to her horse, unfastened the dress that she had carefully bundled for the trip from El Paso, and asked Deborah to carry it home and to hang it up for her. She still liked it and was appreciative that Wade had bought it for her, but some of her joy was gone. When Deborah left, Rand ushered Clem and Wade into his office.

"I'm glad Hadley's at McDonald's place right now," he said. "This will give me some time to get a story

406

ready for him to publish."

"I was going to ask about him," Clem said. "It's not like him not to be in the middle of something like this. Thank God, he wasn't here to learn about Clement. Hadley would have been hellbent to publish it. His duty, he would claim."

"Where's Prentice?" Wade asked. "I can't believe he's not here to meet us."

"He went with Hadley," Rand continued. "He wanted to see a ranch firsthand, thought it would provide him with some interesting subject matter. I expect them back by nightfall."

Wade wandered over to the window. "Tension is high, Rand. You can feel it crackling in the air."

"And with Giovanni's death," Clem said, moving to the drinking pail, "it's not getting any better."

"What happened out there?" Rand asked.

After drinking thirstily, Clem returned the dipper to its peg. Detail by detail, she highlighted the events, beginning with their arrival in San Miguel and concluding with the Italian's death.

"Wade wants Hadley to run an article in the newspaper, so Giuseppe will know for sure that his brother is dead. He also wants Prentice to provide a drawing of him," she said.

"I think this will smoke them out," said Wade. "We know they're somewhere in the triangle of El Paso, Botello, and San Elizario."

"I like the idea," Rand said. "At least, it'll put us on the offensive rather than the defensive, which may be no better, but it'll make me feel better. I've been feeling rather hemmed in lately, trying to figure out what they're going to do next."

Clem glanced around and for the first time since she had entered the office, noticed the prisoner. "What's he doing here?"

"That's Mountain Cat, one of Diablo's braves. He's been my prisoner for several days and is recovering from an illness that is remarkably like smallpox. The soldiers thought for sure he was a goner." Laughing, Rand told her how he and Elm had deceived the troops into leaving him behind. "He says they traced the horse thieves to a camp outside Botello. Since I got your message about the leader speaking Italian, I've been wondering if perhaps we have a common enemy. If we do, this is what I figure we ought to do."

Rand hastened to explain his desire to locate the camp, to determine how large an army of gunfighters Giuseppe had amassed. Once they knew how many they would be facing, they would know how to prepare.

"The brave is our guide to finding the camp," Rand concluded, "but he won't take us until Diablo gets here. I sure hope it's in a hurry."

Wade nodded his agreement. "Giovanni's death puts a new complexion on things. It looks like the Lorenzos were moving their operation from New Orleans out here, Rand, but why? What would they have to gain? Why would they want the salt flats? That's not going to give them that much money. There has to be more."

Rand raked his hand through his hair. "Of course, the obvious reason the Lorenzos are out here is their vendetta against us, but that can't be the sole reason. They're building an army of gunfighters for reasons unknown to me. I can't figure it out. I just wish I had me some heavier guns."

"You have me," Clem said.

"Thanks." Rand fondly patted her shoulder. "But this isn't your fight. The Lorenzos belong to your papa, the Blacksmith, and me."

"They belonged to Clement," Clem corrected, "therefore, I've inherited them. If it hadn't been for him, they wouldn't be here."

Pausing, Rand walked to the stove and poured another cup of coffee; he offered the others some, but they declined by a shake of the head.

"No, they're after all of us, Clem. Giovanni and Giuseppe don't know the details well enough to know who did what, or why they did it. They hate the Joneses generally."

He took several swallows of coffee.

"I can understand why the Blacksmith can't come, but I sure did need him. I guess, though, if I can't have his gun, I'll have to settle for his prayers. Giuseppe will gather as many professional guns as he can, and if he pays the right price—which he will as his desperation mounts—they'll come flocking to him."

"Rand," Clem said, "I'm going to help you. I'm one of the few who is qualified, and I know what I'm doing. Papa had enough confidence in me to want me by his side in case of trouble. Even if I were not a Jones, this is my fight as a citizen of this town."

Wade shoved away from the desk where he had been sitting. "It is," he said, voicing his support and agreement. "She proved herself when she stood up to Powers."

Clem gazed at Wade in amazement. She would have expected him to support Rand.

"You're not concerned about her?" Rand exclaimed.

"Yes," Wade answered, "I am and will be. I'd rather that she didn't, but it's her choice to make. I have confidence in her ability to handle herself. Do you?"

Love for Wade swelled through Clem. "Do you?"

409

she asked Rand.

She and Rand stared at each for a full second, before he nodded.

"You can count on me," Wade said. "I didn't want to put my guns back on, but until the threat is over, I can't take them off. It's funny how you always get tangled up in your past."

"Guess it's fate's way of giving us a chance to straighten it out, so we can move on with the present," Clem remarked, then announced, "I'm going home. I've told you all I know."

"Clem," Wade called, "I want to talk to you."

"Later."

After first taking a leisurely bath and changing into one of her new dresses, Clem set the table, while her mother put the finishing touches on lunch.

"You're worried about the article, aren't you?" Deborah said.

"Yes," Clem murmured. "I don't see why it's necessary for him to print it."

"Sometimes it's difficult for us to see the necessities of someone else's life. Take for instance, I don't see why you should be a law enforcement officer. But I haven't stopped loving you because you are one."

"But this is different," Clem pointed out.

"Not really," Deborah said. "Wade is working at his career, just as you are yours. To him the story is part of his job; it's not something personal. You have to remember, also, your father has to stand on his own, Clem. If his life isn't strong enough for that, no amount of defense will help."

"You don't mind that people all over the United States will read about his involvement with the criminal elements in New Orleans?"

"I would rather they didn't," Deborah answered, "but neither am I going to let it ruin my life. It happened; it's a fact. Clement lived with it; now, so must we."

Clem went to the cabinet and took out the glasses and set them next to the plates.

"No matter whether your father was a criminal or not," Deborah said, "he loved you, and he's lived an upright life since we've been out here. You can be proud of him, Clem, and you can know he wore that damned badge with pride. He truly believed in what it stood for."

"I guess so," Clem said, weary of the subject and unable to come to any conclusion herself.

"With lunch ready," Deborah said, "why don't we sit in the parlor and have a glass of lemonade? Tell me about your trip to San Miguel."

Sitting on the sofa, Clem recounted the story for Deborah, excluding Wade's proposal of marriage.

"I'm glad that one of the Lorenzos no longer poses a threat," Deborah said, "but I'll worry until the last one is gone."

"It's going to be over with soon," Clem promised. "Let's not think about them now. Let's think about happier things." She leaned forward and set her glass on the coffee table. "Wade asked me to marry him."

"And?" Deborah prompted.

"I said yes, but that was before—" Her voice trailed into silence.

Deborah laid her hand over Clem's. "Do you love him?"

"Yes."

Deborah stared at her for endless seconds before she finally asked, "If you marry him, where are you going to live? He'll be returning to—"

"New York."

411

"That's a long way from the people and the land you love."

"Wade said we would be coming out here every year."

"Even if you could," Deborah argued, "that won't be the same as living here. You've never lived anywhere else, Clem."

"I don't know that it matters anymore," she said.

Deborah smiled. "You have plenty of time to think about it. I'm sure the two of you will work things out. All lovers have little quarrels."

"I'd like for us to," Clem admitted. "I want to marry him, Mother, and I want to go to New York."

She truly did. She loved the West and would come back, but she wanted to travel. She wanted to see what the rest of the world was like.

"It doesn't mean that I don't love the West, and that I'll never be back. It simply means that I'm growing and want more out of life. Wade even suggested that one day we buy a ranch out here. Besides, you can move to New York and live with us."

"I can't," Deborah said, "Rand asked me to marry him. It's a little soon after your father's death, but—"

Only weeks ago Clem would have been angry and bitter at such an announcement from her mother, but now she accepted that Deborah and Rand were in love. Her love for Wade opened her eyes to so much that she had been blinded to before.

"I'm happy for you," she said, "and it's not too soon."

"Our wedding will be a small one here at the house," Deborah said. "We've already talked with Pastor James. If it will interfere with yours—that is, if you decide to marry him—I'm sure we—"

"No," Clem said, "it won't interfere."

Deborah shook her head. "Please let me know as

412

soon as you make up your mind. I want you to have a beautiful wedding, and I shall need some time to plan it."

Clem nodded. "I want to invite Doña Pera. And Miss Merica." Then Clem added, "I'm glad you came home. I enjoy having a mother again. I never knew it could be this much fun talking to someone, someone who really understands."

"That's what mothers are for." Deborah smiled. "I enjoy having a daughter like you."

Once again Giuseppe met with Antonio Borajo in the room above the cantina in Botello. This time he called the meeting; he paced the floor.

"Look at this."

Borajo gazed at the opened newspaper on the table.

"Giovanni," Giuseppe said, his voice thick with tears. "He is dead. They did this, knowing that I could not come get his body. He'll be buried in an unmarked grave in an unblessed cemetery." With his index finger he thumped the drawing of his brother. "This is my baby brother, the only one of my family who was left. I raised him. Now he is dead, and they are playing with his soul."

Sitting down, Borajo read the article; Giuseppe continued to talk.

"I had been worried about Giovanni, especially after I found he and Theodoro had talked."

"Have you discussed this with Theodoro?"

"No, Giovanni killed him."

Borajo sighed and shook his head.

"It was not like him to be gone for such a long period of time," Giuseppe continued. "Then one of the men brought me the *Lawful Tribune* and showed

413

me the story. Although Wade Cameron fired the shot, the Joneses are responsible for Giovanni's death. I shall kill them, Antonio. I shall." Giuseppe's hands were shaking so badly, he pressed them against the table.

The priest laid the paper down and bridged his fingers in front of his face. "I'm sorry for your sake, Giuseppe," he eventually said, "but Giovanni's own lust for revenge killed him. A man cannot be driven by his emotions and expect to succeed."

Giuseppe needed something to calm his nervousness. Giovanni's death was more than he could bear, and his cousin's callous attitude, more than he could tolerate. With shaking hands he poured a full glass of whiskey for himself and tilted the bottle to the priest.

"No," he declined, "and you should not be drinking, Giuseppe. It is too early in the day for that. Also you and I have some planning to do. We have to decide how we're going to proceed from here."

"I'll tell you how I'm going to proceed," Giuseppe said, "I'm going to hire more guns and storm Lawful. I have one here now; another is on the way. I'll kill every Jones I can find."

The whiskey warmed him. Already he felt better.

"I'm sure that's what they're hoping you'll do," Borajo said. "And they'll be ready and waiting."

Giuseppe drained the glass and refilled it. "They won't be ready for what I have planned. I have considered this carefully and have the men to do the job."

"What men?" Borajo asked, a frown furrowing his brow.

"I still have Soloman Wise."

"You and he are only two, and I doubt very much that you could do much damage." The priest sighed.

414

"No, my dear cousin, I have someone else. And I have another who is going to join us," Giuseppe drawled and walked to the door and moved to the landing. At the head of the stairs, he called, "Soloman, will you come upstairs?"

"Giuseppe, use some prudence."

His cousin reentered the room, leaving the door ajar. "Listening to you has gotten me nowhere. Now I'll do things my way."

"You've never listened to me," Borajo said. "From the beginning, you have worked behind my back to undermine everything I was working for."

Two hardened gunslingers entered. Giuseppe did not like them, but he respected their expertise with the gun; he admired their total lack of morals. The devil's liaisons, their only code was cruelty and selfishness

"Soloman Wise, you already know," Giuseppe said and waved to the other man. "This is Dac Washburn."

The man tipped his head toward the priest.

"Howdy, preacher."

Giuseppe got perverse satisfaction when Borajo flinched. He disliked Anglos in particular; he disliked irreverence—although he was not a reverent priest—specifically.

"I understand you two have a little problem you want me to take care of." He rubbed the corners of his mouth, the crease filled with dried tobacco juice. "You want me to kill Wade Cameron."

"Wade Cameron!" Borajo rose and placed his hands on the table, balancing his weight on his palms. "This is getting out of hand, Giuseppe. You're losing sight of our goal. Because of you, we're losing our empire. Listen to me."

"We shall have our empire. You shall have the salt

flats and all rights to them, and I shall have Lawful, once I have avenged the death of my family," the Italian declared and pointed to Dac Washburn. "And this man will do it. He hates Cameron."

"Sure do," Washburn agreed. "He sent me to prison when he was a bounty hunter. The only thing that kept me alive was the idea of one day repaying him for what he did to me." His smile revealed tobacco-stained teeth. "For the right price, I'm your man."

"Others will join me," Giuseppe said confidently. "I am getting stronger rather than weaker."

"That's all for now," Borajo said to the gunslingers. He dismissed them with a wave of his hand. "If the two of you will leave us, Giuseppe and I have some personal business to discuss."

The door had no sooner closed behind them than Borajo said, "I'm washing my hands of the entire affair. By hiring men with their own vendettas to settle, you're losing control. No longer are we a good team, Giuseppe. These men have no interest in this land; they're interested only in themselves. If you're wise, you'll get out now. If you don't, you're as *loco* as your brother."

The door closed once more, and Giuseppe poured himself another glass of whiskey. He was beginning to feel quite composed. He was glad that Borajo had walked out. He owed him no loyalty whatever now. After he had killed the Joneses, he would take great pleasure in personally killing Antonio Borajo.

Clem was walking out of the general store, when she saw Doña Pera's carriage roll into town and stop at the hotel. She could hardly believe her eyes. She thought her to be close to San Antonio by now.

Holding her parcels tightly, Clem raced across the street to Emmett's place, to stand on the boardwalk in front of the vehicle.

The door opened, and a footman assisted the doña as she disembarked. Pilar jumped out behind.

"Doña Pera," Clem said, "this is a surprise. I hope your coming back isn't a result of bad news."

"Not at all," she said. "By the time I reached Ft. Stockton, I was weary and wanted to return home. I sent some of my vaqueros on to San Antonio to deliver the wedding gifts."

Peering around her grandmother's skirt, Pilar grinned at Clem. "Your dress is pretty. Do you wear one all the time now?"

"Thank you, and no, not yet. It's taking some getting used to," Clem said. She lifted her skirt enough to show her shoes. "I'm even having to learn to walk in these."

Pilar laughed. "But they look so much better with your dress."

Doña Pera called to one of her servants. "Carry the trunks into the hotel and get me a room."

"You're welcome to stay at our home," Clem said.

"I appreciate the offer, but this time I shall stay here. That way you and your mother need not feel you have to wait on me. I think you and she have other matters on your mind now." Her eyes twinkling, she added, "That is one of the dresses I gave you, no?"

Clem nodded. "I like it very much."

"I'm glad. Is it possible that you have a beau?"

"Yes," Clem murmured. She felt the warmth seep into her cheeks.

"I thought perhaps it would be that way. You have a good man."

"Yes," Clem said, "I do. Please join us for dinner

417

tonight. Rand and Wade will be there."

"So, it is as I thought," Doña Pera said, then smiled. "Of course, I shall be delighted to join you."

"And Pilar is welcome also."

Doña Pera laid her hand on Pilar's shoulder. "I think I shall put her to bed."

"Oh." The child pouted.

"I shall let you visit with Clementina another time. Tonight will be a celebration for the adults, no?"

Clem was not sure if it would be a celebration or not. She had not talked with Wade yet.

Wade could push aside the Lorenzos, but he was worried about Clem. She was still distant and cool, although she wore her yellow calico — the dress he had purchased for her — and following the hair-dresser's instructions, she styled her own hair, using several of the combs he had bought her as decorations.

He was also concerned about Doña Pera. She had been quiet throughout the meal, but he supposed she was tired after her long trip. He wondered why, when she had been so determined to make this trip to San Antonio, she had turned around at Ft. Stockton to return to Lawful.

"Shall we go into the parlor," Deborah said, "and have a glass of lemonade? We'll all visit together and enjoy our evening."

"Lemonade sounds good," Doña Pera said, "but, if you have some wine, I'd rather have a glass of it, please. I'm in need of something more spirited than lemonade."

"Of course," Deborah said, then on soft laughter added, "would you men prefer something stronger than lemonade?"

"Champagne," Rand said. "We need to drink to the bride-to-be."

"And the groom-to-be," Clem added.

Wade looked at Clem, but she said nothing about their engagement.

The glasses were filled and refilled, the toasts moving from the sublime to the ridiculous. At least Rand and Deborah were having a lovely evening, Wade thought. He was uncertain about Clem. As for himself, he was miserable. He ached to get Clem to himself, so he could talk some sense into her. Setting his glass of champagne on the nearby table, he moved to Clem. He decided it was time for them to settle this once and for all. As he reached her, Doña Pera spoke.

"I do not mean to put a sad note on your evening, but I have a confession to make."

The room quieted, and each of them sat down.

"I returned to Lawful because I was carrying a heavy burden. When I was here before, Wade, you asked if I had ever seen or heard of Bryan Dillon, and I said no." She sipped her wine. "I lied to you. I recognized him when you showed me the daguerreotype."

All other thoughts fled from Wade's mind. All movement stopped. No one dared to break the spell that Doña Pera had created with her confession. Putting her wine aside, she reached into her pocket and pulled out the watch. She opened the lid, the click of the lock sounding loudly. It chimed the hour, and all listened to the French melody. With an abrupt movement, she snapped the lid shut and handed the watch to Wade.

"You can see that it is his. The date and the initials are intact."

On that autumn day so long ago when he had

held Nash's watch, Wade had thought this search would be fruitless, like all the others. He had never dreamed that he would hold Bryan's watch in his hand. He ran his finger over the engravings. Then he lifted his head and gazed at Doña Pera.

Her eyes were misty. When she spoke, her voice was faraway. "I was a very young girl married to a much older man. It was a marriage of convenience planned by my parents and my husband. Through the marriage we combined two large estates, which today are the Montelongo holdings. I was to produce a son, a Montelongo, to be the heir to this vast estate. Alberto kept his part of the bargain, but I was unable to fulfill mine. I never conceived a child. Several years after we were married, Alberto hired an American gunman to be his personal body guard. This American and I were thrown together a great deal, and I fell in love with him. His name was Roberto, and he was handsome and dashing."

Wade was so intent on listening to the story, he never thought to record it. As he watched Doña Pera speak, he saw her eyes sparkle. Her voice grew firmer and more confident, as if she took strength from the telling of her story. Even today she loved Roberto.

"Perhaps it was foolish of me, I don't know, but I was unfaithful to my husband. Roberto and I had an affair. We loved each other dearly, and he begged me to leave the hacienda with him. He promised to take care of me."

"My husband learned of the affair and had Roberto arrested on false charges. He also threatened to hurt my family, if I should desert him. I wanted to leave him with or without Roberto, but I could not leave my aged parents to face the wrath of the *hacendado*. He was a cruel man. I bargained with my hus-

420

band. I told him that if he would let Roberto go, I would stay with him for the remainder of my life."

"I'm not sure what he did or how he arranged it, but he had Roberto released from prison. A few nights later, Roberto slipped into my room and asked me to go with him. He was going to take me to his family in New York; he wanted to return to his home. He and a friend were prepared to protect me and my family, but I could not go, because I had promised Alberto."

With trembling hands, Doña Pera picked up the glass of wine and sipped at it.

"Roberto began to tell me something about his family, but his friend called to him. They left, and I never heard or saw him again."

For long minutes after she completed her confession, no one said a word.

Finally Wade asked, "How did you get the watch?"

"Many years later a priest came to see me. Knowing of Roberto's love for me, he delivered the watch. He thought I would want it. He also told me that Alberto arranged for Roberto's release from prison, but betrayed him. The authorities claimed he had escaped. My husband and his vaqueros killed him. I had never confessed my adultery before. No one knew what I had done. That day I confessed to the priest."

"To Father Michael," Wade said.

"To him." She sighed as if the heavy weight had been lifted from her shoulders. "Now you know the story, and you can tell Roberto's—Bryan's brother."

Wade rose. "There's more to your story, isn't there, Doña Pera?"

The other four looked at him in surprise.

Dona Pera nervously played with her fan, folding and unfolding it. When she lifted her head, he could see the fear in her eyes.

"Pilar is all I have," she said. "I could not bear to lose her."

"You conceived Roberto's child."

She was silent a long while before she said, "That's why Alberto wanted me to stay with him. He knew the child was not his, but no one else was to know. The child would carry the Montelongo name. Alberto had visions of training him to be the *haciendado* that he was."

"What was it? A son? Or a daughter?" Wade asked gently.

"A son. He never knew about Roberto. He always thought Alberto was his father. Juan was two when Alberto died. He and my daughter-in-law died in a cholera epidemic four years ago. Pilar would have died, too, had she not been visiting with me."

Tears slowly coursed down her wrinkled cheek. "Through the years I thought about Robert—Bryan's family, and wished I could tell them about the child. I thought about launching a search, but fear of losing my son stopped me. I could envision the family taking him from me, and he was all I had. I did not want to lose him. All I had of Bryan was Juan and the watch. Now, I have only the watch and Pilar. Juan is gone."

She lifted a handkerchief to her eyes. "One day the watch will belong to Pilar, and on the day I give it to her, I will tell her the story about her real grandfather. Until then, I would have liked for her to have something that belonged to him. That's when I thought about having her a watch fashioned after Bryan's."

Wade said, "You sent one of your vaqueros to New Orleans to have a watch made for Pilar."

Doña Pera nodded. "He became frightened when

e saw the interest the watch aroused, and returned
ome directly without the new one. I wanted to give
t to Pilar for her seventh birthday. She loves her
randfather's watch so much. I was afraid to tell you
he story, because I do not want to lose Pilar, not
ven for visits. I am an old woman, and she is the
oy of my life. But I am also an honest woman, and
could not continue my journey to San Antonio, be-
ause I felt so guilty. I could not deny Pilar her heri-
age. She has a right to know her grandfather's
amily. I can also understand that Roberto's brother
vould want to see his grandniece."

Wade returned the watch to Doña Pera. She held
t in the palm of her hand, the lamplight glistening
on it.

"Would you ask Nash Dillon if I may keep the
vatch . . . and have the daguerreotype?"

Clem slipped out of the house unnoticed after
Doña Pera's confession and walked down to the
brook. She stood on the bank, watching the moon-
ight play on the surface of the water. She heard
omeone walk up behind her, and knew it was Wade.
She smelt his herbal cologne.

"You've successfully completed your assignment,"
he said.

"I'll wire Nash tomorrow."

"You have more stories from this trip than you
bargained for."

"I'm a reporter and a publisher, Clem. It's my job
o look for them." He caught her by the shoulders
and turned her around so that she faced him. "Why
didn't you announce our engagement tonight?"

"I needed more time to think."

"You have until tomorrow," Wade said. "I'm going

to send the wire to Nash, and at the same time, want to announce our engagement. I want him t[o] know I won't be home until after the wedding."

"I don't have to wait until then. I have my answe[r] now." She paused, looking fully into his expectan[t] face, visible in the moonlight. "I don't approve o[f] your printing the story about my father. Not becaus[e] of him, but because of the living who will be af[-] fected, like Mother, and Rand, and Father Michael[.] Once the public reads about it, interest will be re[-] vived, and no telling what will happen. But I lov[e] you too much to let this come between us."

Wade opened his arms, and she moved into hi[s] embrace. They clung tightly together. Then h[e] caught her hand in his and led her down the path farther away from the house. When they were in [a] clearing, he began to kiss her again and again, eac[h] one more drugging than the other.

"I want to make love to you," he whispered.

He stroked her shoulders, then moved his finger[s] with tantalizing slowness down her spine, circled he[r] waist, and probed with gentle thoroughness upwar[d] across her rib cage until he cupped her breasts. Be[-] neath her bodice she felt her nipples harden.

"Yes."

Quickly they undressed themselves and stood for [a] moment in the moonlight, looking at each other[.] Then they embraced.

Clem's breasts were swollen and throbbing with desire. She rubbed herself against the taut muscles o[f] his chest. She circled her nipples in the fine dusting of hairs. Wade's hands caressed her; then he bent t[o] tease the tips with tongue and teeth, a gentle nib[-] bling that sent waves of desire undulating through her.

Head back, she clutched his shoulders to keep her

hold on the world. His lips moved upward across the rise of her breasts, the throbbing pulse at her throat, the arched column of her neck. He traveled higher still, until he found her lips, parted and waiting.

The taste of him was more intoxicating than wine. She breathed in the pure male odor of him; she tasted passion on his lips and tongue; she tingled with new and joyous anticipation each place her skin touched against his

Of one accord, they slid to the ground, lying on their pile of clothes. She slanted her mouth under his and slowly parted her lips to guide his into a warm, moist, open kiss. She felt a deep ache start in the center of her being and diffuse through every inch of her body.

Wade's hand moved up her back, pulling her nearer. She felt the heat and probing of his fingers; she felt the heat of his arousal.

The gentle assault became more urgent as both gave in to raw need. His hands touched the burning flesh of her body, sending shimmers of delight through her. He did not leave one inch untouched. His hands, his mouth, his tongue, his endearments, all joined in the loving assault.

They gave themselves to the other, his mouth open and hot on hers, her hands spread against his buttocks as she brought him down again and again on her. His seed exploded with her just as she reached her climax, and they clung tightly together until they settled into a languid sense of well-being.

Much later, after they had dressed, they returned to the brook. Clem sat on a boulder and watched Wade skip pebbles across the placid surface of the water.

"Wade," she asked, "do you think Nash will try to take Pilar away from Doña Pera?"

425

"From what I know about him, I wouldn't think so, but when it comes to family, one never really knows."

"He and Doña Pera are so much alike," Clem said. "Both of them are lonely and have no family except Pilar. It's a shame they live so far from one another."

Wade laughed softly. "Have you turned into a matchmaker, love?"

"I'd like for everyone to be as happy as I am."

Chapter Twenty-two

Dac Washburn lowered his head and spit, the tobacco spittle splattering on the dry earth. He wiped the back of his hand across his mouth.

"I think you stand a better chance if the four of us go in and challenge 'em," he said, "instead of the entire gang."

His hands sunk into his trouser pockets, Giuseppe paced back and forth in front of the cabin. Since his separation from Borajo and the death of Giovanni, he spent most of his time out here with his men. He tried to drill them, but they refused to become a synchronized working unit. Most of them were headstrong and wanted to do only what they wanted, when they wanted.

His gaze moved over the men, who lounged beneath the lean-tos and the tents. They were sluggards at best, taking his money but doing no work for it. The best of the lot were standing with him. Soloman Wise. Dac Washburn. And the kid who had arrived yesterday. Cole Innman. While he was confident of their abilities, he was unsure of their loyalty

"I agree with him in part," Soloman said. "Once we kill off the sheriff and his deputies, then we have the town and all that's in it."

The other three murmured their acknowledgment.

"It seems to me," Giuseppe said, "that we could be ambushed when we enter the town."

The four gunmen laughed, then Washburn said, "We ain't gonna get into town. Rand McGaffney ain't no fool. Since you sent that note, he's likely got scouts positioned on all the roads to town. The minute they spot us, Rand will be notified."

"Yeah," Soloman drawled, "and him and his deputies will ride out to meet us well before we get into town. That's where we'll get rid of 'em. Then the town will be wide open for us."

"Then you bring the gang in to take over," Cole added.

The kid's gaze ran contemptuously over Giuseppe's expensive suit and shoes.

"When I took this job, I didn't know I was working for a dude."

"What I am isn't your concern," Giuseppe said. "You're paid to take orders, and as I long as I pay you, I expect you to follow them without question. Is that agreed? If not, get on your horse and ride out now."

Giuseppe spoke with bravado. Since Borajo had withdrawn his support, he was worried. True, he and Giovanni had money; they had inherited the family fortune in New Orleans, but it was fast dwindling away. He had come to depend on the priest's resources to support him and his men.

"I reckon so," Cole said.

"Good, we shall ride tomorrow." The men were walking away when Giuseppe added, "Gentlemen, I am an expert marksman."

Everyone in Lawful waited. They were not sure for

428

what or for how many, but they waited. The warning note that had followed in the wake of Giovanni's death was indelibly printed on each resident's mind.

I read the account of Giovanni Lorenzo's death in the Lawful Tribune. I hold all of you responsible for my brother's death and will avenge him. I promise I will strike, but you will not know when. You will be punished sorely. Your town totally destroyed.

The note set the tone. Fear and suspicion became the order of the day. All strangers were suspect. By Rand's orders, children were not allowed to play freely on the streets; they were never to be unattended or far from home. He encouraged all proprietors to keep their weapons loaded and easily accessibly at all times. Women were advised never to stray off by themselves; they, too were to have guns.

Clem and Wade were deputized. Twenty-four hour lookouts were posted at both entries into town; no one arrived unannounced. Frightened for their lives, the three men who owned the property around the Chupedera Salt Lakes stayed in town as residents of Frazier's Hotel. Even Maybelle was subdued.

Clem and Wade patrolled the streets by day. Rand and the two other deputies, all on duty at night, were sleeping. The scouting trip to Botello had been cancelled, even if Diablo did arrive. Lawful could not be without its peace officers. They would have to play this one by ear.

"They're trying to frighten us," Clem said, folding her arms over her chest, "by making us play this waiting game. And where I'm concerned, they're succeeding."

Always searching, Wade pinned his gaze to the distant horizon, a characteristic all the residents were adopting lately. "The more jittery we are," he said, "the more of an edge they have."

429

"I know it; I believe it," Clem said, "but knowing and believing doesn't help any. I'm nervous and have the inclination to jump at the least sound."

She began to walk again, Wade easily falling in step with her. By the saloon. Down to the general store. Around the livery barn. Around and around, they traveled the same route time and again during the day. Their eyes were always trained to the distance. They searched; they waited. Their life had become one constant vigil.

"Go get something to eat and rest for a while," Wade said.

Clem did not argue with him. She knew the importance of food and rest; she also knew that if something happened, Wade would send Maybelle and Grady after the others. Rand had been careful to work out a line of communication. He, Clem, and Wade had also worked out a line of defense, should it be needed for the town.

Wagons and barrels and bales of hay were strategically placed. Once the order was issued, the residents would go into action. Each had his own assignment, his own end of town. All hoped they would not have to resort to such measures, but all were willing to if necessary.

Not really hungry and weary only of watching, Clem poured herself a glass of lemonade and sat in one of the chairs on the back porch. Deborah joined her.

"It's hard to plan a wedding," Deborah said, "with such a heavy shadow hanging over the town. Do you think they're going to come?"

Having asked herself that question close to a hundred times, and still having no answer for it, Clem simply shook her head.

She was drinking her second glass of lemonade,

when Maybelle knocked on the front door and called, "Clem, somebody's coming."

Clem's heart beat accelerated; her blood rushed through her body.

Together Clem and Deborah walked to the front door.

Deborah asked, "Shall we awaken Rand?"

Maybelle shook her head. "Wade said to wait. He's putting Grady and Hadley on the top of the saloon. He wants you by him."

"Be careful." Deborah squeezed Clem's hand.

Clem smiled tightly at her mother. Then she leaned down and kissed her cheek. No matter how frightened she might be, no matter how unsure, Clem knew to project an air of confidence. Many lives depended on it. Determined strides carried her up Main Street to the sheriff's office where she joined Wade . . . to wait.

Before they saw the rider, they heard the dull thud of the horse hooves against the dry earth. Wade and Clem straightened; they fell into step and walked down the street, toward the rider. An Indian. A Mescalero.

Clem breathed a sigh of relief. Diablo Negro was here. She wanted to shout his name so the heavens could hear. Instead she kept walking toward him, the smile on her face getting larger. There was one more of them now.

Four of them. Was that enough? How many were they going to have to face?

Diablo Negro slid off the horse. "I am sorry to be late. My grandfather is dying, and I did not want to leave him until the men came."

"I'm sorry," Clem murmured, sorry that she had never gotten by to visit with the old man.

"He is happier," Diablo said. "He has been searching for the Happy Hunting Ground for a long time.

431

His goal seems closer this time."

"I'm glad to see you," Wade said.

The Mescalero acknowledged this with a nod. "They are on their way. kept my braves watching so that I would not be too late. If they continue to travel as they are now, they will be here by sundown."

Again Clem was washed with relief. By knowing they were on their way, and the approximate time of their arrival, the wait was not nearly as nerve-wracking.

Diablo said, "You killed one of the men who speak Italian."

Wade nodded.

"Tell me what he looked like. I want to know if he's the man who led the thieves into our reservation and stole our horses."

"Your hatred for this man has to stem from something more than stolen horses," Wade said.

Diablo nodded his head. "They pillaged our village and raped our women. They killed my sister who was with child."

"I'm sorry," Clem murmured.

"He must die," the Mescalero vowed.

Wade, with help from Clem, gave a description of Giovanni Lorenzo.

"No," Diablo said, a smile finally touching his lips, "that is not the one. I want the one called Giuseppe. He is mine."

Diablo's announcement that the Lorenzo gang was headed for town spread like wildfire, and momentarily the tension was relieved. Knowing when their visitors were expected, people began to move more freely in the streets, and activity in the saloon increased. With renewed fury Horace Newman pounded on the out of tune piano, the discordant notes ringing into the street. For once Clem thought it sounded great.

432

"Is your cousin here?" Diablo asked. After Wade nodded, he said, "If he is not needed to fight the desperados, I would like for him to draw my grandfather's likeness."

"He won't be fighting," Wade said. "He's an artistic man and quite talented, and he doesn't like violence. He's gentle and peaceloving. Let's go to Hadley's house, and ask Prentice if he will do as you ask."

When Prentice heard Diablo Negro's request, he exclaimed, "I'll go. Although I will sketch your grandfather first, may I also draw other villagers?"

Diablo smiled. "You may. I will have two of my braves escort you."

"You brought your braves?" Wade asked.

"I thought perhaps we would need more warriors than you would have in Lawful. My men are seasoned in battle and will be good. Also I know I can trust them. But—" his lips twitched into what might have been a smile. "I have them hidden. I did not want to frighten the townsfolk any more than was necessary, because I did not want them shooting at and killing my men."

Wade and Diablo walked Prentice to the outskirts of town, and after Diablo chirruped several times, a brave came riding out of a small cluster of trees. Diablo gave him instructions in their native tongue, and the brave nodded. He motioned for Prentice to follow him.

As Wade and Diablo walked back to town, Wade said, "If I write your story, may I use it in my magazine?"

Diablo thought a long while before he said, "I would not mind, but the white man is not ready for it."

Elm and Hadley stood in the general store, gazing out the window, looking down the street. Maybelle, unusually quiet, folded her material.

"I never figured on all this when Clement was killed," Elm said. "I thought Rand would step in, and we'd go on just like we had been."

"Why?" Hadley asked, turning a pensive gaze on his friend. "That's the question, Elm. Why has all of this happened? The salt flats aren't something that outlaws would fight over. There's some money in salt, but it isn't gold or silver."

"If it's not the salt, Hadley," Maybelle said, "what is it?"

"I'm wondering if maybe they want the town."

Maybelle and Elm stared at him.

"That's right," he said. "We're close enough to Mexico that they can slip back and forth across the border; we're far enough away from civilization that law enforcement isn't all that good. And we're small enough for them to take us over with no problem. The people who controlled this town would create a haven for outlaws. Of course, they would be charged for the privilege of living here."

Hadley waved a finger through the air. "Now that, my friends, could prove to be a lucrative business. That would be worth fighting for."

"Yep," Elm said, "I reckon so."

"Have you discussed this with Rand?" Maybelle asked.

"No," Hadley answered, "I just figured it out myself. But I will. I think I'll head on over to his office—"

"You'll find him at Deborah's," Maybelle said. "I saw him walking that way a while ago." She picked up a bolt of material and studied it. "I sure hope we can get this settled so those girls can get married. Such a

434

shame this happened right now."

Hadley smiled. He knew Maybelle was thinking about her sales.

"Everything is going to be all right," Hadley promised. "We'll have those weddings, I guarantee you."

Without Clem's knowing or caring how, she had undressed and was lying in Wade's bed at the hotel. She had not come here to make love to him. She wanted to be with him; she wanted him to hold her close. But the urgency of the moment caught them in its grasp.

Wade stood beside the bed, naked also, the sun filtering through the shade to accentuate the sleek hardness of his body. "I didn't mean for this to happen," he murmured.

"I'm glad it did."

"It's been so long." He lay on the bed beside her. "It's difficult for me to stay here in this hotel at night, knowing you are so close, yet so far away. I want you with me all the time. I want to go to sleep with you beside me. I want to wake up with you there also."

"It's only for a little while longer," Clem said.

"Even a little while is too long."

Wade's mouth captured hers in a searing kiss that rocked her to the bottom of her soul, and reminded her of the depth of their love — a love they may not live to see fulfilled. His hand roved over her body, as did his lips. He released her lips to claim her face, strewing kisses wherever his mouth moved, but always they returned to her lips.

"Your body is beautiful," he murmured, his lips touching her breasts.

Clem arched herself forward and threw her head back, her hair pooling on the pillow. A conduit for the

435

passion that flowed from Wade through her, she was utterly lost in passion. She gladly forgot the world outside their lovemaking.

"You don't know how many times I've dreamed of doing this during this past week," he murmured, his hand gently parting her thighs to move up and stroke boldly.

"Or this." His tongue trailed along her neck to the sensual curve of her shoulder.

"Or this." Delicately he cupped her breast in his hand and moved his palm lightly across the tip, at the same time that his tongue paid homage to the other breast.

When both breasts had been thoroughly adored, he nuzzled along her ribs; his hair brushed across her sensitized breasts. Clem moaned when his mouth stopped at her navel, and his warm breath blew across her taut, quivering stomach. Wade flattened his hand on her stomach and thought of her carrying his child — their child. Pleasure raced through him. His fingers began to move at the juncture of her thighs to send pleasure through her body.

Her hands burrowed into Wade's thick hair, and she pulled his head back up to hers. "Now," she demanded, "take me now."

He moved over her, captured her mouth in his, and inserted his strength in her. Clem received and took him deeply within. Moving together as one, they rose and fell with frenzied desperation, losing all reason and concept of time and place.

Giuseppe Lorenzo did not exist; nothing mattered except them and their love for each other.

They cried their victory together.

With the wondrous moment over, Clem slid her hands around Wade's neck and held him tightly. She burrowed her face against his chest A while later,

Wade stirred. "I hate to do this, darling, but we have to get up and get dressed."

"I love you," she murmured.

"I love you."

She watched him dress. "I'm afraid, Wade. Are you?"

"Yes, but it's not a demoralizing fear, darling. It's one that will strengthen us."

About four o'clock in the afternoon, a lone rider burst in town, as if pursued by the hounds of hell themselves. "Where's Rand? They're coming about three miles down the road."

"How many?" Wade called, pushing away from the porch column in front of the saloon. Clem, standing beside him, stepped to the edge of the boardwalk.

"Four."

Rand, Hokie and Turbin rode up.

"I guess the waiting is over," Rand said. "It's time to resolve this matter once and for all. Maybe then we can settle down to our usual quiet pace of living."

"I'm all for that," Clem said.

"Hokie, Turbin," Rand said, "you know what to do, don't you?"

The two men nodded their heads and moved to their positions. Clem and Wade mounted up, and the three of them rode to the south end of Main Street. They watched the dust cloud moving toward them.

"Where's Diablo?" Rand asked.

"I don't know," Wade answered, "but we don't have time to look for him. We'll have to do without him, if he isn't here by the time those riders arrive."

He pulled his hat lower over his face and looked at Rand and Clem. "Let's ride."

Their mounts in step with one another, the three

horsemen moved down the deserted street. The town was silent; people peered through the windows at them. Clem brushed first one hand, then the other down her trousers.

"Still nervous?" Wade asked.

"A little," she replied, "but not as much as I was earlier. I've waited a long time to get the man responsible for my father's death. Nothing will rob me of this moment. Not fear. Not anything."

A good ways out of town, Rand held his hand up, and the three of them dismounted.

"Space yourselves about three feet apart," Rand ordered. "Clem, you take the one to your right, Wade the center, and I'll take the two on the left. If one of us falls, the other two will have to bridge the gap."

Clem nodded. This was no time for an argument; they were tense enough as it was. But she knew that she would try to take down more than one. She figured that Wade felt the same way.

He caught her hand and squeezed tightly before he released it. They waited. Finally the four riders appeared on the horizon; they approached slowly.

"That's far enough," Rand called when they were a few feet from them. "We don't want the likes of you in Lawful."

Four sets of hard, cold eyes surveyed the three lawmen.

"Dac Washburn," Wade said. "It's been a long time since I saw you."

"Too long," the gunman drawled.

"And you must be Rand McGaffney Jones," the man in the center said.

"And you must be Giuseppe Lorenzo," Rand said.

"I thought you'd have more help," Giuseppe said.

"Didn't figure we needed any more," Rand replied. "Your brother was so easy, we figured two of us

438

could look on while the other took care of the four of you," Wade drawled.

Clem knew he was deliberately riling the gunslingers, trying to get under their skin, so they would lose their edge.

"I'm telling you to ride on out," Rand said, "We don't want any trouble."

"You got it," Dac said. "I ain't leaving until I kill Wade Cameron."

"I thought you were still in prison," Wade said.

"No prison could ever keep me from you. I've lived for this day."

"If you persist in this showdown, it's going to be your last."

The gunman's dark eyes never left Wade's hands. If he were nervous or frightened, he never showed it. Clem's hands were clammy, and she wanted to rub them against her clothes, but did not.

A blood-curdling battle cry sounded, and before any of them could react, Indians—all armed with rifles—came from all directions to surround them. It seemed to Clem that they materialized out of nowhere. Their faces painted for war, they were fierce looking.

Diablo Negro rode up to the gunslingers.

"My braves have orders to shoot any of you who move," he said, his gaze including all of them. "I only want one man. When we get him, the rest of you may do whatever you wish."

"Diablo," Rand said, "this is a matter for the law."

"Law will ensure that justice is served, my friend. Mescalero law."

"I can't let you do this."

"You can't stop me. If you try, my braves will shoot you. I wouldn't want to, but I would."

"Which one of us do you want?" Washburn asked.

439

Diablo urged his horse forward, stopping when he was in front of Giuseppe. He stared into the Italian's face. Giuseppe began to fidget in the saddle. He went for his gun, clearing leather, but Diablo moved faster. He slapped the gun away from Giuseppe with one hand and caught him around the throat with the other.

"You will not die this easy, Italian. You will remember your deeds to the Mescalero Apaches a thousand times before you die."

"No," Giuseppe screamed, "you can't do this!"

"Diablo," Rand shouted, "you can't."

Diablo motioned to his braves, and several of them closed the circle around Giuseppe, forcing him to go with them.

"Rand," he yelled, "you've got to stop them."

One of the braves struck Giuseppe with the butt of his gun, dazing him.

"Now," Diablo said, waving his braves on. He pulled his rifle from the saddle holster. "It is a fair fight. It is three to three."

Without taking his eyes from the group who gathered in the center of the road, he quickly rode away, soon lost to sight.

"Well, what will it be?" Rand said. "It's your choice."

"Nothing's changed," Dac Washburn said. "Cameron's mine."

"Reckon I stand with Dac," the younger of the desperados said. "How about you, Wise?"

"Yeah," he answered, "I reckon with the three of you out of the way, the town will be helpless and easy pickings."

The three dismounted to stand in front of the lawmen. Again each measured his adversary. Dac had chosen Wade, so it fell that Wise was facing Rand,

and the youngest gunslinger faced Clem.

Tension built as they stared, as they studied, as they contemplated. Then, as if by silent command, they all went for their guns, the shots ringing out, three falling dead in the road.

Dressed in an ecru ball gown, Clem walked into the parlor where Wade waited. "As usual, love," he said, "you're lovely."

She walked into his outstretched arms. "And you're handsome."

Glad that Deborah and Rand were already gone, he kissed her deeply, both of them breathing heavily when he released her mouth to murmur, "Are you ready to go?"

She laughed softly. "I'd much rather be going to bed with you than to a party."

"We'll do that later," he promised.

Totally immersed with one another, they walked into town to join the happy people of Lawful in their celebration. Long before they reached the ballroom at the hotel, they heard the music. As they moved through the crowd, people gave Wade friendly slaps on the back and congratulated him and Clem on the way they took care of the gunfighters, and on their coming marriage.

Across the crowded room, Miss Merica spotted them and waved; then she began to weave her way toward them.

"And just when is the big day?" she asked.

"June 14th," Clem answered.

The old lady beamed and nodded her head. "I always knew he was the one fer you, Clem. I always knew it." She turned to Wade. "You was a green'un when I first met you, but you've aged pretty good.

You and Clem are gonna be happy together. Now, remember, I want to come to the wedding."

Wade slipped his arm around Clem's waist and drew her to him. "Shall we dance, love?"

Chapter Twenty-three

Vines, growing in profusion on the lattice work, shaded the patio of the Montelongo Hacienda from the summer sun. Clem and Wade waited with Nash Dillon for the entrance of Doña Pera and Pilar.

"Do you think the child will like me?" Nash asked, and reached up to run his finger around his collar. He was perspiring, but not from the heat. He was nervous. The minute he received Wade's letter, he began making plans to travel to El Paso to visit with Doña Pera and his grandniece. Three long months had passed since then, but he was here.

"Of course, she will," Wade assured him.

"You may have to give her time to know and to love you," Clem explained, "but that shouldn't take too long. She's a loving child. Doña Pera has done an exceptional job in rearing her."

"Thank you, Clem." Doña Pera, her back straight, her shoulders square, moved onto the patio.

Nash and Wade rose.

"Doña Pera," Wade said, "this is Nash Dillon, Bryan's brother and Pilar's great uncle."

Standing in front of Nash, Doña Pera extended her hand, and Nash raised it to his mouth, briefly touching the top with his lips. She was a handsome woman; he could imagine how beautiful she had been in her youth. The type of woman his brother would have fallen in love with.

"Hello, *Senor* Dillon. Welcome to the Hacienda de Montelongo."

"Thank you for inviting me."

"Doña Pera, Nash," Wade said, "Clem and I are going to leave you alone to talk."

"That is good," she told them.

Nash nodded. He sensed that Doña Pera was as nervous as he, and he would feel more comfortable if the two of them were alone and could talk. He hoped she felt the same way.

When they were alone, she said, "*Senor* Dillon, I wish I could say that this is a happy occasion for me, but I would be lying if I did."

"You're hand was trembling a moment ago," Nash said.

"I—I am frightened."

Nash caught both her hands, and led her to the chair next to his, and sat her down.

"Doña Pera," he said, a smile playing on his lips, "I must confess that I'm as frightened as you are. I don't know what to expect from the woman who loved my brother and who bore him a son. Why are you frightened of me? Do you think I'm going to try to take Pilar from you?"

She raised her eyes to him. "Yes."

"I wouldn't do that. I know how much you love the child."

"Because of my fear, I did not immediately admit to knowing your brother," she confessed. "But neither could I keep Pilar from her heritage. She has a right to know who her grandfather was and to meet his family. She is having her lessons now. When she takes her afternoon break, I shall bring her to see you."

She reached into her pocket and withdrew the

444

daguerreotype.

"Thank you for letting me keep this. Robert—
Bryan looked like this when I first met him. Please,
tell me about him."

"Hello, Pilar," Nash said.

She stood in the doorway and stared at him, sol-
emn-faced.

Nash slowly moved toward her, speaking in what he
hoped was a reassuring tone. "Did your grandmother
tell you about me?"

"She said you came for Wade's and Clem's wedding."

"I did," he answered.

"It's next week," she announced. "A June wedding.
My grandmother says that is the right time to have a
wedding. She is taking me."

"Did your grandmother tell you that I brought you
a gift?"

She nodded.

Smiling, Nash said, "If you'll come closer, I'll give it
to you."

She stepped onto the patio and walked to him.
"What is it?"

He reached into his pocket and pulled out a small
gold watch on a black grosgrain ribbon. He tied it
about her neck, so that the watch lay on her chest.

She touched it; then looked up at him with a large
smile. "This is like my grandmother's watch."

Biting back the tears, Nash only nodded.

"I always wanted one like it."

"Now you have it."

"Thank you," she said. "If you'll kneel down, I
would like to give you a kiss."

Nash obeyed her, and she leaned forward to place a

tentative kiss on his cheek. Stepping back, she asked, "What am I to call you?"

"Uncle Nash."

"Uncle Nash," she repeated, and it was all Nash could do to keep from catching her in his arms and hugging her tightly. But he knew he must proceed slowly.

"I like that." She ran into the house, calling, "Grandmother, Uncle Nash gave me a watch . . . a watch like yours."

The June day was beautiful; the perfect day for a wedding. Bouquets of wildflowers decorated the church; their fragrance wafting through the small frame building. Wade, in his black suit, stood at the altar in front of Pastor James. Standing next to him was Prentice.

Friends and well-wishers filled the church to capacity. Sitting on the Jones' family pew were Elm, Hadley, Maybelle, and Miss Merica. Remembering Clem's promise to her, Wade had made a special trip to bring Miss Merica to town yesterday. She had spent the night with Clem's mother and stepfather.

"I knew it," she said to Wade as they drove in yesterday. "I knew when I first laid eyes on you, Wade Cameron, that you was the man for Clem. I knew a'fore too long the two of you would be married." She was quiet for a moment before she had added, "I also figured Rand and Deborah would git married. They've been in love a mighty long time. Glad they did. They're mighty happy."

Wade smiled at Miss Merica and Maybelle, who kept dabbing a large white kerchief to her eyes; both returned the smile. Hokie and Turbin, grinning big but looking uncomfortable in their Sunday-go-toneeting clothes, were there.

On the left front pew, Nash Dillon sat next to Doña
Pera, Pilar between them. Around her neck hung the
small gold timepiece.

Pilar laid her head on her great uncle's shoulder,
and looked up at him, smiling. He patted her fondly
and looked over her head at Doña Pera. They, too,
shared a smile.

Prentice leaned over and whispered into Wade's ear,
"You know, Nash and Doña Pera are getting mighty
friendly. His short visit is growing quickly into a long
one. Rumor has it that Doña Pera will not be making
her annual pilgrimage to San Antonio. Rather she's
going to New York. I wonder why?"

Wade grinned, and replied in a soft tone, "Clem
has tried her hand at matchmaking. You, too?"

"They really look good together," Prentice insisted.

Wade's gaze again moved over the crowd. The
Mayor and Mrs. Bedford. William Pinely and family.
The Emmett Fraziers. More whom Wade recognized
by face but not by name.

Toward the back sat Father Michael Murphy and
Diablo Negro.

Eagerly Wade awaited his bride to be. It seemed to
him that everyone in Lawful but him had seen Clem
in her wedding dress, and all remarked how beautiful
she looked. He impatiently awaited her arrival and
entrance.

Mrs. James sat down at the organ and began to
play the wedding march. Wearing her own wedding
dress, Deborah, Clem's only attendant and matron of
honor, walked down the aisle. She was lovely, but
Wade's attention was focused on the door. He eagerly
anticipated his bride stepping into view.

She did, the soft rays of the sun surrounding her.
Wade caught his breath. Radiantly lovely, she stood in

the vestibule, her hand resting on Rand's arm. Through the veil she smiled at him. Slowly she and Rand followed Deborah.

Each step brought her nearer to Wade. All his adult life he had fought marriage, and had considered it a trap. Now he had deliberately ensnared himself in Clem's magic web, and silently implored her never to free him from her love.

She stopped in front of him. He held out his hand, waiting for her to join him. Wade stepped next to his bride, the two of them holding hands as Pastor James performed the wedding ceremony. Wade heard the words; he was sure they were wonderful and true, but he really was not listening. He was looking at his bride; he was loving her with all his heart and soul.

"Do you take this woman . . ."

"I do."

"To love, honor, and cherish . . ."

"I do."

"With this ring . . ."

Wade took the wide gold band from Prentice and slipped it on the fourth finger of Clem's left hand.

She did the same to him.

"You may kiss the bride."

Wade lifted the veil and doubled it over her head; then he took her into his arms. Before his lips touched hers, he whispered, "I love you, Mrs. Cameron."

"I love you."

Then Wade kissed his bride.